ONCE UPON TIME,
THERE WAS A WIZARD...

THEN IT ALL
WENT TO
HELL.

IMAGE COMICS, INC.
Robert Kirkman—Chief Operating Officer
Erik Larsen—Chief Financial Officer
Todd McFarlane—President
Marc Silvestri—Chief Executive Officer
Jim Valentino—Vice President
Eric Stephenson—Publisher/Chief Creative Officer
Corey Hart—Director of Sales
Jeff Boison—Director of Publishing Planning
& Book Trade Sales
Chris Ross—Director of Digital Sales
Jeff Stang—Director of Specialty Sales
Kat Salazar—Director of PR & Marketing
Drew Gill—Art Director
Heather Doornink—Production Director
Nicole Lapalme—Controller
IMAGECOMICS.COM

CURSE WORDS VOLUME #4: QUEEN MARGARET, FIRST PRINTING. MARCH 2019. Published by Image Comics, Inc. Office of publication: 2701 NW Vaughn St., Suite 780, Portland, OR 97210. Copyright © 2019 SILENT E PRODUCTIONS, LLC. All rights reserved. Contains material originally published in single magazine form as CURSE WORDS #16-20 and the CURSE WORDS SUMMER SWIMSUIT SPECIAL. "CURSE WORDS," its logos, and the likenesses of all characters herein are trademarks of SILENT E PRODUCTIONS, LLC, unless otherwise noted. "Image" and the Image Comics logos are registered trademarks of Image Comics, Inc. No part of this publication may be reproduced or transmitted, in any form or by any means (except for short excerpts for journalistic or review purposes), without the express written permission of SILENT E PRODUCTIONS, LLC, or Image Comics, Inc. All names, characters, events, and locales in this publication are entirely fictional. Any resemblance to actual persons (living or dead), events, or places, without satirical intent, is coincidental. Printed in the USA. For information regarding the CPSIA on this printed material call: 203-595-3636. For international rights, contact: foreignlicensing@imagecomics.com. ISBN: 978-1-5343-1049-0.

CURSE WORDS

VOLUME FOUR: QUEEN MARGARET

CREATED BY

CHARLES SOULE &
RYAN BROWNE

COLORS BY
ADDISON DUKE

LETTERS BY
CHRIS CRANK

SUMMER SWIMSUIT SPECIAL DRAWN BY
JOE QUINONES & JOE RIVERA

BOOK DESIGN BY
RYAN BROWNE

PRODUCTION BY
ERIKA SCHNATZ

COLOR ASSISTS BY
ANDREW MISISCO

LOGO BY
SEAN DOVE

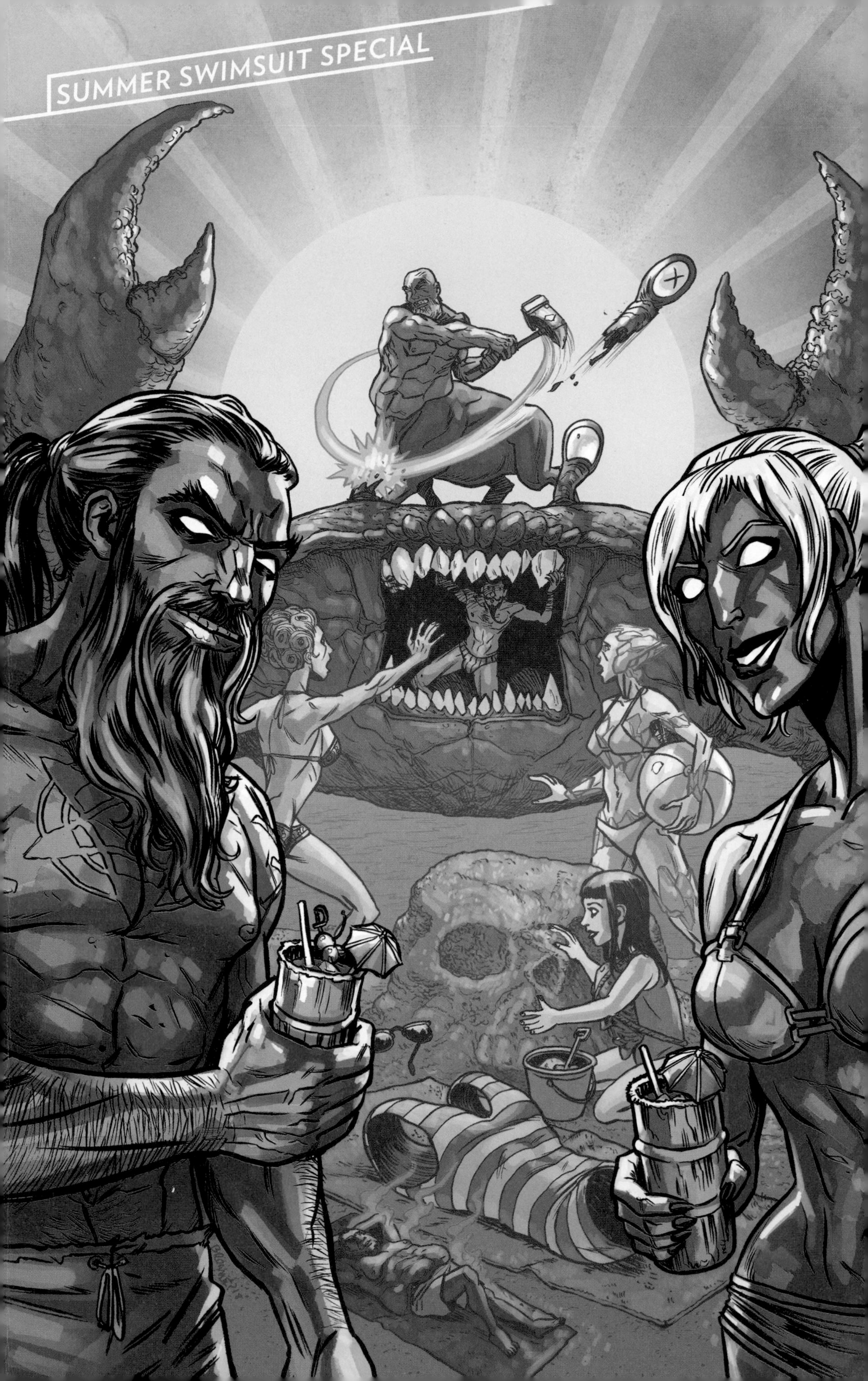
SUMMER SWIMSUIT SPECIAL

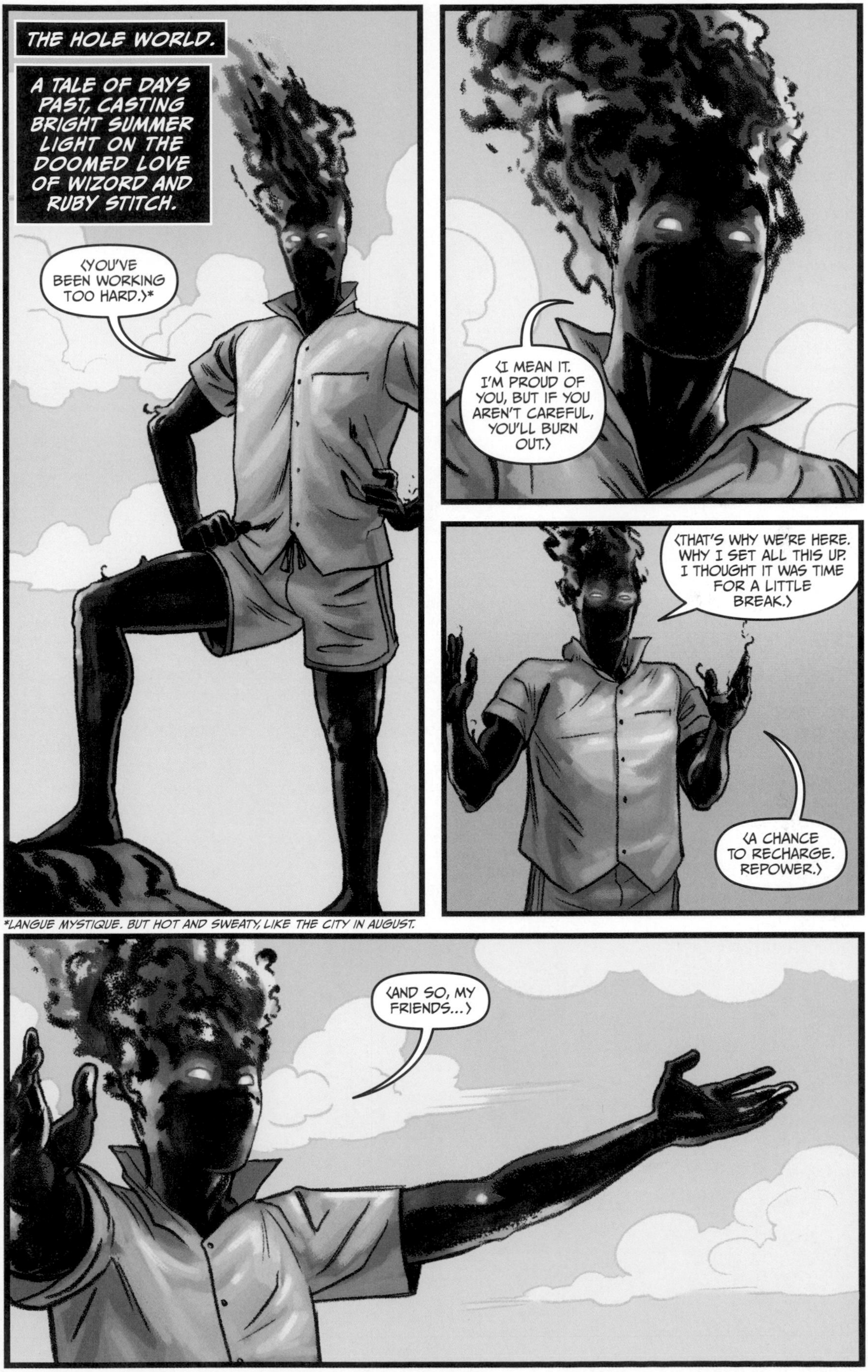
THE HOLE WORLD.
A TALE OF DAYS PAST, CASTING BRIGHT SUMMER LIGHT ON THE DOOMED LOVE OF WIZORD AND RUBY STITCH.
‹YOU'VE BEEN WORKING TOO HARD.›*
‹I MEAN IT. I'M PROUD OF YOU, BUT IF YOU AREN'T CAREFUL, YOU'LL BURN OUT.›
‹THAT'S WHY WE'RE HERE. WHY I SET ALL THIS UP. I THOUGHT IT WAS TIME FOR A LITTLE BREAK.›
‹A CHANCE TO RECHARGE. REPOWER.›
*LANGUE MYSTIQUE. BUT HOT AND SWEATY, LIKE THE CITY IN AUGUST.
‹AND SO, MY FRIENDS...›

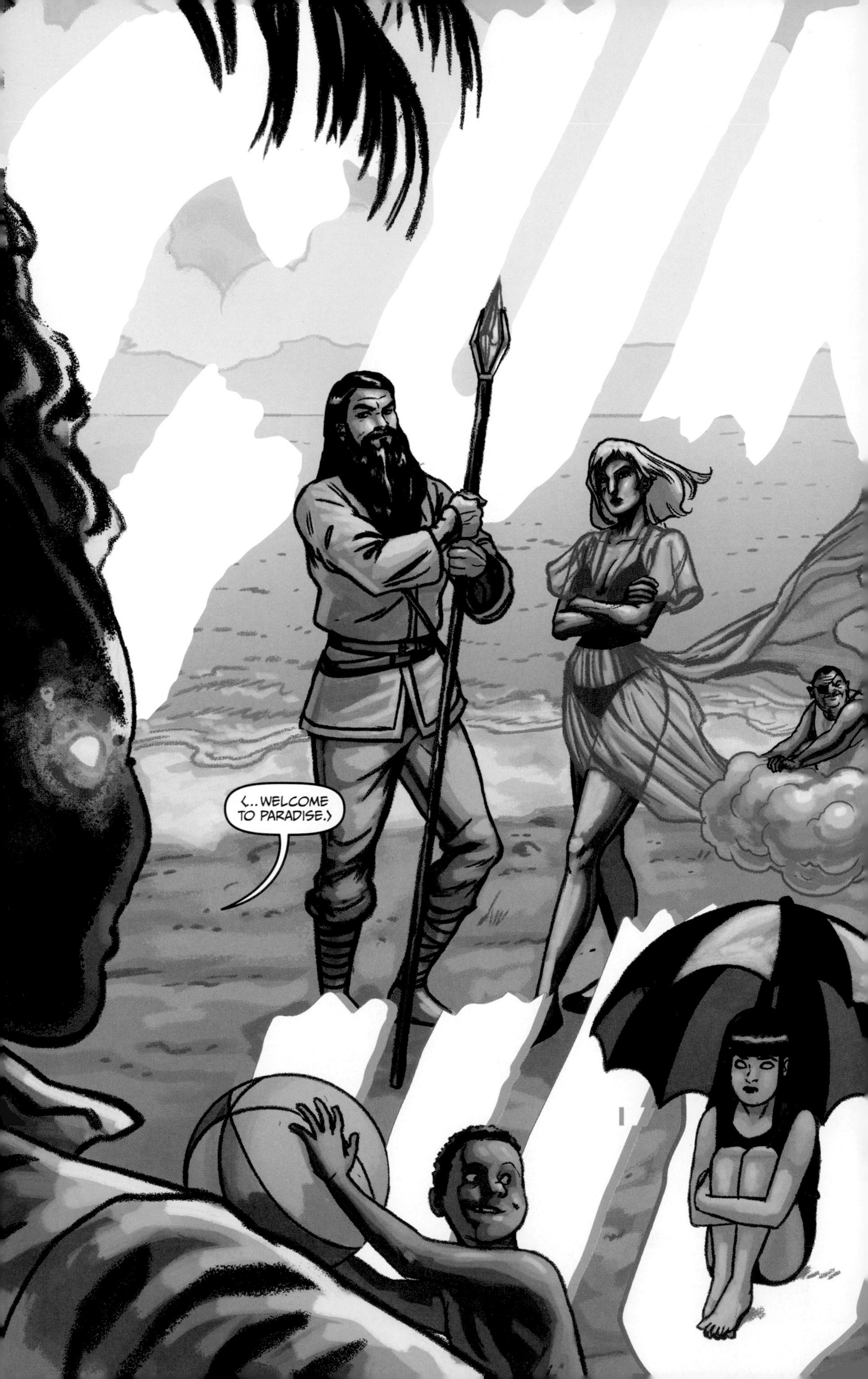
‹...WELCOME TO PARADISE.›

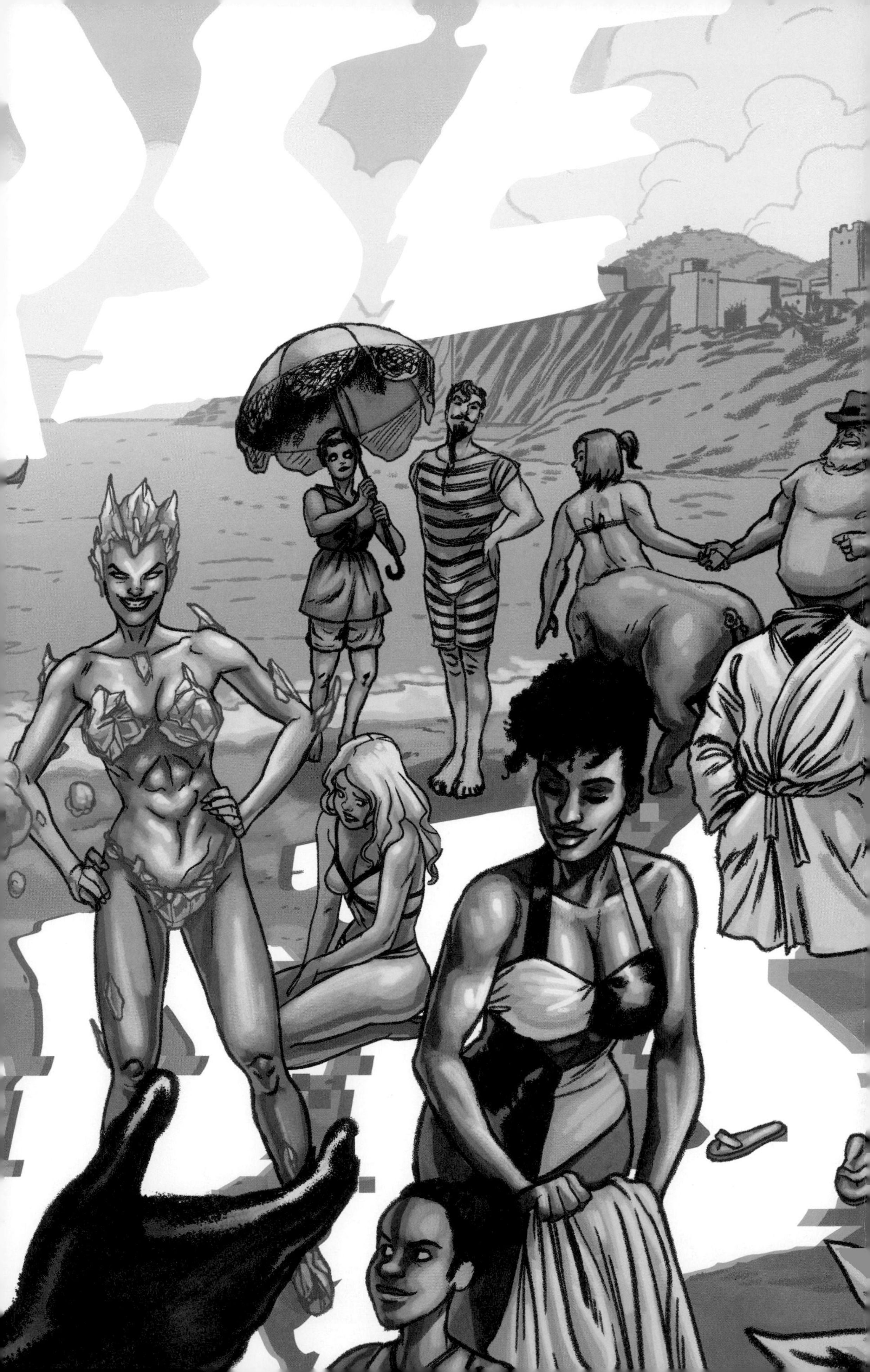

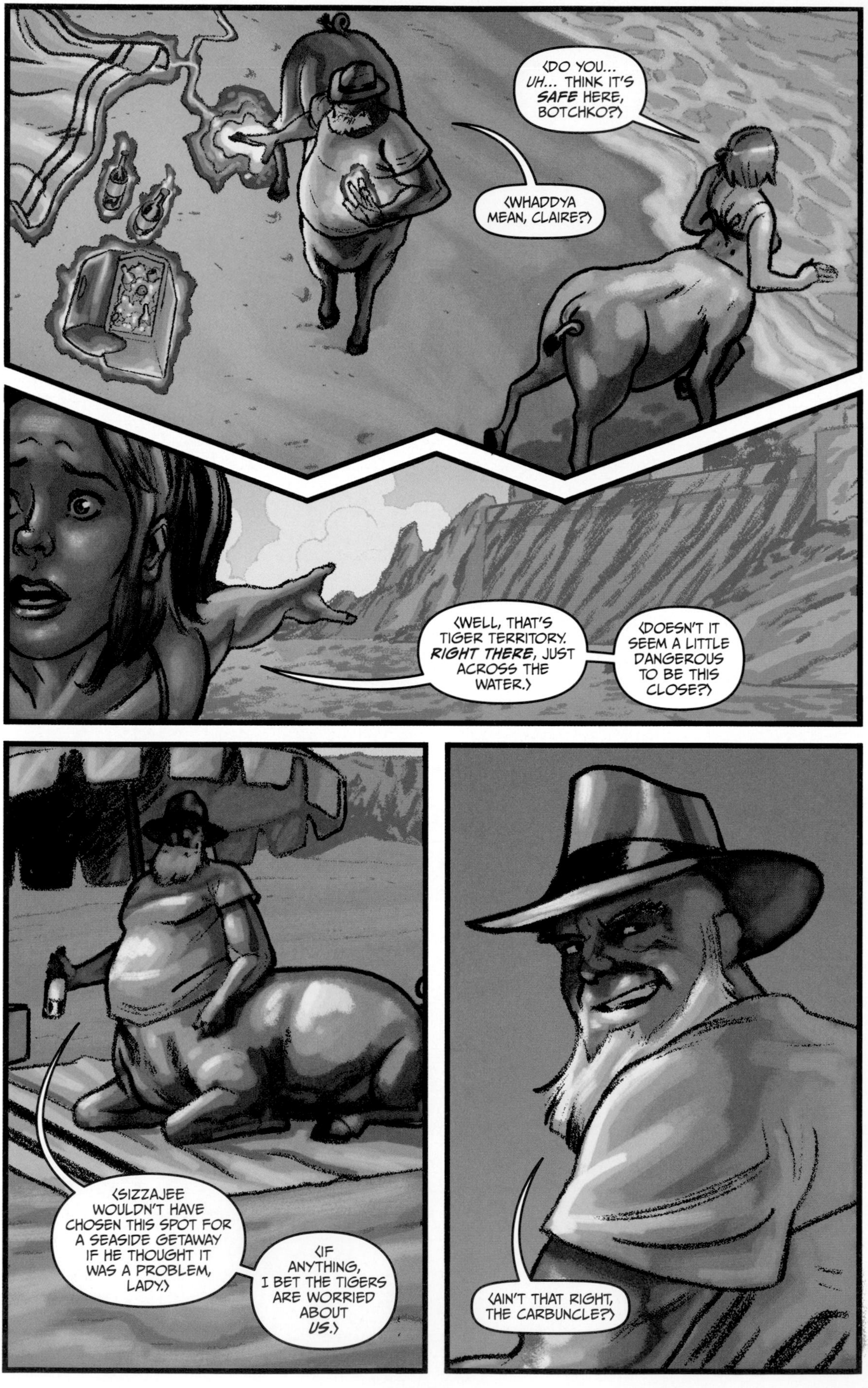

‹DO YOU... *UH*... THINK IT'S **SAFE** HERE, BOTCHKO?›
‹WHADDYA MEAN, CLAIRE?›
‹WELL, THAT'S TIGER TERRITORY. **RIGHT THERE**, JUST ACROSS THE WATER.›
‹DOESN'T IT SEEM A LITTLE DANGEROUS TO BE THIS CLOSE?›
‹SIZZAJEE WOULDN'T HAVE CHOSEN THIS SPOT FOR A SEASIDE GETAWAY IF HE THOUGHT IT WAS A PROBLEM, LADY.›
‹IF ANYTHING, I BET THE TIGERS ARE WORRIED ABOUT *US*.›
‹AIN'T THAT RIGHT, THE CARBUNCLE?›

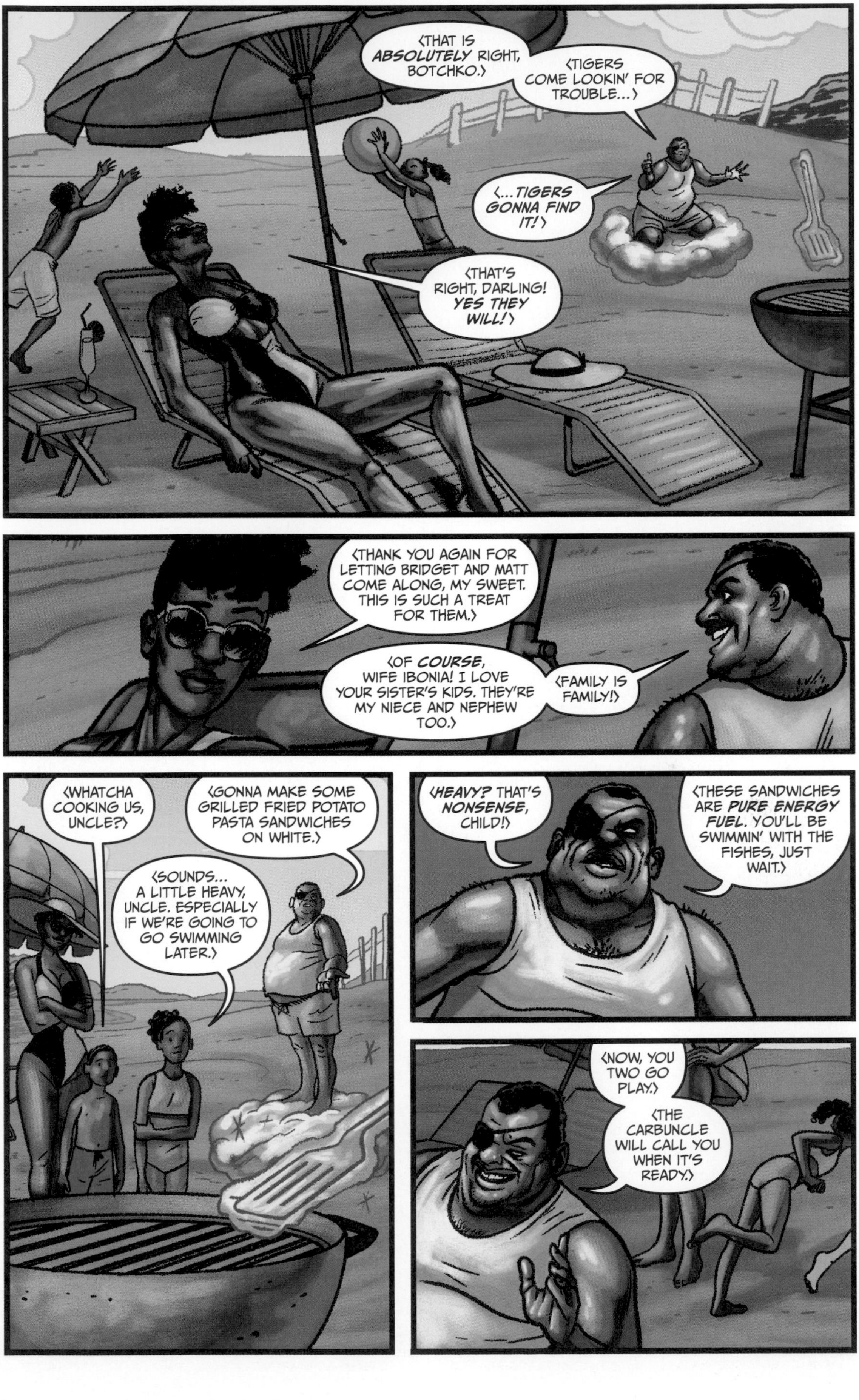

⟨THAT IS ABSOLUTELY RIGHT, BOTCHKO.⟩
⟨TIGERS COME LOOKIN' FOR TROUBLE...⟩
⟨...TIGERS GONNA FIND IT!⟩
⟨THAT'S RIGHT, DARLING! YES THEY WILL!⟩
⟨THANK YOU AGAIN FOR LETTING BRIDGET AND MATT COME ALONG, MY SWEET. THIS IS SUCH A TREAT FOR THEM.⟩
⟨OF COURSE, WIFE IBONIA! I LOVE YOUR SISTER'S KIDS. THEY'RE MY NIECE AND NEPHEW TOO.⟩
⟨FAMILY IS FAMILY!⟩
⟨WHATCHA COOKING US, UNCLE?⟩
⟨GONNA MAKE SOME GRILLED FRIED POTATO PASTA SANDWICHES ON WHITE.⟩
⟨SOUNDS... A LITTLE HEAVY, UNCLE. ESPECIALLY IF WE'RE GOING TO GO SWIMMING LATER.⟩
⟨HEAVY? THAT'S NONSENSE, CHILD!⟩
⟨THESE SANDWICHES ARE PURE ENERGY FUEL. YOU'LL BE SWIMMIN' WITH THE FISHES, JUST WAIT.⟩
⟨NOW, YOU TWO GO PLAY.⟩
⟨THE CARBUNCLE WILL CALL YOU WHEN IT'S READY.⟩

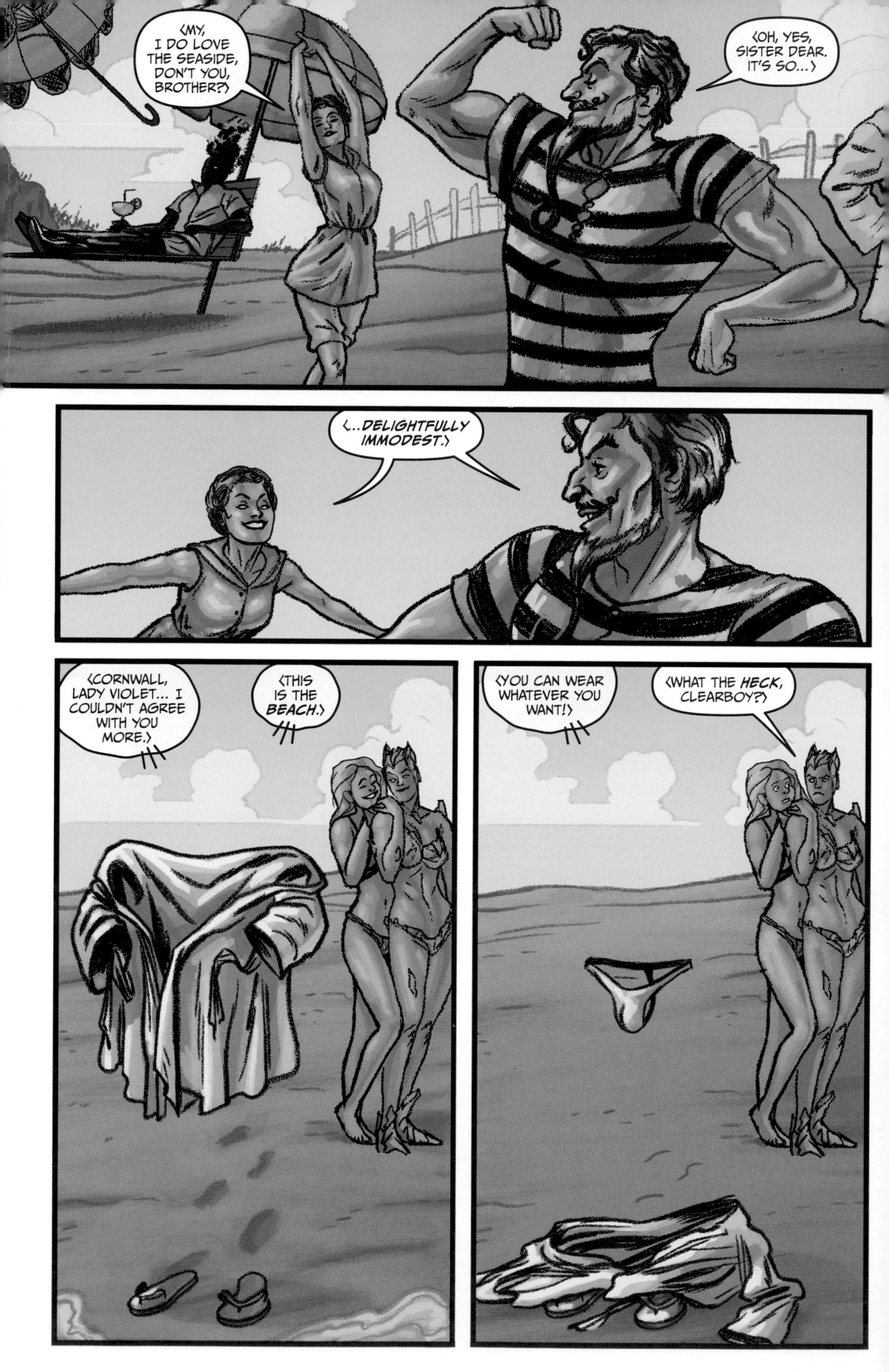

‹MY, I DO LOVE THE SEASIDE, DON'T YOU, BROTHER?›
‹OH, YES, SISTER DEAR. IT'S SO...›
‹...DELIGHTFULLY IMMODEST.›
‹CORNWALL, LADY VIOLET... I COULDN'T AGREE WITH YOU MORE.›
‹THIS IS THE BEACH.›
‹YOU CAN WEAR WHATEVER YOU WANT!›
‹WHAT THE HECK, CLEARBOY?›

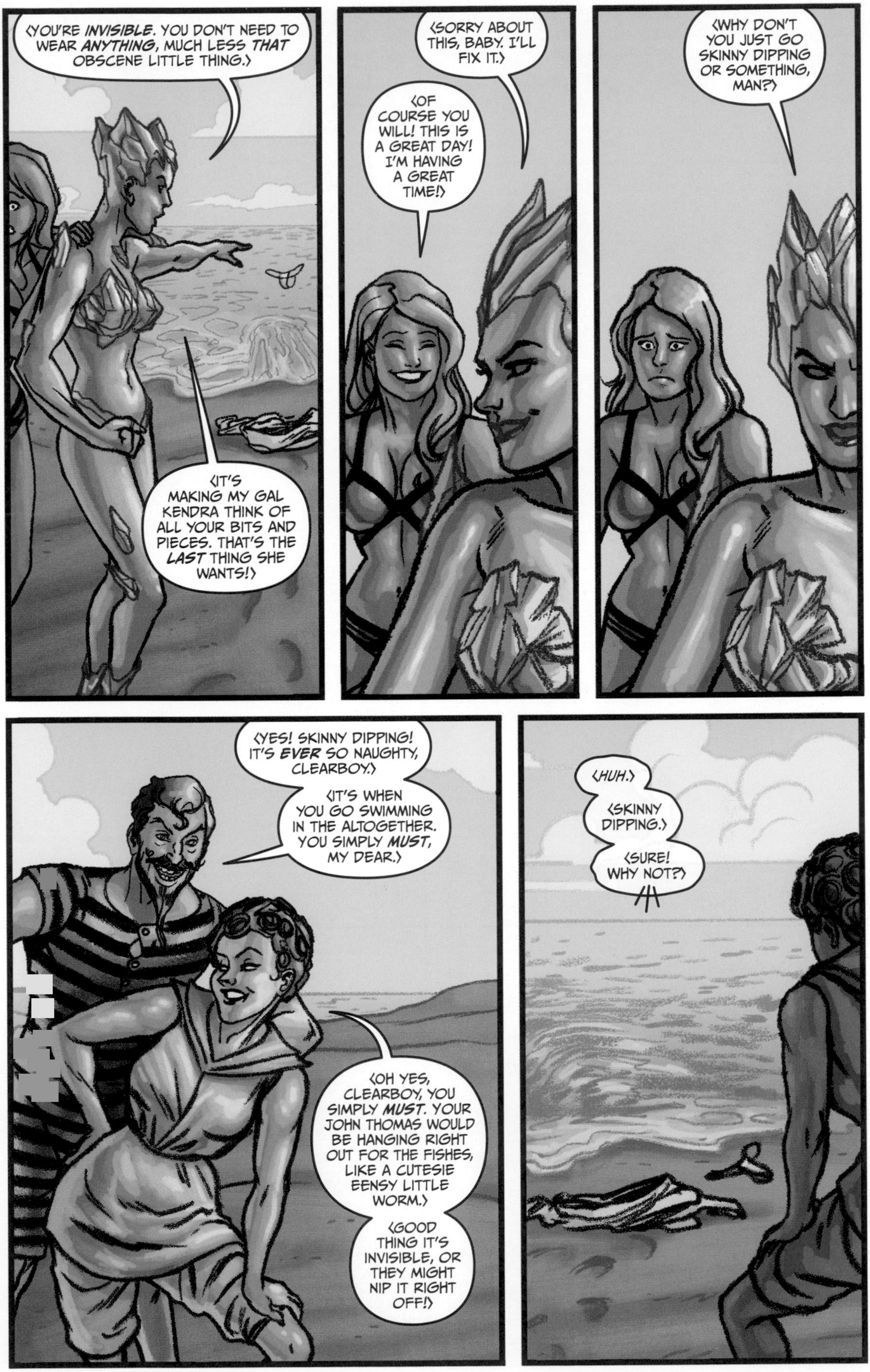
‹YOU'RE INVISIBLE. YOU DON'T NEED TO WEAR ANYTHING, MUCH LESS THAT OBSCENE LITTLE THING.›
‹IT'S MAKING MY GAL KENDRA THINK OF ALL YOUR BITS AND PIECES. THAT'S THE LAST THING SHE WANTS!›
‹SORRY ABOUT THIS, BABY. I'LL FIX IT.›
‹OF COURSE YOU WILL! THIS IS A GREAT DAY! I'M HAVING A GREAT TIME!›
‹WHY DON'T YOU JUST GO SKINNY DIPPING OR SOMETHING, MAN?›
‹YES! SKINNY DIPPING! IT'S EVER SO NAUGHTY, CLEARBOY.›
‹IT'S WHEN YOU GO SWIMMING IN THE ALTOGETHER. YOU SIMPLY MUST, MY DEAR.›
‹OH YES, CLEARBOY, YOU SIMPLY MUST. YOUR JOHN THOMAS WOULD BE HANGING RIGHT OUT FOR THE FISHES, LIKE A CUTESIE EENSY LITTLE WORM.›
‹GOOD THING IT'S INVISIBLE, OR THEY MIGHT NIP IT RIGHT OFF!›
‹HUH.›
‹SKINNY DIPPING.›
‹SURE! WHY NOT?›

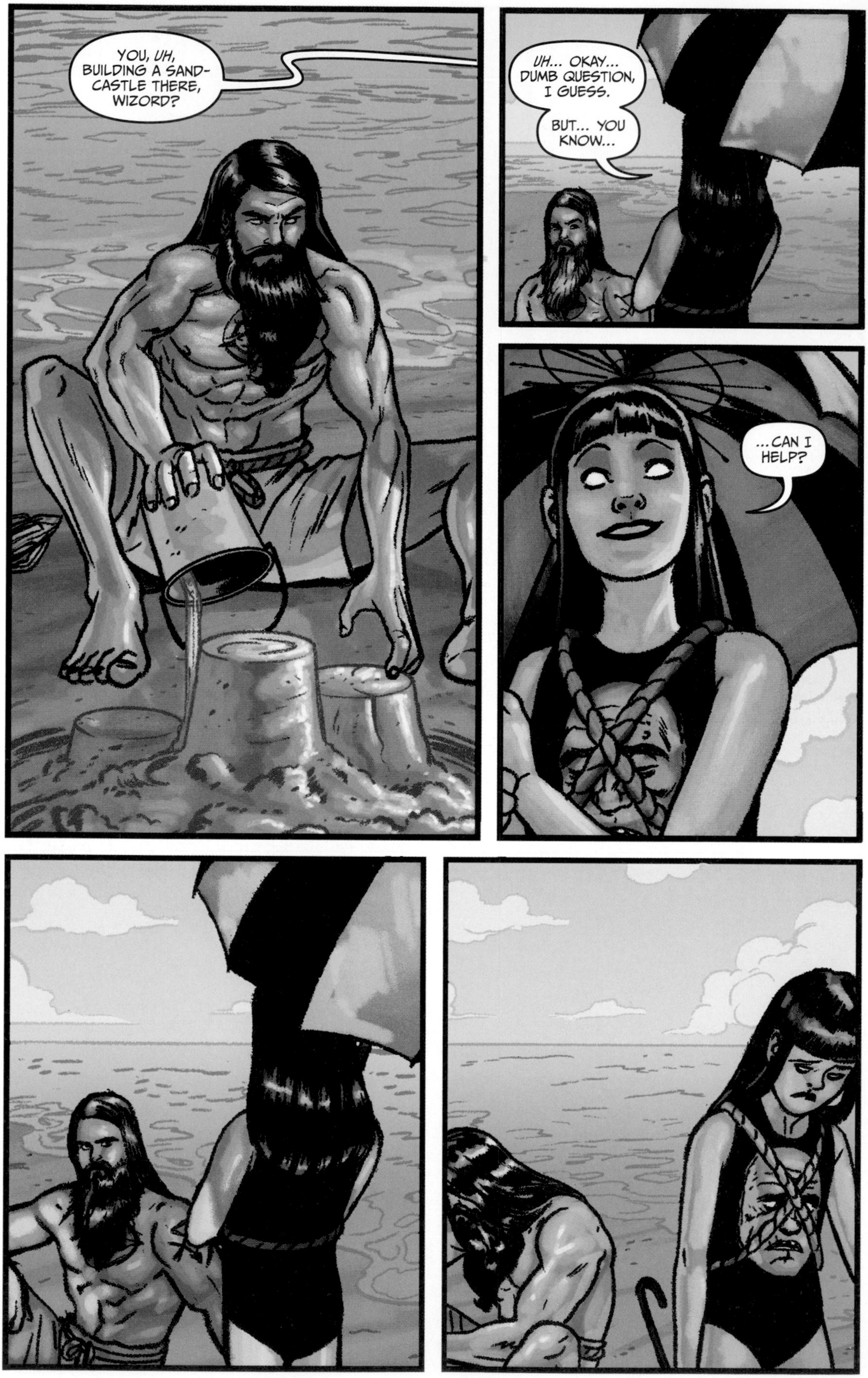
YOU, UH, BUILDING A SAND-CASTLE THERE, WIZORD?
UH... OKAY... DUMB QUESTION, I GUESS.
BUT... YOU KNOW...
...CAN I HELP?

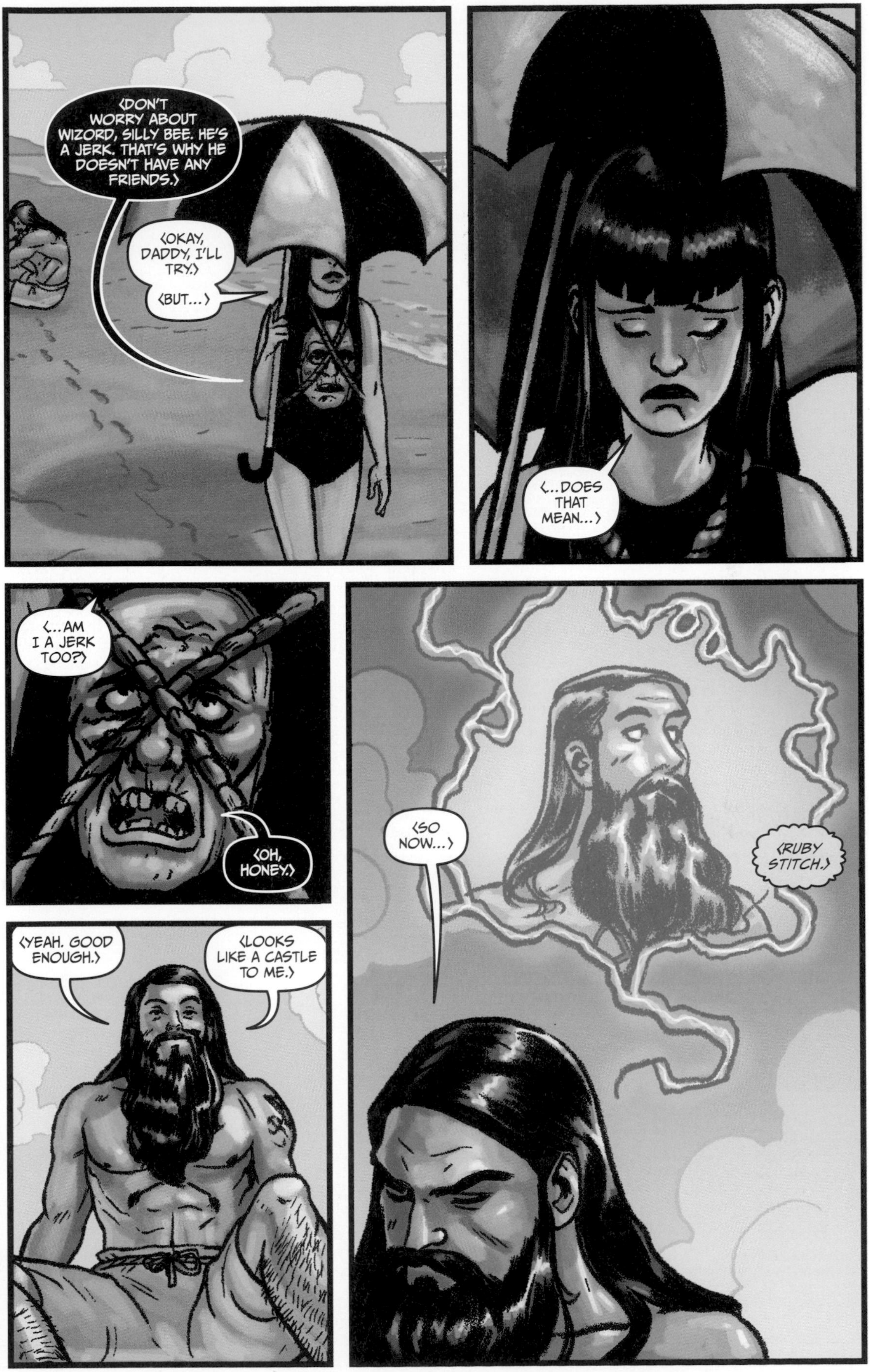
<DON'T WORRY ABOUT WIZORD, SILLY BEE. HE'S A JERK. THAT'S WHY HE DOESN'T HAVE ANY FRIENDS.>
<OKAY, DADDY, I'LL TRY.>
<BUT...>
<...DOES THAT MEAN...>
<...AM I A JERK TOO?>
<OH, HONEY.>
<YEAH. GOOD ENOUGH.>
<LOOKS LIKE A CASTLE TO ME.>
<SO NOW...>
<RUBY STITCH.>

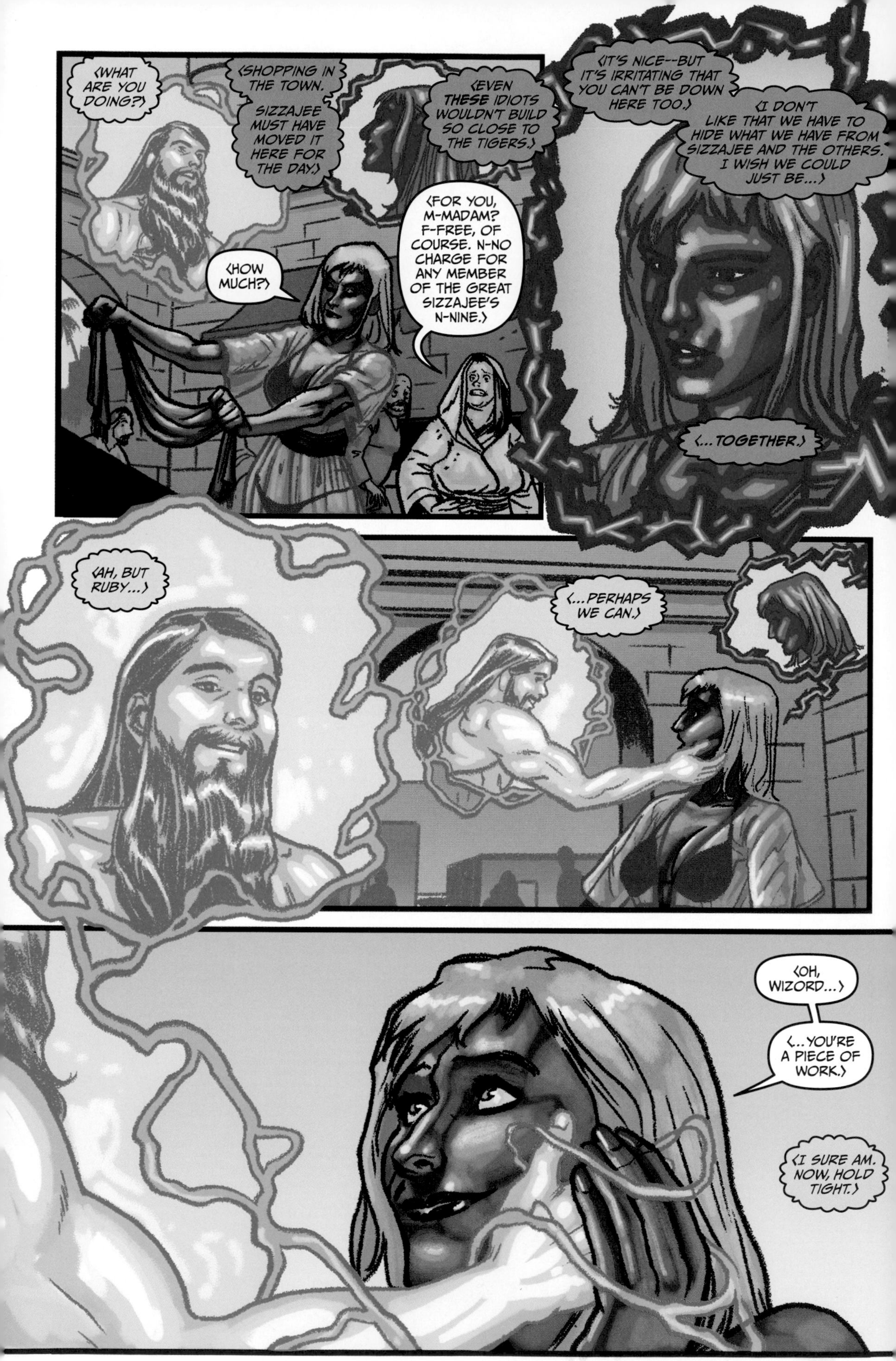

‹WHAT ARE YOU DOING?›
‹SHOPPING IN THE TOWN.
SIZZAJEE MUST HAVE MOVED IT HERE FOR THE DAY.›
‹EVEN THESE IDIOTS WOULDN'T BUILD SO CLOSE TO THE TIGERS.›
‹HOW MUCH?›
‹FOR YOU, M-MADAM? F-FREE, OF COURSE. N-NO CHARGE FOR ANY MEMBER OF THE GREAT SIZZAJEE'S N-NINE.›
‹IT'S NICE--BUT IT'S IRRITATING THAT YOU CAN'T BE DOWN HERE TOO.›
‹I DON'T LIKE THAT WE HAVE TO HIDE WHAT WE HAVE FROM SIZZAJEE AND THE OTHERS. I WISH WE COULD JUST BE...›
‹...TOGETHER.›
‹AH, BUT RUBY...›
‹...PERHAPS WE CAN.›
‹OH, WIZORD...›
‹...YOU'RE A PIECE OF WORK.›
‹I SURE AM. NOW, HOLD TIGHT.›

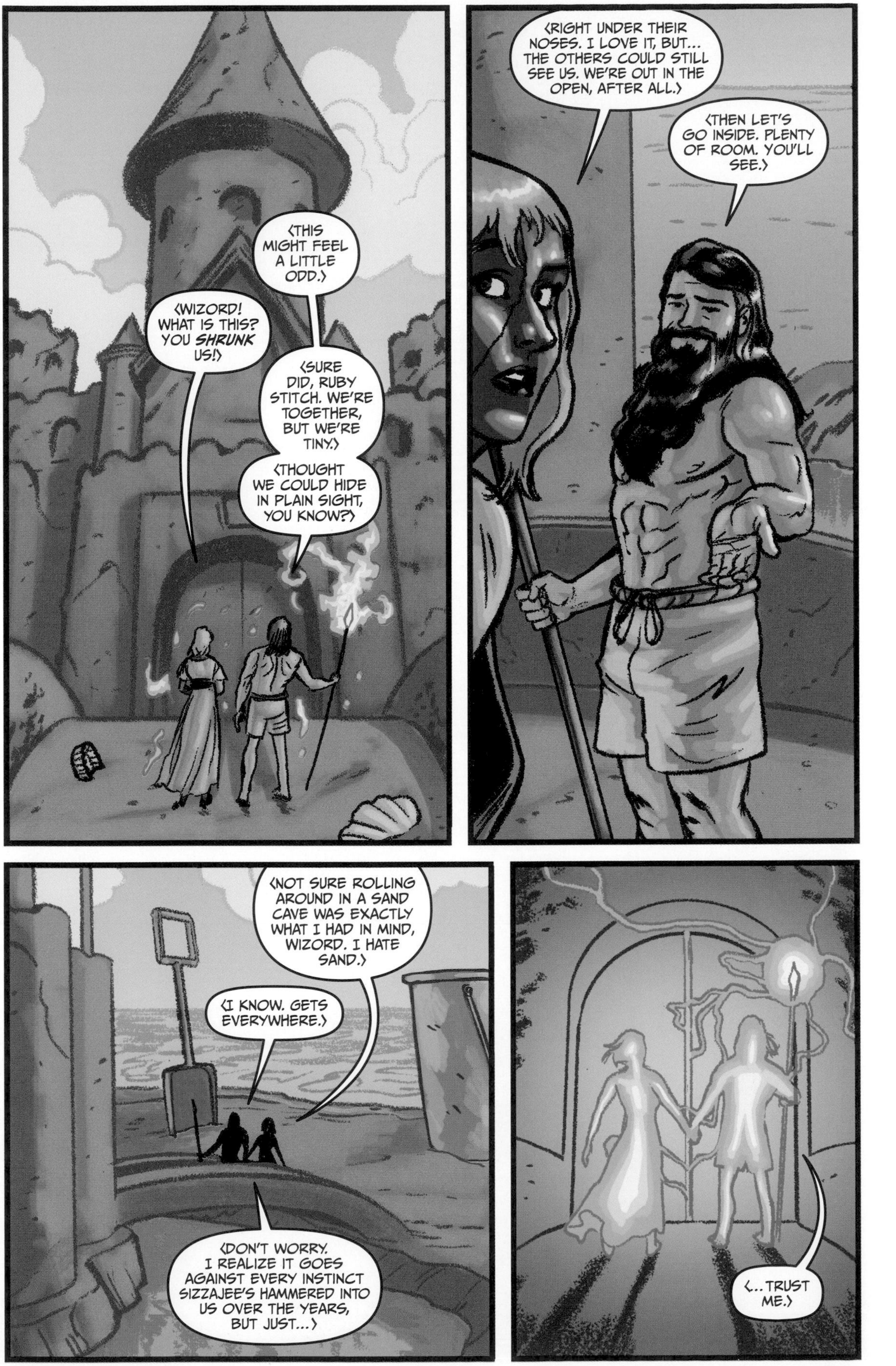
<THIS MIGHT FEEL A LITTLE ODD.>
<WIZORD! WHAT IS THIS? YOU **SHRUNK** US!>
<SURE DID, RUBY STITCH. WE'RE TOGETHER, BUT WE'RE TINY.>
<THOUGHT WE COULD HIDE IN PLAIN SIGHT, YOU KNOW?>
<RIGHT UNDER THEIR NOSES. I LOVE IT, BUT... THE OTHERS COULD STILL SEE US. WE'RE OUT IN THE OPEN, AFTER ALL.>
<THEN LET'S GO INSIDE. PLENTY OF ROOM. YOU'LL SEE.>
<NOT SURE ROLLING AROUND IN A SAND CAVE WAS EXACTLY WHAT I HAD IN MIND, WIZORD. I HATE SAND.>
<I KNOW. GETS EVERYWHERE.>
<DON'T WORRY. I REALIZE IT GOES AGAINST EVERY INSTINCT SIZZAJEE'S HAMMERED INTO US OVER THE YEARS, BUT JUST...>
<...TRUST ME.>

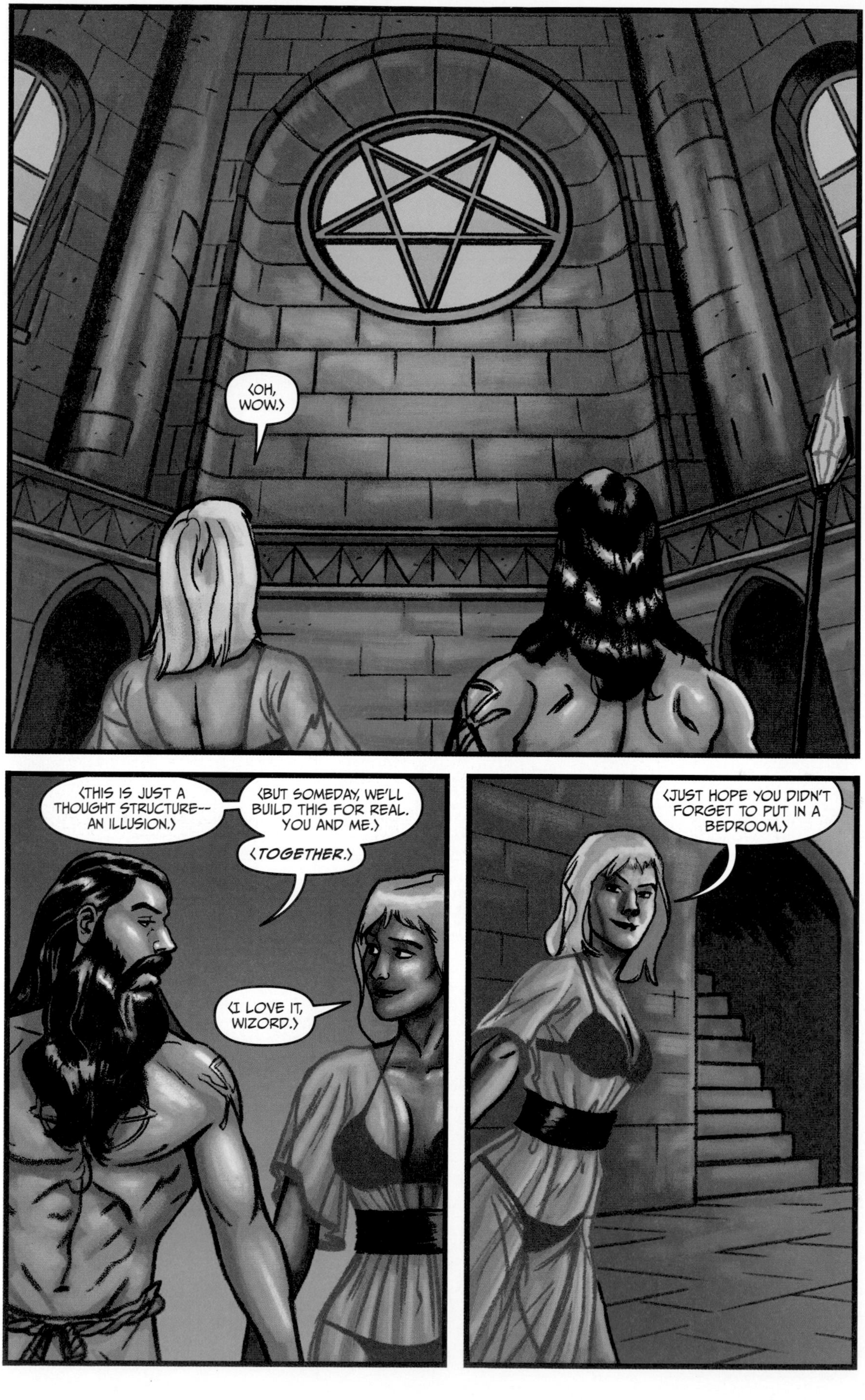

⟨OH, WOW.⟩
⟨THIS IS JUST A THOUGHT STRUCTURE-- AN ILLUSION.⟩
⟨BUT SOMEDAY, WE'LL BUILD THIS FOR REAL. YOU AND ME.⟩
⟨*TOGETHER.*⟩
⟨I LOVE IT, WIZORD.⟩
⟨JUST HOPE YOU DIDN'T FORGET TO PUT IN A BEDROOM.⟩

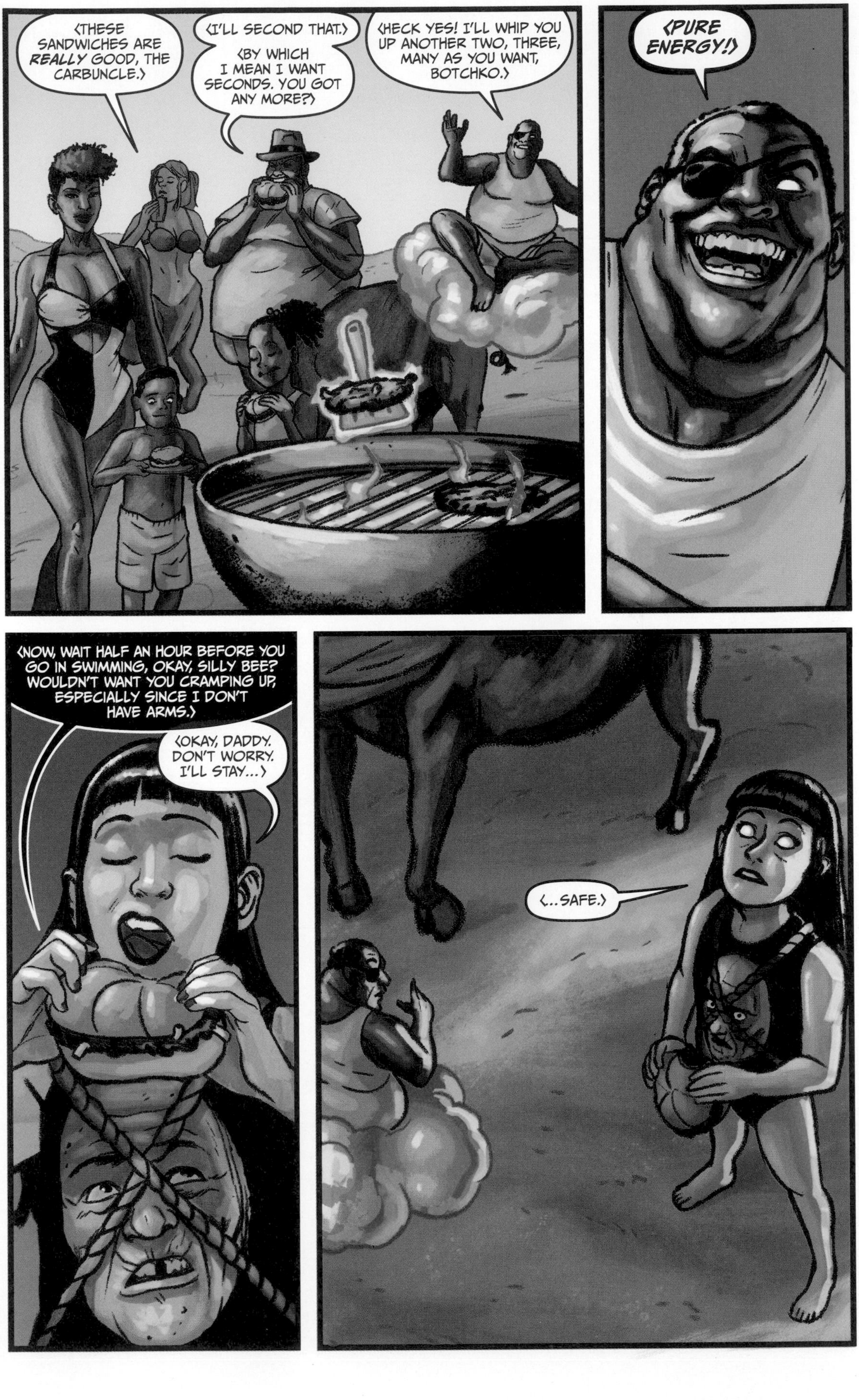

<THESE SANDWICHES ARE REALLY GOOD, THE CARBUNCLE.>
<I'LL SECOND THAT.>
<BY WHICH I MEAN I WANT SECONDS. YOU GOT ANY MORE?>
<HECK YES! I'LL WHIP YOU UP ANOTHER TWO, THREE, MANY AS YOU WANT, BOTCHKO.>
<PURE ENERGY!>
<NOW, WAIT HALF AN HOUR BEFORE YOU GO IN SWIMMING, OKAY, SILLY BEE? WOULDN'T WANT YOU CRAMPING UP, ESPECIALLY SINCE I DON'T HAVE ARMS.>
<OKAY, DADDY. DON'T WORRY. I'LL STAY...>
<...SAFE.>

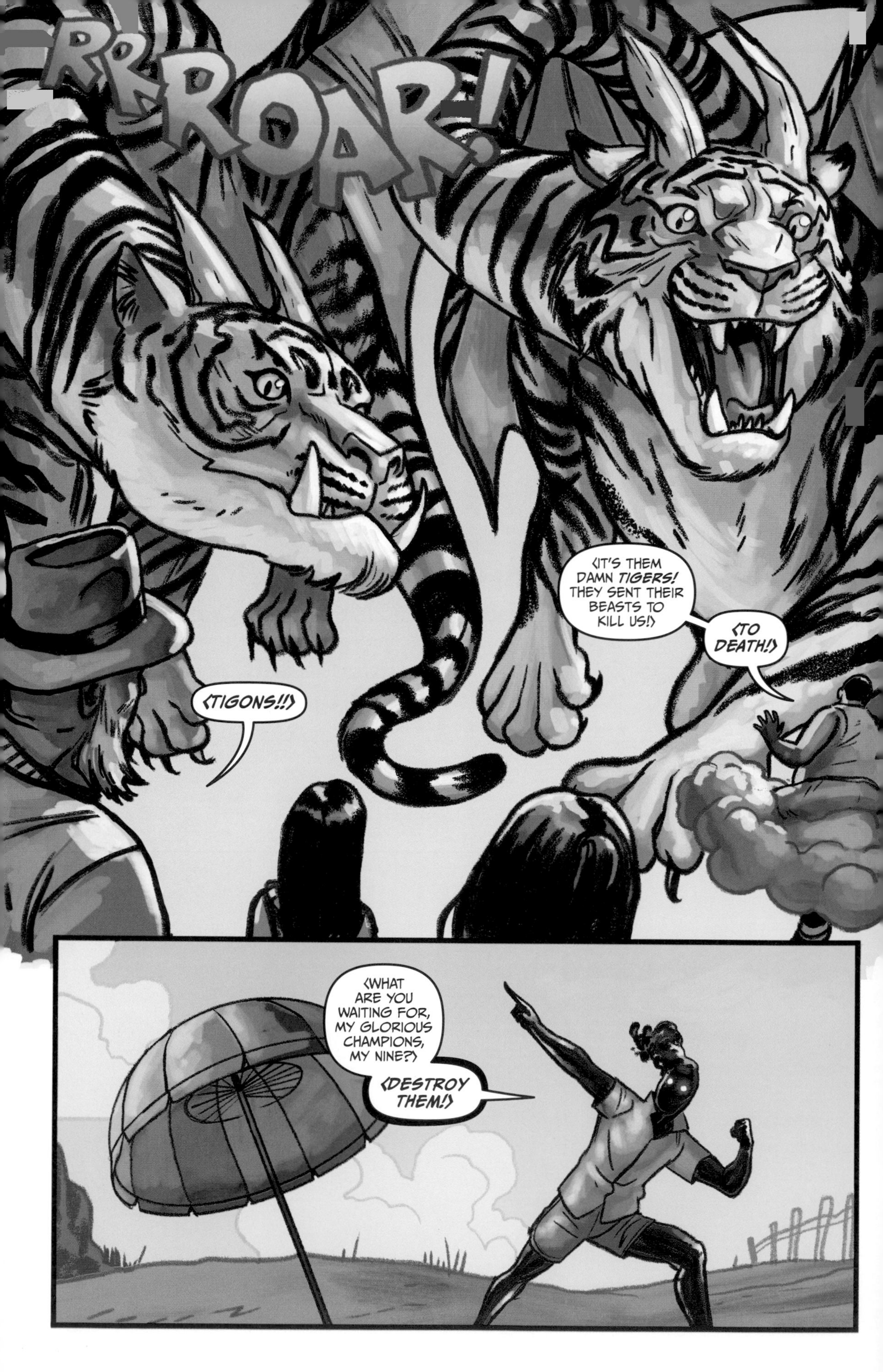
RRROAR!
⟨IT'S THEM DAMN TIGERS! THEY SENT THEIR BEASTS TO KILL US!⟩
⟨TO DEATH!⟩
⟨TIGONS!!⟩
⟨WHAT ARE YOU WAITING FOR, MY GLORIOUS CHAMPIONS, MY NINE?⟩
⟨DESTROY THEM!⟩

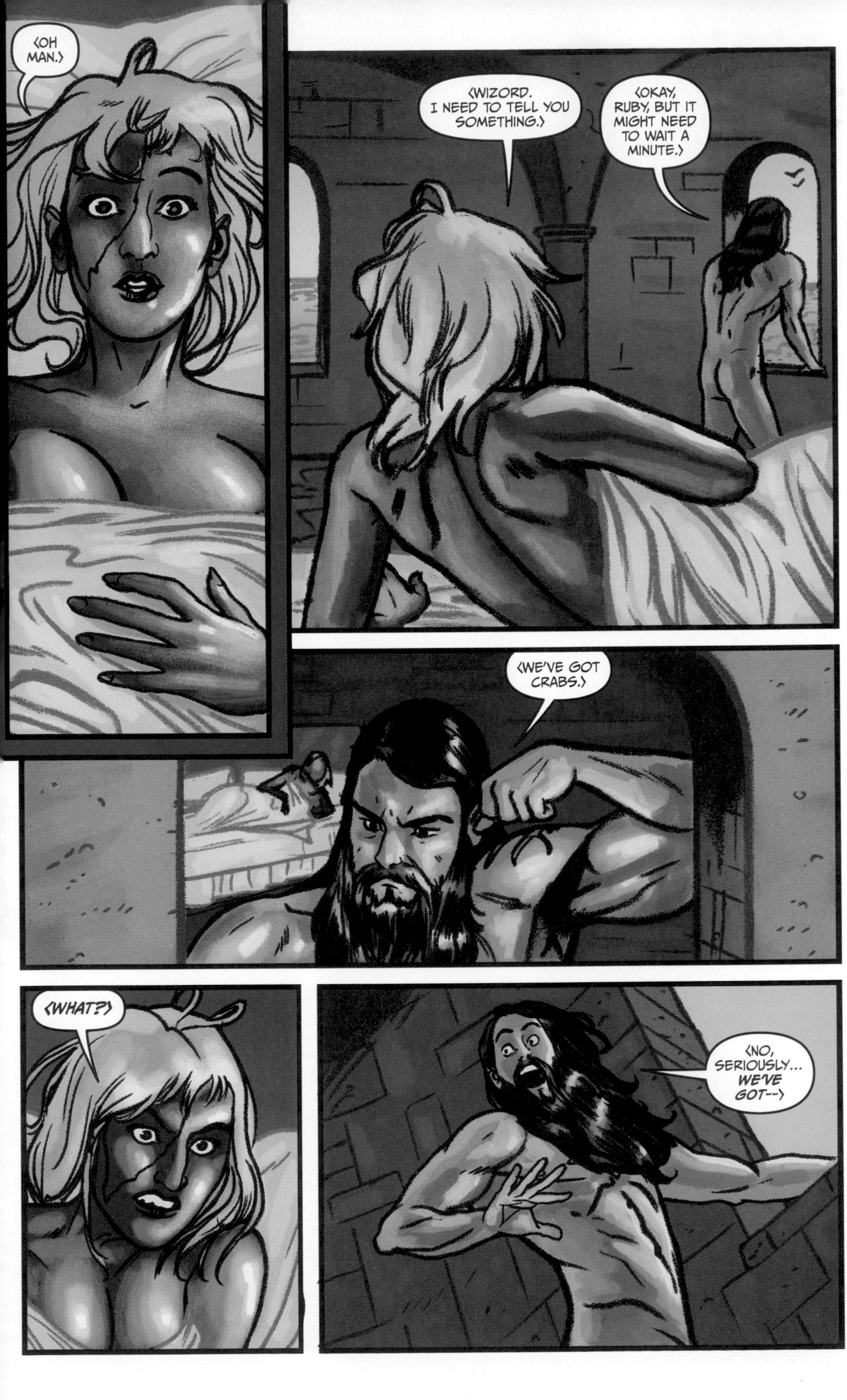
‹OH MAN.›
‹WIZORD. I NEED TO TELL YOU SOMETHING.›
‹OKAY, RUBY, BUT IT MIGHT NEED TO WAIT A MINUTE.›
‹WE'VE GOT CRABS.›
‹WHAT?›
‹NO, SERIOUSLY... WE'VE GOT--›

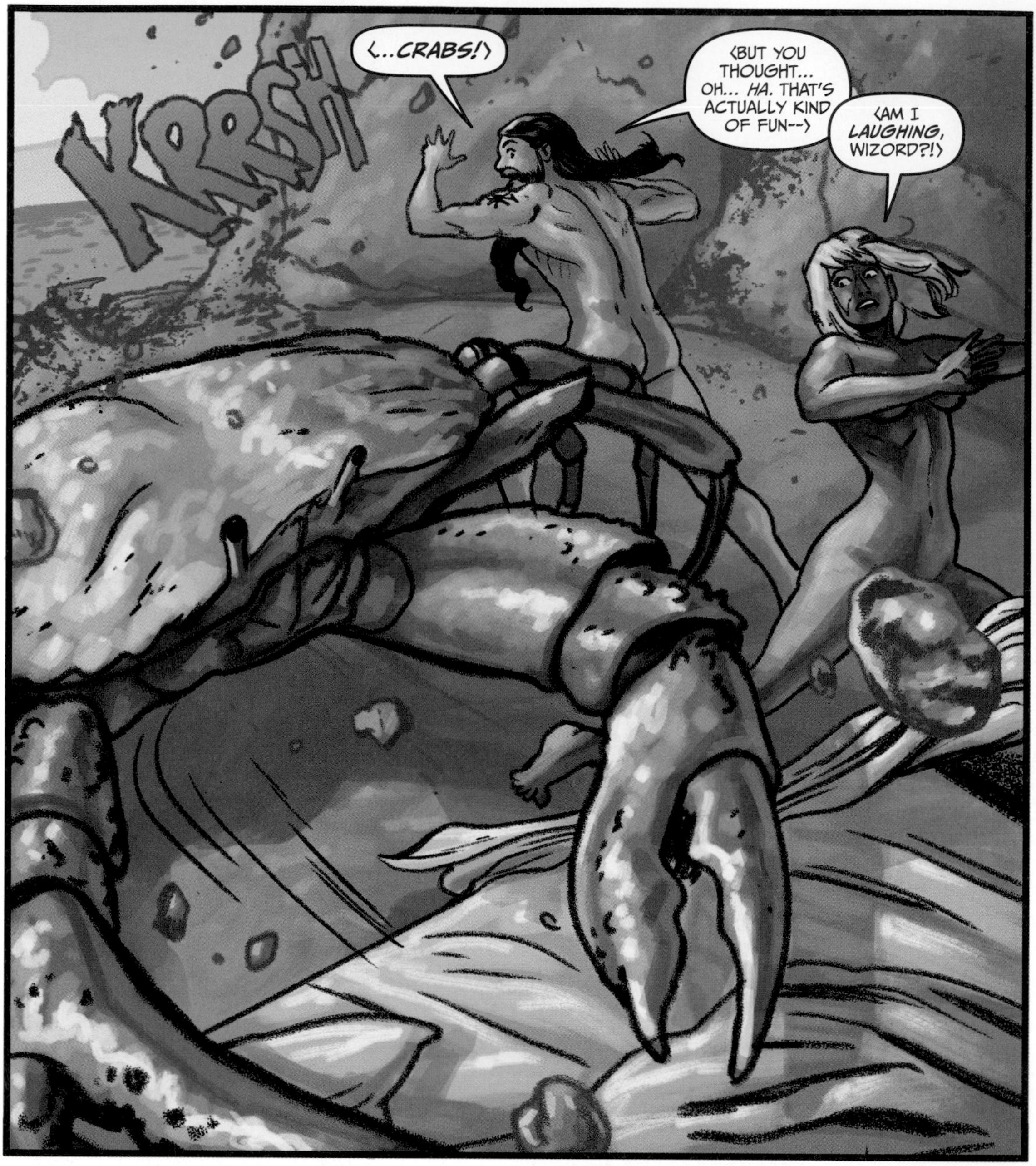
KRRSH
‹...CRABS!›
‹BUT YOU THOUGHT... OH... HA. THAT'S ACTUALLY KIND OF FUN--›
‹AM I LAUGHING, WIZORD?!›

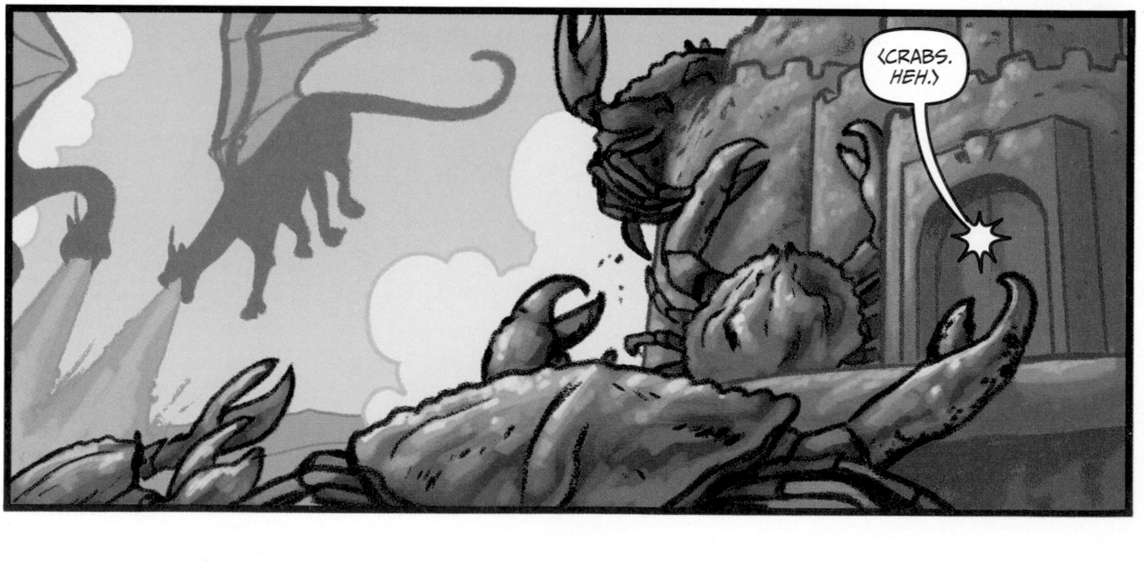
‹CRABS. HEH.›

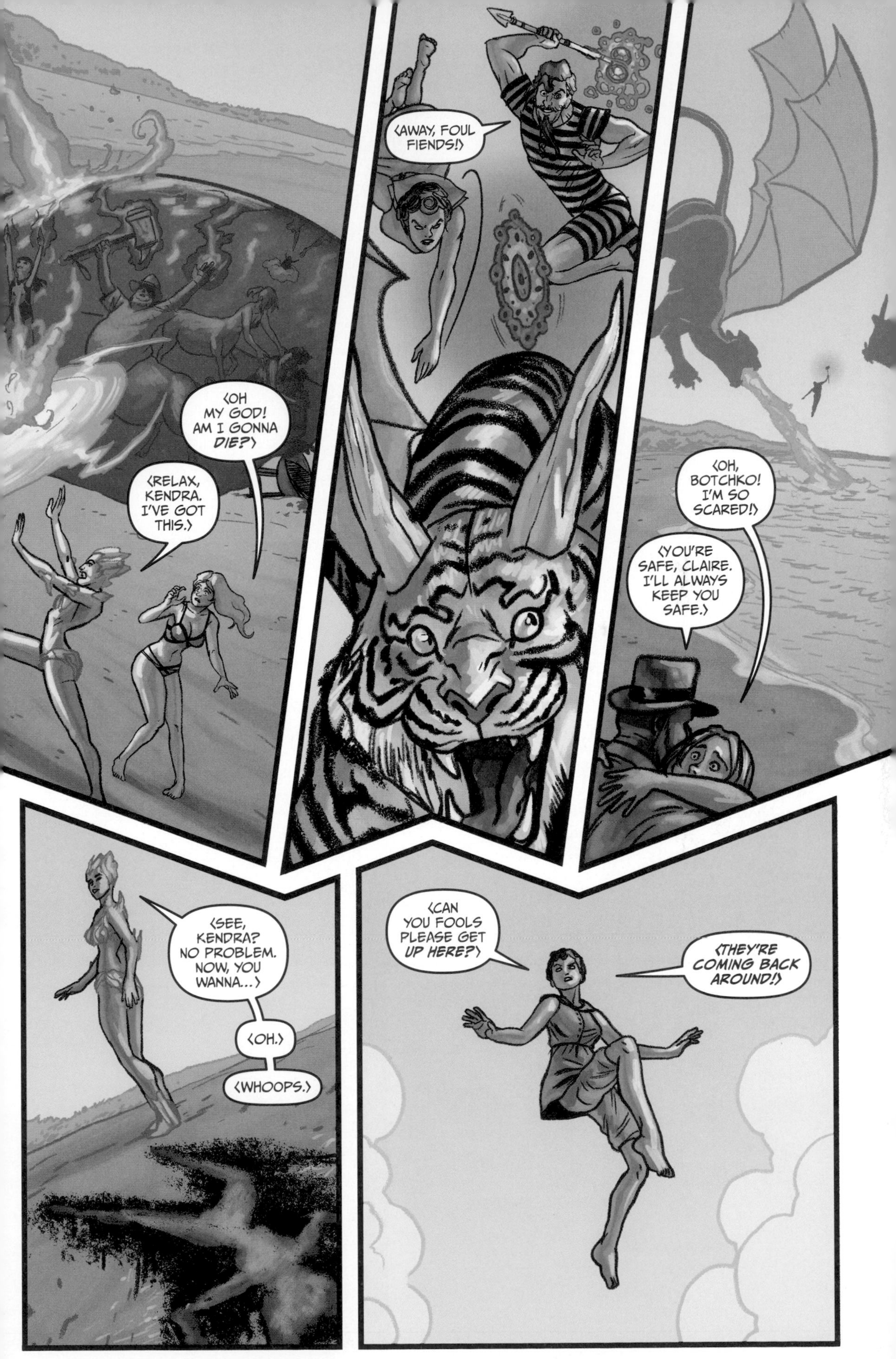

‹OH MY GOD! AM I GONNA DIE?›
‹RELAX, KENDRA. I'VE GOT THIS.›
‹AWAY, FOUL FIENDS!›
‹OH, BOTCHKO! I'M SO SCARED!›
‹YOU'RE SAFE, CLAIRE. I'LL ALWAYS KEEP YOU SAFE.›
‹SEE, KENDRA? NO PROBLEM. NOW, YOU WANNA...›
‹OH.›
‹WHOOPS.›
‹CAN YOU FOOLS PLEASE GET UP HERE?›
‹THEY'RE COMING BACK AROUND!›

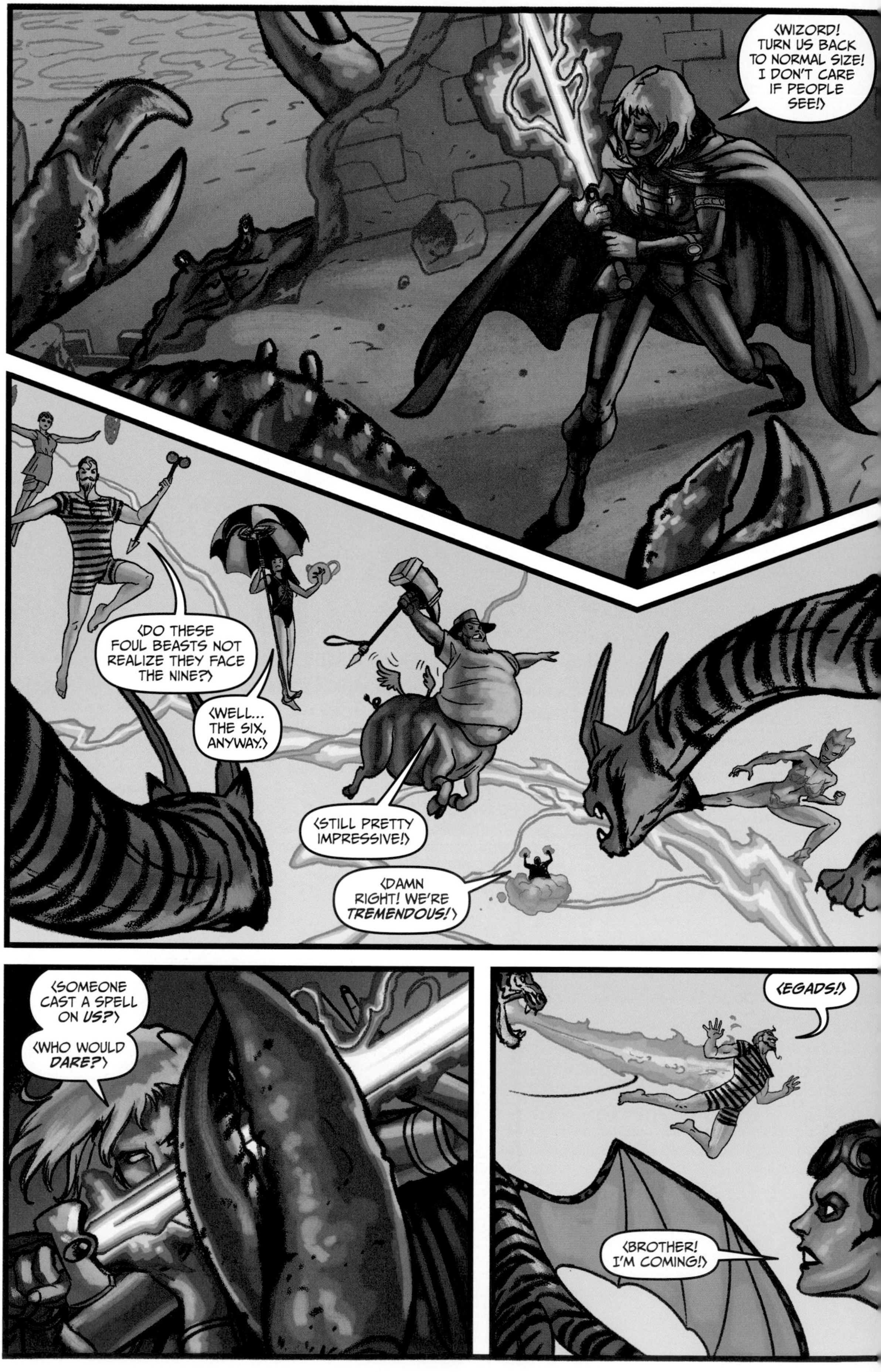
〈WIZORD! TURN US BACK TO NORMAL SIZE! I DON'T CARE IF PEOPLE SEE!〉
〈DO THESE FOUL BEASTS NOT REALIZE THEY FACE THE NINE?〉
〈WELL... THE SIX, ANYWAY.〉
〈STILL PRETTY IMPRESSIVE!〉
〈DAMN RIGHT! WE'RE *TREMENDOUS!*〉
〈SOMEONE CAST A SPELL ON *US?*〉
〈WHO WOULD *DARE?*〉
〈*EGADS!*〉
〈BROTHER! I'M COMING!〉

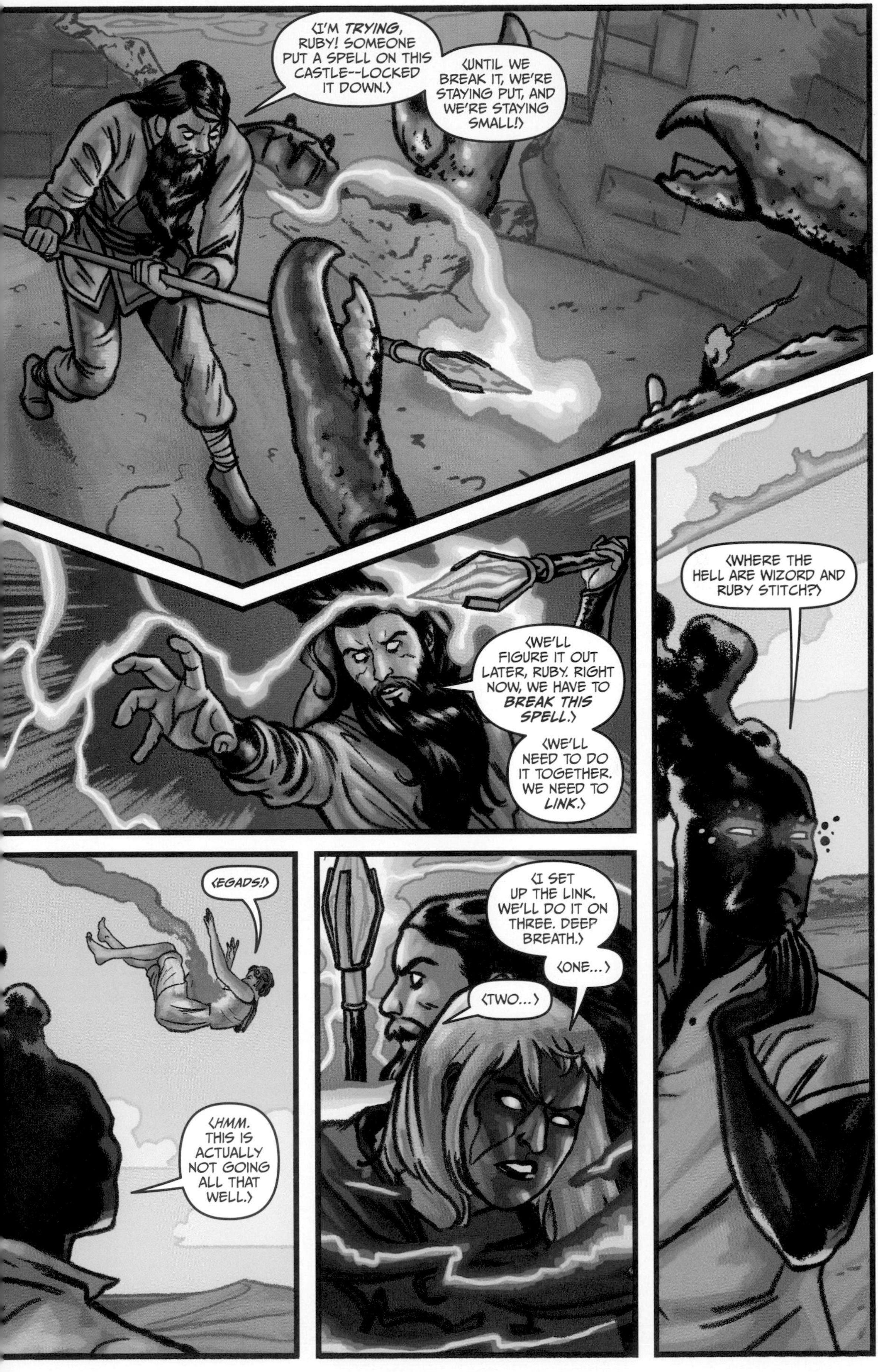
⟨I'M *TRYING*, RUBY! SOMEONE PUT A SPELL ON THIS CASTLE--LOCKED IT DOWN.⟩
⟨UNTIL WE BREAK IT, WE'RE STAYING PUT, AND WE'RE STAYING SMALL!⟩
⟨WE'LL FIGURE IT OUT LATER, RUBY. RIGHT NOW, WE HAVE TO ***BREAK THIS SPELL***.⟩
⟨WE'LL NEED TO DO IT TOGETHER. WE NEED TO *LINK*.⟩
⟨WHERE THE HELL ARE WIZORD AND RUBY STITCH?⟩
⟨*EGADS!*⟩
⟨*HMM.* THIS IS ACTUALLY NOT GOING ALL THAT WELL.⟩
⟨I SET UP THE LINK. WE'LL DO IT ON THREE. DEEP BREATH.⟩
⟨ONE...⟩
⟨TWO...⟩

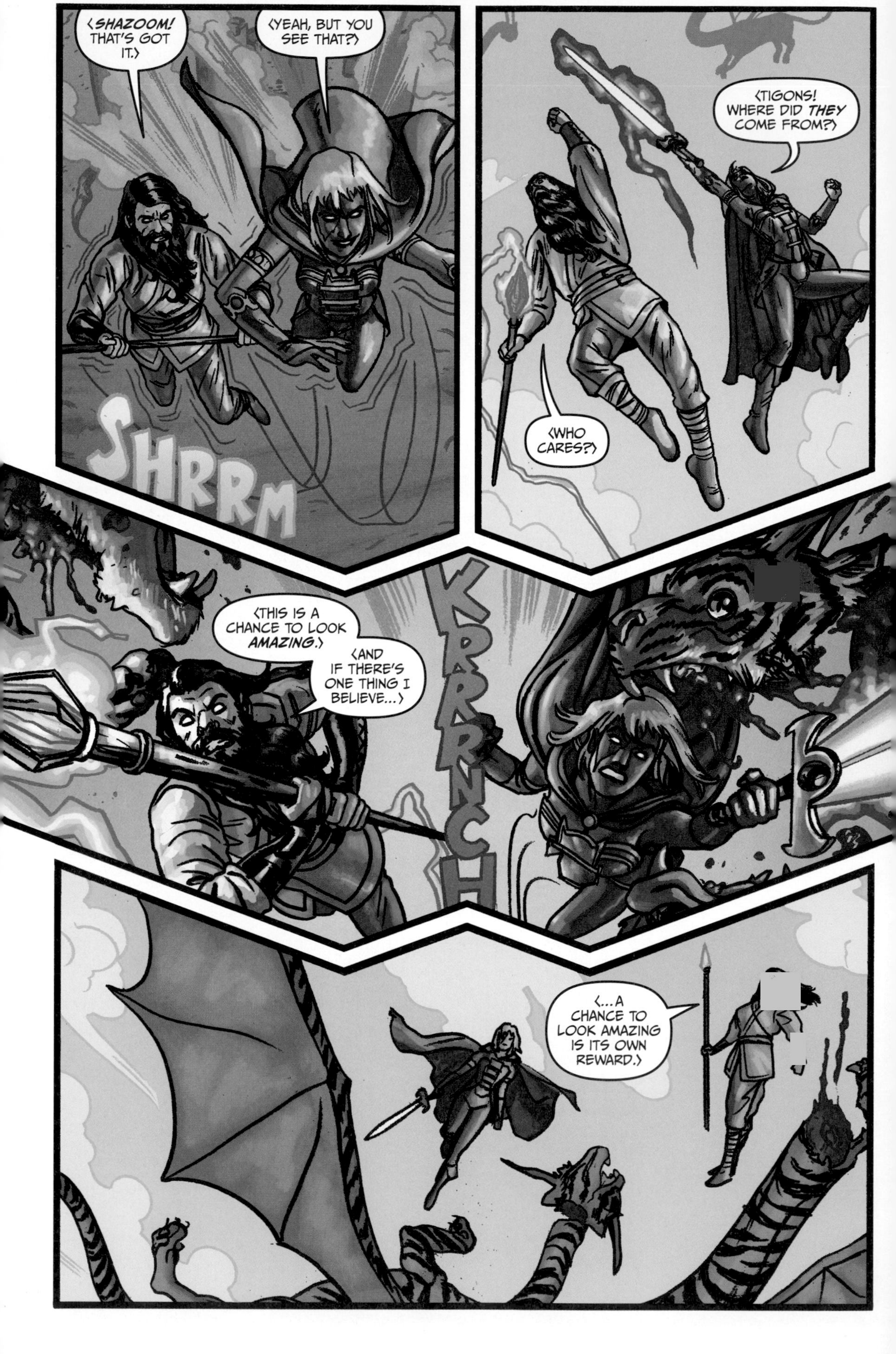
‹SHAZOOM! THAT'S GOT IT.›
‹YEAH, BUT YOU SEE THAT?›
SHRRM
‹TIGONS! WHERE DID THEY COME FROM?›
‹WHO CARES?›
‹THIS IS A CHANCE TO LOOK AMAZING.›
‹AND IF THERE'S ONE THING I BELIEVE...›
KRRRNCH
‹...A CHANCE TO LOOK AMAZING IS ITS OWN REWARD.›

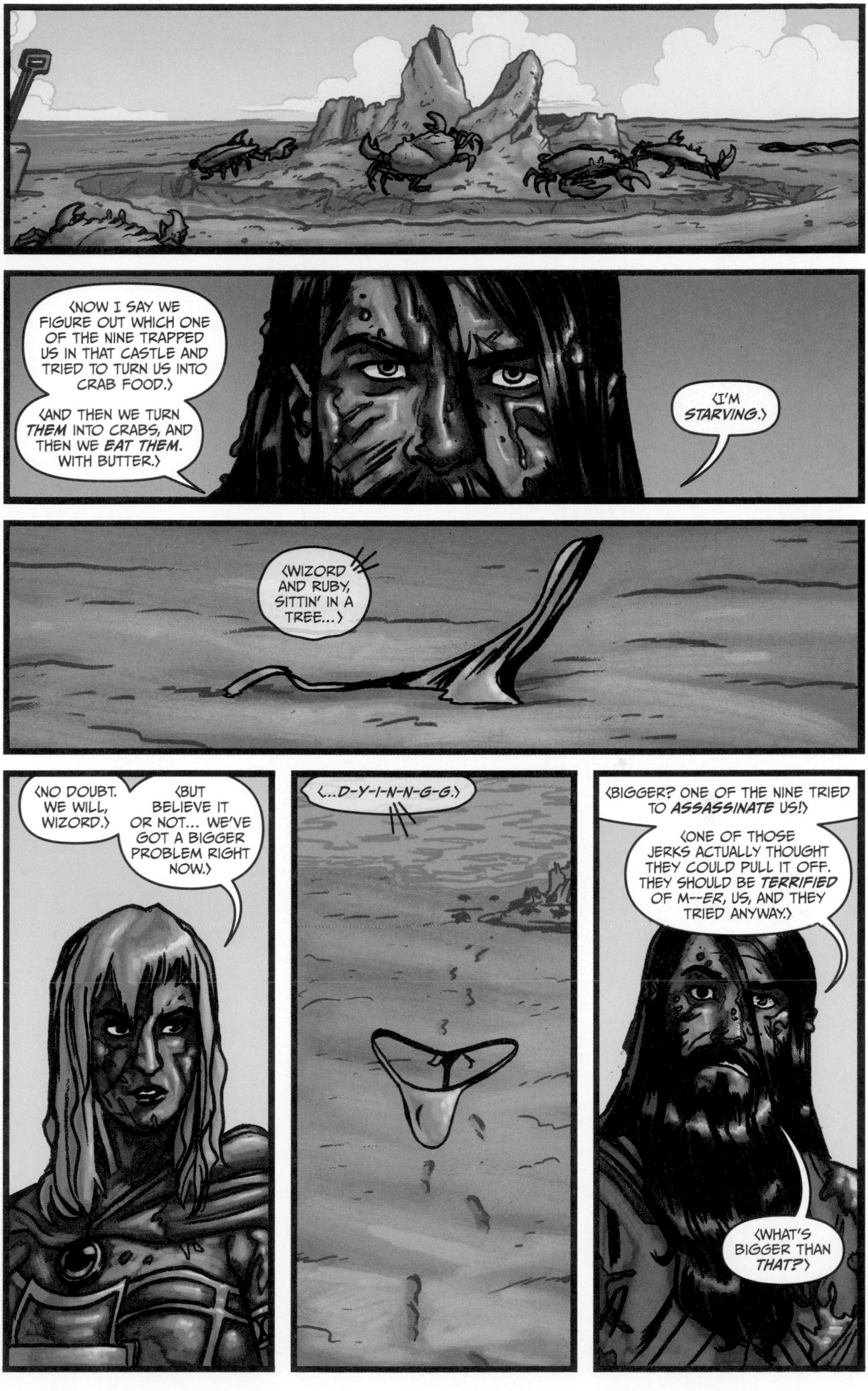
〈NOW I SAY WE FIGURE OUT WHICH ONE OF THE NINE TRAPPED US IN THAT CASTLE AND TRIED TO TURN US INTO CRAB FOOD.〉
〈AND THEN WE TURN *THEM* INTO CRABS, AND THEN WE *EAT THEM*. WITH BUTTER.〉
〈I'M *STARVING*.〉
〈WIZORD AND RUBY, SITTIN' IN A TREE...〉
〈NO DOUBT. WE WILL, WIZORD.〉
〈BUT BELIEVE IT OR NOT... WE'VE GOT A BIGGER PROBLEM RIGHT NOW.〉
〈...D-Y-I-N-N-G-G.〉
〈BIGGER? ONE OF THE NINE TRIED TO *ASSASSINATE* US!〉
〈ONE OF THOSE JERKS ACTUALLY THOUGHT THEY COULD PULL IT OFF. THEY SHOULD BE *TERRIFIED* OF M--*ER*, US, AND THEY TRIED ANYWAY.〉
〈WHAT'S BIGGER THAN *THAT?*〉

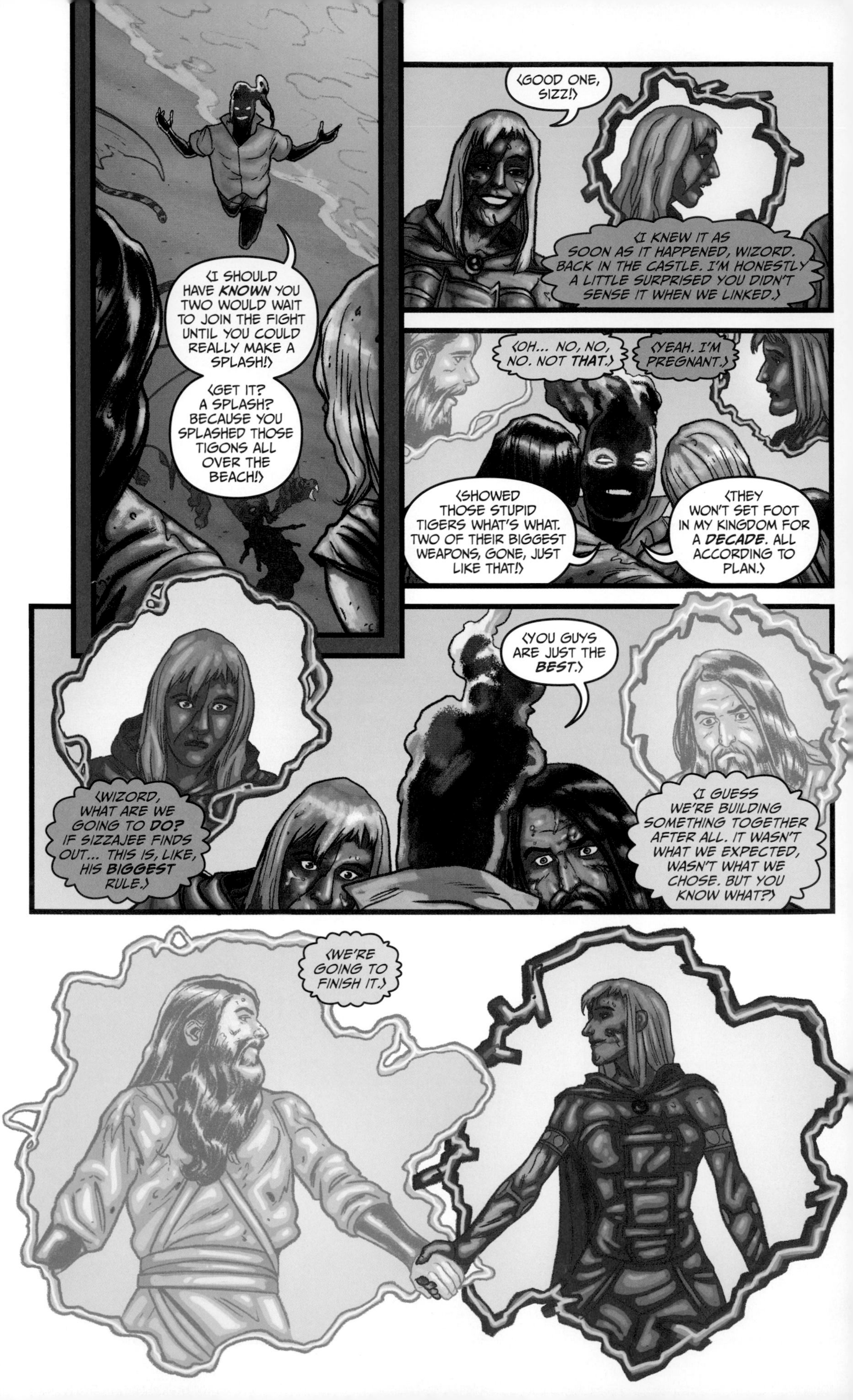
‹I SHOULD HAVE KNOWN YOU TWO WOULD WAIT TO JOIN THE FIGHT UNTIL YOU COULD REALLY MAKE A SPLASH!›
‹GET IT? A SPLASH? BECAUSE YOU SPLASHED THOSE TIGONS ALL OVER THE BEACH!›
‹GOOD ONE, SIZZ!›
‹I KNEW IT AS SOON AS IT HAPPENED, WIZORD. BACK IN THE CASTLE. I'M HONESTLY A LITTLE SURPRISED YOU DIDN'T SENSE IT WHEN WE LINKED.›
‹OH... NO, NO, NO. NOT THAT.›
‹YEAH. I'M PREGNANT.›
‹SHOWED THOSE STUPID TIGERS WHAT'S WHAT. TWO OF THEIR BIGGEST WEAPONS, GONE, JUST LIKE THAT!›
‹THEY WON'T SET FOOT IN MY KINGDOM FOR A DECADE. ALL ACCORDING TO PLAN.›
‹YOU GUYS ARE JUST THE BEST.›
‹WIZORD, WHAT ARE WE GOING TO DO? IF SIZZAJEE FINDS OUT... THIS IS, LIKE, HIS BIGGEST RULE.›
‹I GUESS WE'RE BUILDING SOMETHING TOGETHER AFTER ALL. IT WASN'T WHAT WE EXPECTED, WASN'T WHAT WE CHOSE. BUT YOU KNOW WHAT?›
‹WE'RE GOING TO FINISH IT.›

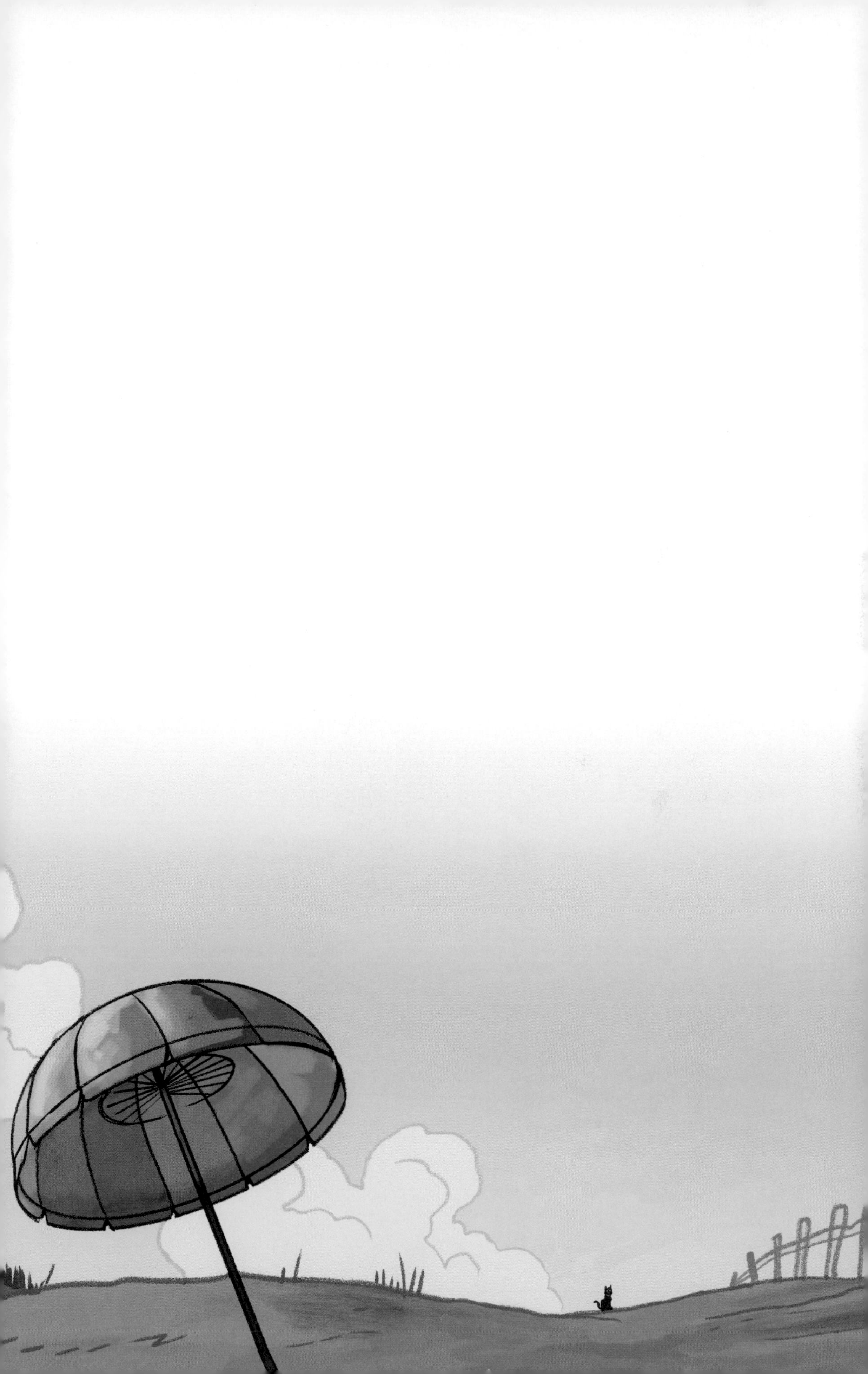

SIXTEEN

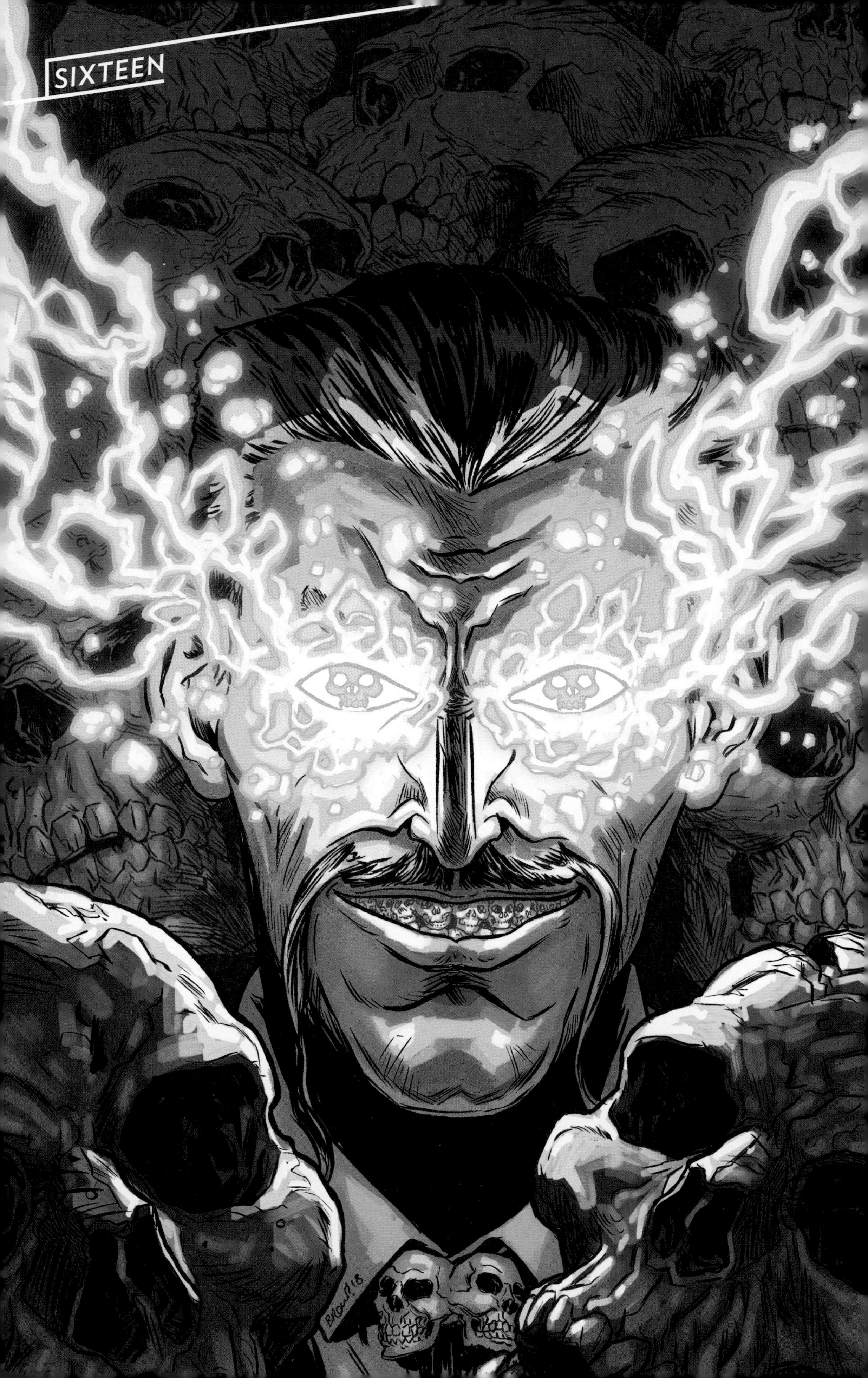

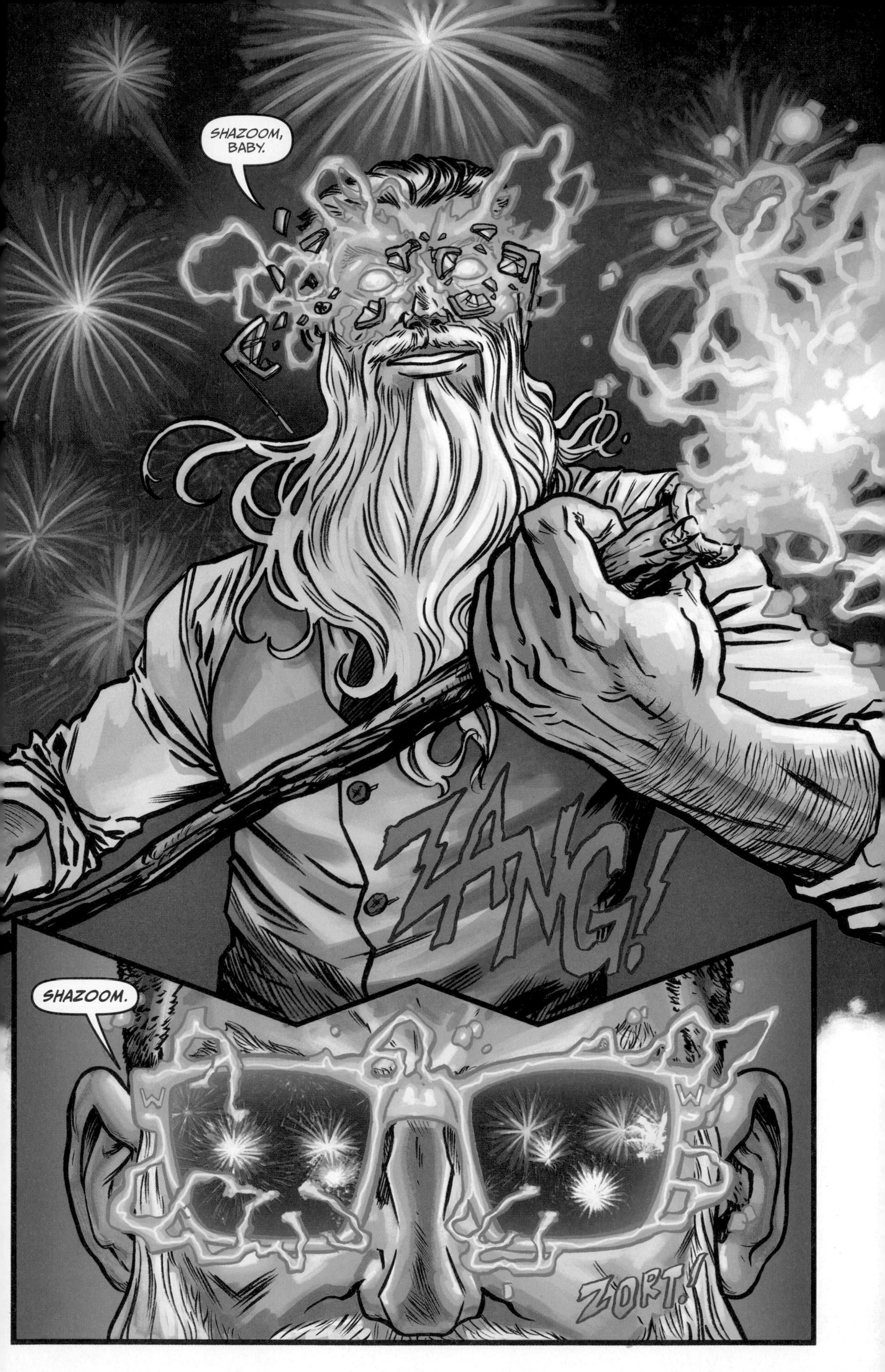
SHAZOOM, BABY.
ZANG!
SHAZOOM.
ZORT!

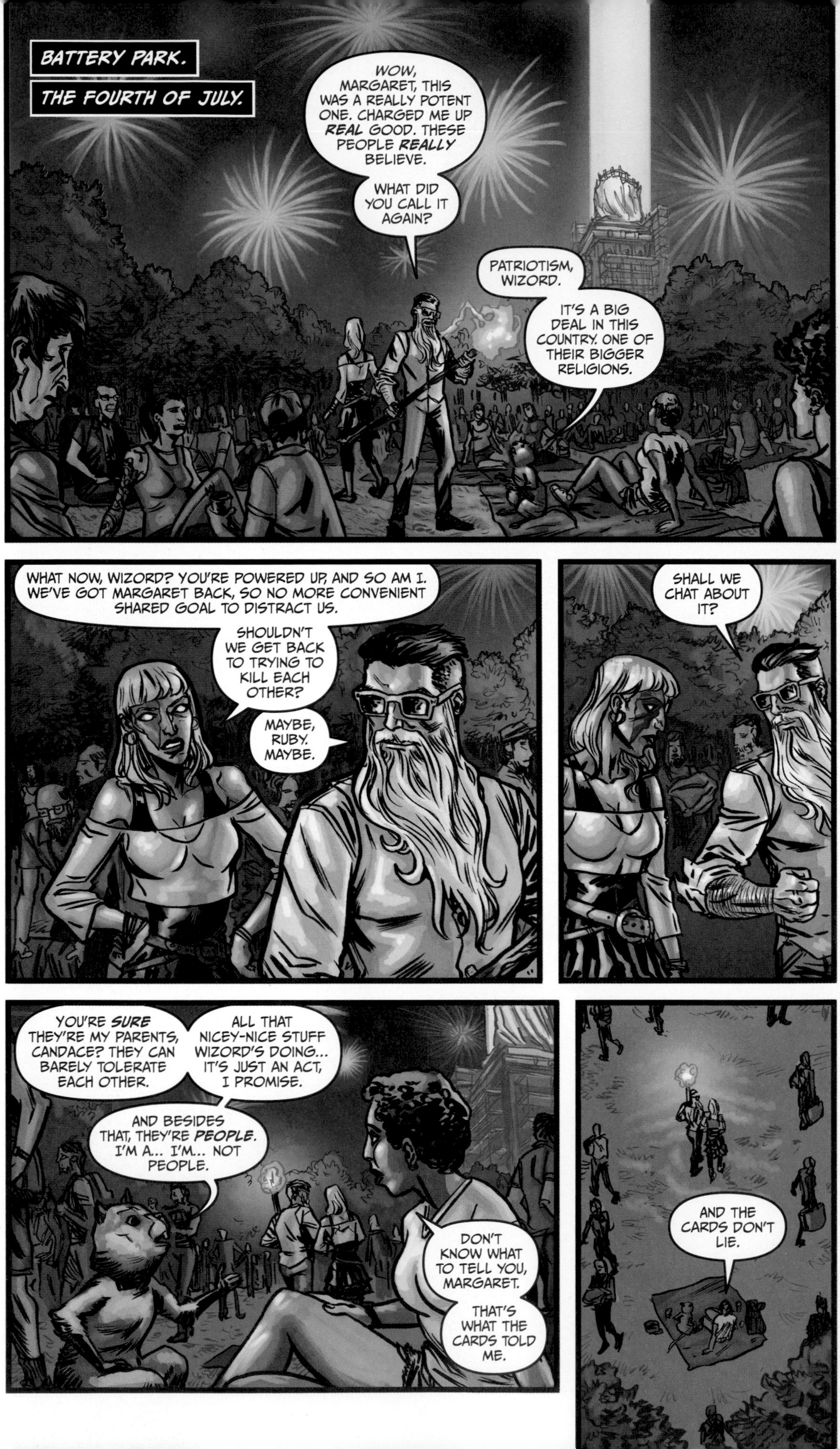

BATTERY PARK.
THE FOURTH OF JULY.
WOW, MARGARET, THIS WAS A REALLY POTENT ONE. CHARGED ME UP *REAL* GOOD. THESE PEOPLE *REALLY* BELIEVE.
WHAT DID YOU CALL IT AGAIN?
PATRIOTISM, WIZORD.
IT'S A BIG DEAL IN THIS COUNTRY. ONE OF THEIR BIGGER RELIGIONS.
WHAT NOW, WIZORD? YOU'RE POWERED UP, AND SO AM I. WE'VE GOT MARGARET BACK, SO NO MORE CONVENIENT SHARED GOAL TO DISTRACT US.
SHOULDN'T WE GET BACK TO TRYING TO KILL EACH OTHER?
MAYBE, RUBY. MAYBE.
SHALL WE CHAT ABOUT IT?
YOU'RE *SURE* THEY'RE MY PARENTS, CANDACE? THEY CAN BARELY TOLERATE EACH OTHER.
ALL THAT NICEY-NICE STUFF WIZORD'S DOING... IT'S JUST AN ACT, I PROMISE.
AND BESIDES THAT, THEY'RE *PEOPLE*. I'M A... I'M... NOT PEOPLE.
DON'T KNOW WHAT TO TELL YOU, MARGARET.
THAT'S WHAT THE CARDS TOLD ME.
AND THE CARDS DON'T LIE.

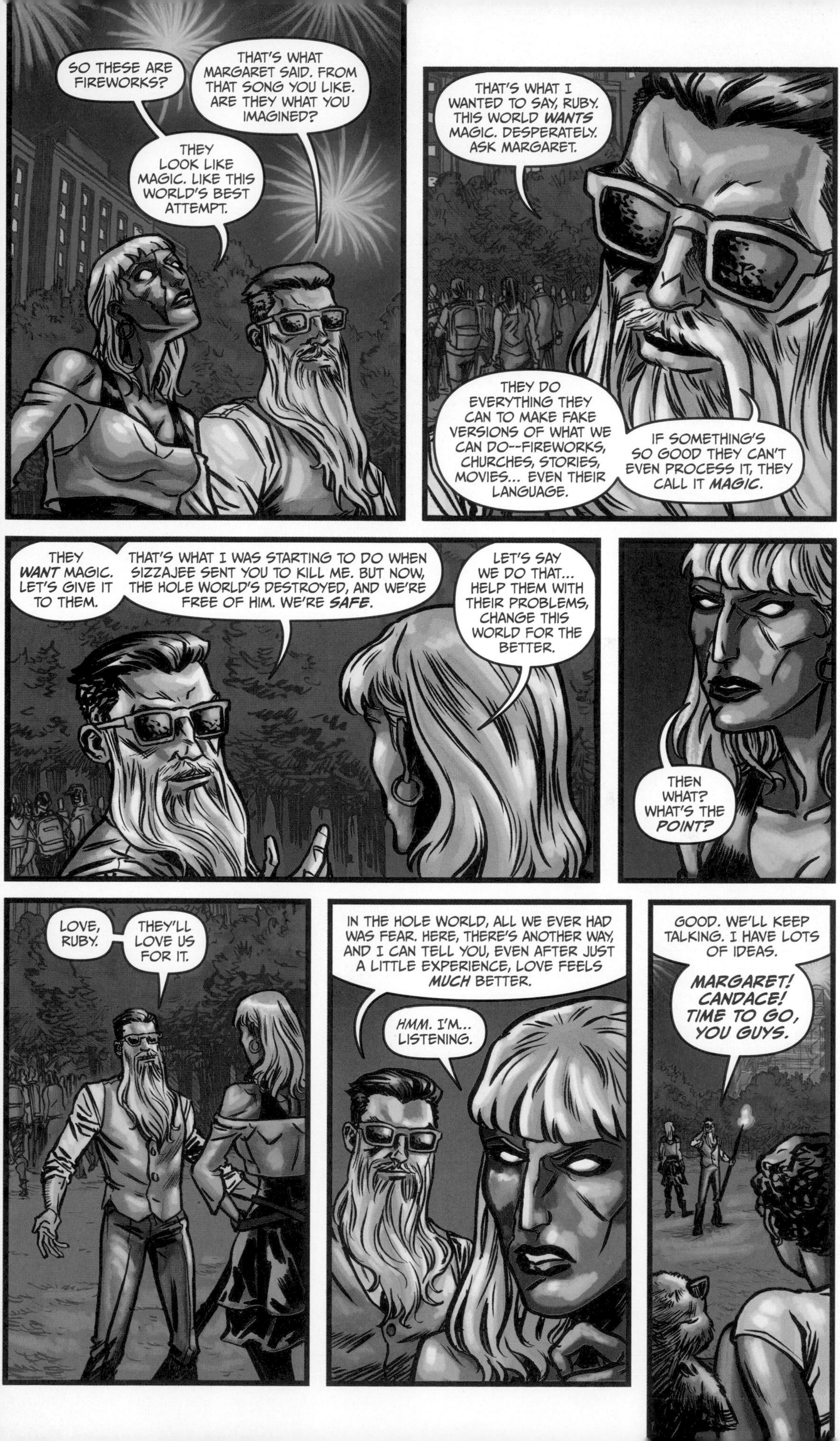
SO THESE ARE FIREWORKS?
THAT'S WHAT MARGARET SAID. FROM THAT SONG YOU LIKE. ARE THEY WHAT YOU IMAGINED?
THEY LOOK LIKE MAGIC. LIKE THIS WORLD'S BEST ATTEMPT.
THAT'S WHAT I WANTED TO SAY, RUBY. THIS WORLD WANTS MAGIC. DESPERATELY. ASK MARGARET.
THEY DO EVERYTHING THEY CAN TO MAKE FAKE VERSIONS OF WHAT WE CAN DO--FIREWORKS, CHURCHES, STORIES, MOVIES... EVEN THEIR LANGUAGE.
IF SOMETHING'S SO GOOD THEY CAN'T EVEN PROCESS IT, THEY CALL IT MAGIC.
THEY WANT MAGIC. LET'S GIVE IT TO THEM.
THAT'S WHAT I WAS STARTING TO DO WHEN SIZZAJEE SENT YOU TO KILL ME. BUT NOW, THE HOLE WORLD'S DESTROYED, AND WE'RE FREE OF HIM. WE'RE SAFE.
LET'S SAY WE DO THAT... HELP THEM WITH THEIR PROBLEMS, CHANGE THIS WORLD FOR THE BETTER.
THEN WHAT? WHAT'S THE POINT?
LOVE, RUBY.
THEY'LL LOVE US FOR IT.
IN THE HOLE WORLD, ALL WE EVER HAD WAS FEAR. HERE, THERE'S ANOTHER WAY, AND I CAN TELL YOU, EVEN AFTER JUST A LITTLE EXPERIENCE, LOVE FEELS MUCH BETTER.
HMM. I'M... LISTENING.
GOOD. WE'LL KEEP TALKING. I HAVE LOTS OF IDEAS.
MARGARET! CANDACE! TIME TO GO, YOU GUYS.

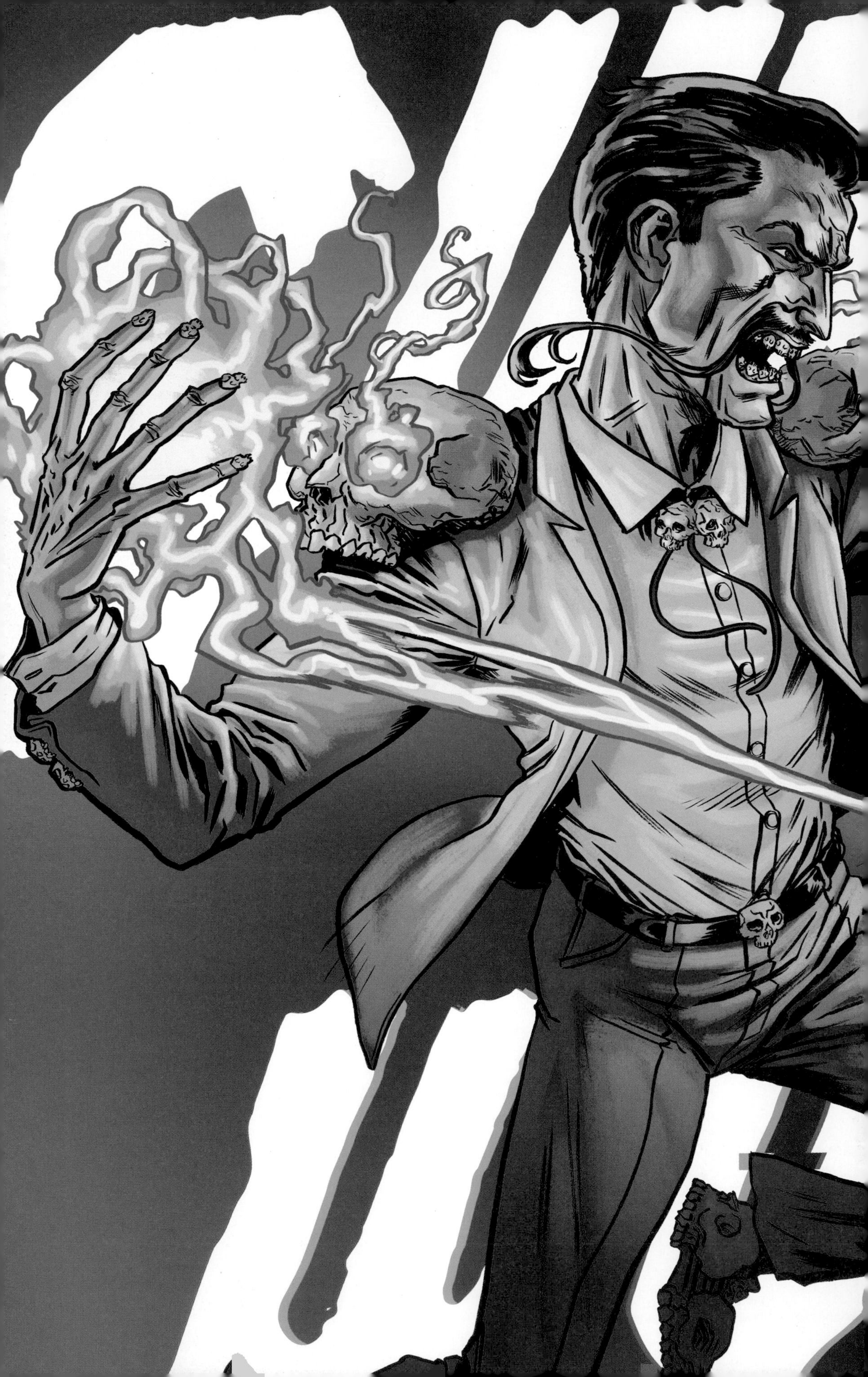

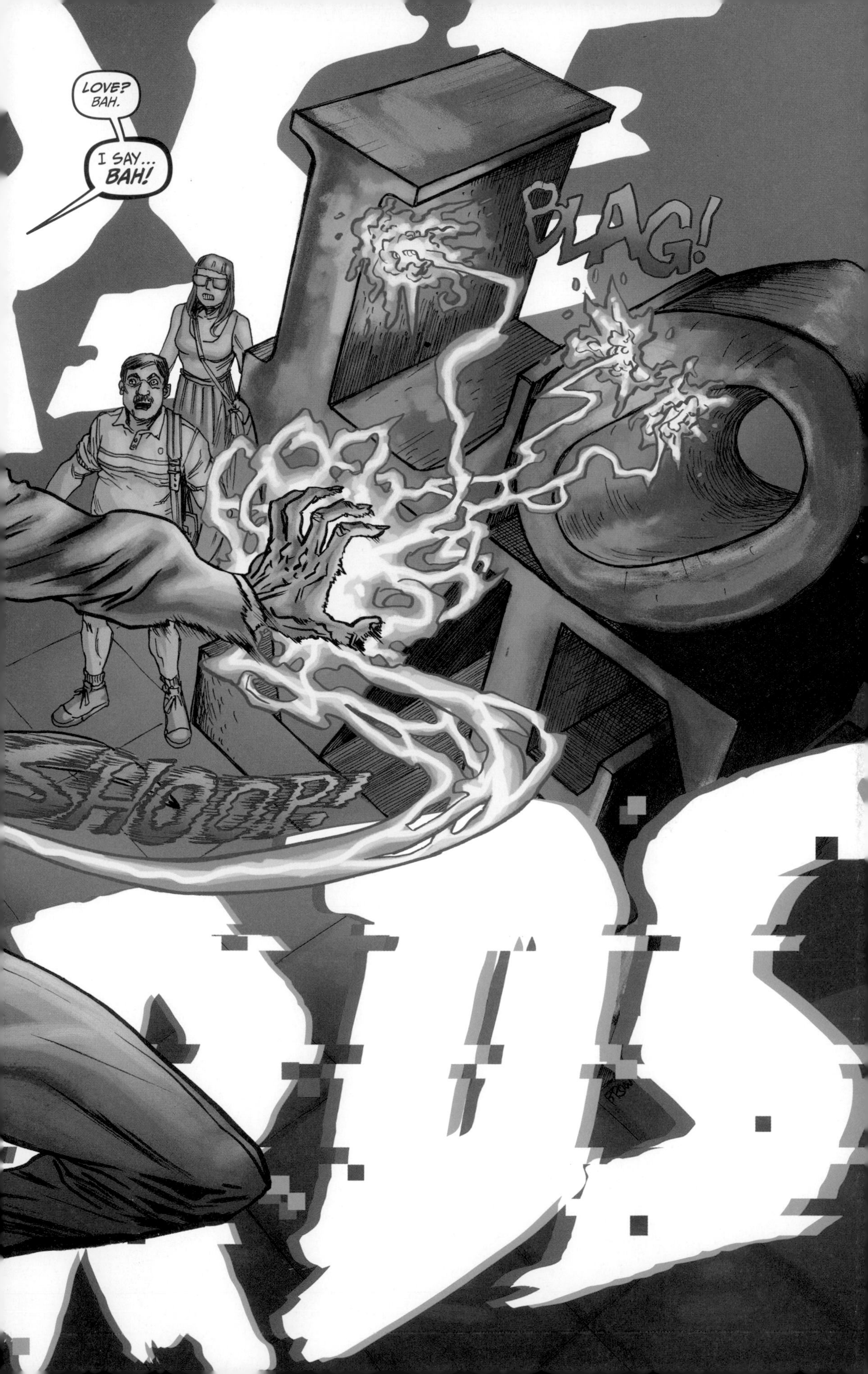
LOVE? BAH.
I SAY... BAH!
BLAG!
SHOOP!

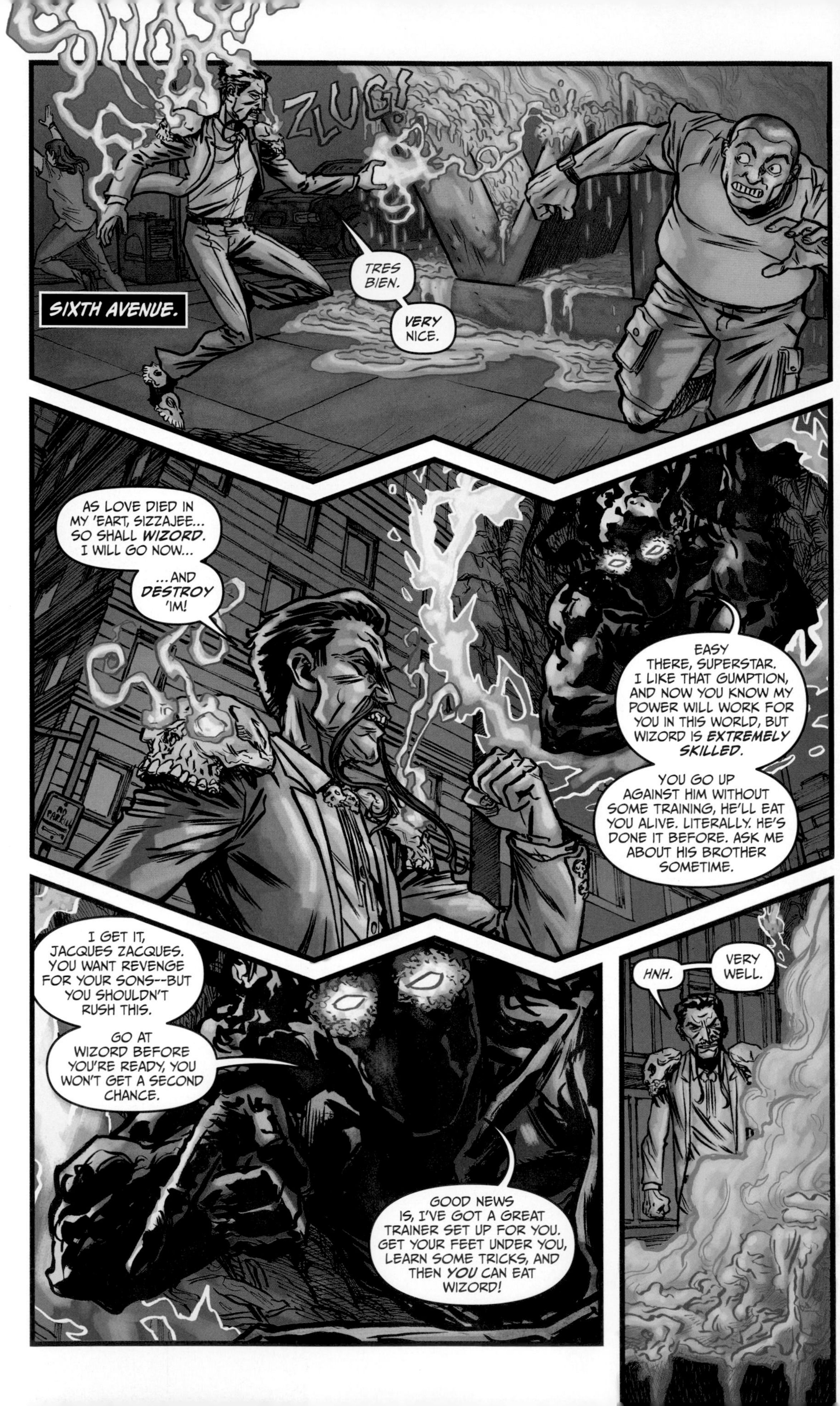
SHHOOF
ZLUG!
SIXTH AVENUE.
TRES BIEN.
VERY NICE.
AS LOVE DIED IN MY 'EART, SIZZAJEE... SO SHALL WIZORD. I WILL GO NOW...
...AND DESTROY 'IM!
EASY THERE, SUPERSTAR. I LIKE THAT GUMPTION, AND NOW YOU KNOW MY POWER WILL WORK FOR YOU IN THIS WORLD, BUT WIZORD IS EXTREMELY SKILLED.
YOU GO UP AGAINST HIM WITHOUT SOME TRAINING, HE'LL EAT YOU ALIVE. LITERALLY. HE'S DONE IT BEFORE. ASK ME ABOUT HIS BROTHER SOMETIME.
I GET IT, JACQUES ZACQUES. YOU WANT REVENGE FOR YOUR SONS--BUT YOU SHOULDN'T RUSH THIS.
GO AT WIZORD BEFORE YOU'RE READY, YOU WON'T GET A SECOND CHANCE.
GOOD NEWS IS, I'VE GOT A GREAT TRAINER SET UP FOR YOU. GET YOUR FEET UNDER YOU, LEARN SOME TRICKS, AND THEN YOU CAN EAT WIZORD!
HNH.
VERY WELL.

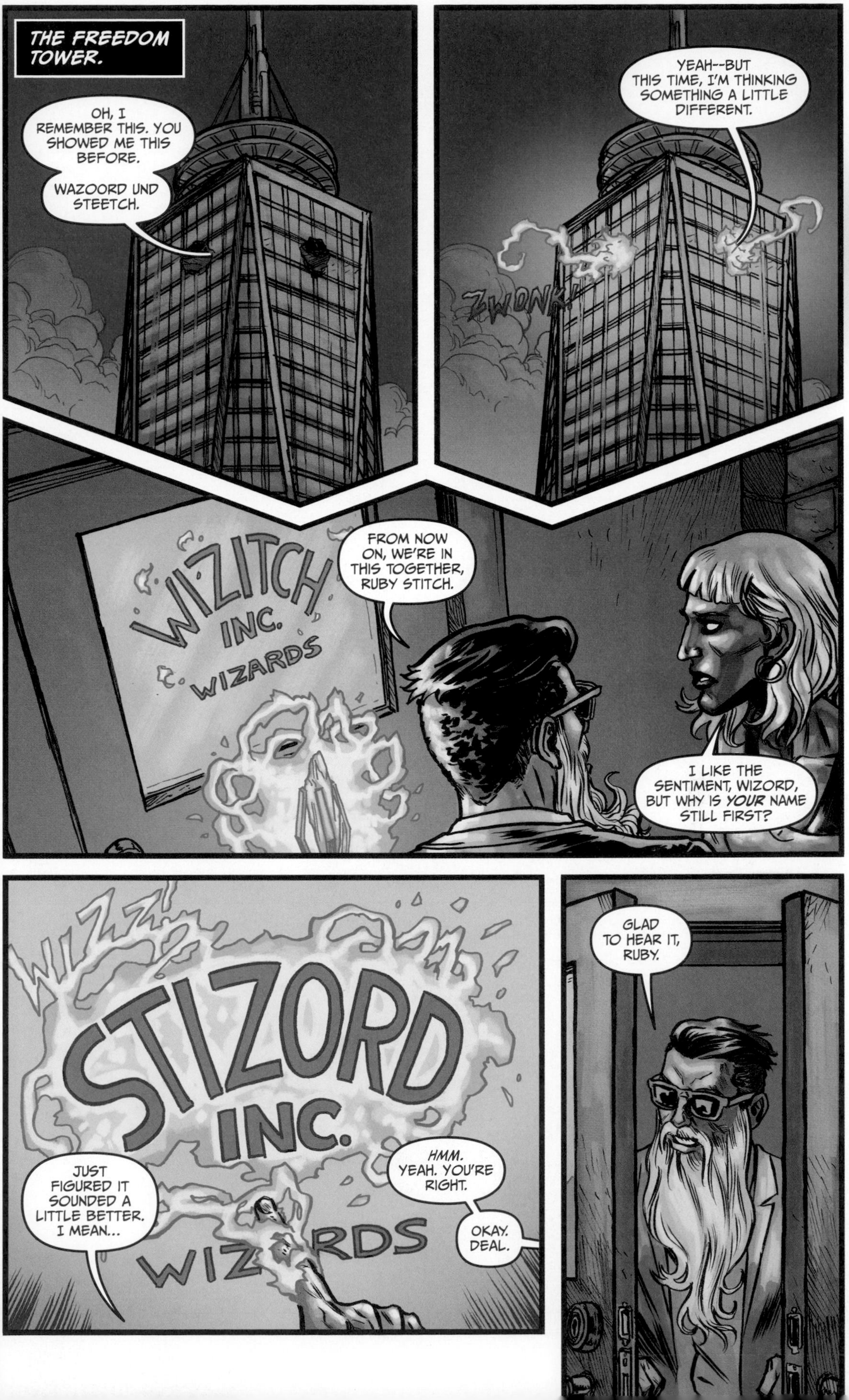
THE FREEDOM TOWER.
OH, I REMEMBER THIS. YOU SHOWED ME THIS BEFORE.
WAZOORD UND STEETCH.
YEAH--BUT THIS TIME, I'M THINKING SOMETHING A LITTLE DIFFERENT.
ZWONK!
WIZITCH INC. WIZARDS
FROM NOW ON, WE'RE IN THIS TOGETHER, RUBY STITCH.
I LIKE THE SENTIMENT, WIZORD, BUT WHY IS YOUR NAME STILL FIRST?
WIZZZ!
STIZORD INC.
WIZ RDS
JUST FIGURED IT SOUNDED A LITTLE BETTER. I MEAN...
HMM. YEAH. YOU'RE RIGHT.
OKAY. DEAL.
GLAD TO HEAR IT, RUBY.

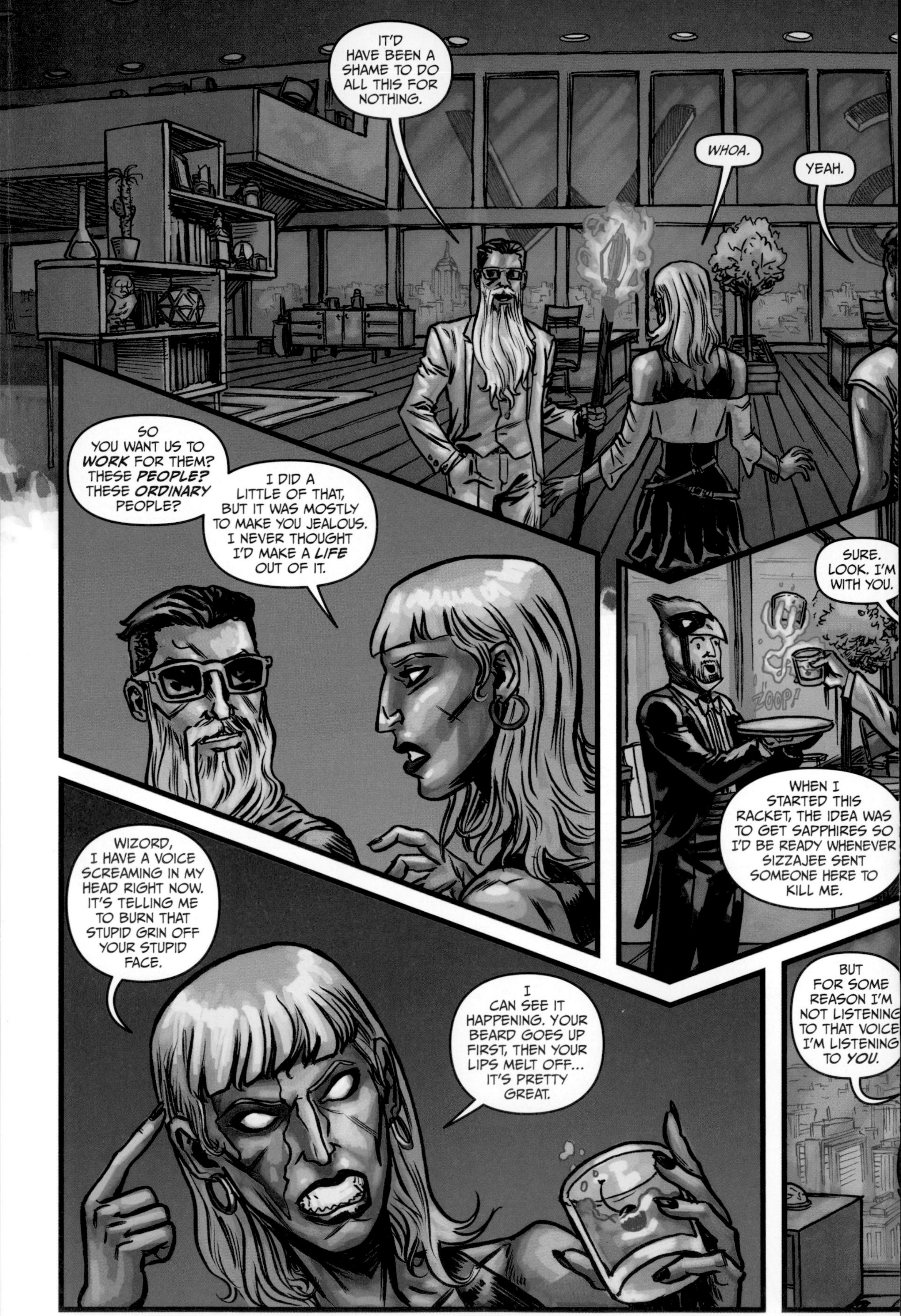
IT'D HAVE BEEN A SHAME TO DO ALL THIS FOR NOTHING.
WHOA.
YEAH.
SO YOU WANT US TO WORK FOR THEM? THESE PEOPLE? THESE ORDINARY PEOPLE?
I DID A LITTLE OF THAT, BUT IT WAS MOSTLY TO MAKE YOU JEALOUS. I NEVER THOUGHT I'D MAKE A LIFE OUT OF IT.
SURE. LOOK. I'M WITH YOU.
ZOOP!
WHEN I STARTED THIS RACKET, THE IDEA WAS TO GET SAPPHIRES SO I'D BE READY WHENEVER SIZZAJEE SENT SOMEONE HERE TO KILL ME.
WIZORD, I HAVE A VOICE SCREAMING IN MY HEAD RIGHT NOW. IT'S TELLING ME TO BURN THAT STUPID GRIN OFF YOUR STUPID FACE.
I CAN SEE IT HAPPENING. YOUR BEARD GOES UP FIRST, THEN YOUR LIPS MELT OFF... IT'S PRETTY GREAT.
BUT FOR SOME REASON I'M NOT LISTENING TO THAT VOICE. I'M LISTENING TO YOU.

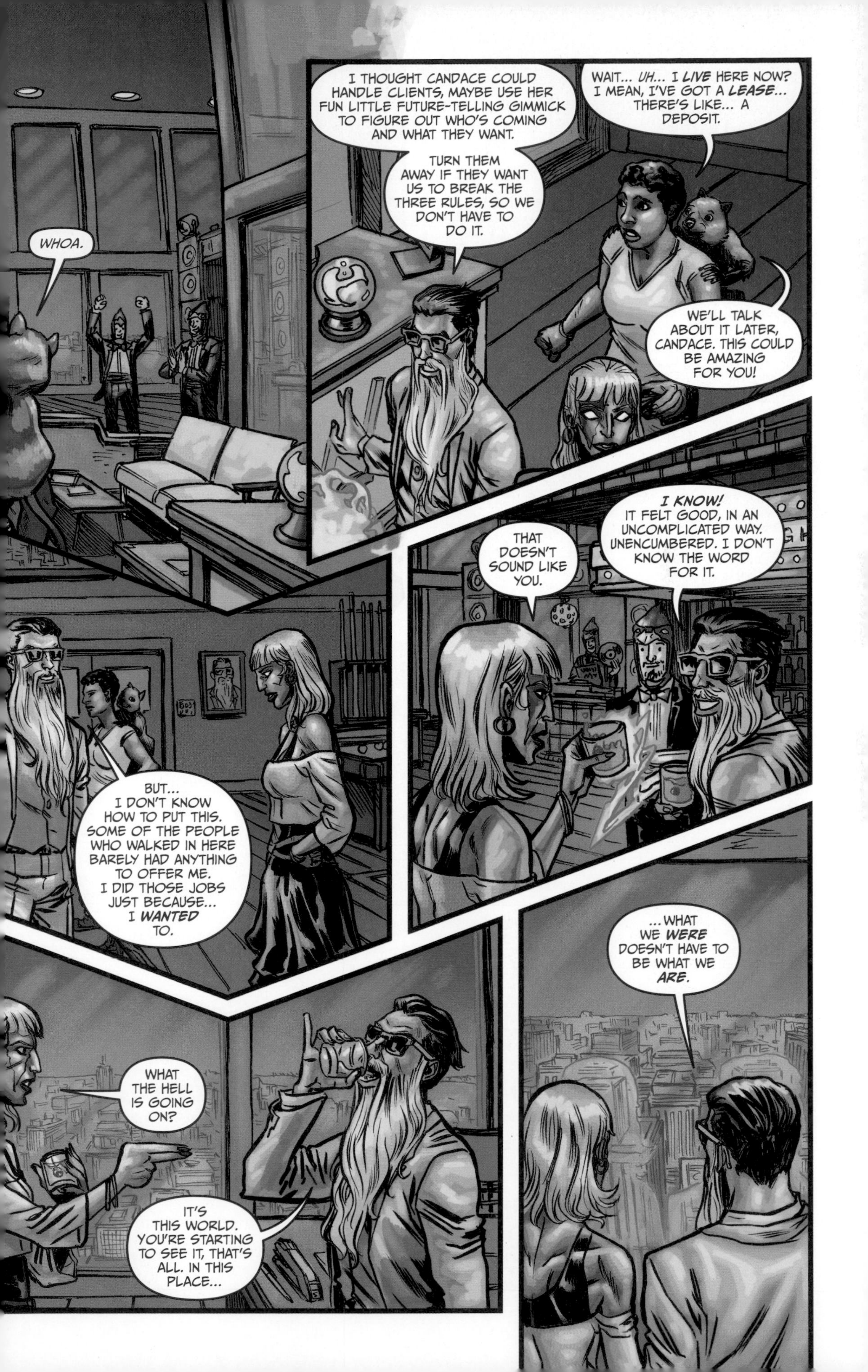
WHOA.
I THOUGHT CANDACE COULD HANDLE CLIENTS, MAYBE USE HER FUN LITTLE FUTURE-TELLING GIMMICK TO FIGURE OUT WHO'S COMING AND WHAT THEY WANT.
TURN THEM AWAY IF THEY WANT US TO BREAK THE THREE RULES, SO WE DON'T HAVE TO DO IT.
WAIT... UH... I LIVE HERE NOW? I MEAN, I'VE GOT A LEASE... THERE'S LIKE... A DEPOSIT.
WE'LL TALK ABOUT IT LATER, CANDACE. THIS COULD BE AMAZING FOR YOU!
BUT... I DON'T KNOW HOW TO PUT THIS. SOME OF THE PEOPLE WHO WALKED IN HERE BARELY HAD ANYTHING TO OFFER ME. I DID THOSE JOBS JUST BECAUSE... I WANTED TO.
THAT DOESN'T SOUND LIKE YOU.
I KNOW! IT FELT GOOD, IN AN UNCOMPLICATED WAY. UNENCUMBERED. I DON'T KNOW THE WORD FOR IT.
WHAT THE HELL IS GOING ON?
IT'S THIS WORLD. YOU'RE STARTING TO SEE IT, THAT'S ALL. IN THIS PLACE...
...WHAT WE WERE DOESN'T HAVE TO BE WHAT WE ARE.

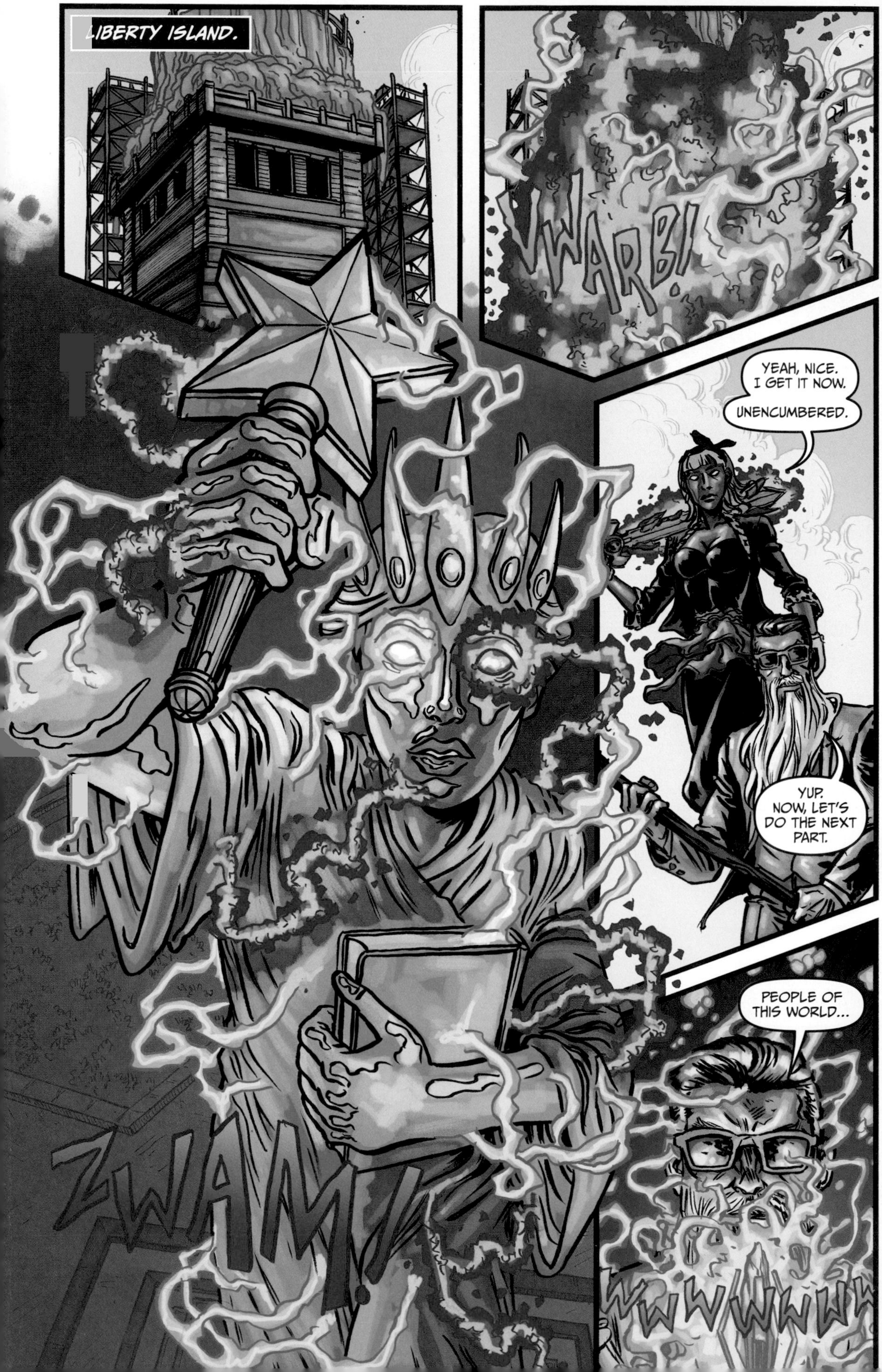
LIBERTY ISLAND.
VWARB!
YEAH, NICE. I GET IT NOW.
UNENCUMBERED.
YUP. NOW, LET'S DO THE NEXT PART.
ZWAM!
PEOPLE OF THIS WORLD...
WWWWWWW

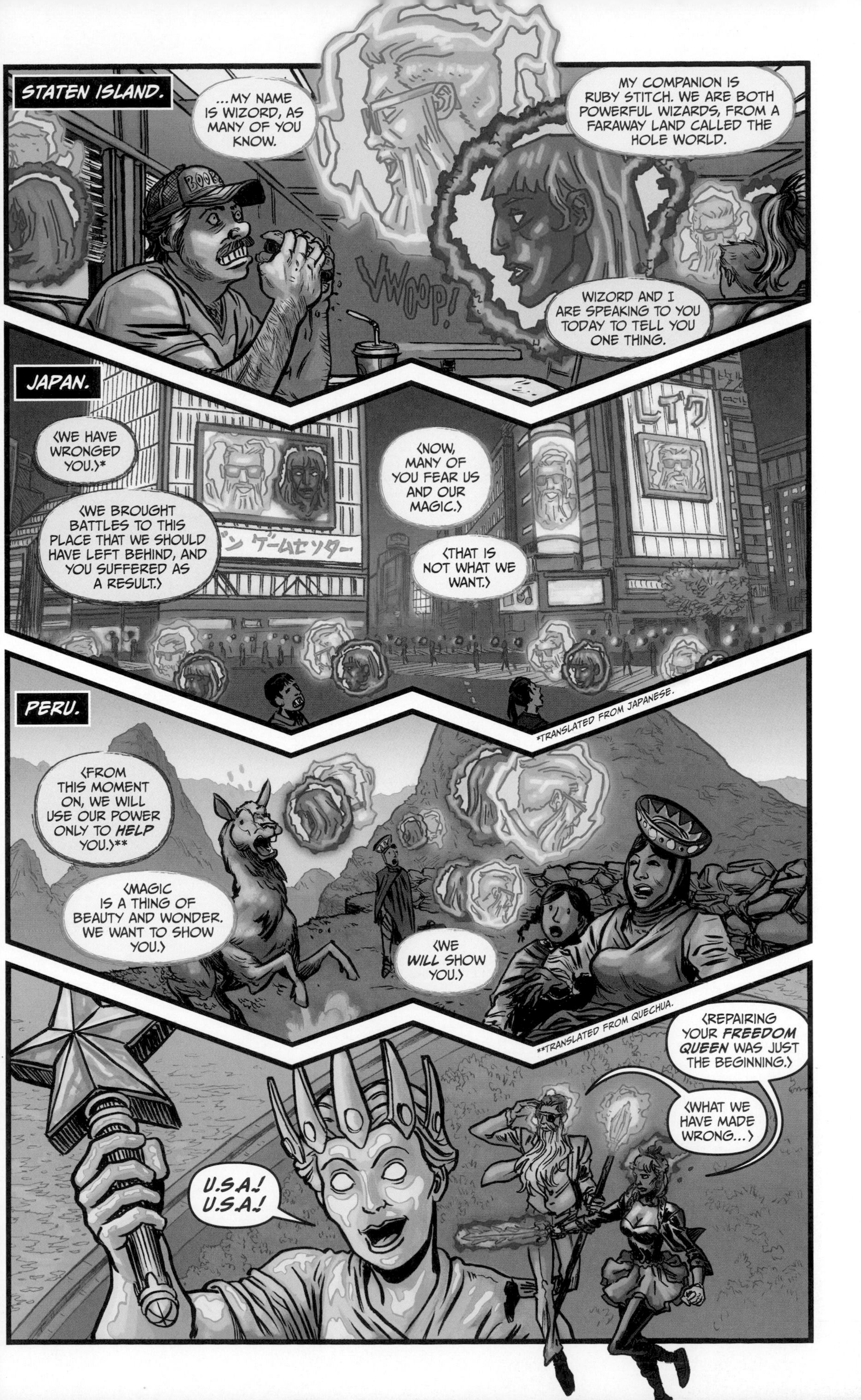
STATEN ISLAND.
...MY NAME IS WIZORD, AS MANY OF YOU KNOW.
MY COMPANION IS RUBY STITCH. WE ARE BOTH POWERFUL WIZARDS, FROM A FARAWAY LAND CALLED THE HOLE WORLD.
VWOOP!
WIZORD AND I ARE SPEAKING TO YOU TODAY TO TELL YOU ONE THING.
JAPAN.
‹WE HAVE WRONGED YOU.›*
‹WE BROUGHT BATTLES TO THIS PLACE THAT WE SHOULD HAVE LEFT BEHIND, AND YOU SUFFERED AS A RESULT.›
‹NOW, MANY OF YOU FEAR US AND OUR MAGIC.›
‹THAT IS NOT WHAT WE WANT.›
*TRANSLATED FROM JAPANESE.
PERU.
‹FROM THIS MOMENT ON, WE WILL USE OUR POWER ONLY TO ***HELP*** YOU.›**
‹MAGIC IS A THING OF BEAUTY AND WONDER. WE WANT TO SHOW YOU.›
‹WE ***WILL*** SHOW YOU.›
**TRANSLATED FROM QUECHUA.
‹REPAIRING YOUR ***FREEDOM QUEEN*** WAS JUST THE BEGINNING.›
‹WHAT WE HAVE MADE WRONG...›
U.S.A.! U.S.A.!

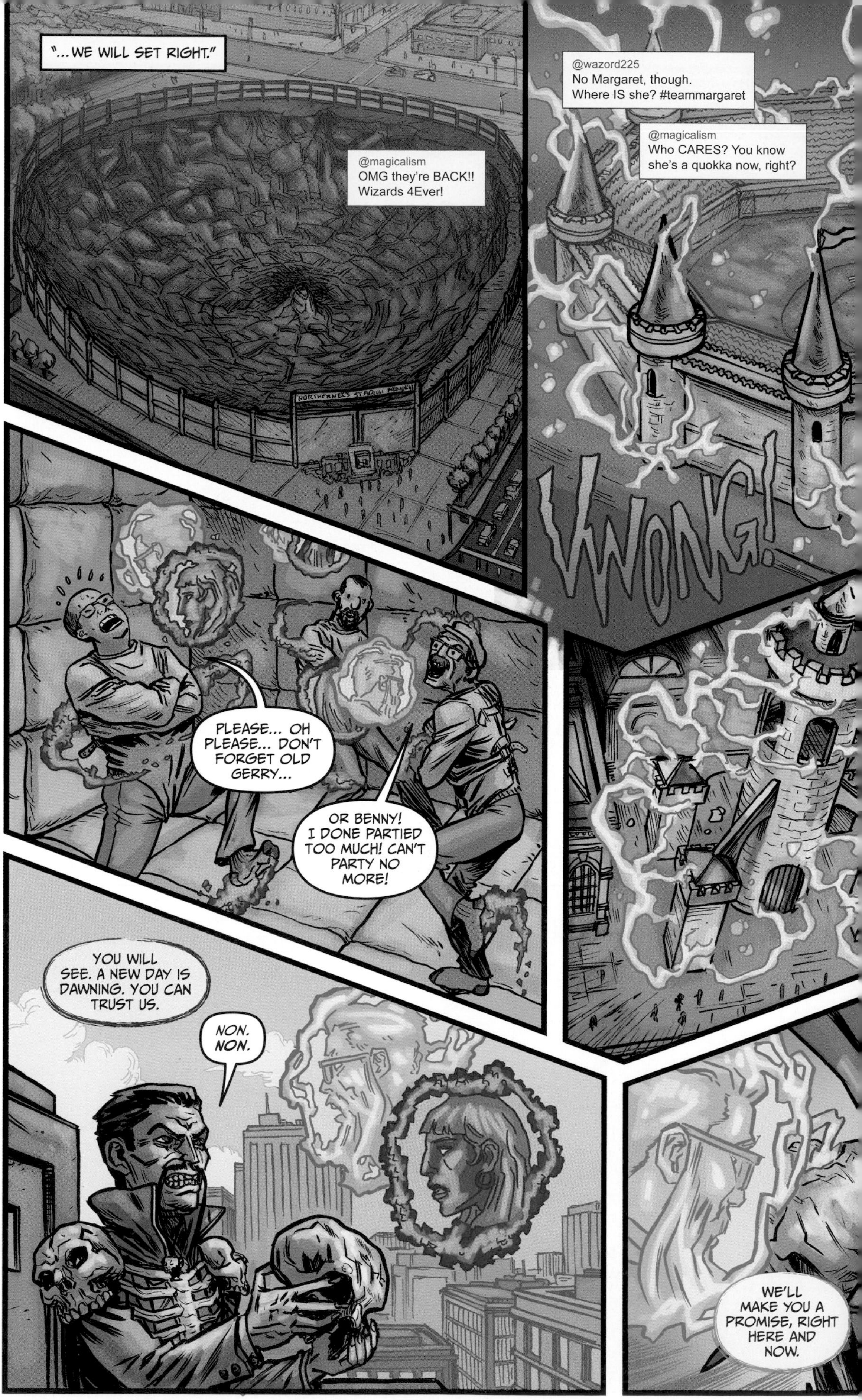

"...WE WILL SET RIGHT."
@magicalism
OMG they're BACK!! Wizards 4Ever!
@wazord225
No Margaret, though. Where IS she? #teammargaret
@magicalism
Who CARES? You know she's a quokka now, right?
VWONG!
PLEASE... OH PLEASE... DON'T FORGET OLD GERRY...
OR BENNY! I DONE PARTIED TOO MUCH! CAN'T PARTY NO MORE!
YOU WILL SEE. A NEW DAY IS DAWNING. YOU CAN TRUST US.
NON. NON.
WE'LL MAKE YOU A PROMISE, RIGHT HERE AND NOW.

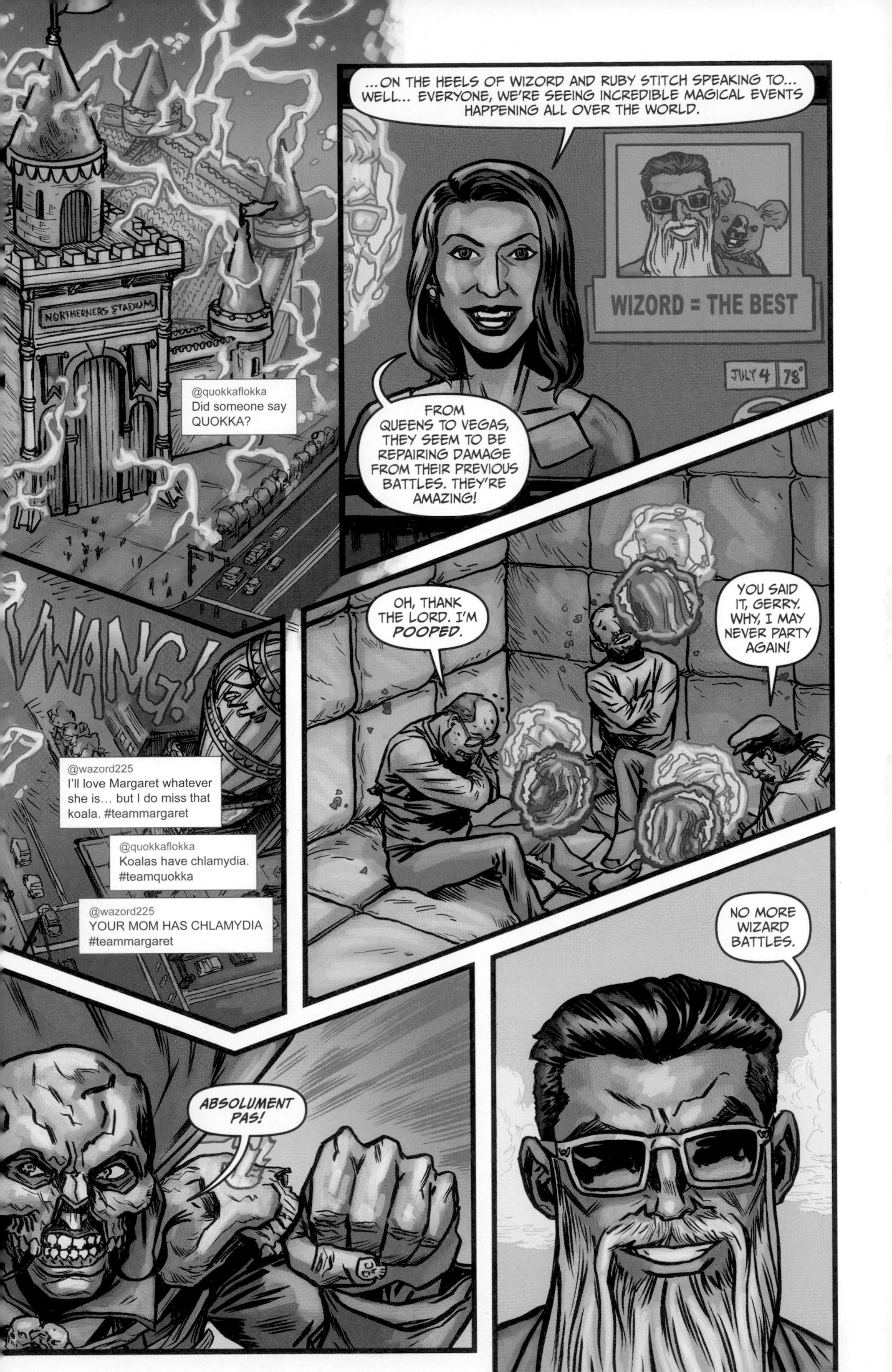
NORTHERNERS STADIUM
@quokkaflokka
Did someone say QUOKKA?
...ON THE HEELS OF WIZORD AND RUBY STITCH SPEAKING TO... WELL... EVERYONE, WE'RE SEEING INCREDIBLE MAGICAL EVENTS HAPPENING ALL OVER THE WORLD.
WIZORD = THE BEST
JULY 4 78°
FROM QUEENS TO VEGAS, THEY SEEM TO BE REPAIRING DAMAGE FROM THEIR PREVIOUS BATTLES. THEY'RE AMAZING!
VWANG!
@wazord225
I'll love Margaret whatever she is… but I do miss that koala. #teammargaret
@quokkaflokka
Koalas have chlamydia. #teamquokka
@wazord225
YOUR MOM HAS CHLAMYDIA #teammargaret
OH, THANK THE LORD. I'M POOPED.
YOU SAID IT, GERRY. WHY, I MAY NEVER PARTY AGAIN!
ABSOLUMENT PAS!
NO MORE WIZARD BATTLES.

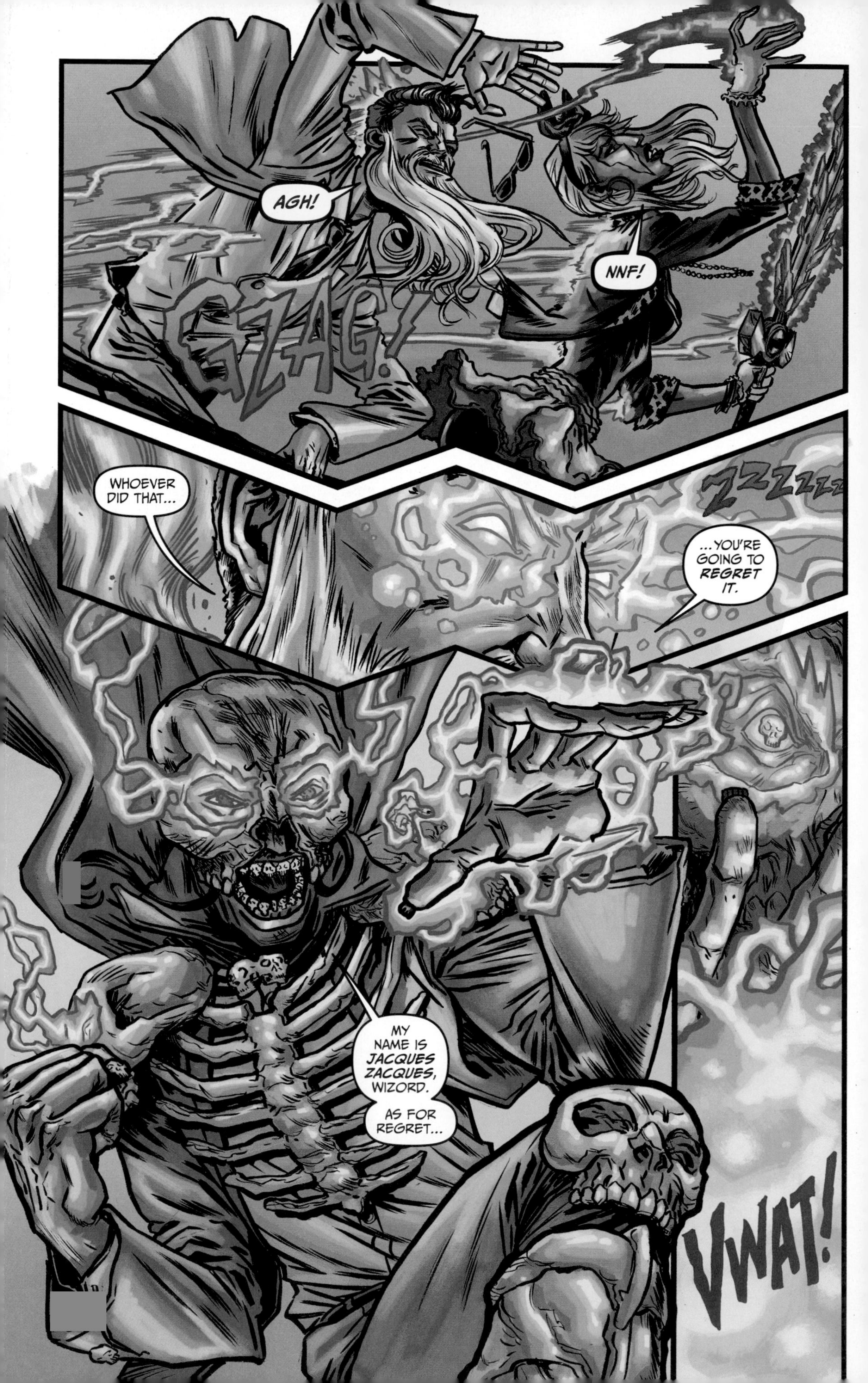
AGH!
NNF!
GZAG!
WHOEVER DID THAT...
ZZZZZZZ
...YOU'RE GOING TO REGRET IT.
MY NAME IS JACQUES ZACQUES, WIZORD.
AS FOR REGRET...
VWAT!

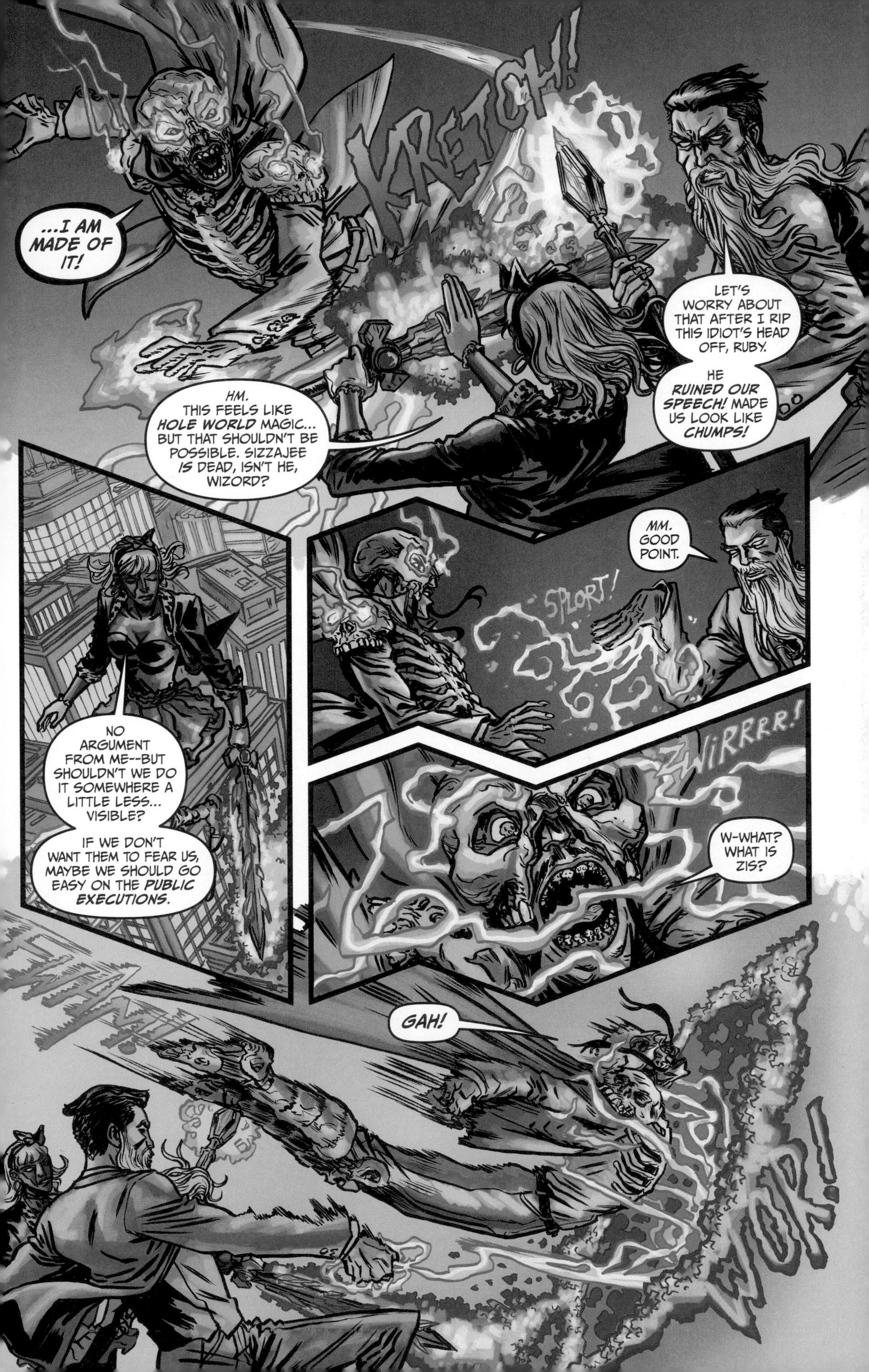
KRETCH!
...I AM MADE OF IT!
LET'S WORRY ABOUT THAT AFTER I RIP THIS IDIOT'S HEAD OFF, RUBY.
HE RUINED OUR SPEECH! MADE US LOOK LIKE CHUMPS!
HM. THIS FEELS LIKE HOLE WORLD MAGIC... BUT THAT SHOULDN'T BE POSSIBLE. SIZZAJEE IS DEAD, ISN'T HE, WIZORD?
NO ARGUMENT FROM ME--BUT SHOULDN'T WE DO IT SOMEWHERE A LITTLE LESS... VISIBLE?
IF WE DON'T WANT THEM TO FEAR US, MAYBE WE SHOULD GO EASY ON THE PUBLIC EXECUTIONS.
MM. GOOD POINT.
SPLORT!
ZWIRRRR!
W-WHAT? WHAT IS ZIS?
GAH!
WOP!

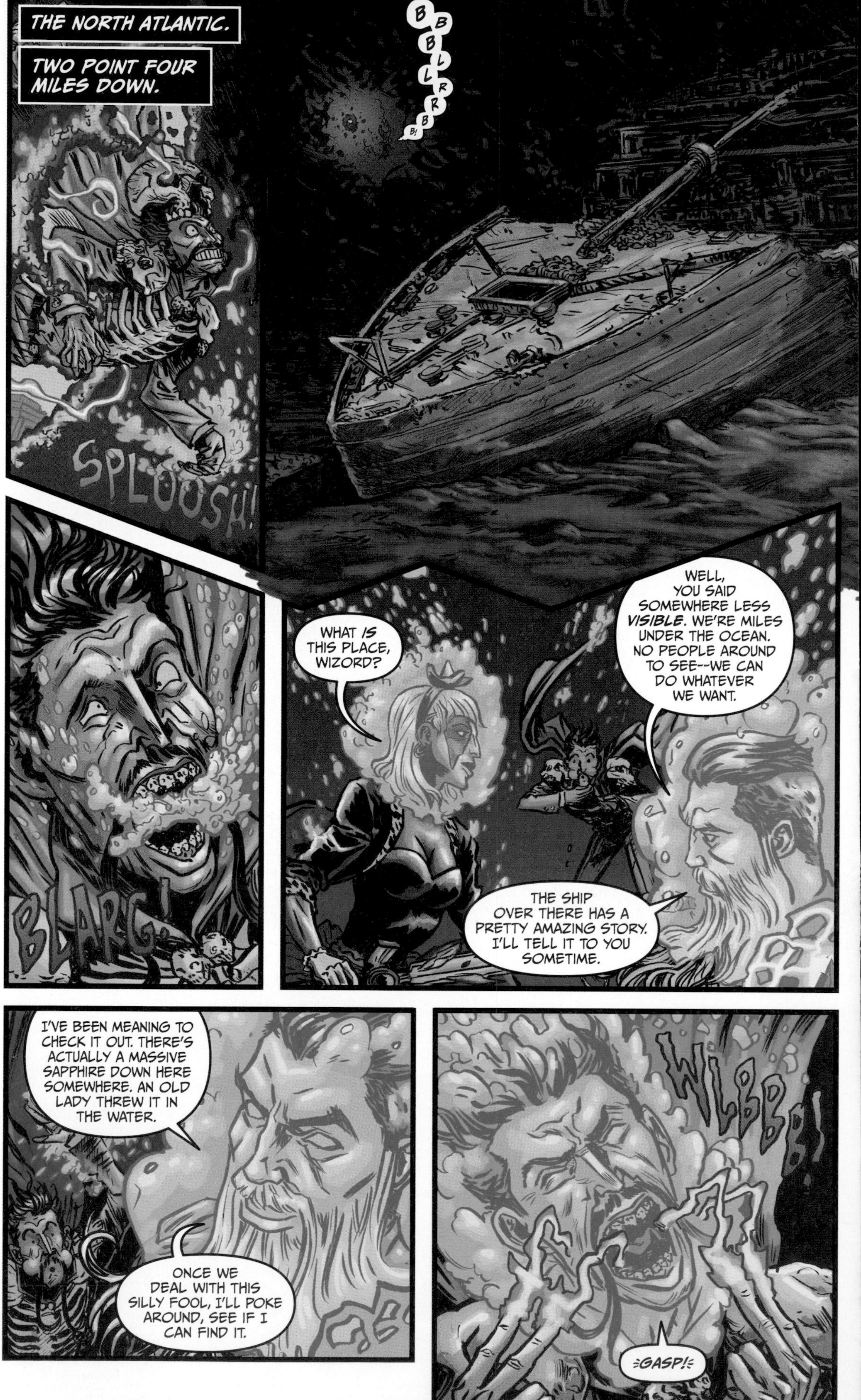
THE NORTH ATLANTIC.
TWO POINT FOUR MILES DOWN.
BBBLLRRBB!
SPLOOSH!
BLARG!
WHAT IS THIS PLACE, WIZORD?
WELL, YOU SAID SOMEWHERE LESS VISIBLE. WE'RE MILES UNDER THE OCEAN. NO PEOPLE AROUND TO SEE--WE CAN DO WHATEVER WE WANT.
THE SHIP OVER THERE HAS A PRETTY AMAZING STORY. I'LL TELL IT TO YOU SOMETIME.
I'VE BEEN MEANING TO CHECK IT OUT. THERE'S ACTUALLY A MASSIVE SAPPHIRE DOWN HERE SOMEWHERE. AN OLD LADY THREW IT IN THE WATER.
ONCE WE DEAL WITH THIS SILLY FOOL, I'LL POKE AROUND, SEE IF I CAN FIND IT.
WLBBB!
GASP!

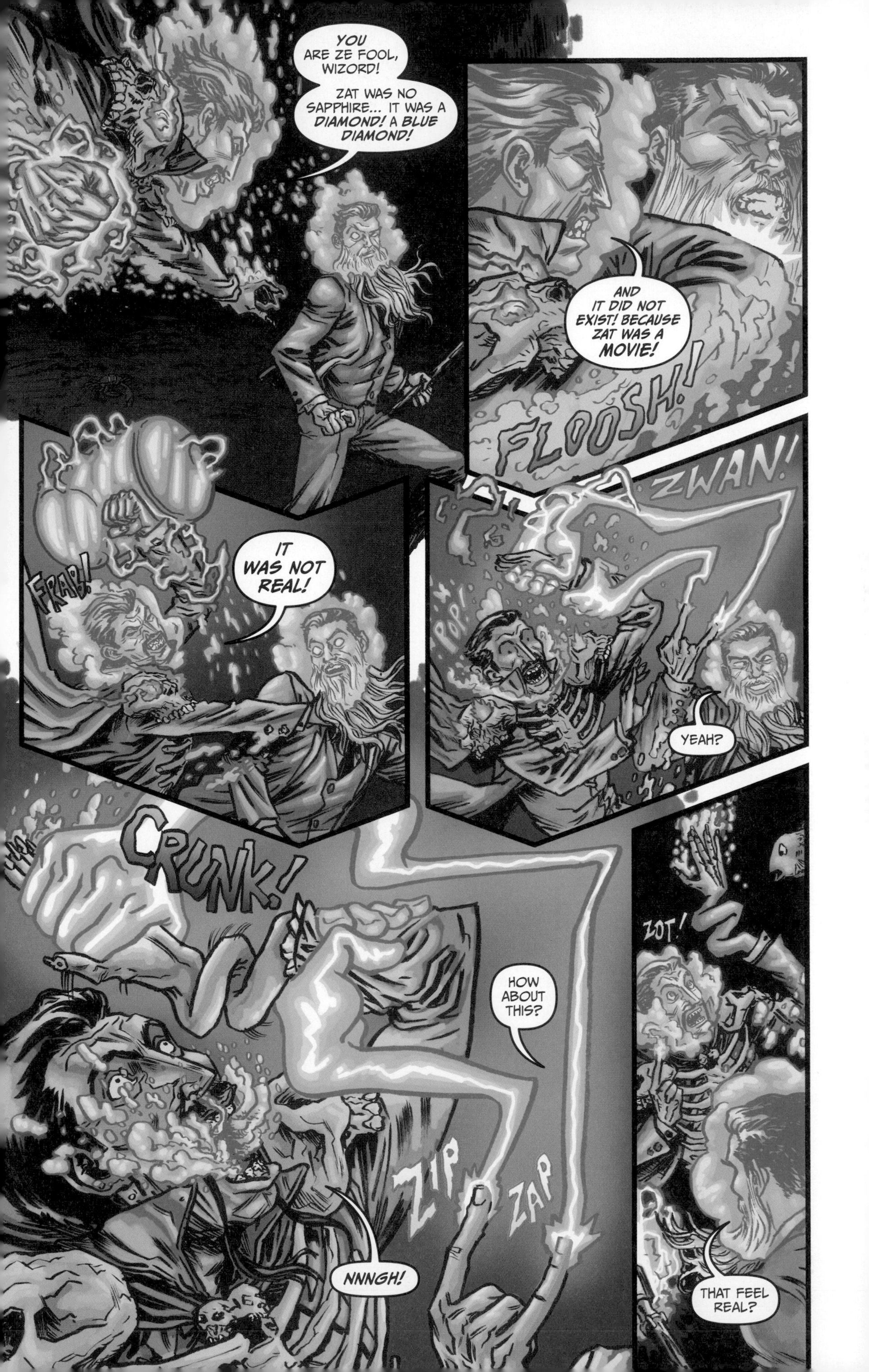
YOU ARE ZE FOOL, WIZORD!
ZAT WAS NO SAPPHIRE... IT WAS A DIAMOND! A BLUE DIAMOND!
AND IT DID NOT EXIST! BECAUSE ZAT WAS A MOVIE!
FLOOSH!
FRAB!
IT WAS NOT REAL!
ZWAN!
POP!
YEAH?
CRUNK!
HOW ABOUT THIS?
ZIP
ZAP
NNNGH!
ZOT!
THAT FEEL REAL?

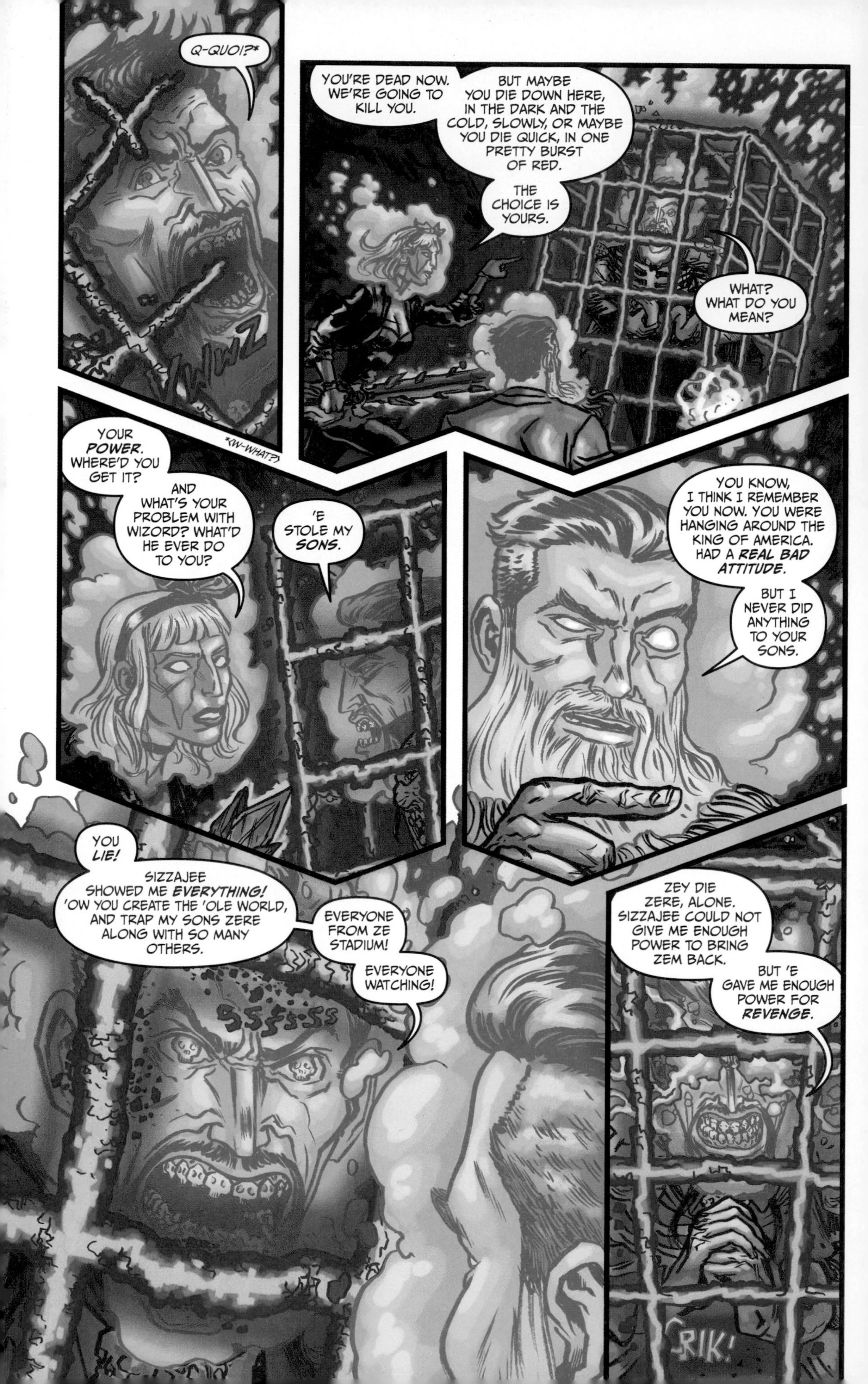
Q-QUOI?*
VWWZ
*(W-WHAT?)
YOU'RE DEAD NOW. WE'RE GOING TO KILL YOU.
BUT MAYBE YOU DIE DOWN HERE, IN THE DARK AND THE COLD, SLOWLY, OR MAYBE YOU DIE QUICK, IN ONE PRETTY BURST OF RED.
THE CHOICE IS YOURS.
WHAT? WHAT DO YOU MEAN?
YOUR POWER. WHERE'D YOU GET IT?
AND WHAT'S YOUR PROBLEM WITH WIZORD? WHAT'D HE EVER DO TO YOU?
'E STOLE MY SONS.
YOU KNOW, I THINK I REMEMBER YOU NOW. YOU WERE HANGING AROUND THE KING OF AMERICA. HAD A REAL BAD ATTITUDE.
BUT I NEVER DID ANYTHING TO YOUR SONS.
YOU LIE!
SIZZAJEE SHOWED ME EVERYTHING! 'OW YOU CREATE THE 'OLE WORLD, AND TRAP MY SONS ZERE ALONG WITH SO MANY OTHERS.
EVERYONE FROM ZE STADIUM!
EVERYONE WATCHING!
SSSSSS
ZEY DIE ZERE, ALONE. SIZZAJEE COULD NOT GIVE ME ENOUGH POWER TO BRING ZEM BACK.
BUT 'E GAVE ME ENOUGH POWER FOR REVENGE.
CRIK!

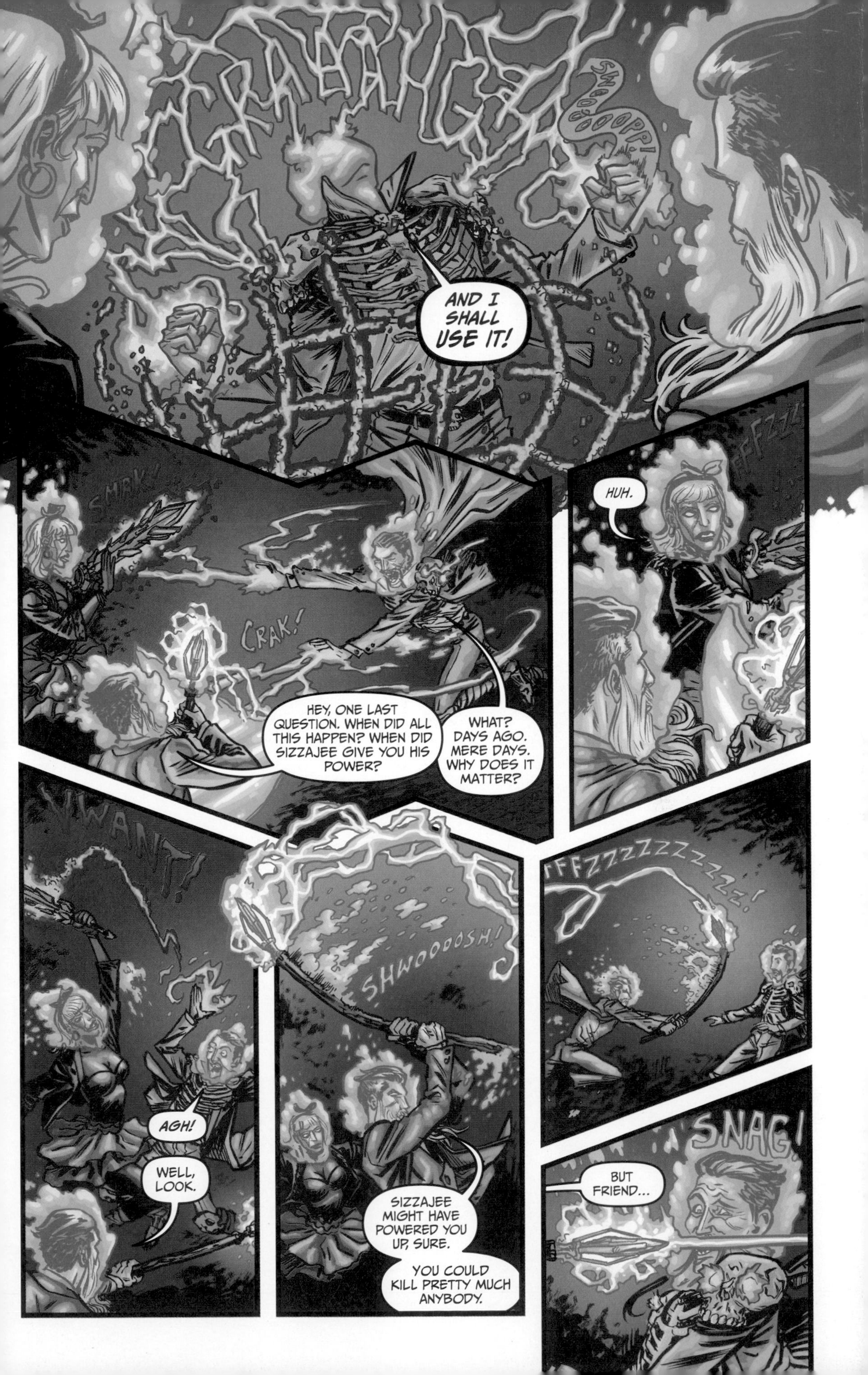
SHWOOOOOPP!
AND I SHALL USE IT!
SMAK!
CRAK!
HEY, ONE LAST QUESTION. WHEN DID ALL THIS HAPPEN? WHEN DID SIZZAJEE GIVE YOU HIS POWER?
WHAT? DAYS AGO. MERE DAYS. WHY DOES IT MATTER?
HUH.
VWANT!
AGH!
WELL, LOOK.
SHWOOOOSH!
SIZZAJEE MIGHT HAVE POWERED YOU UP, SURE.
YOU COULD KILL PRETTY MUCH ANYBODY.
FFFZZZZZZZZZZZz!
SNAG!
BUT FRIEND...

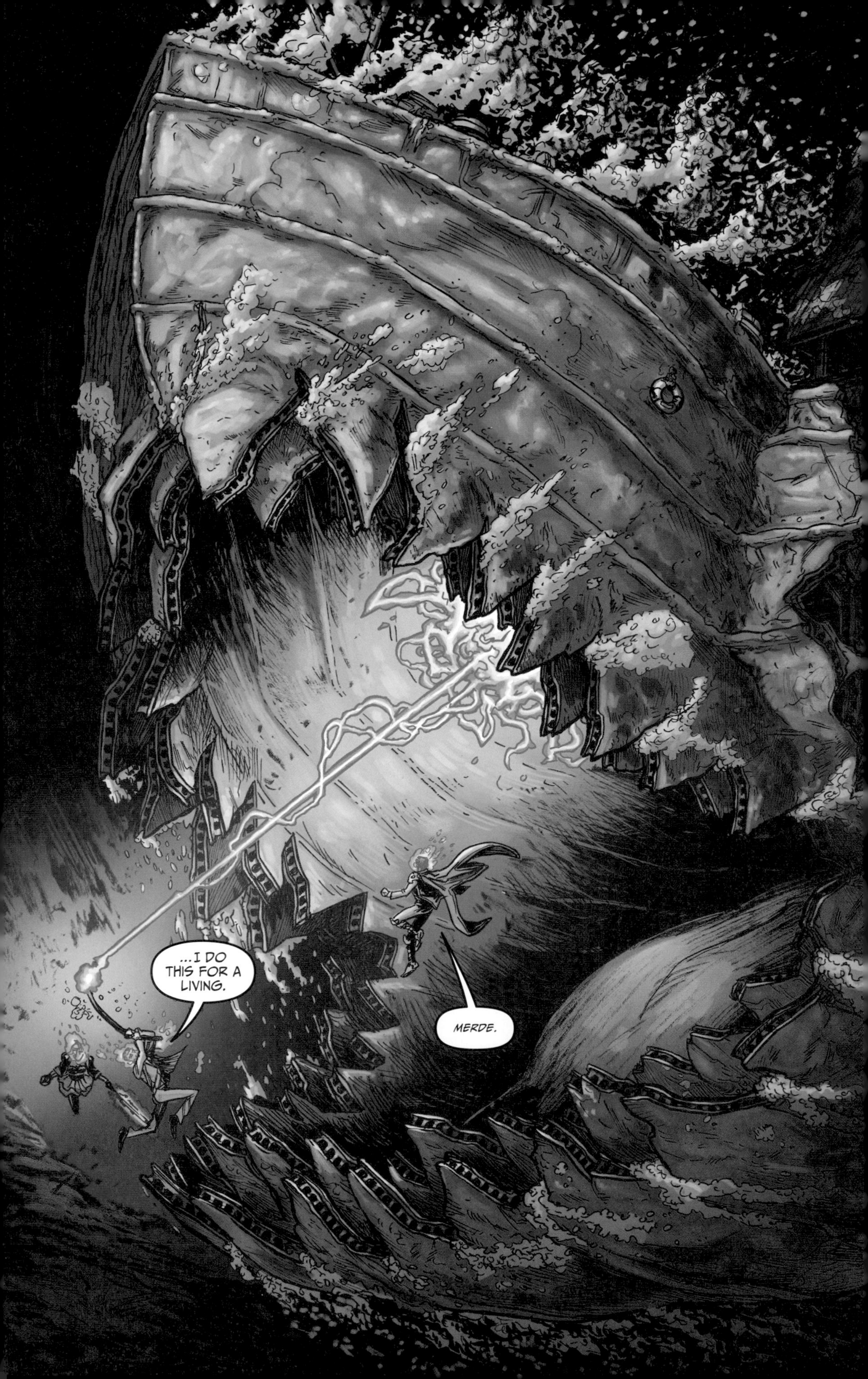
...I DO THIS FOR A LIVING.
MERDE.

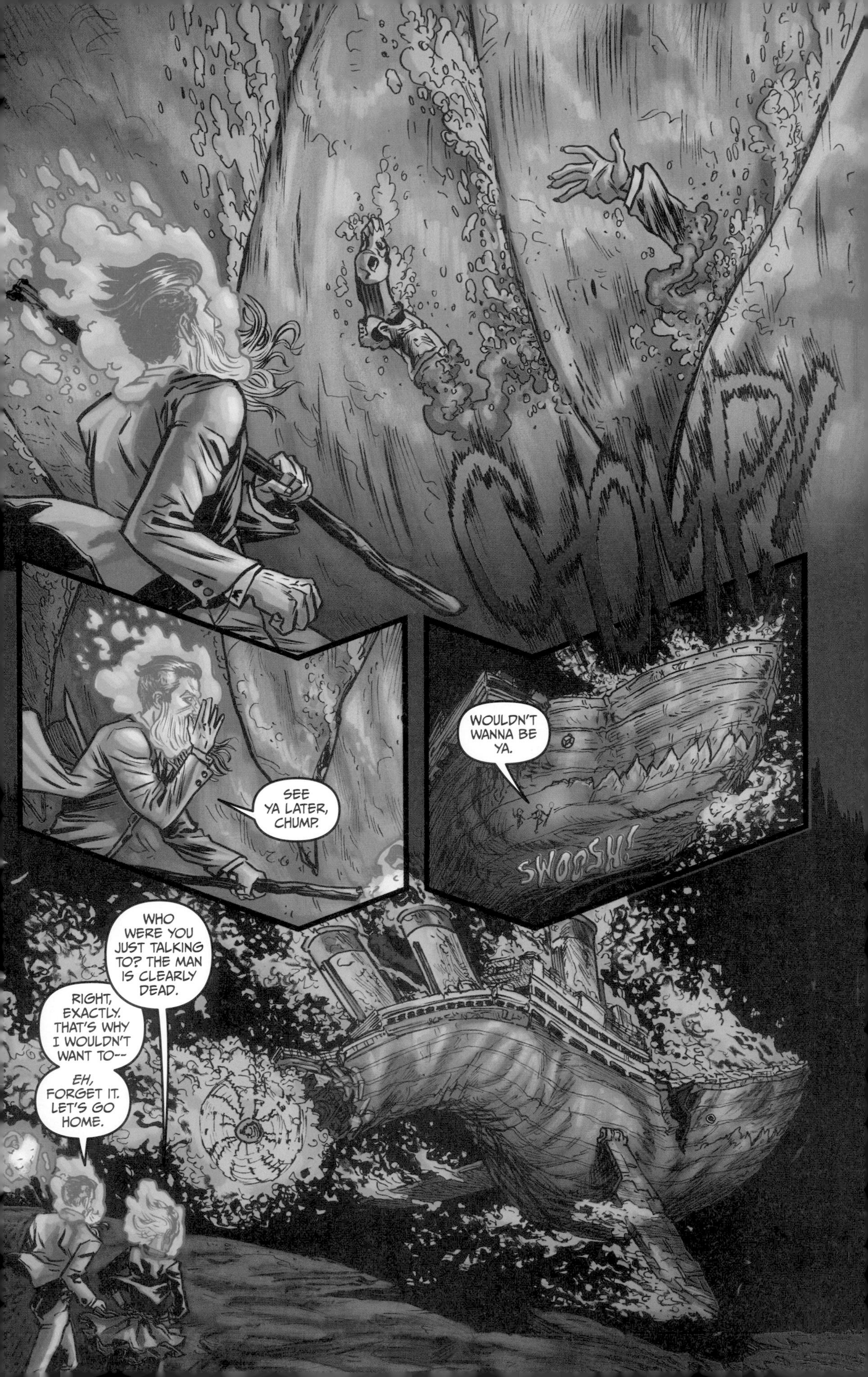
SEE YA LATER, CHUMP.
WOULDN'T WANNA BE YA.
SWOOSH!
WHO WERE YOU JUST TALKING TO? THE MAN IS CLEARLY DEAD.
RIGHT, EXACTLY. THAT'S WHY I WOULDN'T WANT TO--
EH, FORGET IT. LET'S GO HOME.

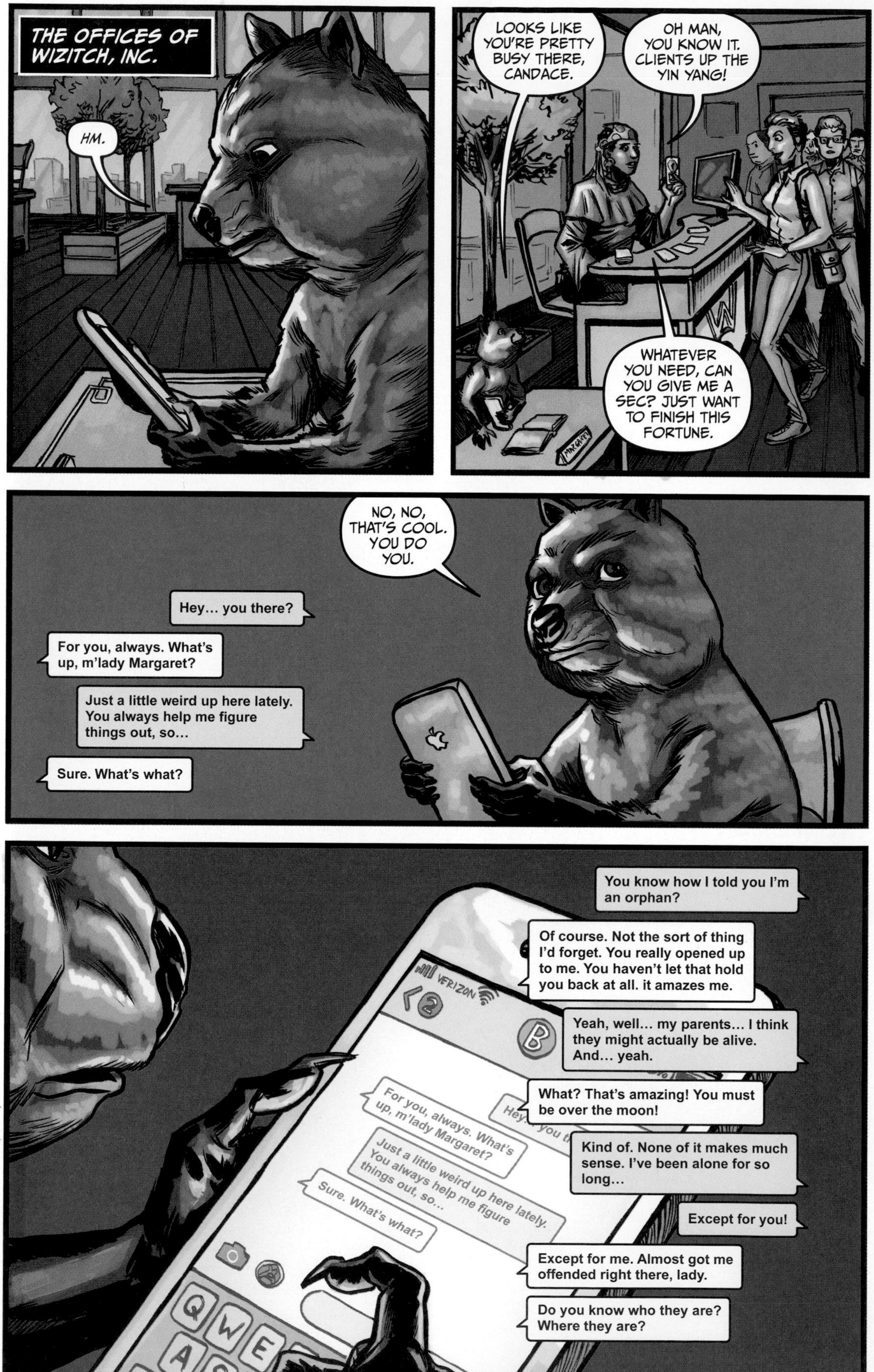
THE OFFICES OF WIZITCH, INC.
HM.
LOOKS LIKE YOU'RE PRETTY BUSY THERE, CANDACE.
OH MAN, YOU KNOW IT. CLIENTS UP THE YIN YANG!
WHATEVER YOU NEED, CAN YOU GIVE ME A SEC? JUST WANT TO FINISH THIS FORTUNE.
NO, NO, THAT'S COOL. YOU DO YOU.
Hey… you there?
For you, always. What's up, m'lady Margaret?
Just a little weird up here lately. You always help me figure things out, so…
Sure. What's what?
You know how I told you I'm an orphan?
Of course. Not the sort of thing I'd forget. You really opened up to me. You haven't let that hold you back at all. it amazes me.
Yeah, well… my parents… I think they might actually be alive. And… yeah.
What? That's amazing! You must be over the moon!
Kind of. None of it makes much sense. I've been alone for so long…
Except for you!
Except for me. Almost got me offended right there, lady.
Do you know who they are? Where they are?

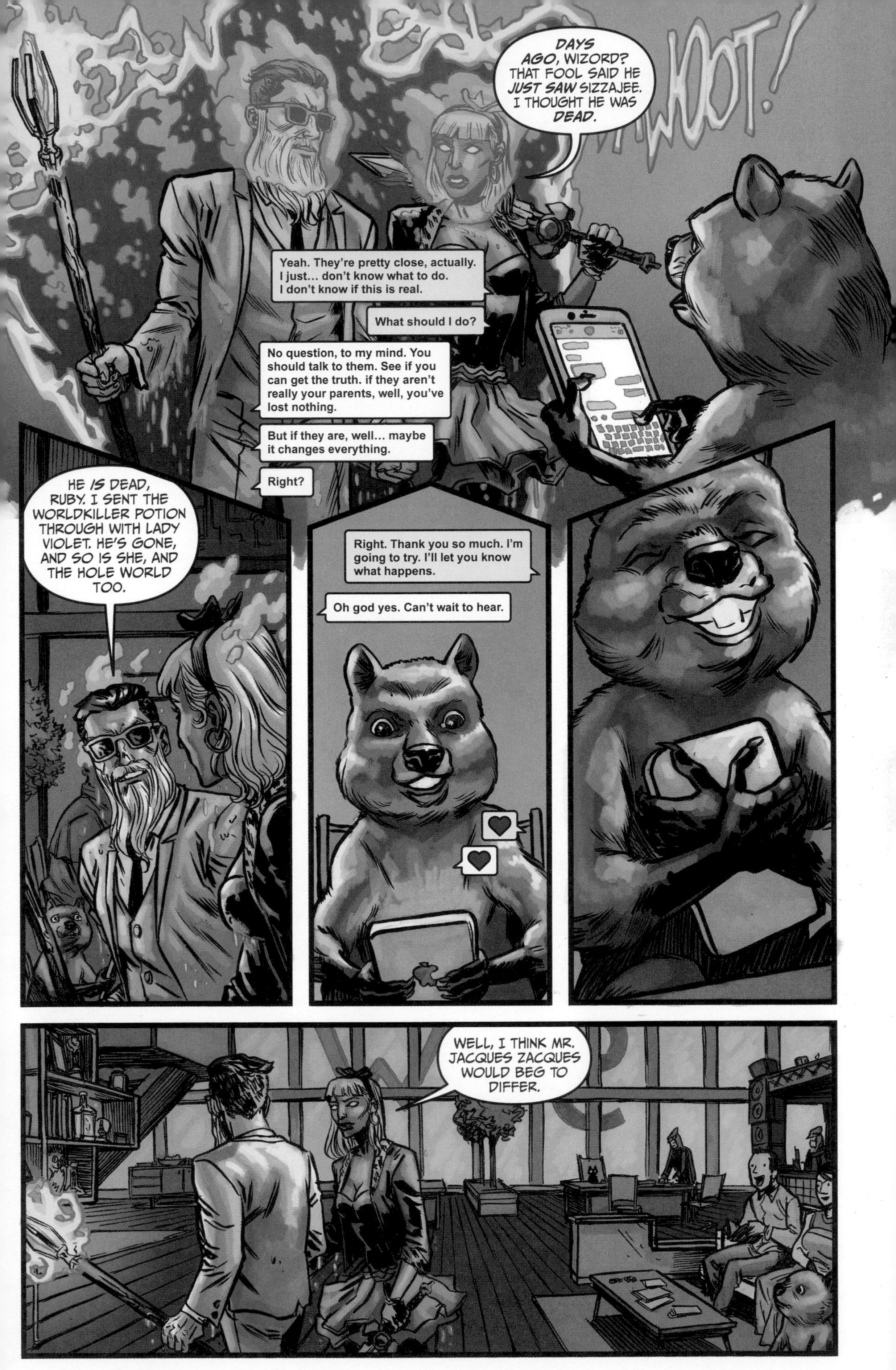

DAYS AGO, WIZORD? THAT FOOL SAID HE JUST SAW SIZZAJEE. I THOUGHT HE WAS DEAD.
WOOT!
Yeah. They're pretty close, actually. I just… don't know what to do. I don't know if this is real.
What should I do?
No question, to my mind. You should talk to them. See if you can get the truth. if they aren't really your parents, well, you've lost nothing.
But if they are, well… maybe it changes everything.
Right?
HE IS DEAD, RUBY. I SENT THE WORLDKILLER POTION THROUGH WITH LADY VIOLET. HE'S GONE, AND SO IS SHE, AND THE HOLE WORLD TOO.
Right. Thank you so much. I'm going to try. I'll let you know what happens.
Oh god yes. Can't wait to hear.
WELL, I THINK MR. JACQUES ZACQUES WOULD BEG TO DIFFER.

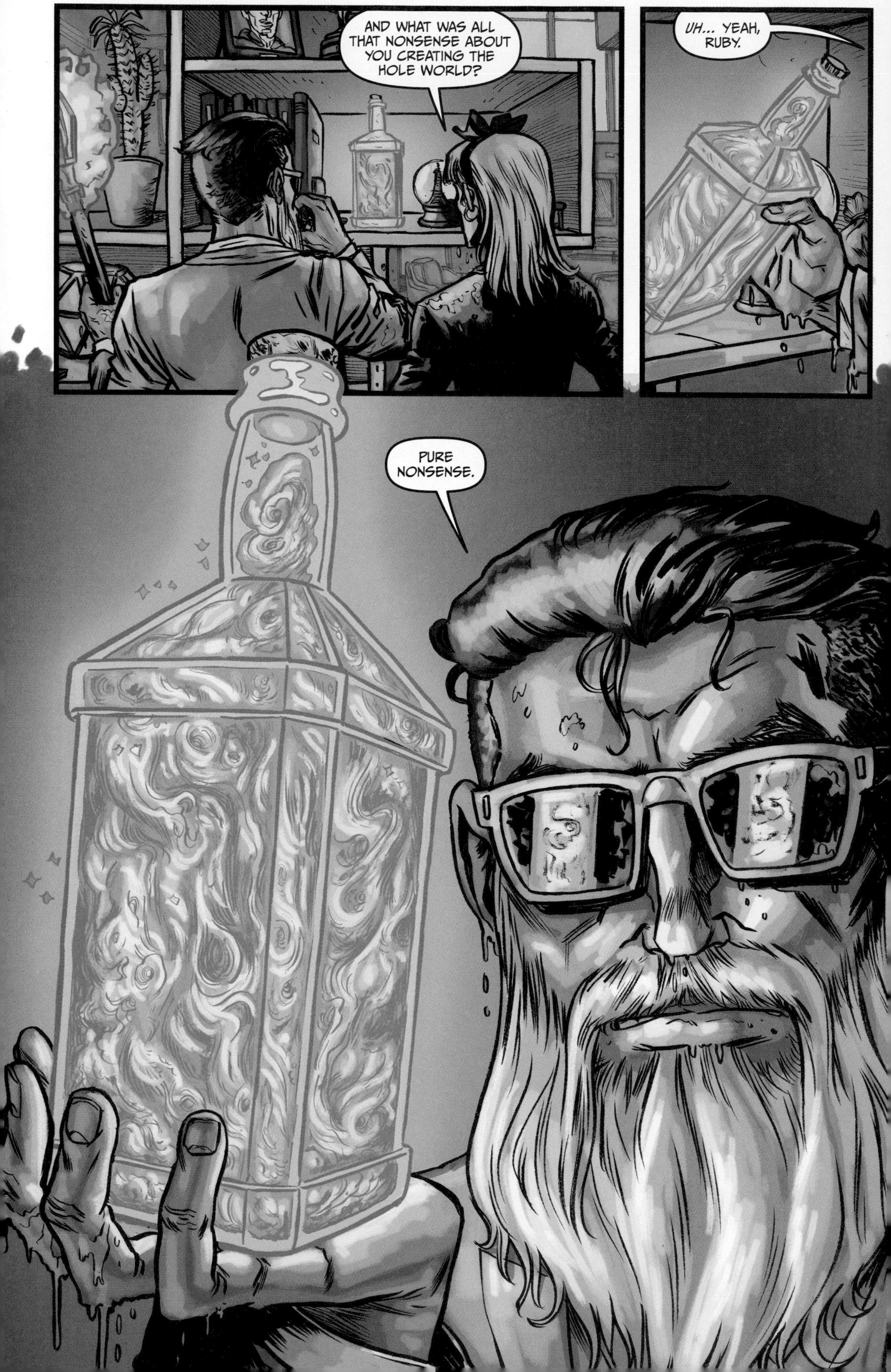
AND WHAT WAS ALL THAT NONSENSE ABOUT YOU CREATING THE HOLE WORLD?
UH... YEAH, RUBY.
PURE NONSENSE.

SEVENTEEN

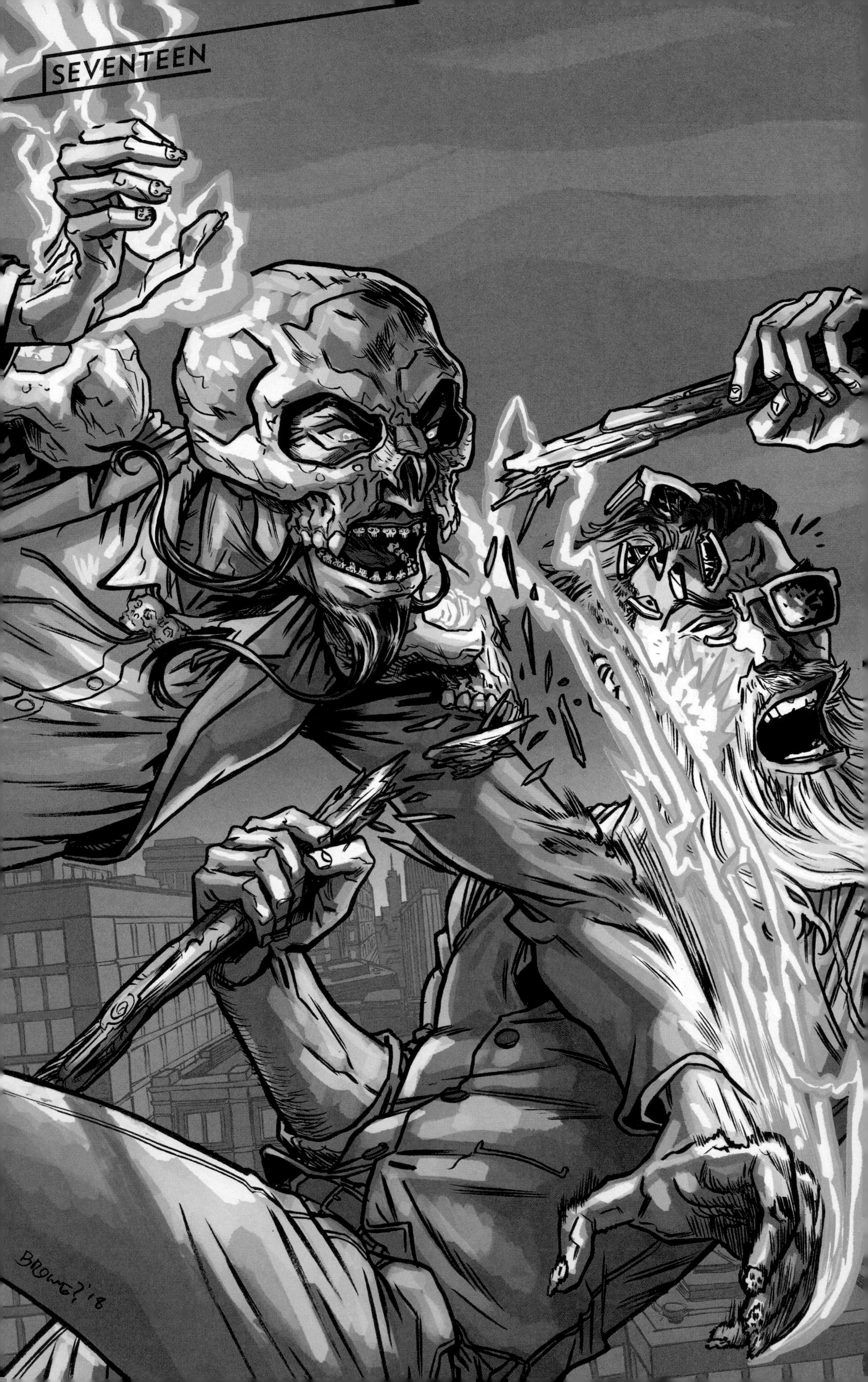

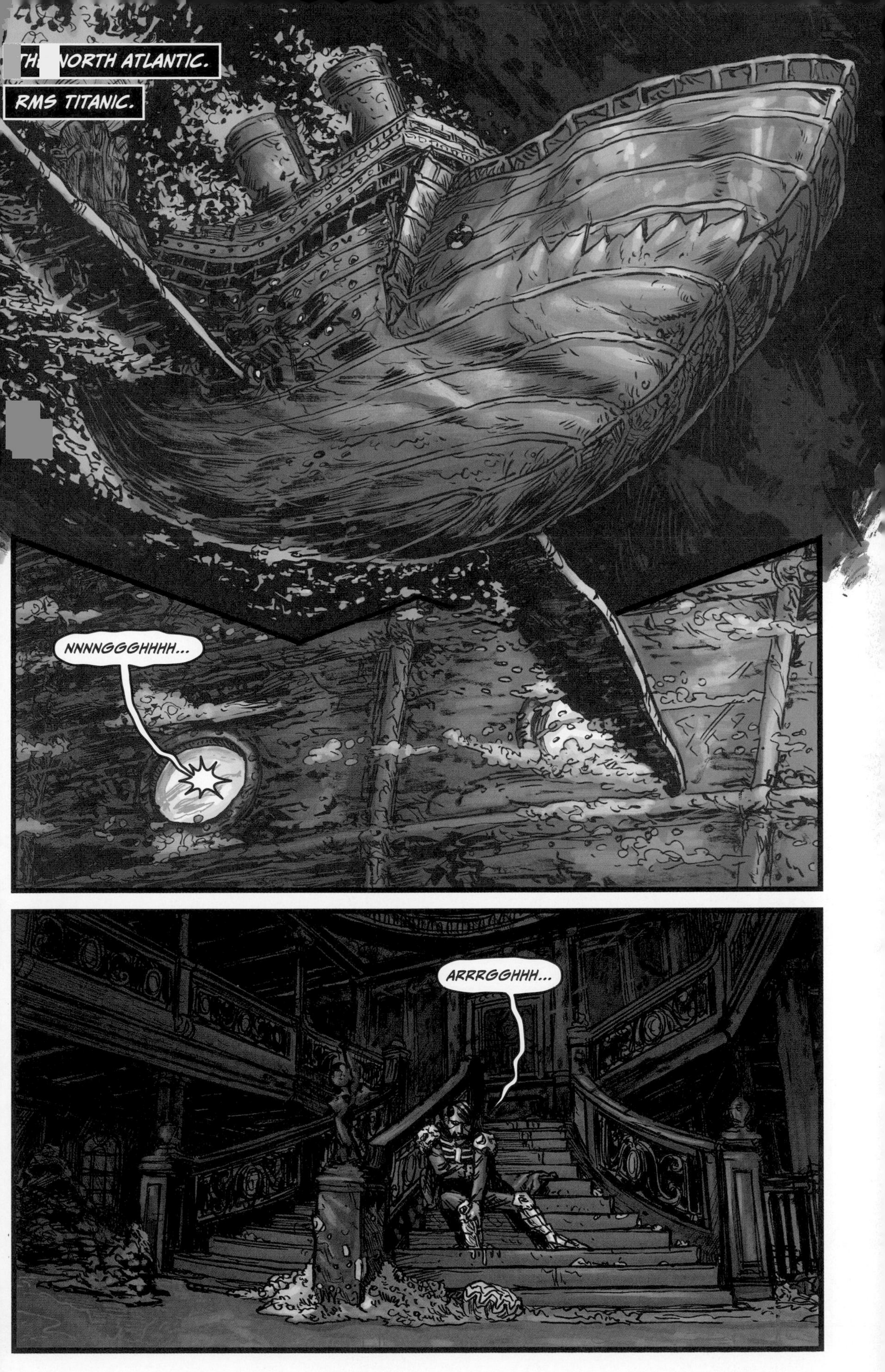
THE NORTH ATLANTIC.
RMS TITANIC.
NNNNGGGHHHH...
ARRRGGHHH...

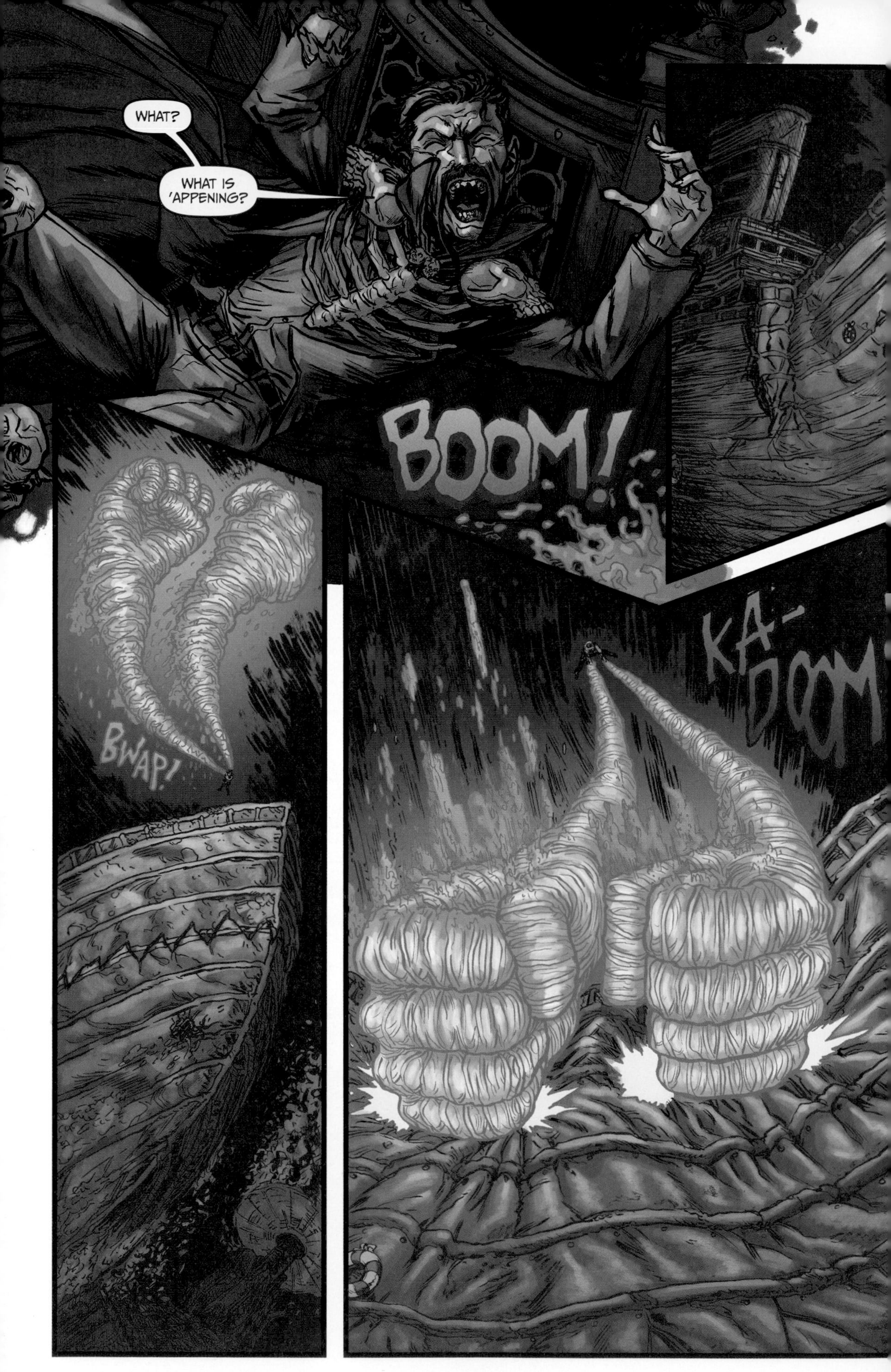
WHAT?
WHAT IS 'APPENING?
BOOM!
BWAP!
KA-DOOM

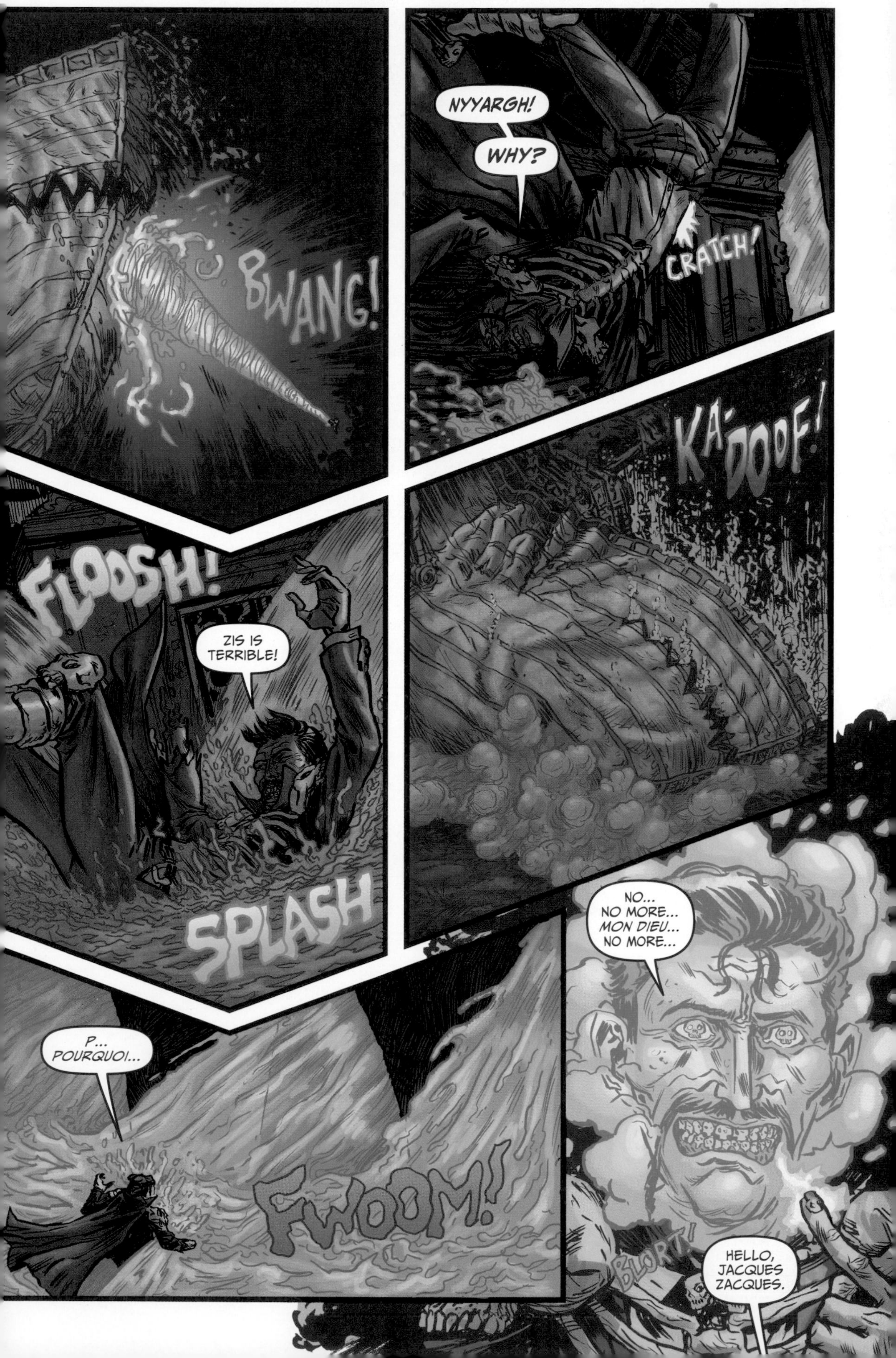
BWANG!
NYYARGH!
WHY?
CRATCH!
KA-DOOF!
FLOOSH!
ZIS IS TERRIBLE!
SPLASH
NO... NO MORE... MON DIEU... NO MORE...
P... POURQUOI...
FWOOM!
BLORT!
HELLO, JACQUES ZACQUES.

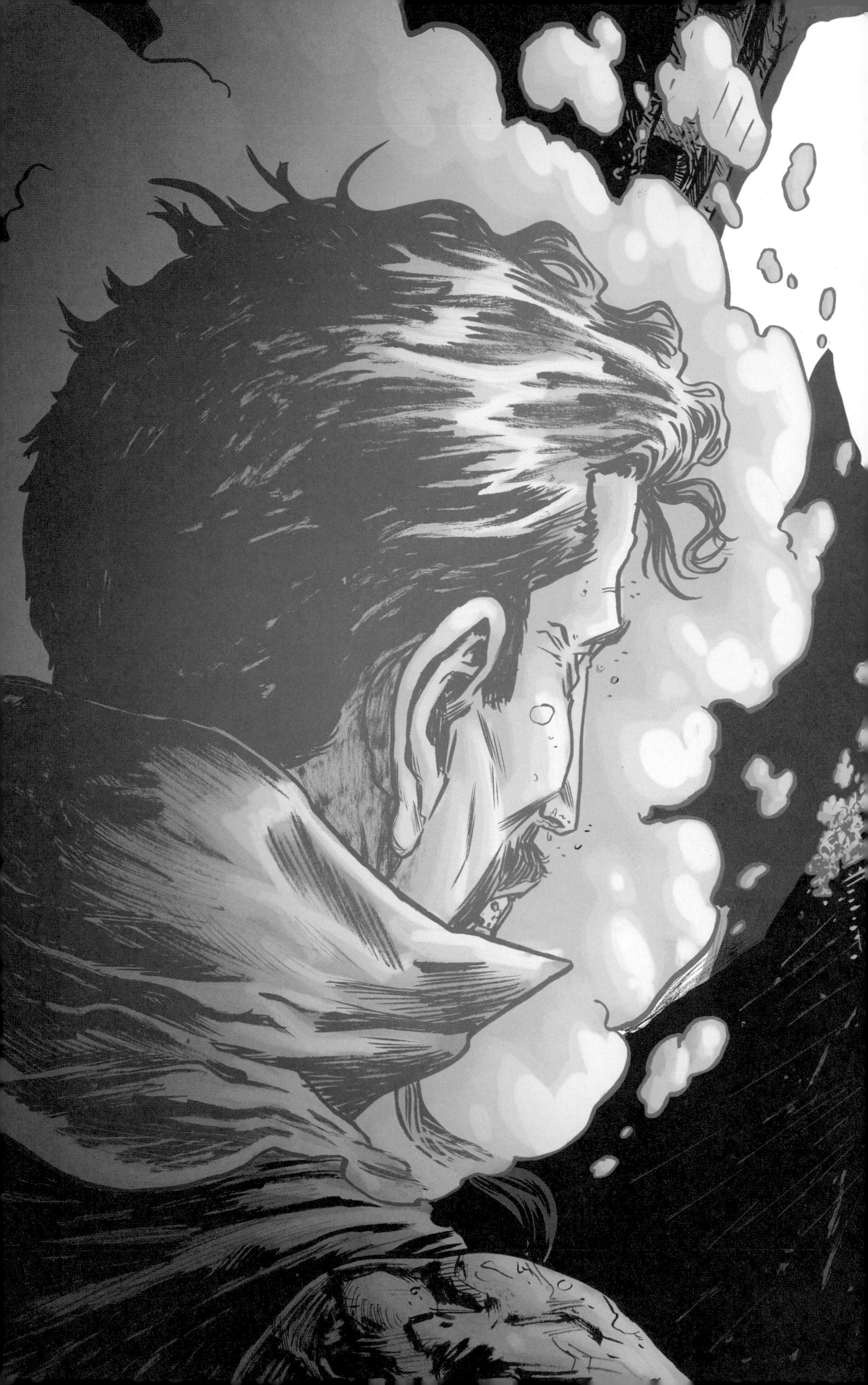

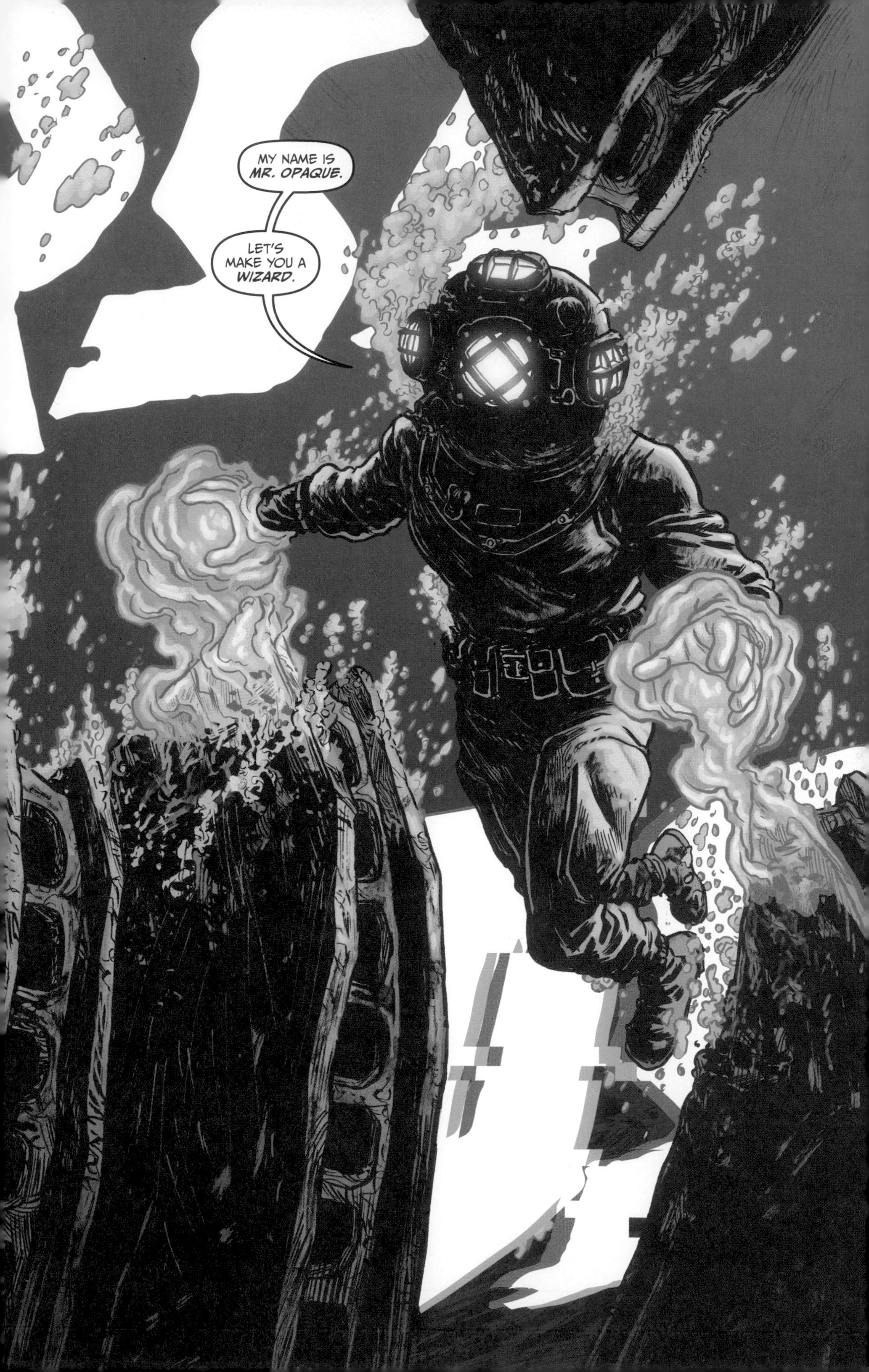
MY NAME IS MR. OPAQUE.
LET'S MAKE YOU A WIZARD.

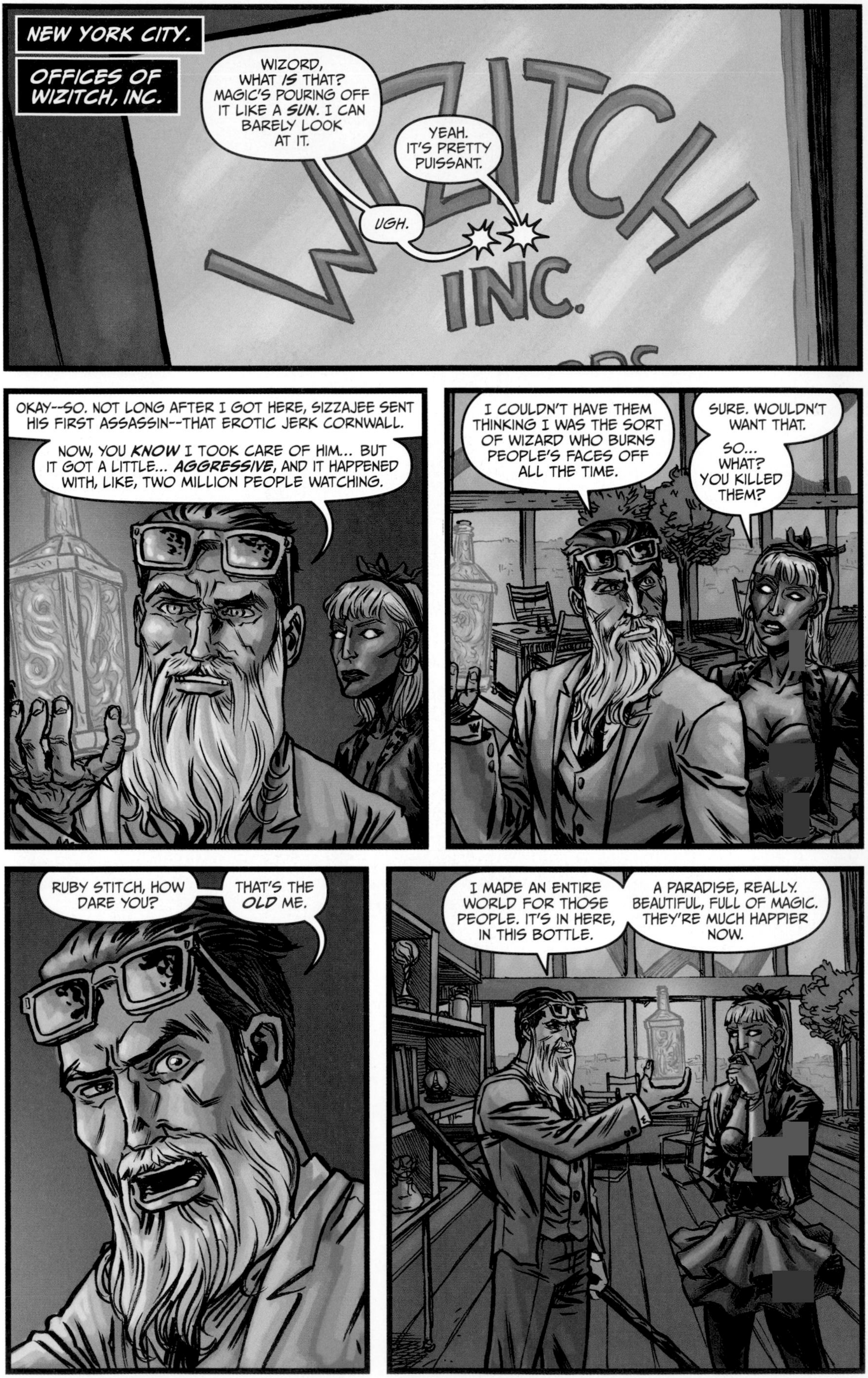
NEW YORK CITY.
OFFICES OF WIZITCH, INC.
WIZORD, WHAT *IS* THAT? MAGIC'S POURING OFF IT LIKE A ***SUN***. I CAN BARELY LOOK AT IT.
YEAH. IT'S PRETTY PUISSANT.
UGH.
WIZITCH INC.
OKAY--SO. NOT LONG AFTER I GOT HERE, SIZZAJEE SENT HIS FIRST ASSASSIN--THAT EROTIC JERK CORNWALL.
NOW, YOU ***KNOW*** I TOOK CARE OF HIM... BUT IT GOT A LITTLE... ***AGGRESSIVE***, AND IT HAPPENED WITH, LIKE, TWO MILLION PEOPLE WATCHING.
I COULDN'T HAVE THEM THINKING I WAS THE SORT OF WIZARD WHO BURNS PEOPLE'S FACES OFF ALL THE TIME.
SURE. WOULDN'T WANT THAT.
SO... WHAT? YOU KILLED THEM?
RUBY STITCH, HOW DARE YOU?
THAT'S THE ***OLD*** ME.
I MADE AN ENTIRE WORLD FOR THOSE PEOPLE. IT'S IN HERE, IN THIS BOTTLE.
A PARADISE, REALLY. BEAUTIFUL, FULL OF MAGIC. THEY'RE MUCH HAPPIER NOW.

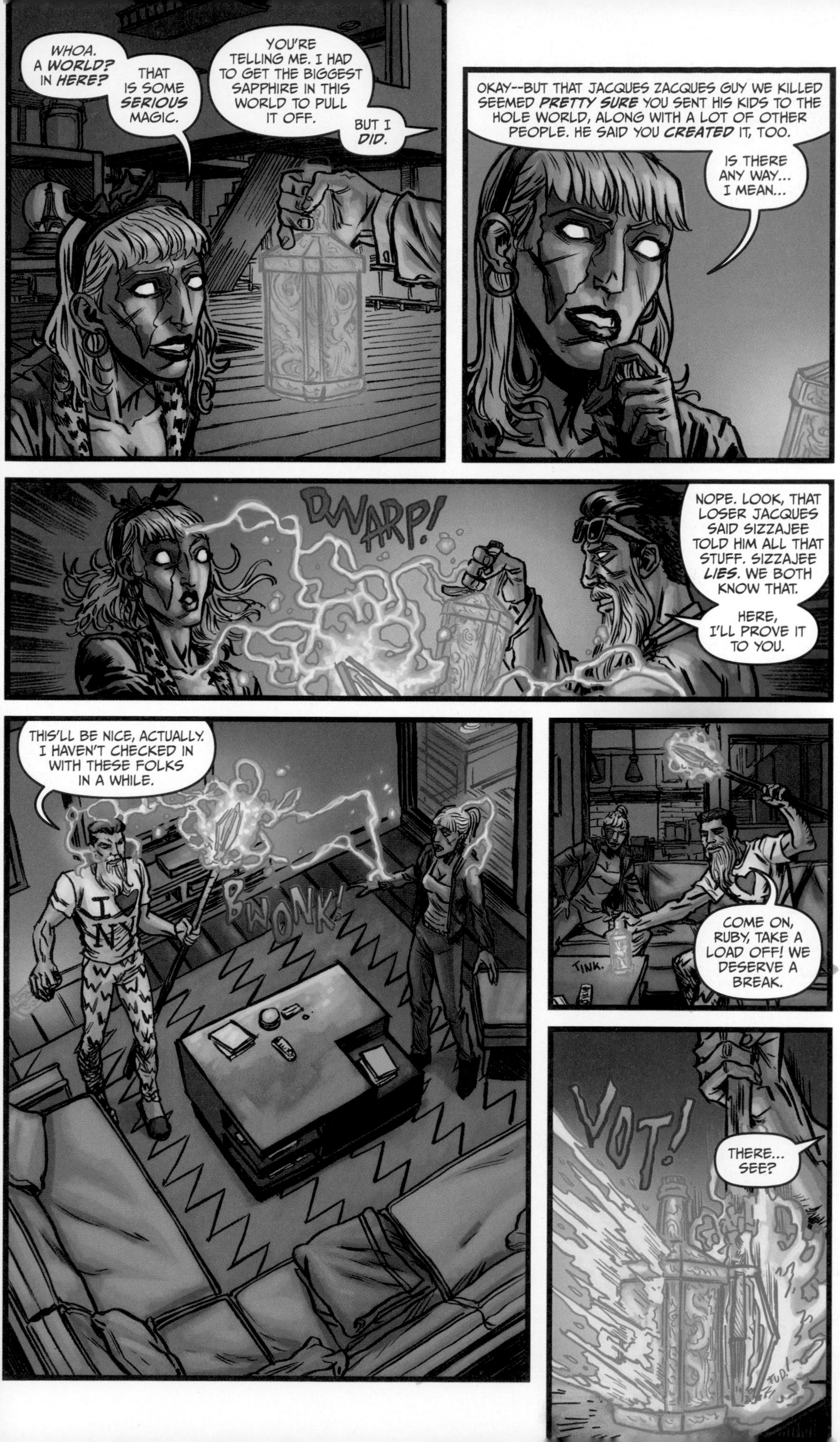

WHOA. A WORLD? IN HERE?
THAT IS SOME SERIOUS MAGIC.
YOU'RE TELLING ME. I HAD TO GET THE BIGGEST SAPPHIRE IN THIS WORLD TO PULL IT OFF.
BUT I DID.
OKAY--BUT THAT JACQUES ZACQUES GUY WE KILLED SEEMED PRETTY SURE YOU SENT HIS KIDS TO THE HOLE WORLD, ALONG WITH A LOT OF OTHER PEOPLE. HE SAID YOU CREATED IT, TOO.
IS THERE ANY WAY... I MEAN...
DWARP!
NOPE. LOOK, THAT LOSER JACQUES SAID SIZZAJEE TOLD HIM ALL THAT STUFF. SIZZAJEE LIES. WE BOTH KNOW THAT.
HERE, I'LL PROVE IT TO YOU.
THIS'LL BE NICE, ACTUALLY. I HAVEN'T CHECKED IN WITH THESE FOLKS IN A WHILE.
BWONK!
I ♥ NY
COME ON, RUBY, TAKE A LOAD OFF! WE DESERVE A BREAK.
TINK.
VOT!
THERE... SEE?
TUD!

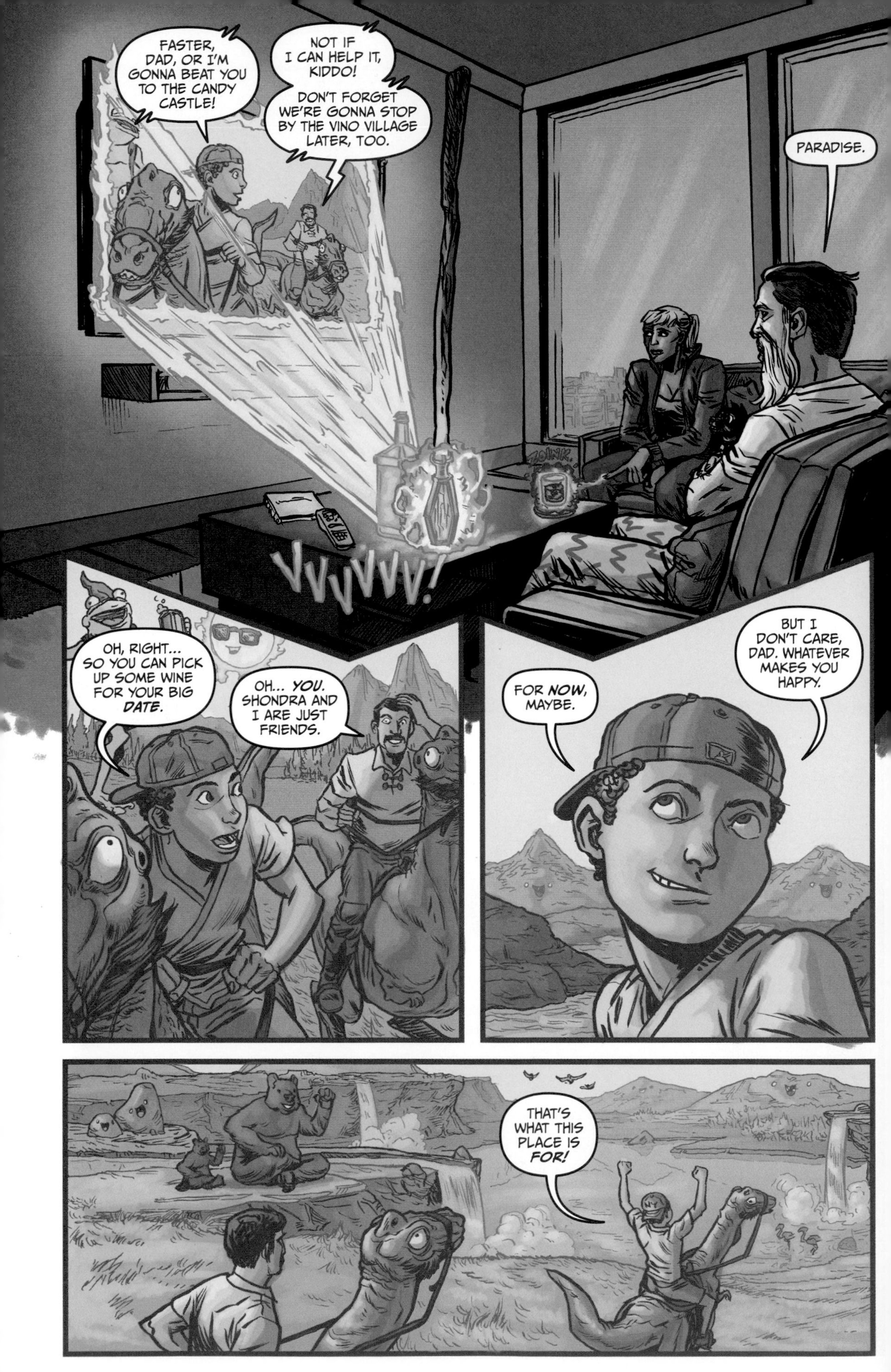
FASTER, DAD, OR I'M GONNA BEAT YOU TO THE CANDY CASTLE!
NOT IF I CAN HELP IT, KIDDO!
DON'T FORGET WE'RE GONNA STOP BY THE VINO VILLAGE LATER, TOO.
PARADISE.
ZOINK.
VVVVVV!
OH, RIGHT... SO YOU CAN PICK UP SOME WINE FOR YOUR BIG *DATE*.
OH... *YOU*. SHONDRA AND I ARE JUST FRIENDS.
FOR *NOW*, MAYBE.
BUT I DON'T CARE, DAD. WHATEVER MAKES YOU HAPPY.
THAT'S WHAT THIS PLACE IS *FOR!*

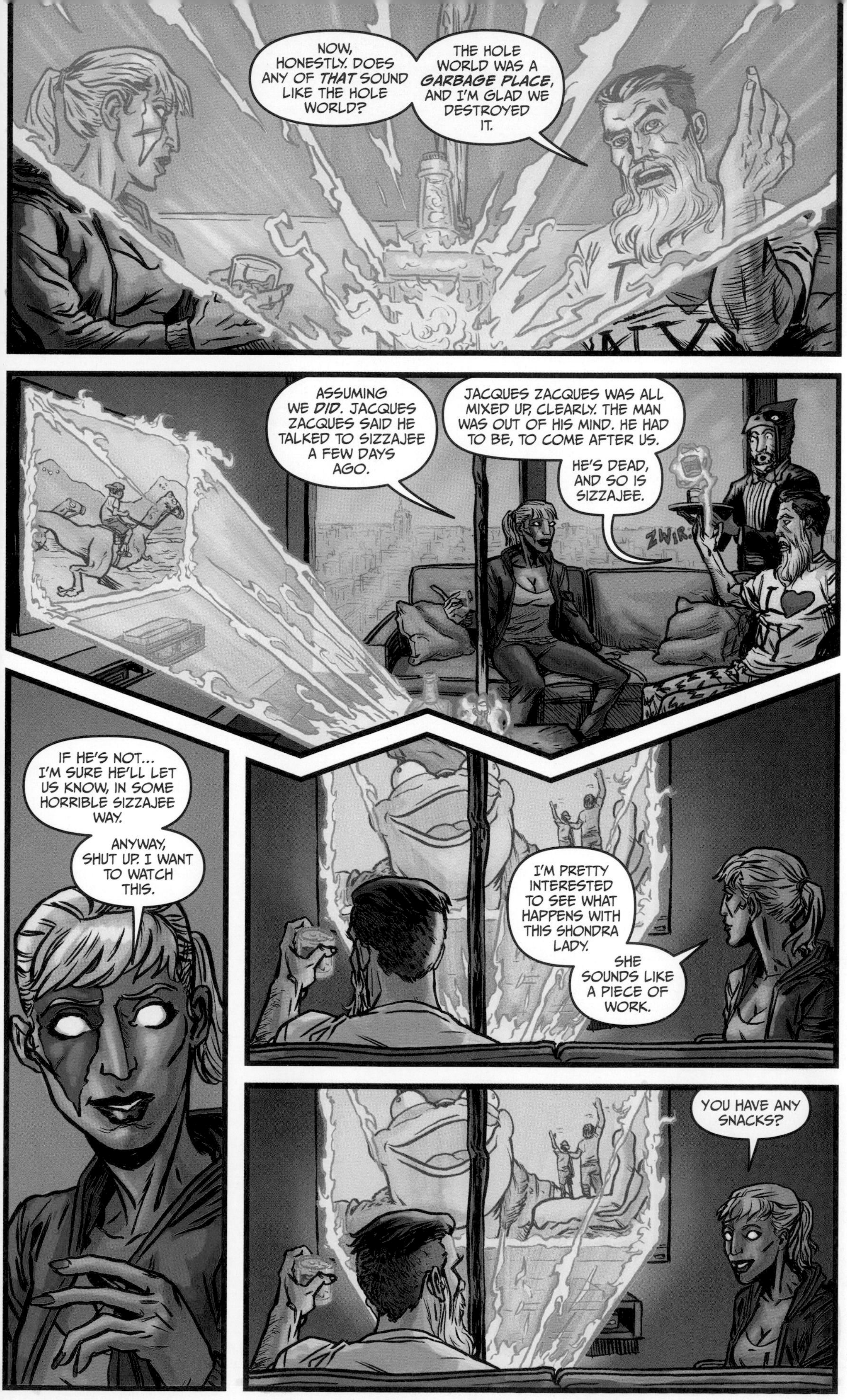
NOW, HONESTLY. DOES ANY OF THAT SOUND LIKE THE HOLE WORLD?
THE HOLE WORLD WAS A GARBAGE PLACE, AND I'M GLAD WE DESTROYED IT.
ASSUMING WE DID. JACQUES ZACQUES SAID HE TALKED TO SIZZAJEE A FEW DAYS AGO.
JACQUES ZACQUES WAS ALL MIXED UP, CLEARLY. THE MAN WAS OUT OF HIS MIND. HE HAD TO BE, TO COME AFTER US.
HE'S DEAD, AND SO IS SIZZAJEE.
ZWIR.
IF HE'S NOT... I'M SURE HE'LL LET US KNOW, IN SOME HORRIBLE SIZZAJEE WAY.
ANYWAY, SHUT UP. I WANT TO WATCH THIS.
I'M PRETTY INTERESTED TO SEE WHAT HAPPENS WITH THIS SHONDRA LADY.
SHE SOUNDS LIKE A PIECE OF WORK.
YOU HAVE ANY SNACKS?

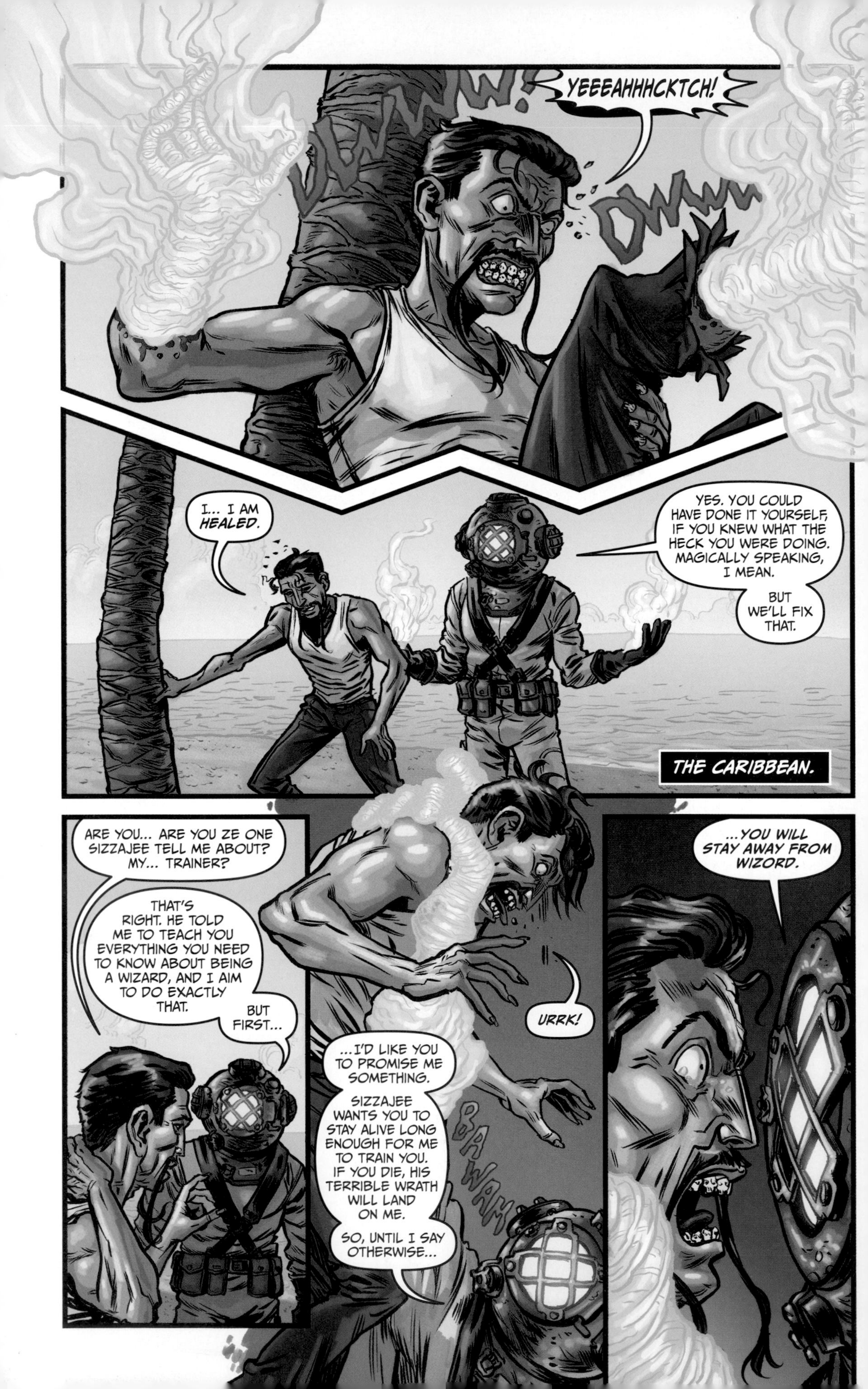
DWWWW!
YEEEAHHHCKTCH!
DWWW
I... I AM HEALED.
YES. YOU COULD HAVE DONE IT YOURSELF, IF YOU KNEW WHAT THE HECK YOU WERE DOING. MAGICALLY SPEAKING, I MEAN.
BUT WE'LL FIX THAT.
THE CARIBBEAN.
ARE YOU... ARE YOU ZE ONE SIZZAJEE TELL ME ABOUT? MY... TRAINER?
THAT'S RIGHT. HE TOLD ME TO TEACH YOU EVERYTHING YOU NEED TO KNOW ABOUT BEING A WIZARD, AND I AIM TO DO EXACTLY THAT.
BUT FIRST...
...I'D LIKE YOU TO PROMISE ME SOMETHING.
SIZZAJEE WANTS YOU TO STAY ALIVE LONG ENOUGH FOR ME TO TRAIN YOU. IF YOU DIE, HIS TERRIBLE WRATH WILL LAND ON ME.
SO, UNTIL I SAY OTHERWISE...
URRK!
BAWAM
...YOU WILL STAY AWAY FROM WIZORD.

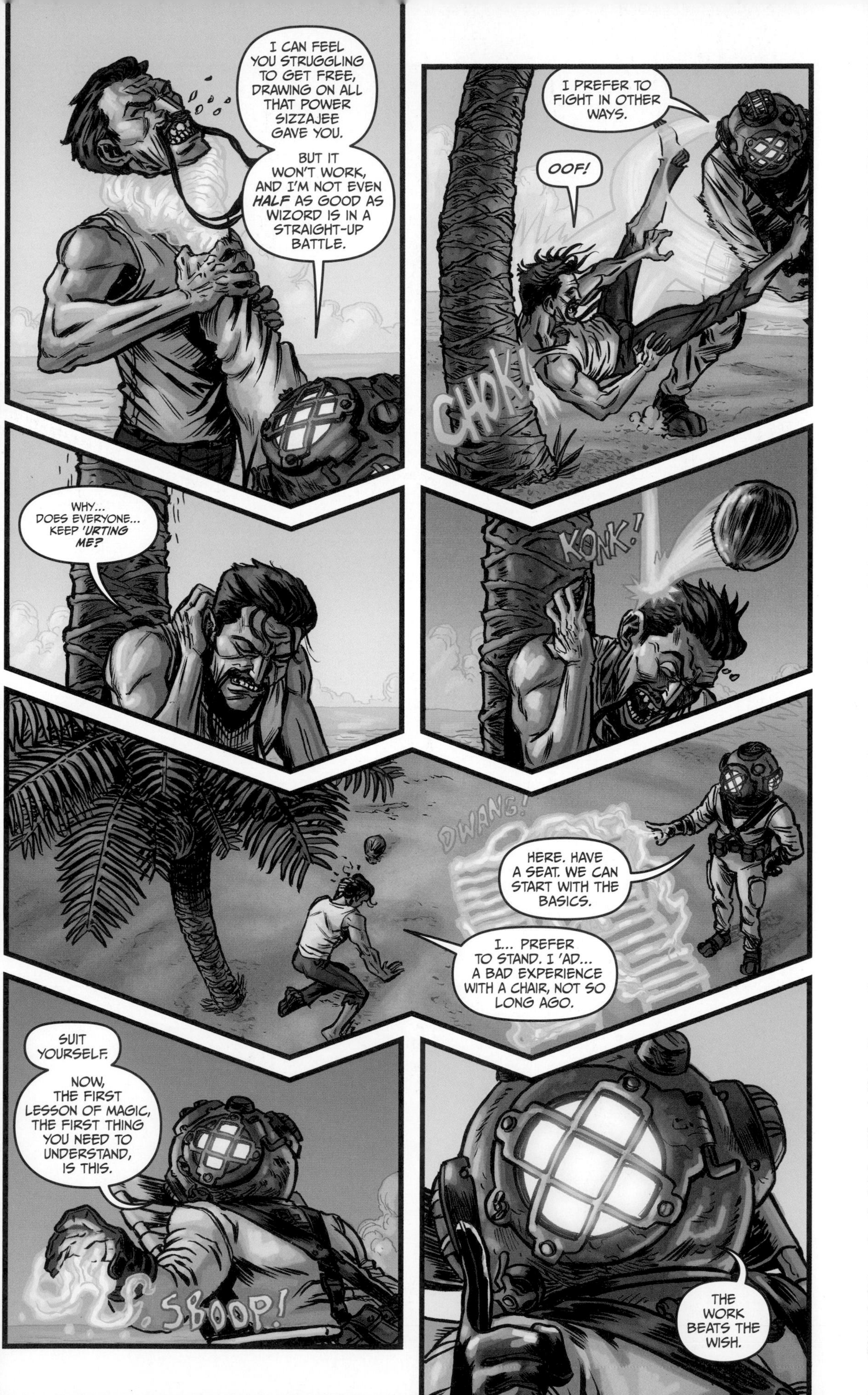
I CAN FEEL YOU STRUGGLING TO GET FREE, DRAWING ON ALL THAT POWER SIZZAJEE GAVE YOU.
BUT IT WON'T WORK, AND I'M NOT EVEN HALF AS GOOD AS WIZORD IS IN A STRAIGHT-UP BATTLE.
I PREFER TO FIGHT IN OTHER WAYS.
OOF!
CHOK!
WHY... DOES EVERYONE... KEEP 'URTING ME?
KONK!
DWANG!
HERE. HAVE A SEAT. WE CAN START WITH THE BASICS.
I... PREFER TO STAND. I 'AD... A BAD EXPERIENCE WITH A CHAIR, NOT SO LONG AGO.
SUIT YOURSELF.
NOW, THE FIRST LESSON OF MAGIC, THE FIRST THING YOU NEED TO UNDERSTAND, IS THIS.
SBOOP!
THE WORK BEATS THE WISH.

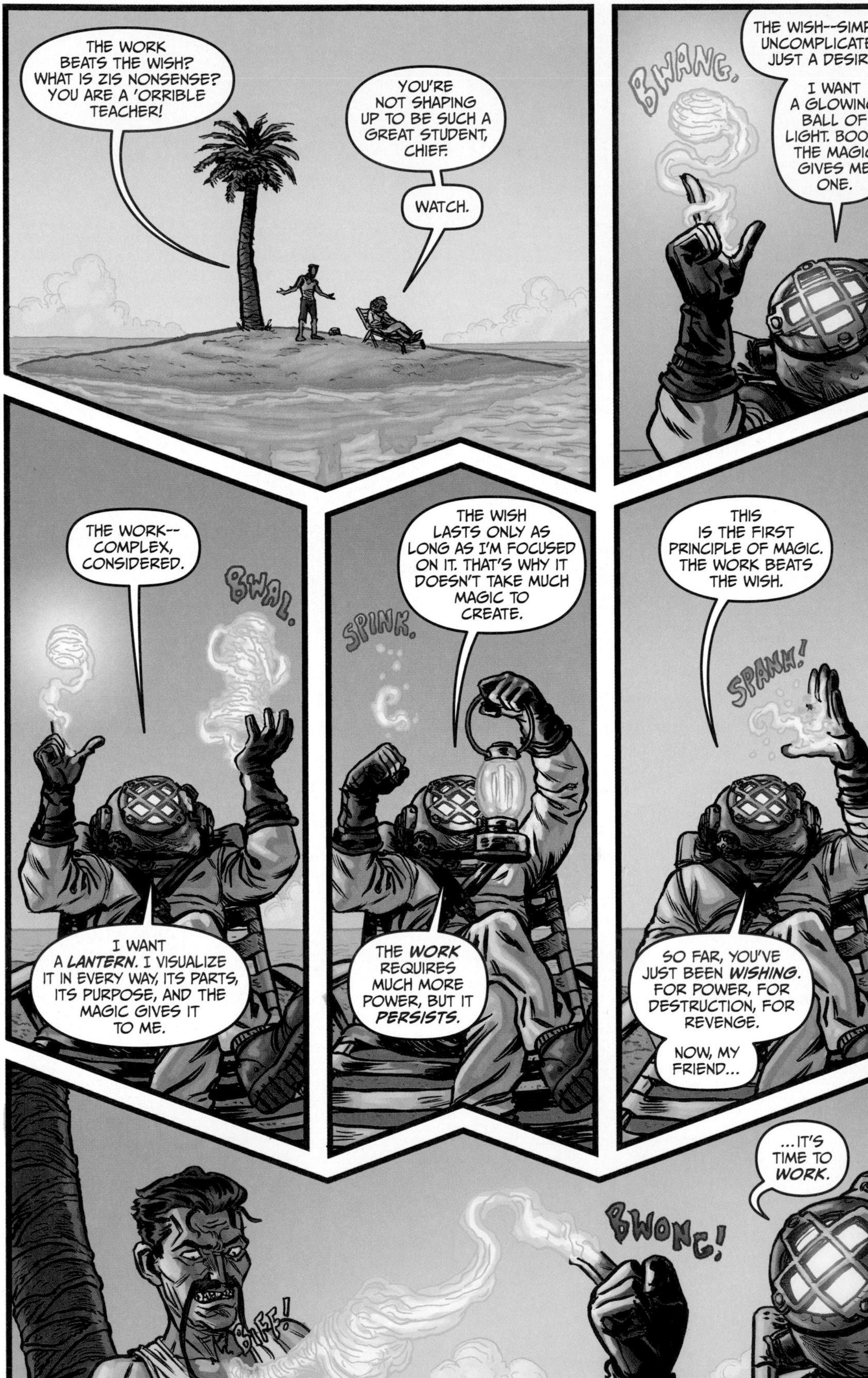
THE WORK BEATS THE WISH? WHAT IS ZIS NONSENSE? YOU ARE A 'ORRIBLE TEACHER!
YOU'RE NOT SHAPING UP TO BE SUCH A GREAT STUDENT, CHIEF.
WATCH.
BWANG.
THE WISH--SIMPLE, UNCOMPLICATED, JUST A DESIRE.
I WANT A GLOWING BALL OF LIGHT. BOOM, THE MAGIC GIVES ME ONE.
THE WORK--COMPLEX, CONSIDERED.
BWAL.
I WANT A *LANTERN*. I VISUALIZE IT IN EVERY WAY, ITS PARTS, ITS PURPOSE, AND THE MAGIC GIVES IT TO ME.
THE WISH LASTS ONLY AS LONG AS I'M FOCUSED ON IT. THAT'S WHY IT DOESN'T TAKE MUCH MAGIC TO CREATE.
SPINK.
THE *WORK* REQUIRES MUCH MORE POWER, BUT IT *PERSISTS*.
THIS IS THE FIRST PRINCIPLE OF MAGIC. THE WORK BEATS THE WISH.
SPANK!
SO FAR, YOU'VE JUST BEEN *WISHING*. FOR POWER, FOR DESTRUCTION, FOR REVENGE.
NOW, MY FRIEND...
...IT'S TIME TO *WORK*.
BWONG!
FWOOF!

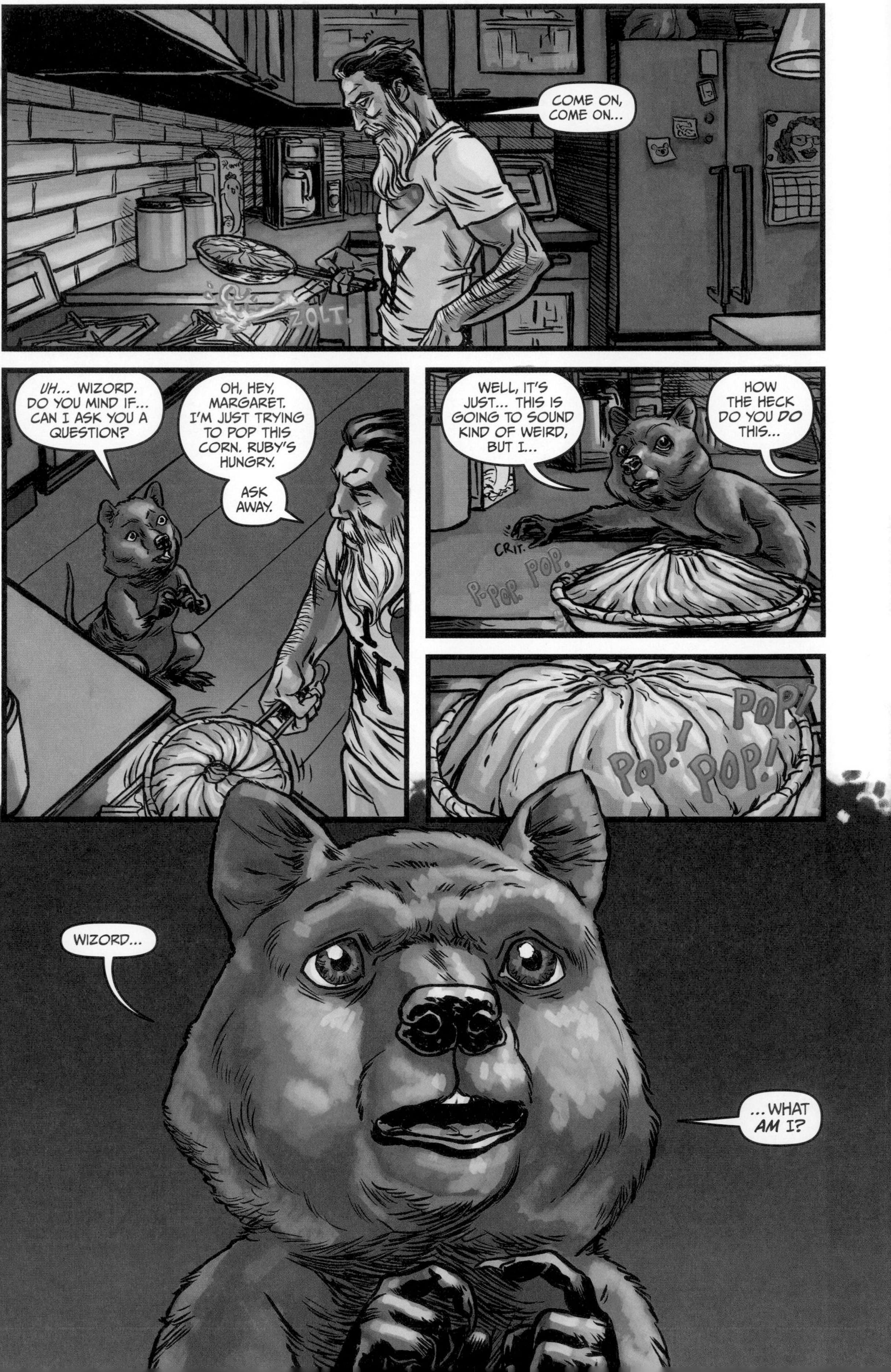

COME ON, COME ON...
ZOLT.
UH... WIZORD. DO YOU MIND IF... CAN I ASK YOU A QUESTION?
OH, HEY, MARGARET. I'M JUST TRYING TO POP THIS CORN. RUBY'S HUNGRY.
ASK AWAY.
WELL, IT'S JUST... THIS IS GOING TO SOUND KIND OF WEIRD, BUT I...
HOW THE HECK DO YOU DO THIS...
CRIT.
P-POP. POP.
POP! POP! POP!
WIZORD...
...WHAT AM I?

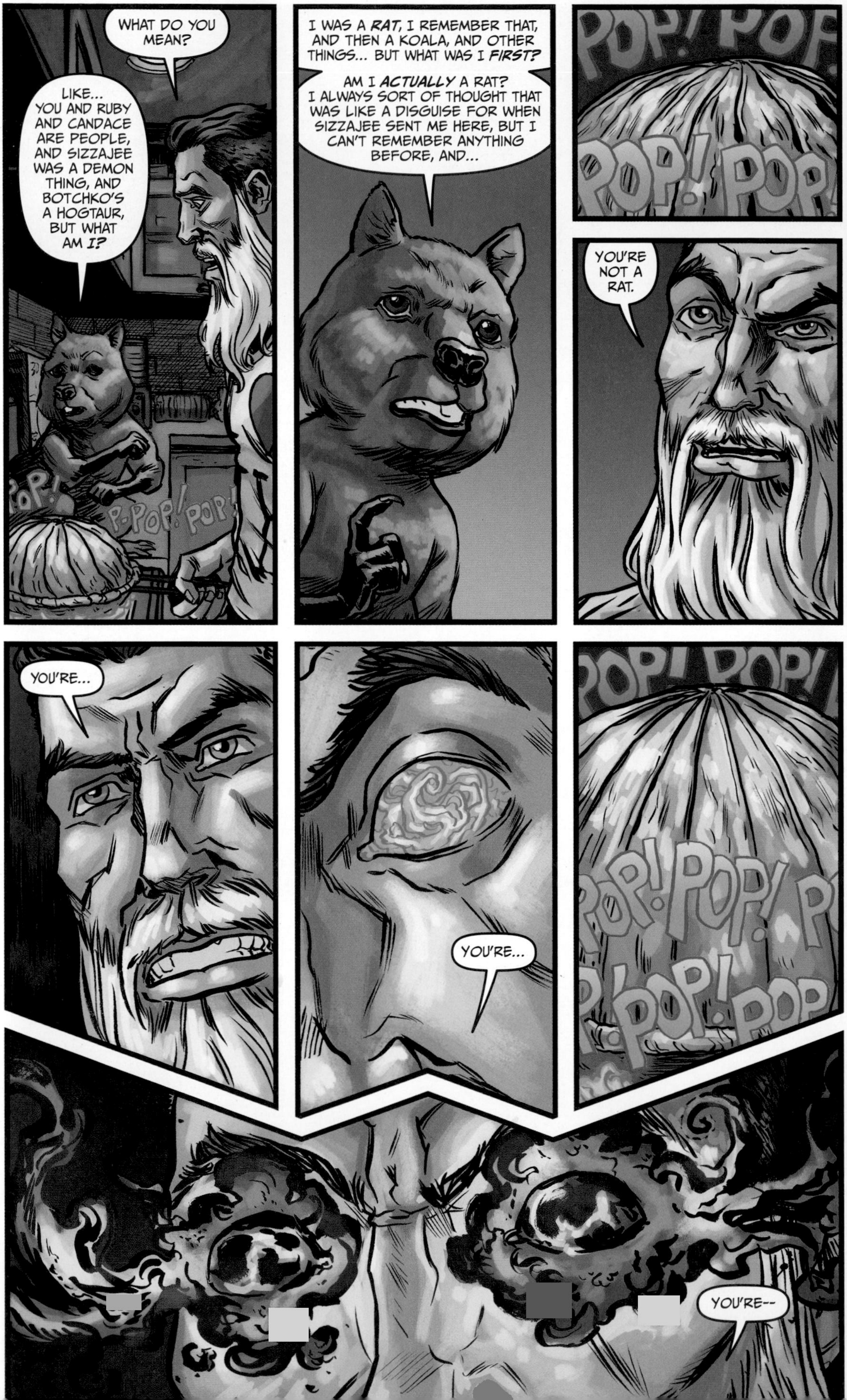
WHAT DO YOU MEAN?
LIKE... YOU AND RUBY AND CANDACE ARE PEOPLE, AND SIZZAJEE WAS A DEMON THING, AND BOTCHKO'S A HOGTAUR, BUT WHAT AM I?
POP! P-POP! POP!
I WAS A RAT, I REMEMBER THAT, AND THEN A KOALA, AND OTHER THINGS... BUT WHAT WAS I FIRST?
AM I ACTUALLY A RAT? I ALWAYS SORT OF THOUGHT THAT WAS LIKE A DISGUISE FOR WHEN SIZZAJEE SENT ME HERE, BUT I CAN'T REMEMBER ANYTHING BEFORE, AND...
POP! POP! POP! POP!
YOU'RE NOT A RAT.
YOU'RE...
YOU'RE...
POP! POP! POP! POP! POP! POP! POP!
YOU'RE--

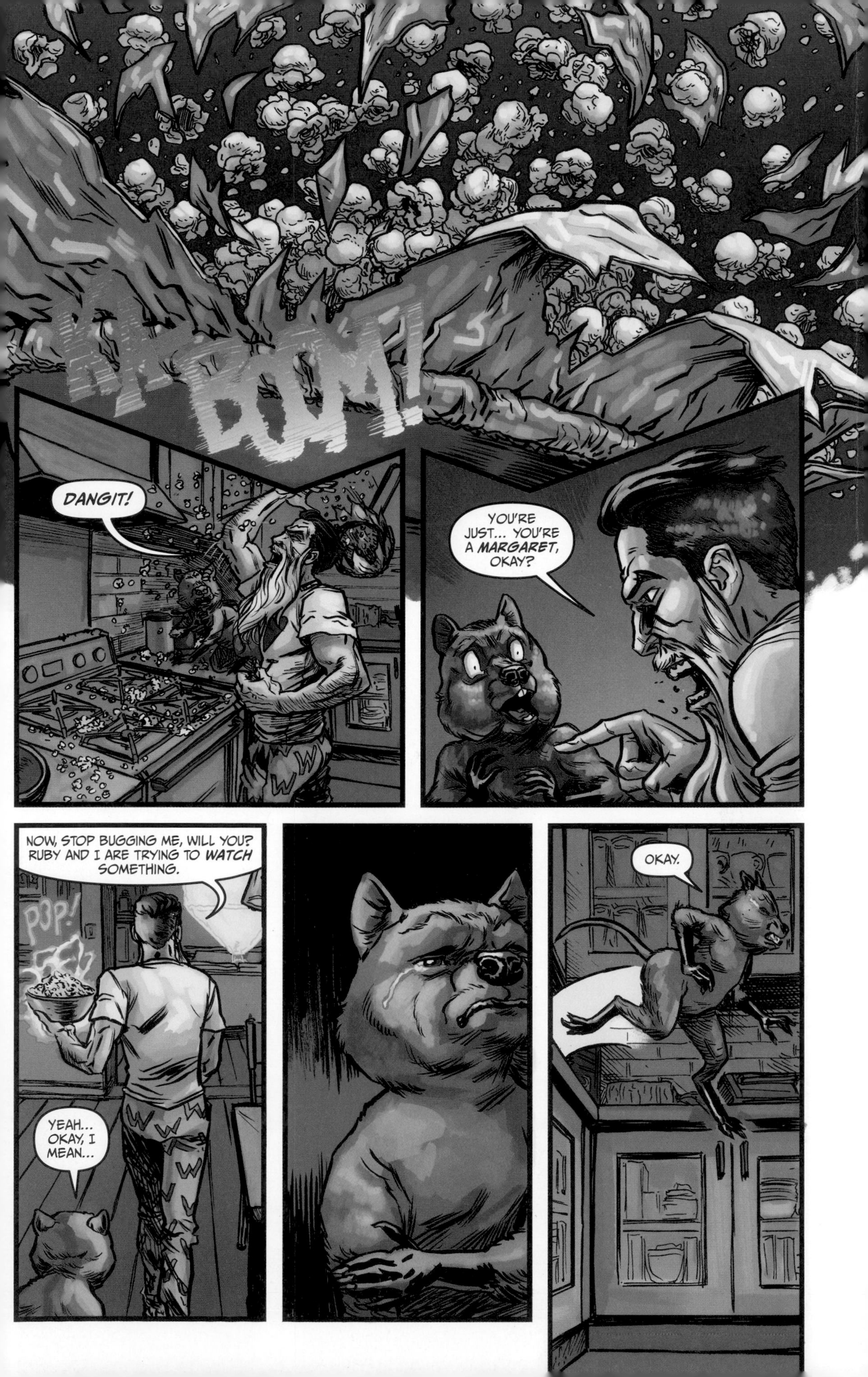
BOOM!
DANGIT!
YOU'RE JUST... YOU'RE A MARGARET, OKAY?
NOW, STOP BUGGING ME, WILL YOU? RUBY AND I ARE TRYING TO WATCH SOMETHING.
POP!
YEAH... OKAY, I MEAN...
OKAY.

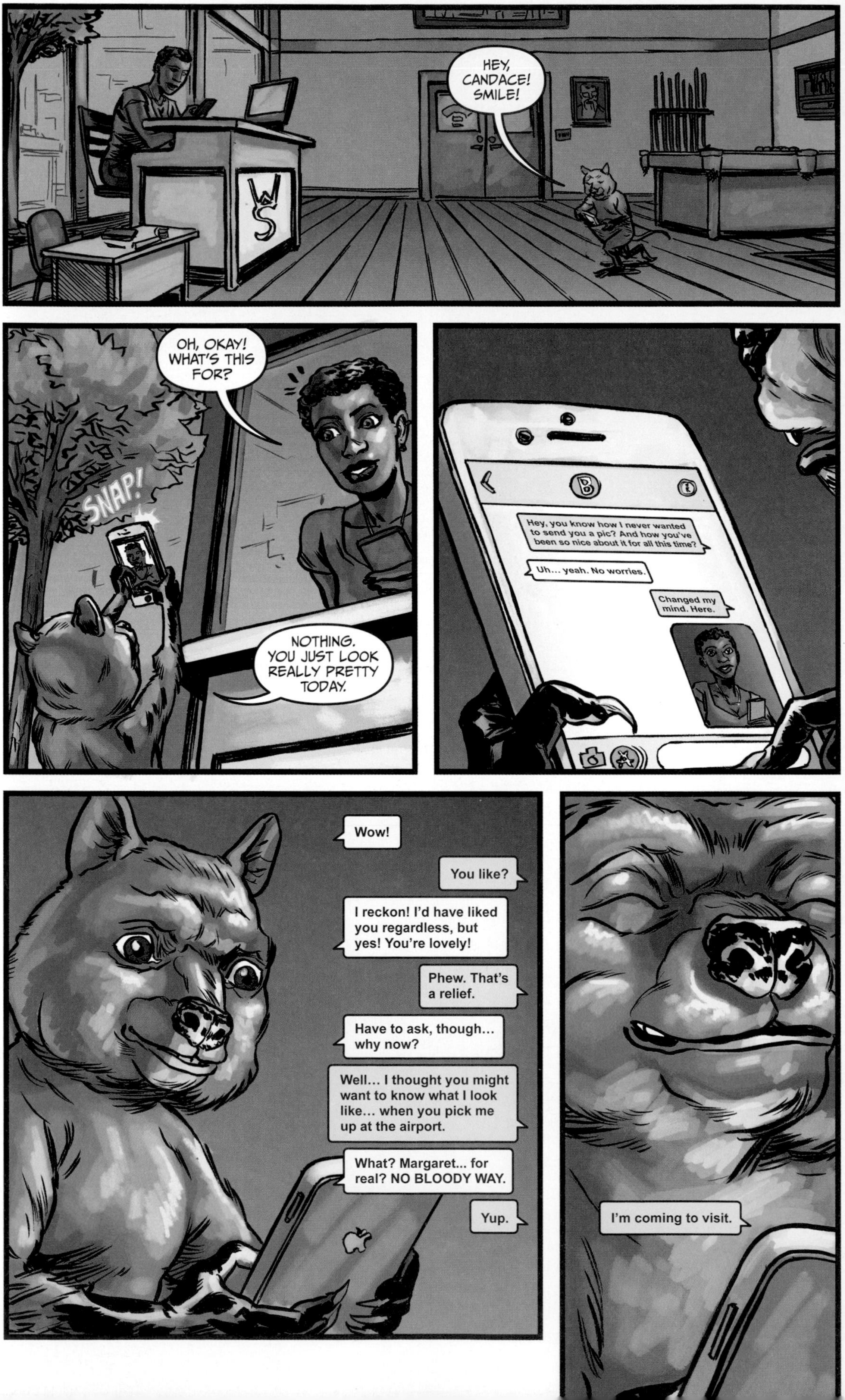
HEY, CANDACE! SMILE!
OH, OKAY! WHAT'S THIS FOR?
SNAP!
NOTHING. YOU JUST LOOK REALLY PRETTY TODAY.
Hey, you know how I never wanted to send you a pic? And how you've been so nice about it for all this time?
Uh... yeah. No worries.
Changed my mind. Here.
Wow!
You like?
I reckon! I'd have liked you regardless, but yes! You're lovely!
Phew. That's a relief.
Have to ask, though... why now?
Well... I thought you might want to know what I look like... when you pick me up at the airport.
What? Margaret... for real? NO BLOODY WAY.
Yup.
I'm coming to visit.

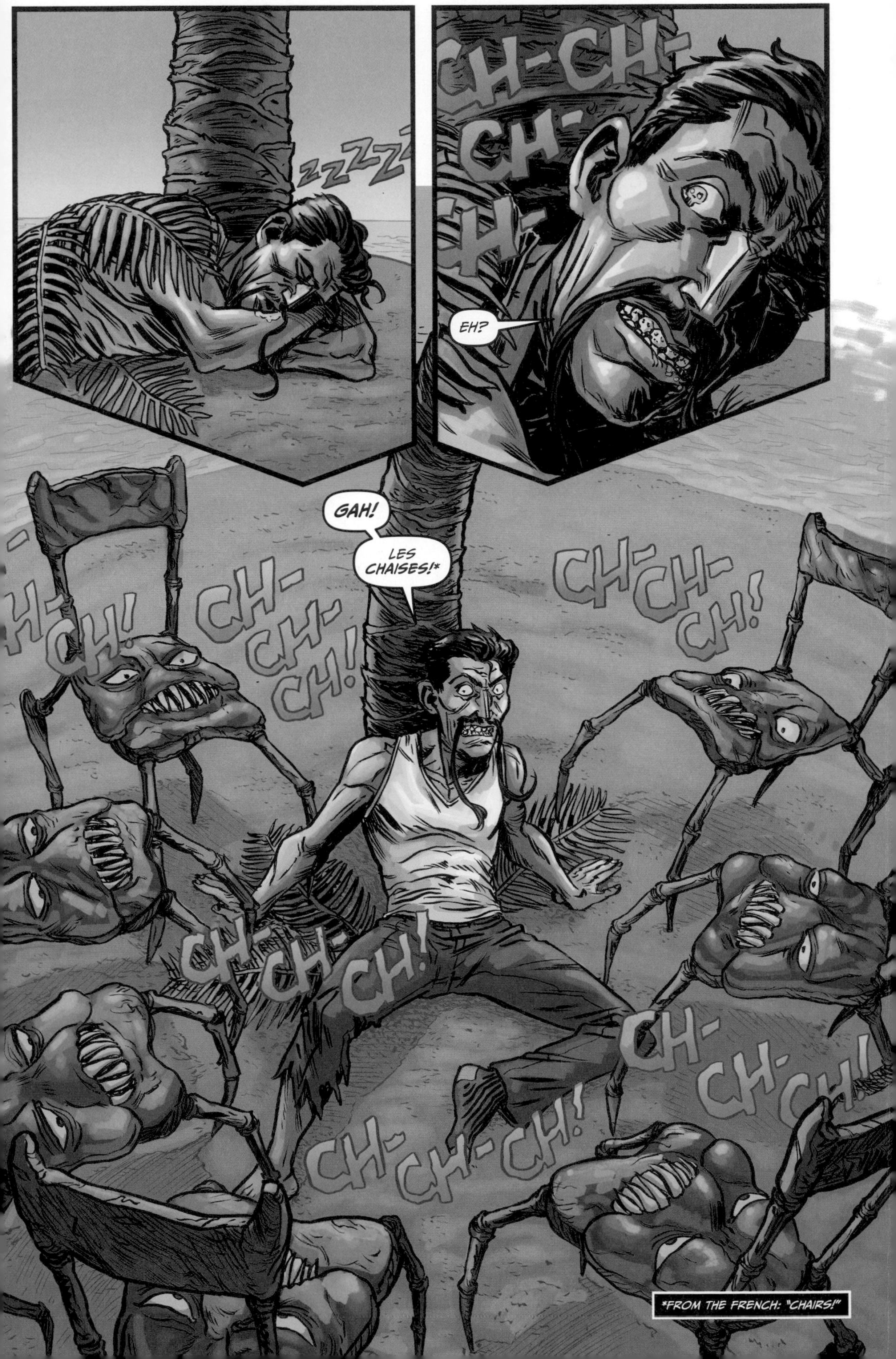
ZZZZZ
CH-CH-CH-CH-
EH?
GAH!
LES CHAISES!*
CH-CH!
CH-CH-CH!
CH-CH-CH!
CH-CH-CH!
CH-CH-CH!
CH-CH-CH!
CH-CH-CH!
*FROM THE FRENCH: "CHAIRS!"

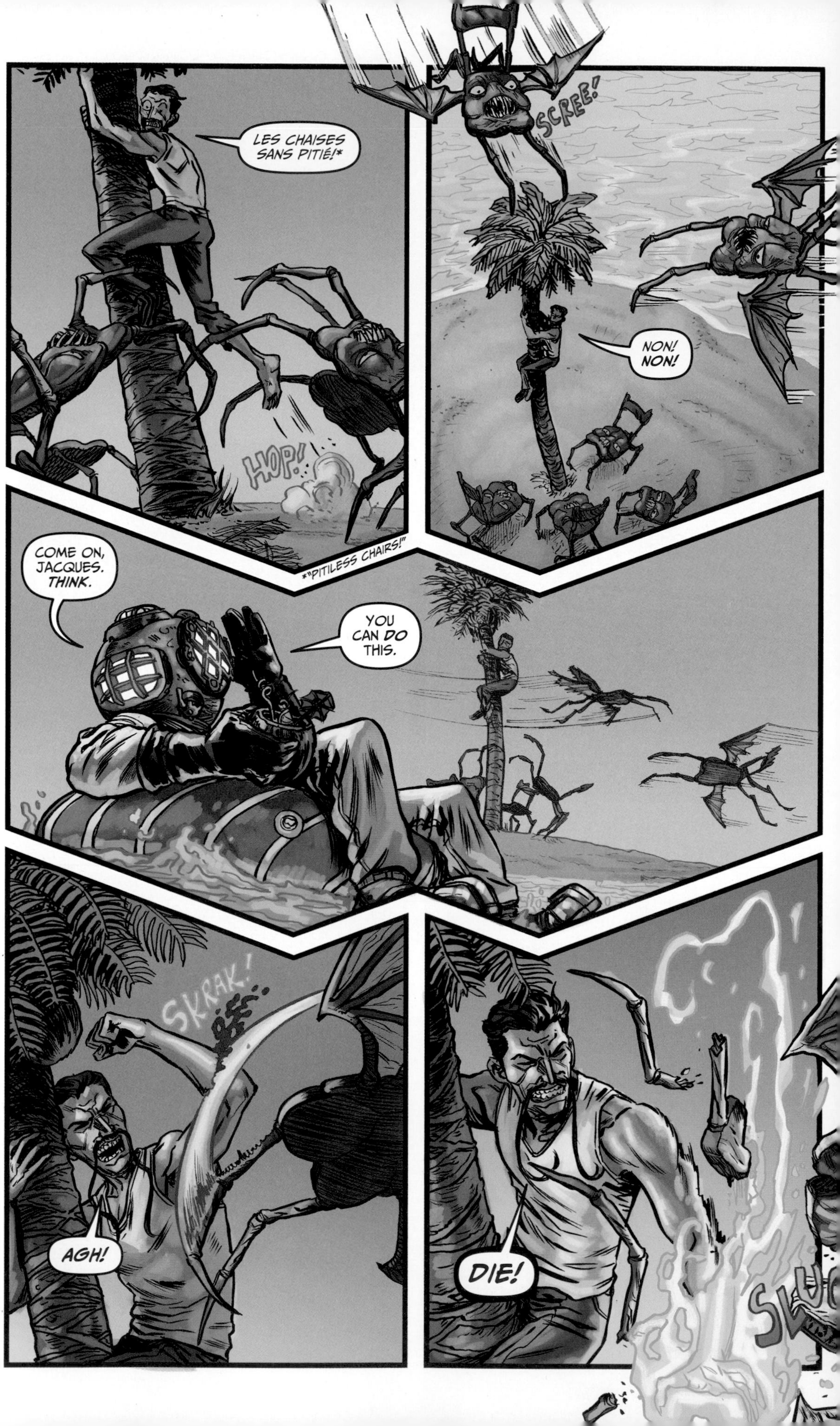
LES CHAISES SANS PITIÉ!*
HOP!
*"PITILESS CHAIRS!"
SCREE!
NON! NON!
COME ON, JACQUES. THINK.
YOU CAN DO THIS.
SKRAK!
AGH!
DIE!

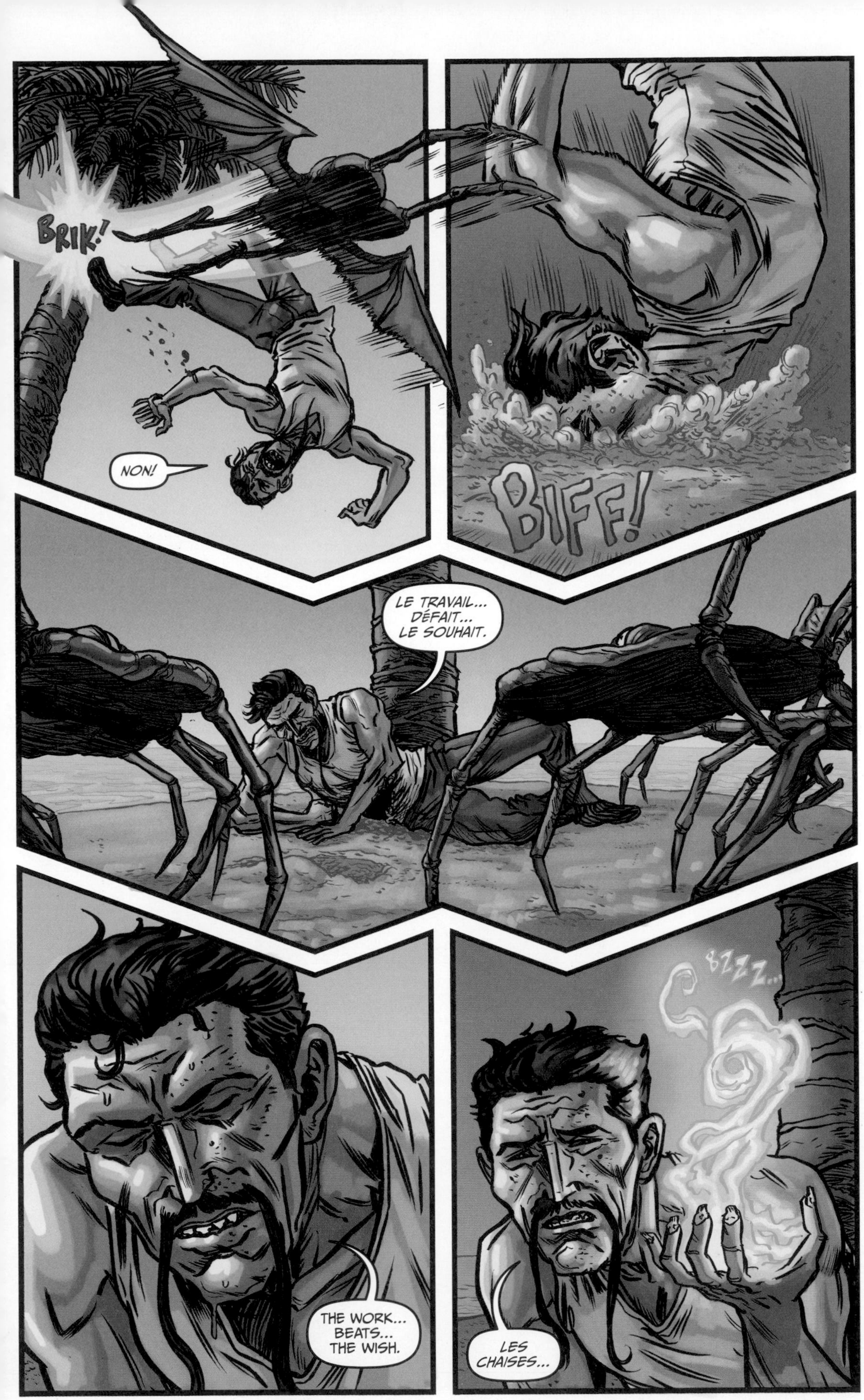
BRIK!
NON!
BIFF!
LE TRAVAIL... DÉFAIT... LE SOUHAIT.
THE WORK... BEATS... THE WISH.
BZZZ...
LES CHAISES...

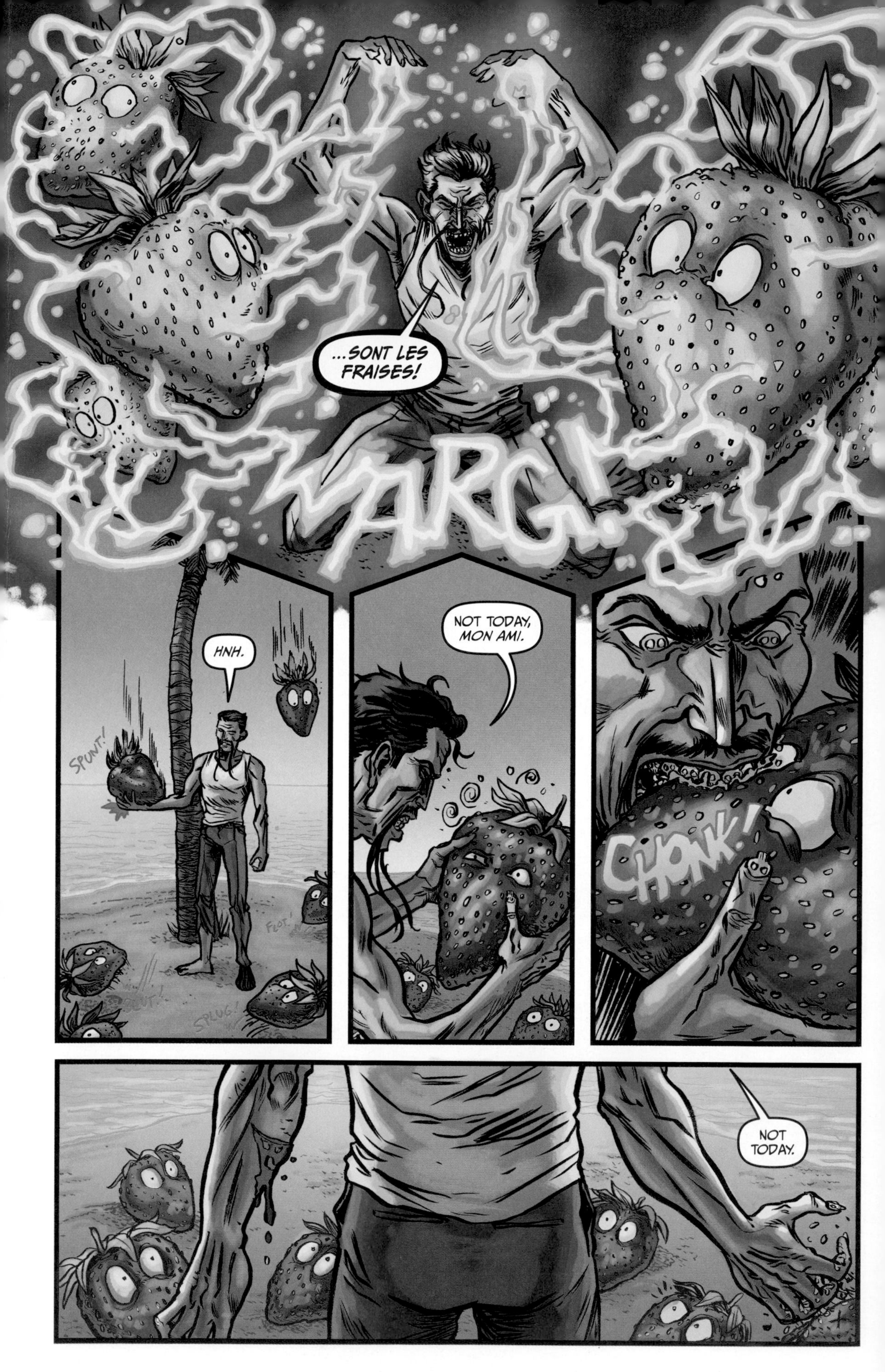
...SONT LES FRAISES!
VARG!
HNH.
SPUNT!
FLOT!
SPLUG!
NOT TODAY, MON AMI.
CHONK!
NOT TODAY.

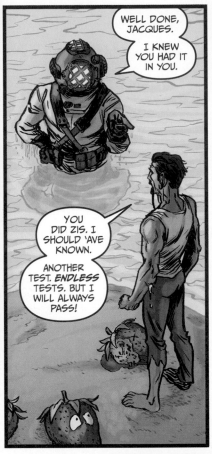

WELL DONE, JACQUES.

I KNEW YOU HAD IT IN YOU.

YOU DID ZIS. I SHOULD 'AVE KNOWN.

ANOTHER TEST. *ENDLESS* TESTS. BUT I WILL ALWAYS PASS!

SORT OF AN UNORTHODOX SOLUTION HERE, THOUGH, I HAVE TO SAY.

AH... YES. IN MY LANGUAGE, ZE CHAIRS ARE "LES CHAISES." WHEN I TRY TO CHANGE ZEM TO SOMETHING 'ARMLESS, "LES FRAISES" CAME TO MIND. STRAWBERRIES.

ZE RHYME, YOU SEE. I AM A BIT EMBARRASSED. ZE CHOICE OF A CHILD. SILLY.

THAT'S FASCINATING. WE ALL HAVE OUR SPECIALTIES. I WONDER IF YOU'LL END UP BEING A *WORDZARD*.

ANYWAY, LOOK, IN MANY WAYS, MAGIC *IS* SILLY, JACQUES. THAT'S WHY IT'S GREAT. YOU'LL SEE.

PERHAPS. BUT I REALIZE SOMETHING IMPORTANT TODAY.

IF IT 'AD BEEN ONLY ZE *ONE* CHAIR, I COULD 'AVE DESTROYED IT EASILY. BUT... IT WAS *MANY*.

ATTACKING FROM ALL DIRECTIONS. I COULD NOT FOCUS. I NEARLY *DIED*.

WHEN I DESTROY WIZORD, I MUST USE THIS LESSON.

BEFORE I ATTACK HIM NEXT, I MUST BUILD...

ZZZ

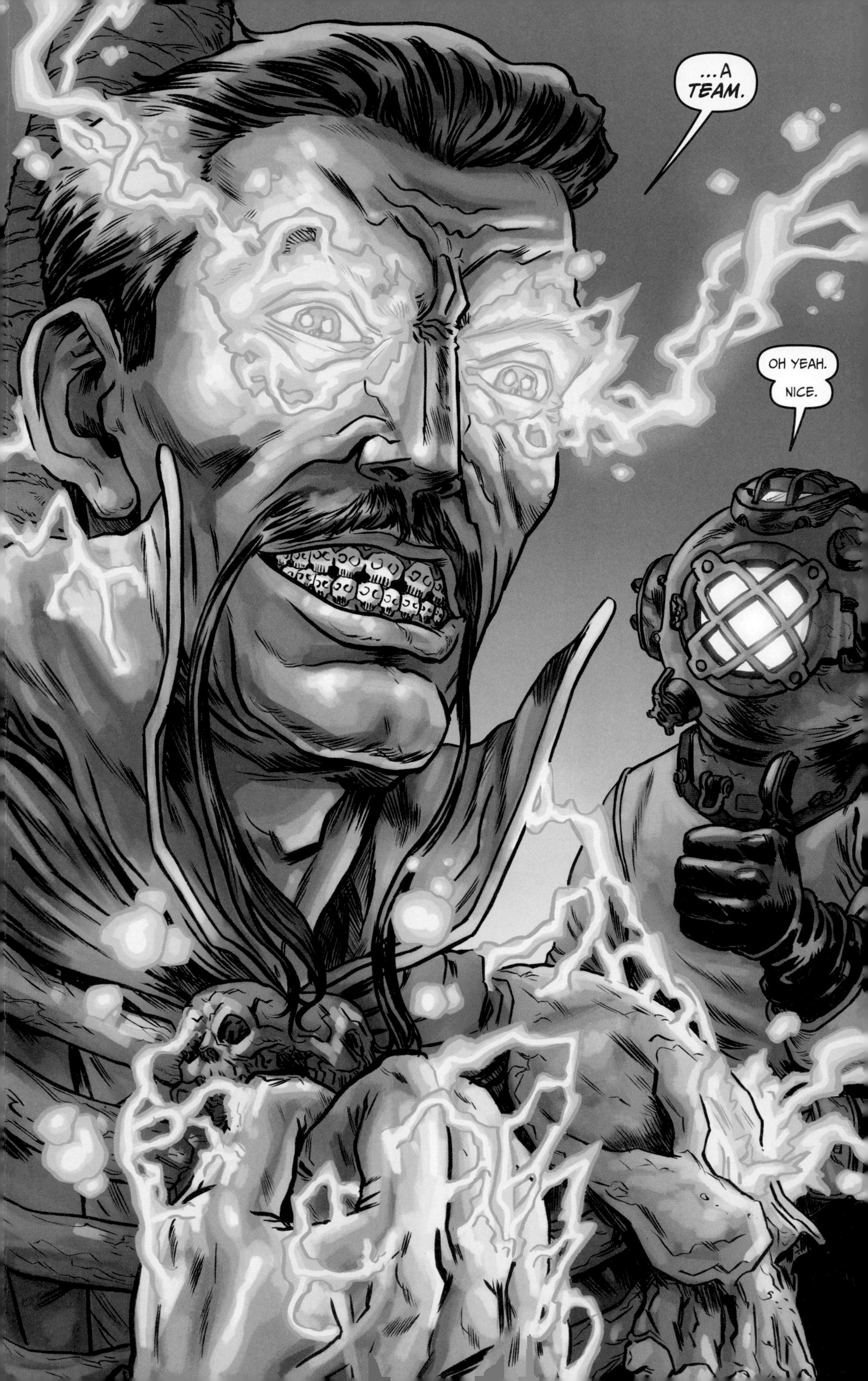
...A TEAM.
OH YEAH. NICE.

EIGHTEEN

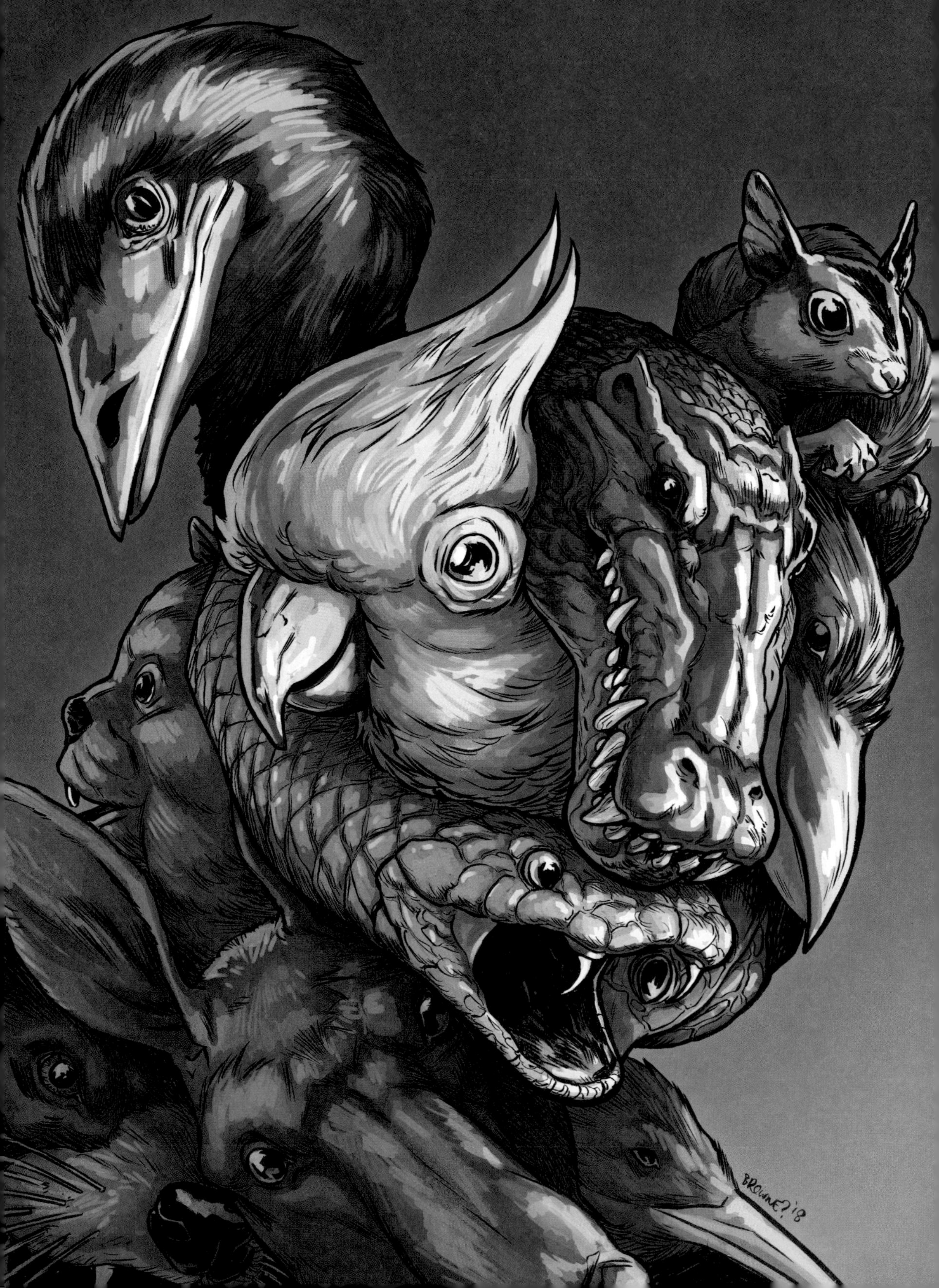

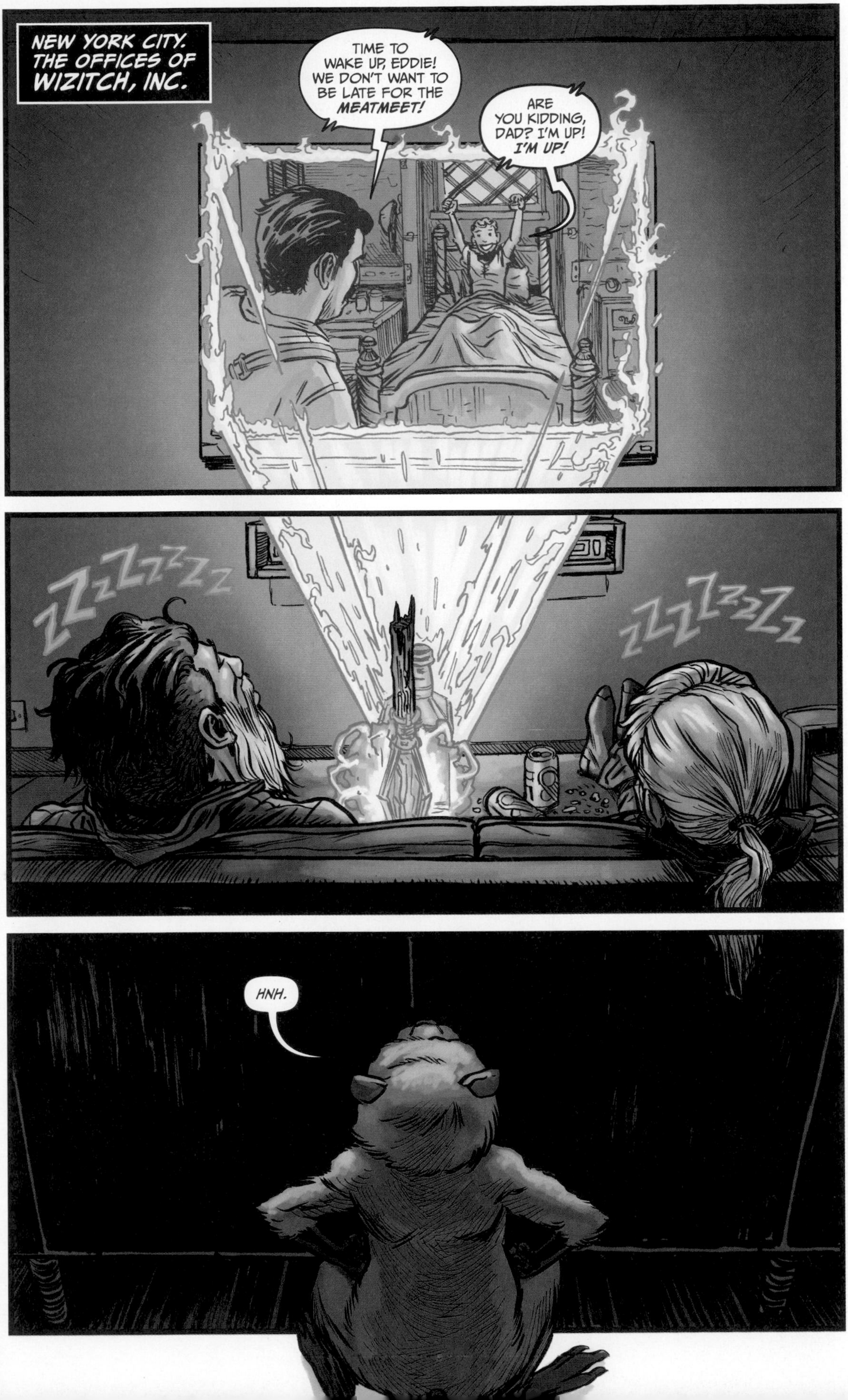
NEW YORK CITY. THE OFFICES OF WIZITCH, INC.
TIME TO WAKE UP, EDDIE! WE DON'T WANT TO BE LATE FOR THE MEATMEET!
ARE YOU KIDDING, DAD? I'M UP! I'M UP!
ZZZZZZZZ
ZZZZZZZZ
HNH.

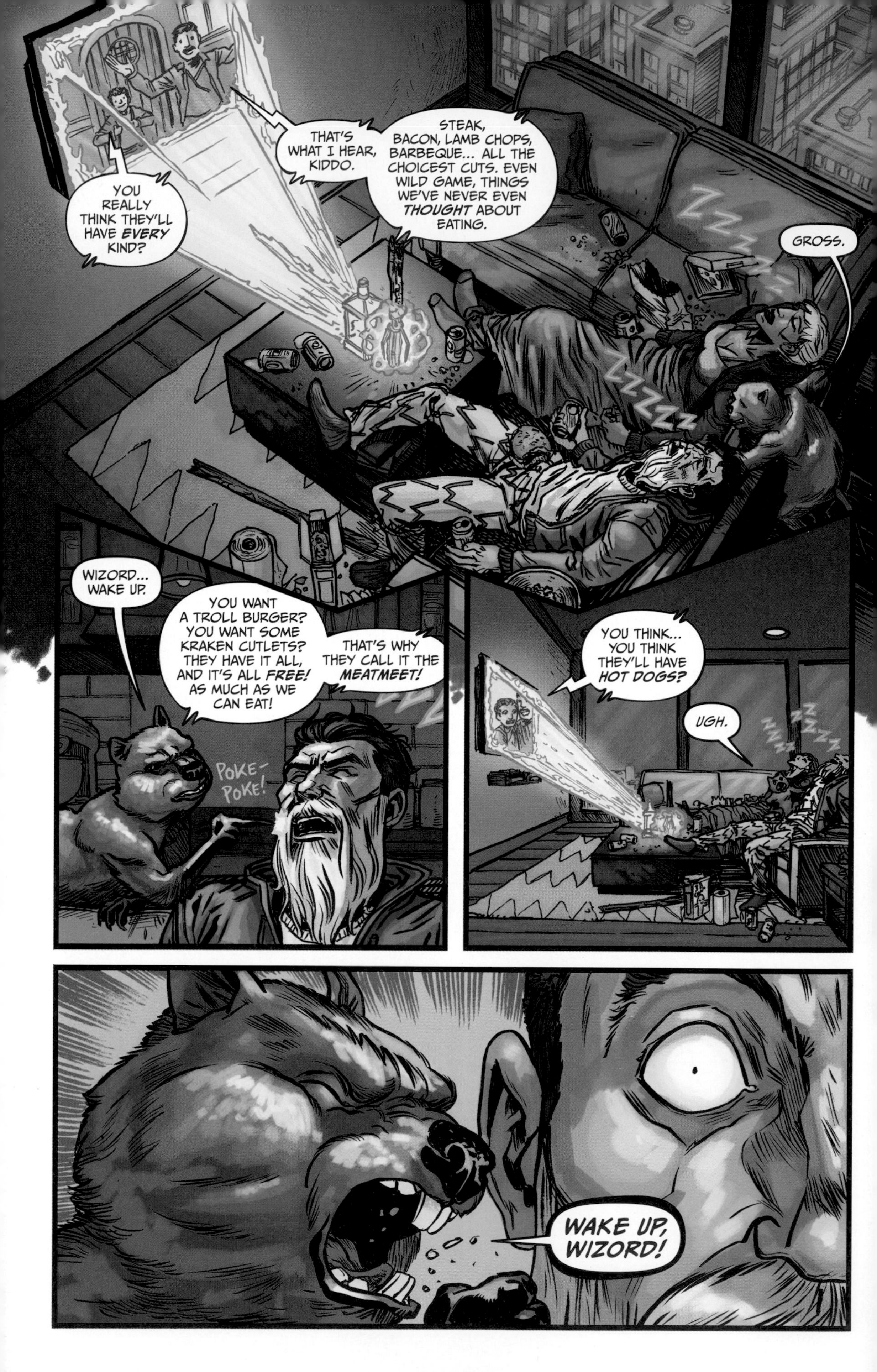
YOU REALLY THINK THEY'LL HAVE *EVERY* KIND?
THAT'S WHAT I HEAR, KIDDO.
STEAK, BACON, LAMB CHOPS, BARBEQUE... ALL THE CHOICEST CUTS. EVEN WILD GAME, THINGS WE'VE NEVER EVEN *THOUGHT* ABOUT EATING.
GROSS.
WIZORD... WAKE UP.
YOU WANT A TROLL BURGER? YOU WANT SOME KRAKEN CUTLETS? THEY HAVE IT ALL, AND IT'S ALL *FREE!* AS MUCH AS WE CAN EAT!
THAT'S WHY THEY CALL IT THE *MEATMEET!*
POKE-POKE!
YOU THINK... YOU THINK THEY'LL HAVE *HOT DOGS?*
UGH.
WAKE UP, WIZORD!

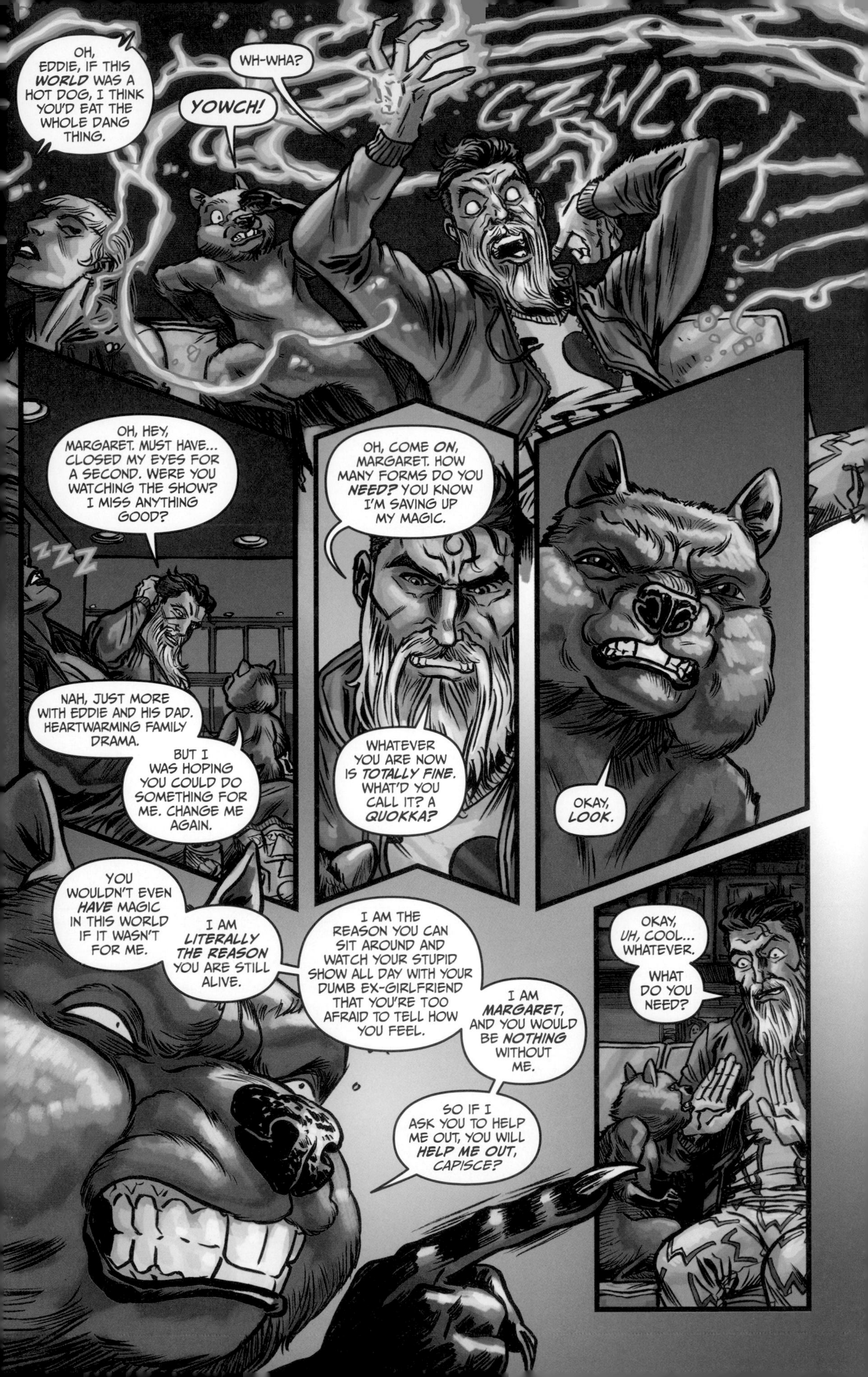

OH, EDDIE, IF THIS WORLD WAS A HOT DOG, I THINK YOU'D EAT THE WHOLE DANG THING.
WH-WHA?
YOWCH!
GZWCCK
OH, HEY, MARGARET. MUST HAVE... CLOSED MY EYES FOR A SECOND. WERE YOU WATCHING THE SHOW? I MISS ANYTHING GOOD?
ZZZ
NAH, JUST MORE WITH EDDIE AND HIS DAD. HEARTWARMING FAMILY DRAMA.
BUT I WAS HOPING YOU COULD DO SOMETHING FOR ME. CHANGE ME AGAIN.
OH, COME ON, MARGARET. HOW MANY FORMS DO YOU NEED? YOU KNOW I'M SAVING UP MY MAGIC.
WHATEVER YOU ARE NOW IS TOTALLY FINE. WHAT'D YOU CALL IT? A QUOKKA?
OKAY, LOOK.
YOU WOULDN'T EVEN HAVE MAGIC IN THIS WORLD IF IT WASN'T FOR ME.
I AM LITERALLY THE REASON YOU ARE STILL ALIVE.
I AM THE REASON YOU CAN SIT AROUND AND WATCH YOUR STUPID SHOW ALL DAY WITH YOUR DUMB EX-GIRLFRIEND THAT YOU'RE TOO AFRAID TO TELL HOW YOU FEEL.
I AM MARGARET, AND YOU WOULD BE NOTHING WITHOUT ME.
SO IF I ASK YOU TO HELP ME OUT, YOU WILL HELP ME OUT, CAPISCE?
OKAY, UH, COOL... WHATEVER.
WHAT DO YOU NEED?

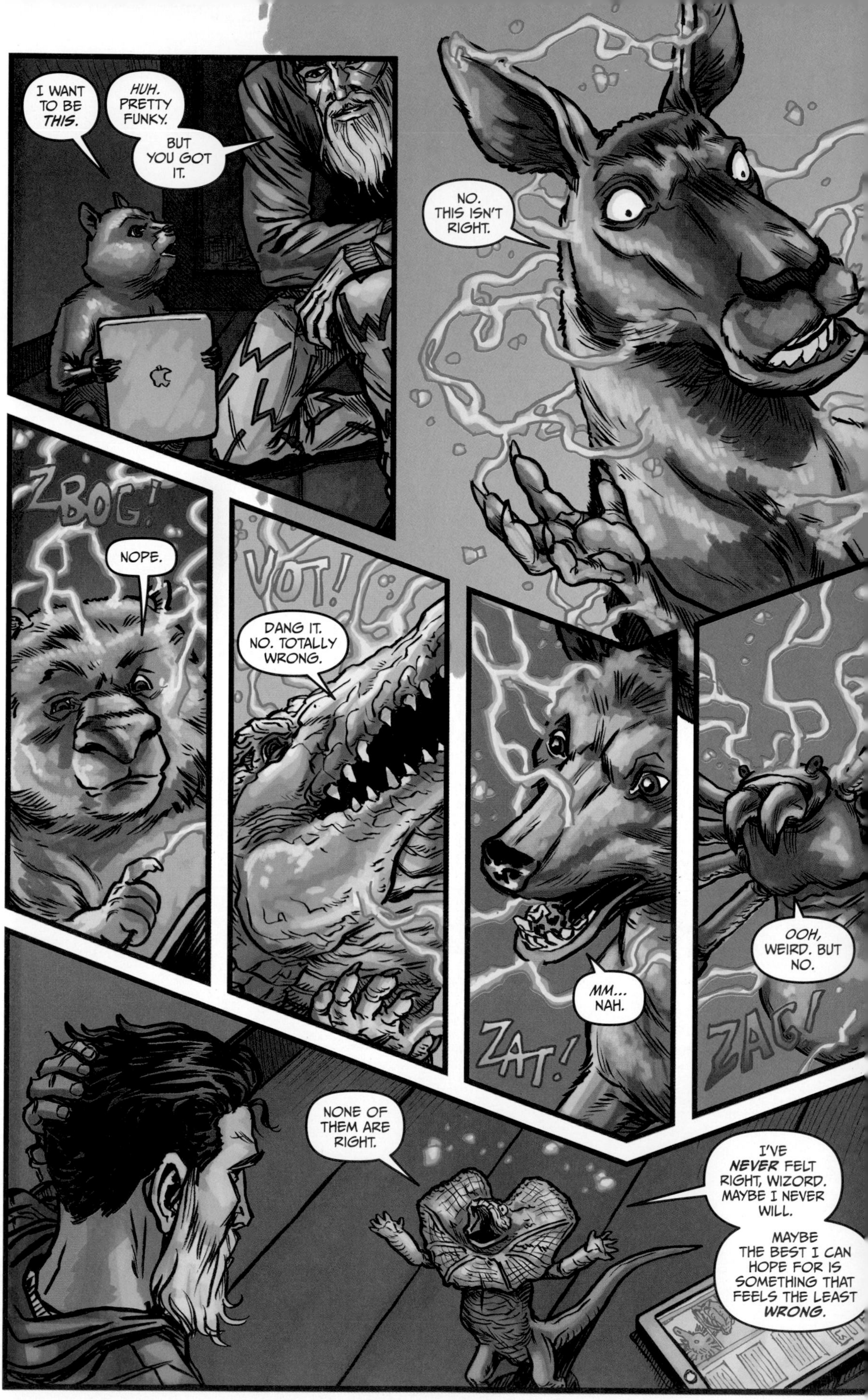
I WANT TO BE *THIS*.
HUH. PRETTY FUNKY.
BUT YOU GOT IT.
NO. THIS ISN'T RIGHT.
ZBOG!
NOPE.
VOT!
DANG IT. NO. TOTALLY WRONG.
MM... NAH.
ZAT!
OOH, WEIRD. BUT NO.
ZAG!
NONE OF THEM ARE RIGHT.
I'VE ***NEVER*** FELT RIGHT, WIZORD. MAYBE I NEVER WILL.
MAYBE THE BEST I CAN HOPE FOR IS SOMETHING THAT FEELS THE LEAST ***WRONG***.

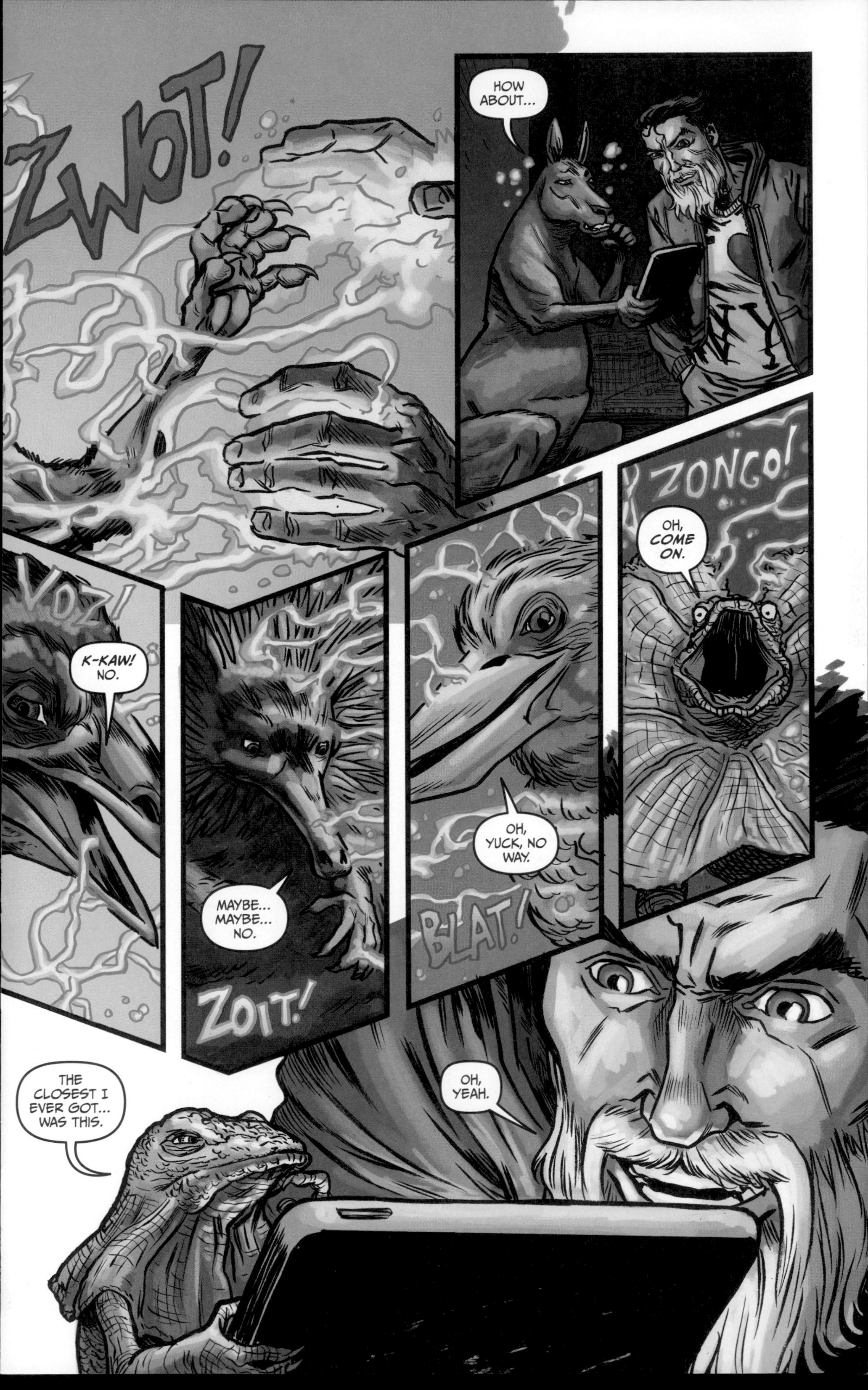
ZWOT!
HOW ABOUT...
VOZ!
K-KAW! NO.
MAYBE... MAYBE... NO.
ZOIT!
OH, YUCK, NO WAY.
BLAT!
ZONGO!
OH, COME ON.
THE CLOSEST I EVER GOT... WAS THIS.
OH, YEAH.

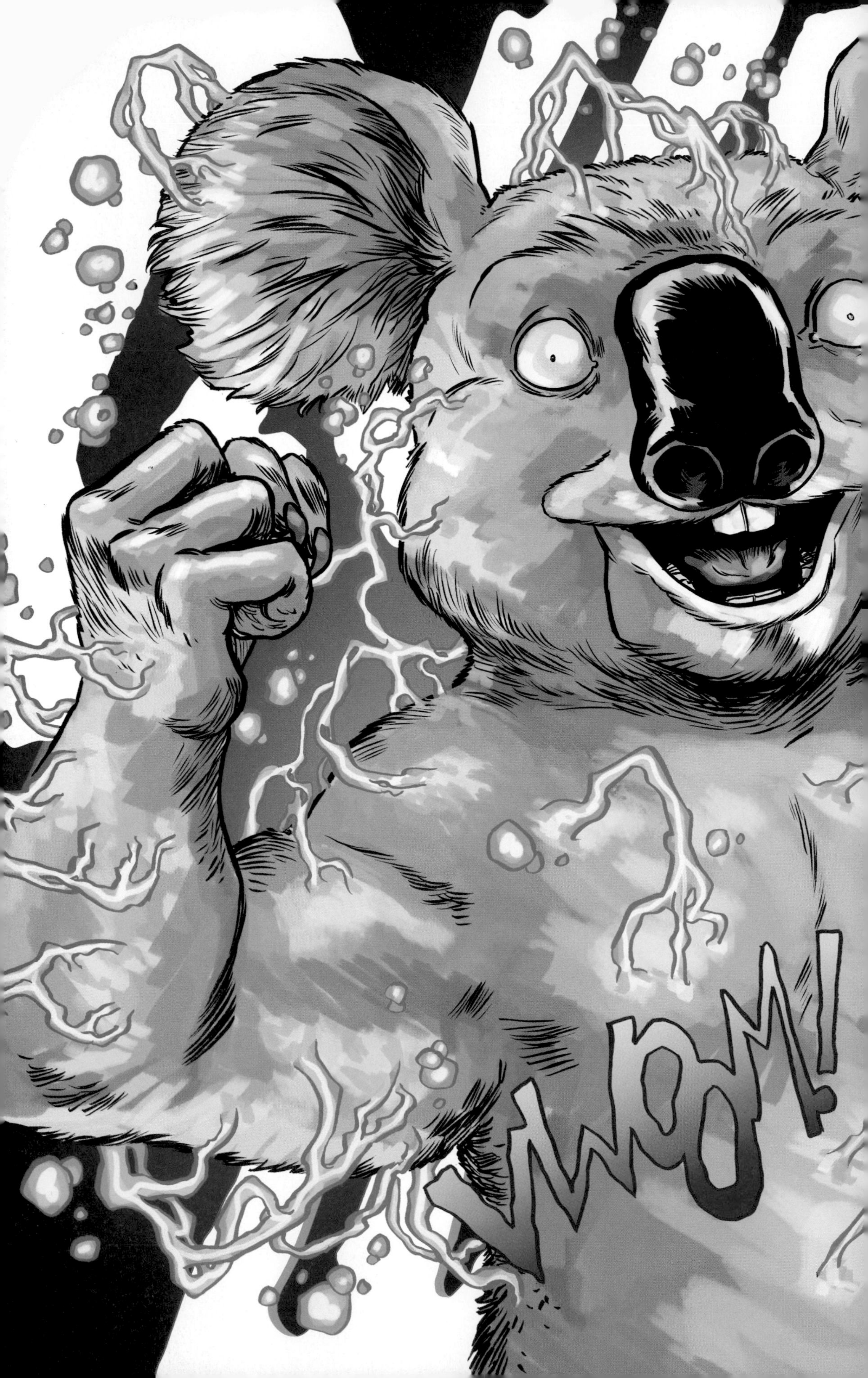
WOOM!

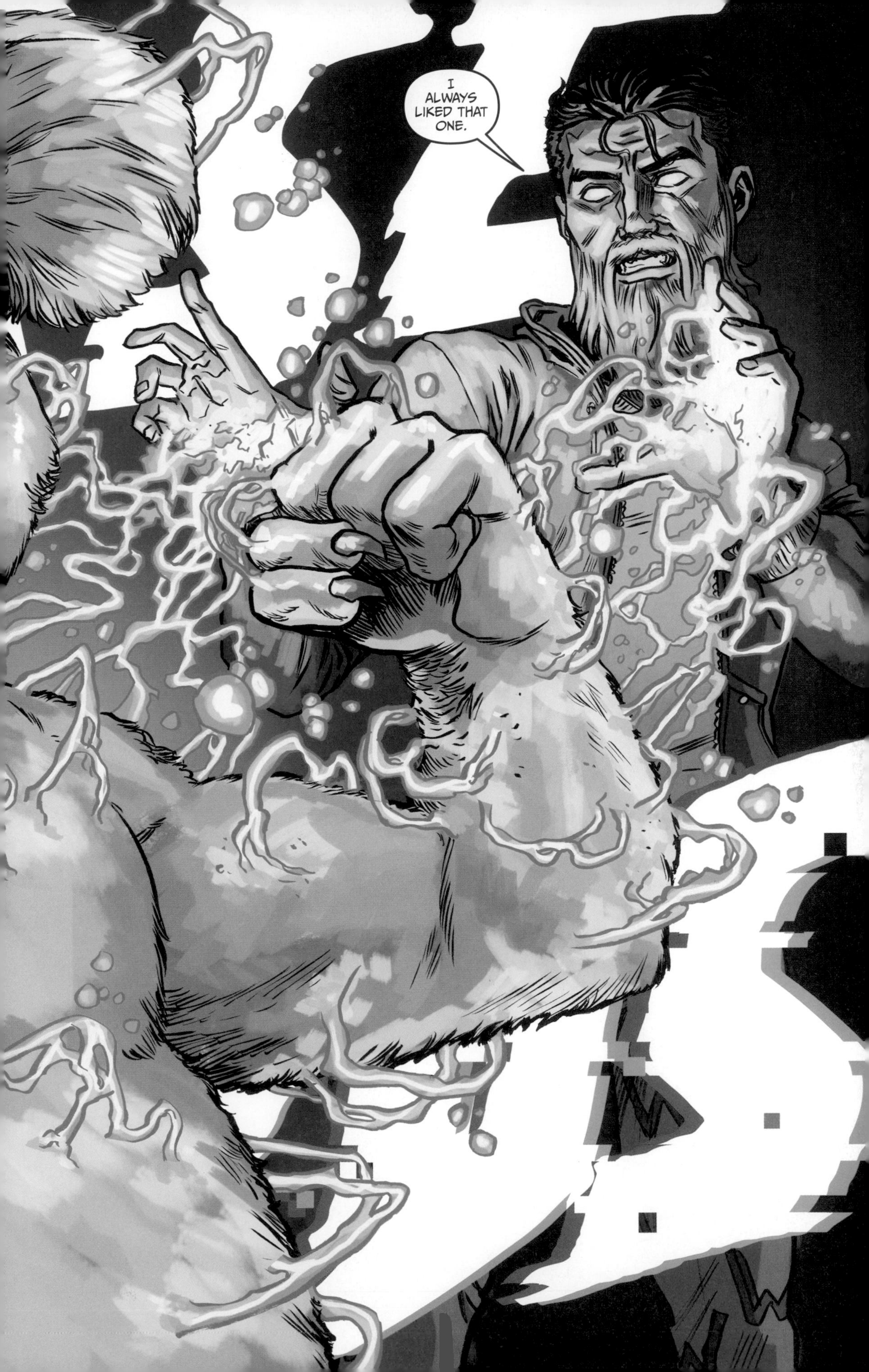
I ALWAYS LIKED THAT ONE.

PARIS, FRANCE.

AH, OUI, MONSIEUR OPAQUE... DO YOU SEE MY CITY, MY 'OME...?

ZERE IS NOTHING LIKE IT IN ALL ZE WORLD.

OH, YEAH. AMAZING, JACQUES ZACQUES. THIS IS A PRETTY... *UH...* STUPENDOUS ARCH YOU'VE GOT HERE.

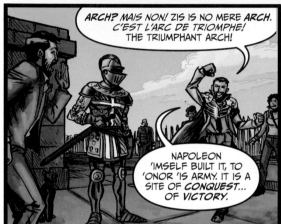

ARCH? MAIS NON! ZIS IS NO MERE *ARCH.* C'EST L'ARC DE TRIOMPHE! THE TRIUMPHANT ARCH!

NAPOLEON 'IMSELF BUILT IT, TO 'ONOR 'IS ARMY. IT IS A SITE OF *CONQUEST...* OF *VICTORY.*

A FITTING PLACE FOR MY OWN TRIUMPH OVER WIZORD...

...TO BEGIN!!

RIGHT ON, RIGHT ON. BUT YOU SAID YOU WERE GOING TO BUILD A *TEAM* TO HELP YOU KILL WIZORD, RIGHT?

I'M ALL FOR THAT. THE MORE THE BETTER. WIZORD'S SCARY ENOUGH BY HIMSELF, AND IF HE'S GOT RUBY STITCH FIGHTING WITH HIM TOO... YEAH. THE MORE THE BETTER.

YES, OF COURSE. WE 'AVE ME... WE 'AVE YOU...

ONLY IN A MANNER OF SPEAKING. I'M HERE TO GUIDE YOU, TO TEACH YOU MAGIC--BUT AS FAR AS A FULL-FRONTAL ASSAULT... THAT'S NOT MY BAG.

I PREFER TO FIGHT IN DIFFERENT WAYS.

HEH. "FULL-FRONTAL." THAT'S ACTUALLY PRETTY FUNNY, IF YOU THINK ABOUT IT.

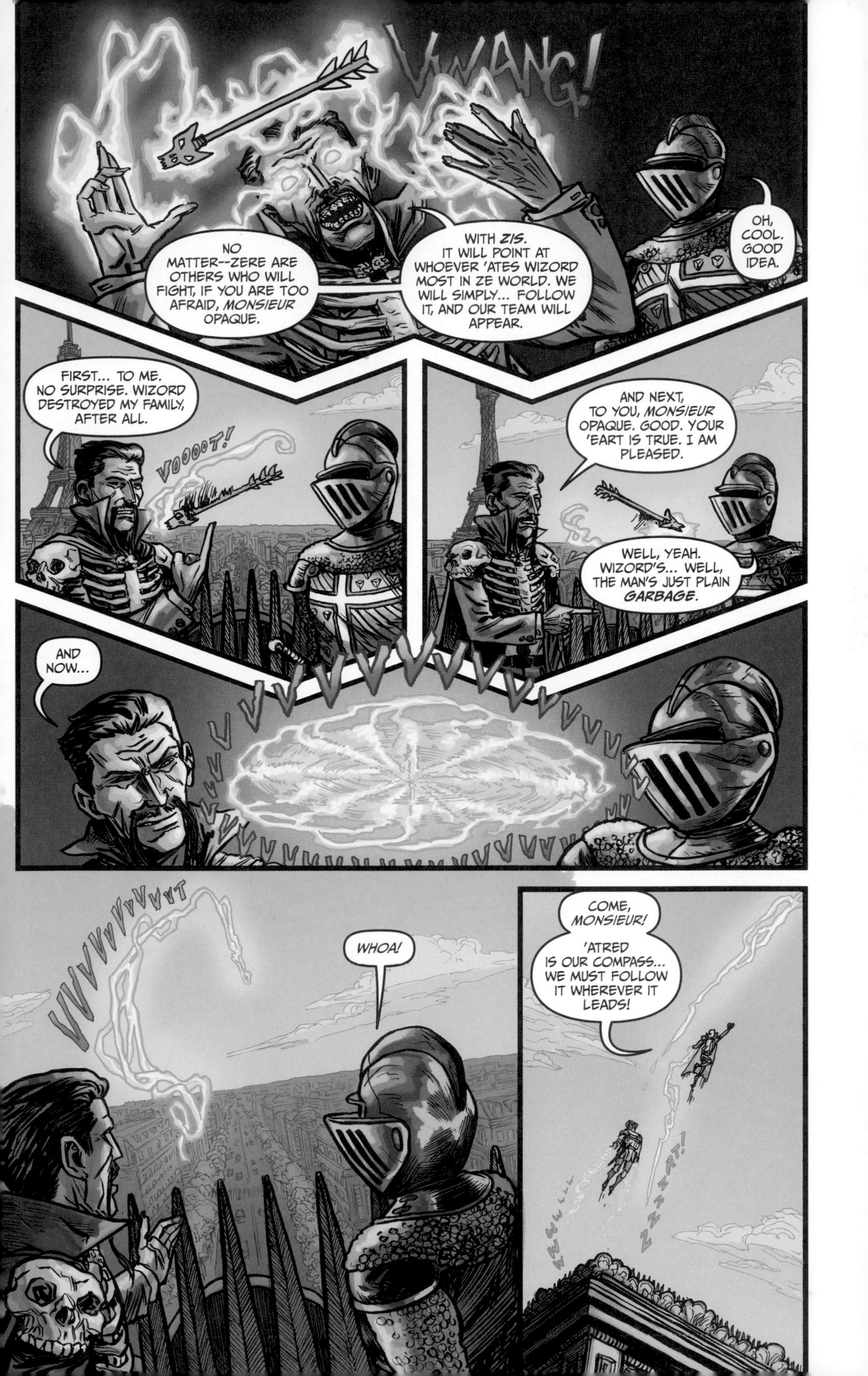
VWANG!
NO MATTER--ZERE ARE OTHERS WHO WILL FIGHT, IF YOU ARE TOO AFRAID, MONSIEUR OPAQUE.
WITH ZIS. IT WILL POINT AT WHOEVER 'ATES WIZORD MOST IN ZE WORLD. WE WILL SIMPLY... FOLLOW IT, AND OUR TEAM WILL APPEAR.
OH, COOL. GOOD IDEA.
FIRST... TO ME. NO SURPRISE. WIZORD DESTROYED MY FAMILY, AFTER ALL.
VOOOOT!
AND NEXT, TO YOU, MONSIEUR OPAQUE. GOOD. YOUR 'EART IS TRUE. I AM PLEASED.
WELL, YEAH. WIZORD'S... WELL, THE MAN'S JUST PLAIN GARBAGE.
AND NOW...
WHOA!
COME, MONSIEUR!
'ATRED IS OUR COMPASS... WE MUST FOLLOW IT WHEREVER IT LEADS!
ZZZAT!

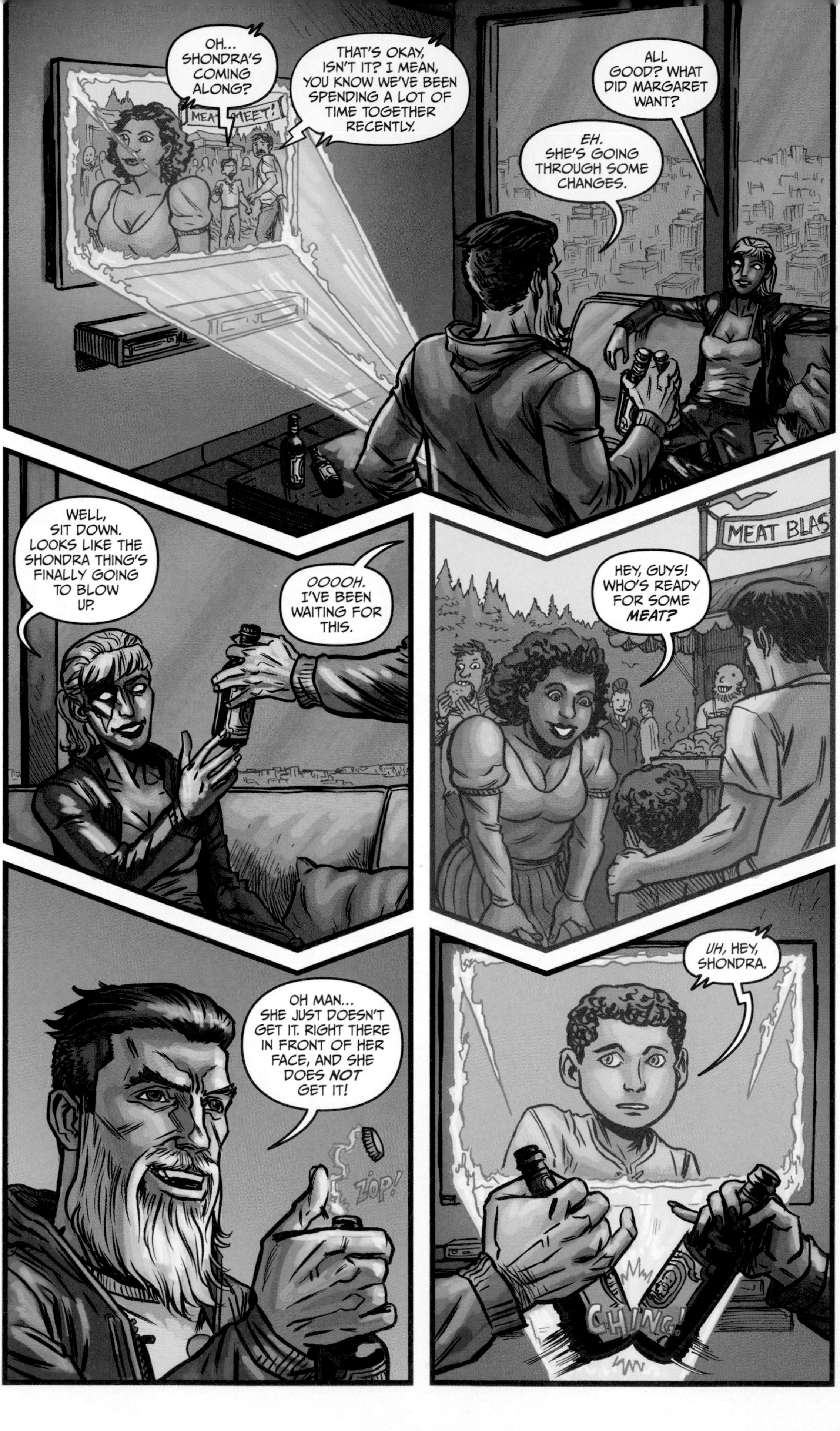
MEAT
MEET!
OH... SHONDRA'S COMING ALONG?
THAT'S OKAY, ISN'T IT? I MEAN, YOU KNOW WE'VE BEEN SPENDING A LOT OF TIME TOGETHER RECENTLY.
ALL GOOD? WHAT DID MARGARET WANT?
EH. SHE'S GOING THROUGH SOME CHANGES.
WELL, SIT DOWN. LOOKS LIKE THE SHONDRA THING'S FINALLY GOING TO BLOW UP.
OOOOH. I'VE BEEN WAITING FOR THIS.
MEAT BLAS
HEY, GUYS! WHO'S READY FOR SOME *MEAT?*
OH MAN... SHE JUST DOESN'T GET IT. RIGHT THERE IN FRONT OF HER FACE, AND SHE DOES *NOT* GET IT!
ZOP!
UH, HEY, SHONDRA.
CHING!

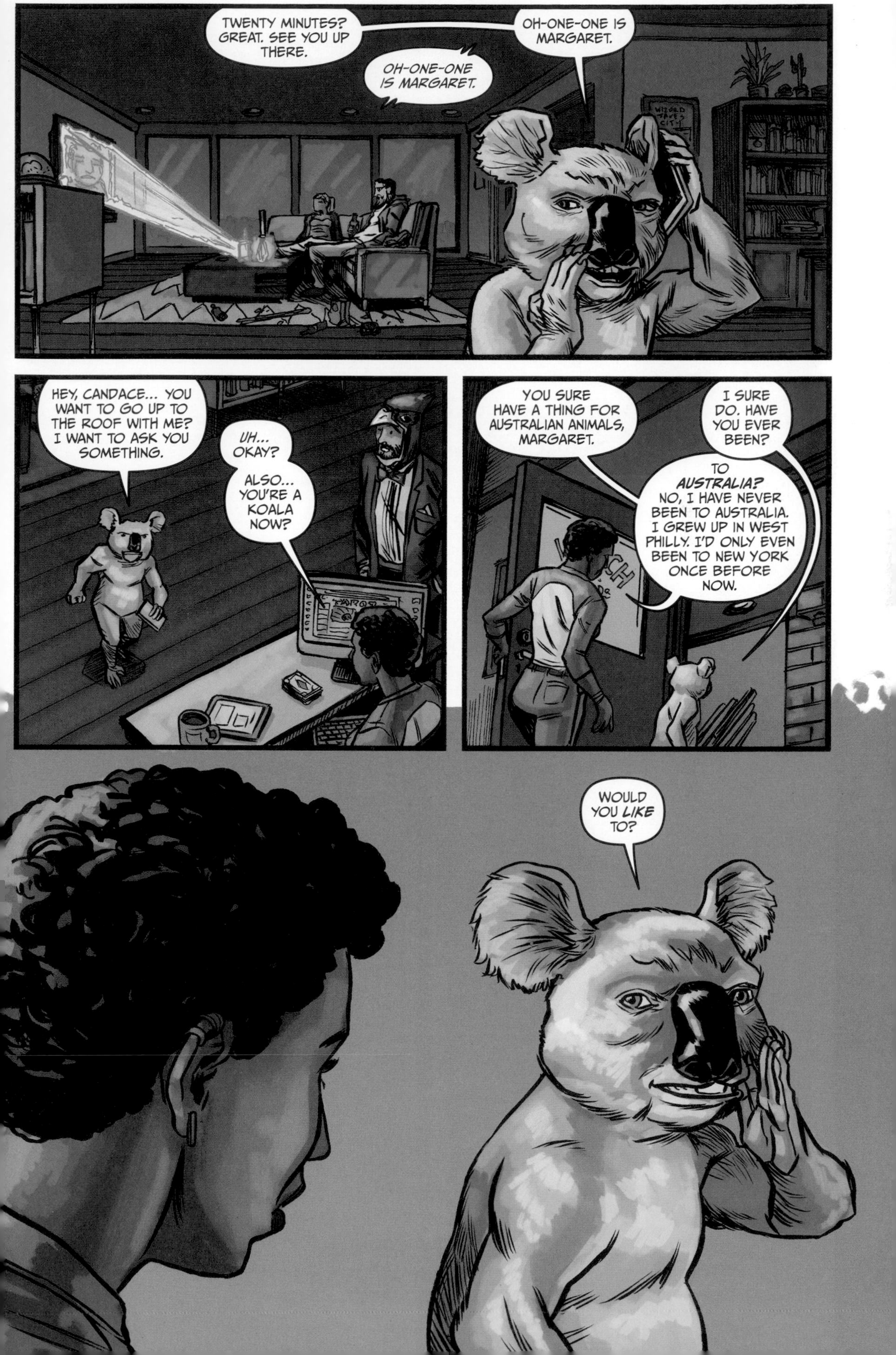
TWENTY MINUTES? GREAT. SEE YOU UP THERE.
OH-ONE-ONE IS MARGARET.
OH-ONE-ONE IS MARGARET.
WIZARD SAVES CITY
HEY, CANDACE... YOU WANT TO GO UP TO THE ROOF WITH ME? I WANT TO ASK YOU SOMETHING.
UH... OKAY?
ALSO... YOU'RE A KOALA NOW?
YOU SURE HAVE A THING FOR AUSTRALIAN ANIMALS, MARGARET.
I SURE DO. HAVE YOU EVER BEEN?
TO *AUSTRALIA?* NO, I HAVE NEVER BEEN TO AUSTRALIA. I GREW UP IN WEST PHILLY. I'D ONLY EVEN BEEN TO NEW YORK ONCE BEFORE NOW.
WOULD YOU *LIKE* TO?

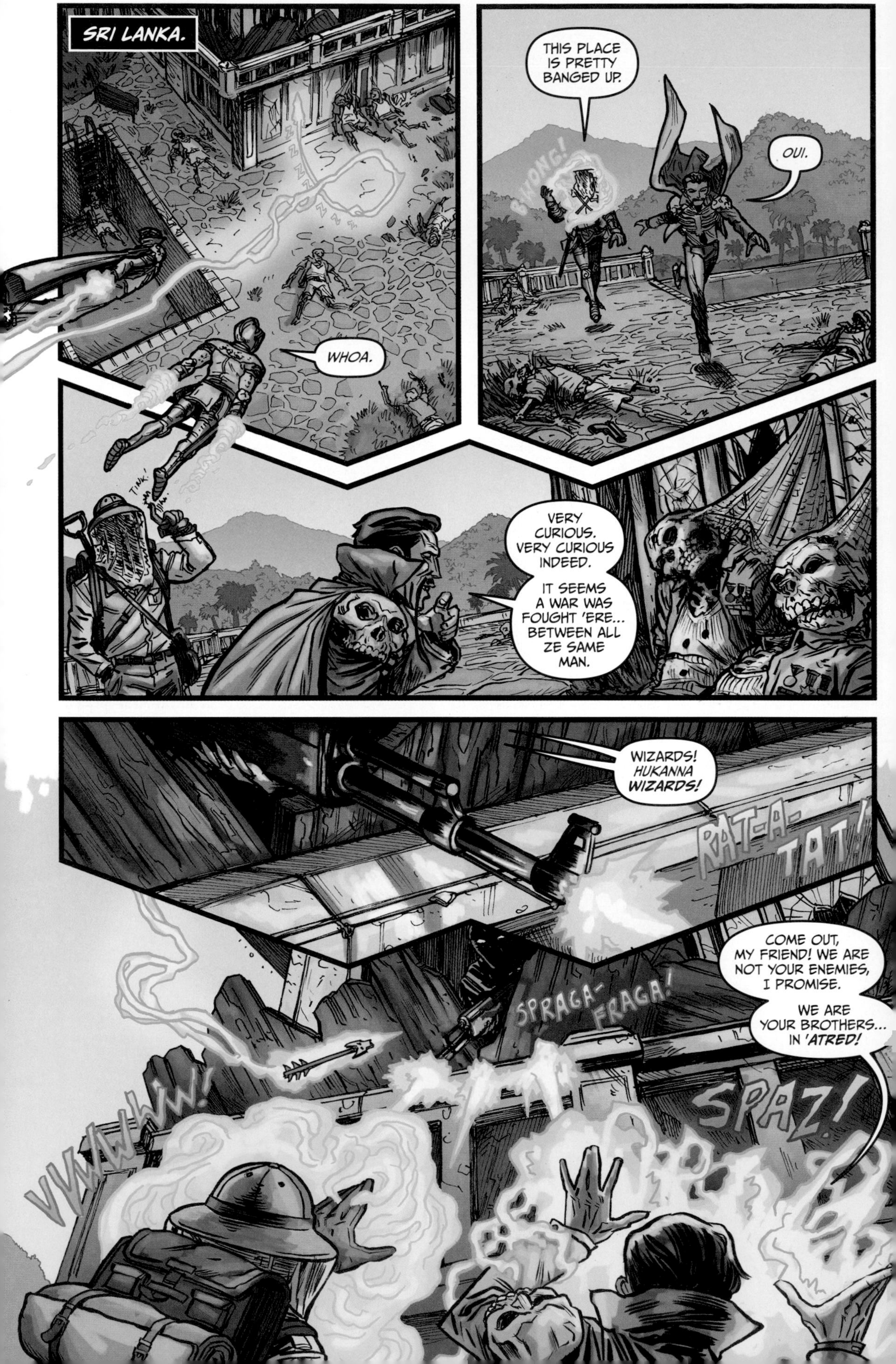
SRI LANKA.
WHOA.
BWONG!
THIS PLACE IS PRETTY BANGED UP.
OUI.
TINK!
VERY CURIOUS. VERY CURIOUS INDEED.
IT SEEMS A WAR WAS FOUGHT 'ERE... BETWEEN ALL ZE SAME MAN.
WIZARDS! HUKANNA WIZARDS!
RAT-A-TAT!
COME OUT, MY FRIEND! WE ARE NOT YOUR ENEMIES, I PROMISE.
WE ARE YOUR BROTHERS... IN 'ATRED!
SPRAGA-FRAGA!
VVVWWWW!
SPAZ!

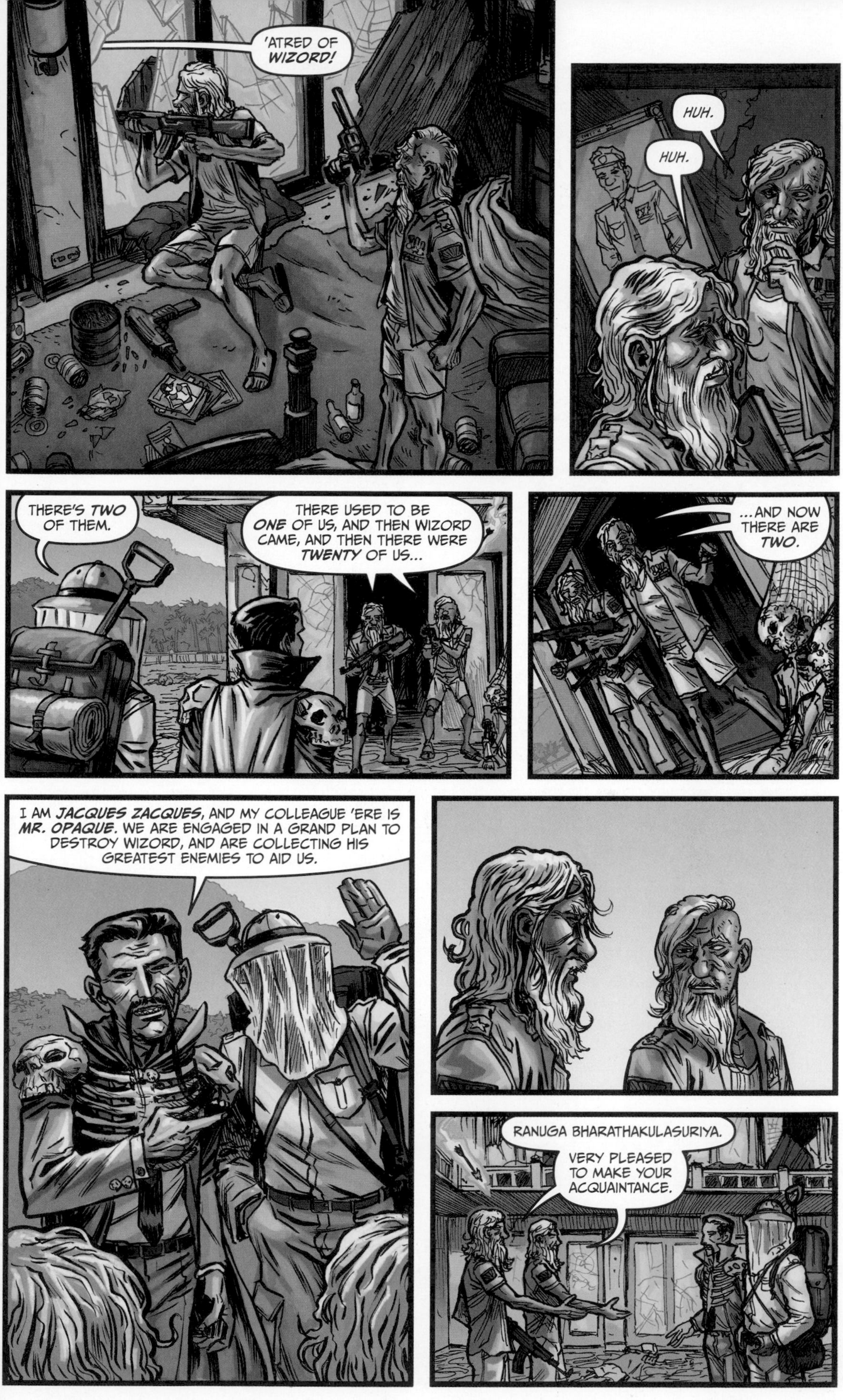
'ATRED OF WIZORD!
HUH.
HUH.
THERE'S TWO OF THEM.
THERE USED TO BE ONE OF US, AND THEN WIZORD CAME, AND THEN THERE WERE TWENTY OF US...
...AND NOW THERE ARE TWO.
I AM JACQUES ZACQUES, AND MY COLLEAGUE 'ERE IS MR. OPAQUE. WE ARE ENGAGED IN A GRAND PLAN TO DESTROY WIZORD, AND ARE COLLECTING HIS GREATEST ENEMIES TO AID US.
RANUGA BHARATHAKULASURIYA.
VERY PLEASED TO MAKE YOUR ACQUAINTANCE.

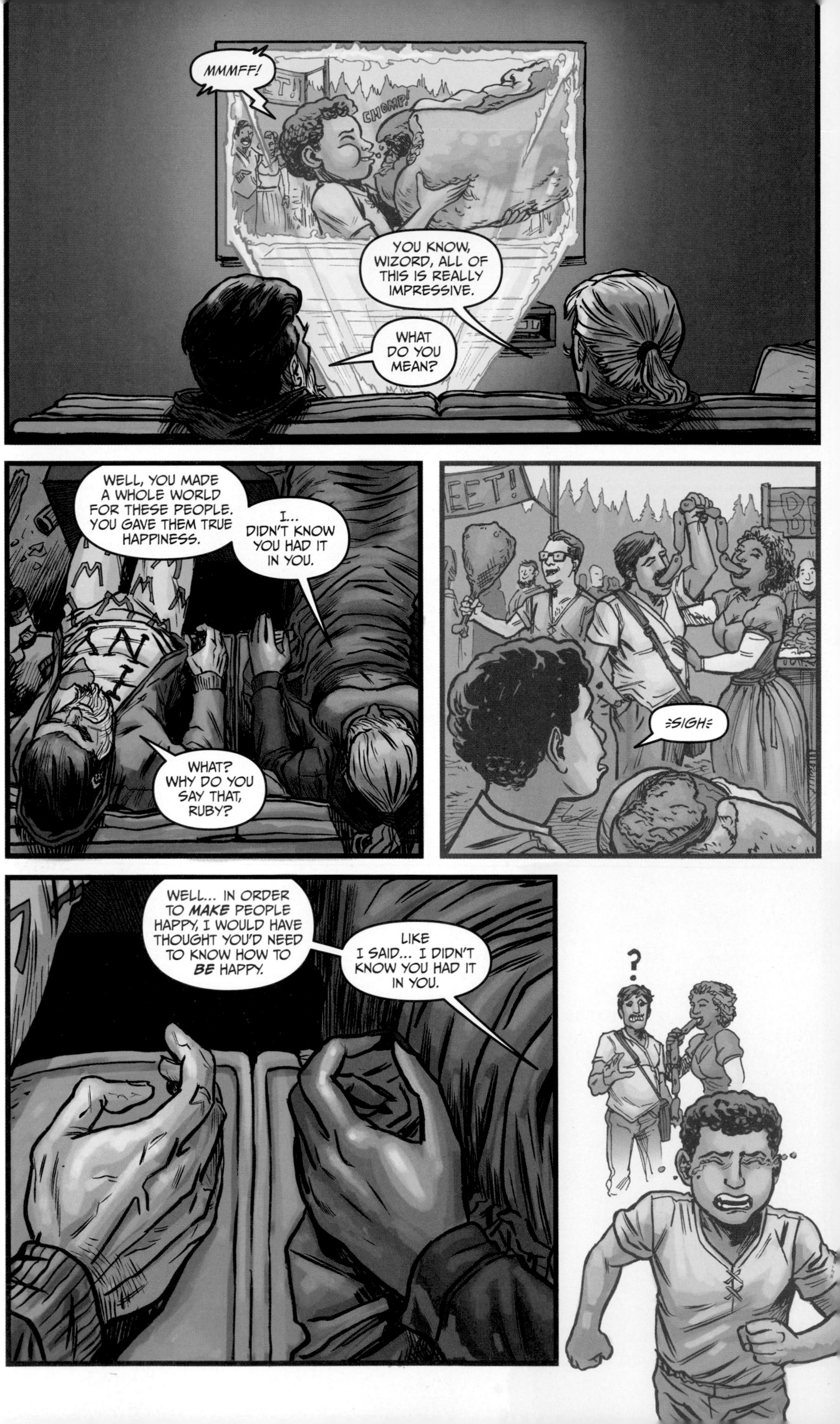
MMMFF!
CHOMP!
YOU KNOW, WIZORD, ALL OF THIS IS REALLY IMPRESSIVE.
WHAT DO YOU MEAN?
WELL, YOU MADE A WHOLE WORLD FOR THESE PEOPLE. YOU GAVE THEM TRUE HAPPINESS.
I... DIDN'T KNOW YOU HAD IT IN YOU.
WHAT? WHY DO YOU SAY THAT, RUBY?
EET!
≈SIGH≈
WELL... IN ORDER TO MAKE PEOPLE HAPPY, I WOULD HAVE THOUGHT YOU'D NEED TO KNOW HOW TO BE HAPPY.
LIKE I SAID... I DIDN'T KNOW YOU HAD IT IN YOU.
?

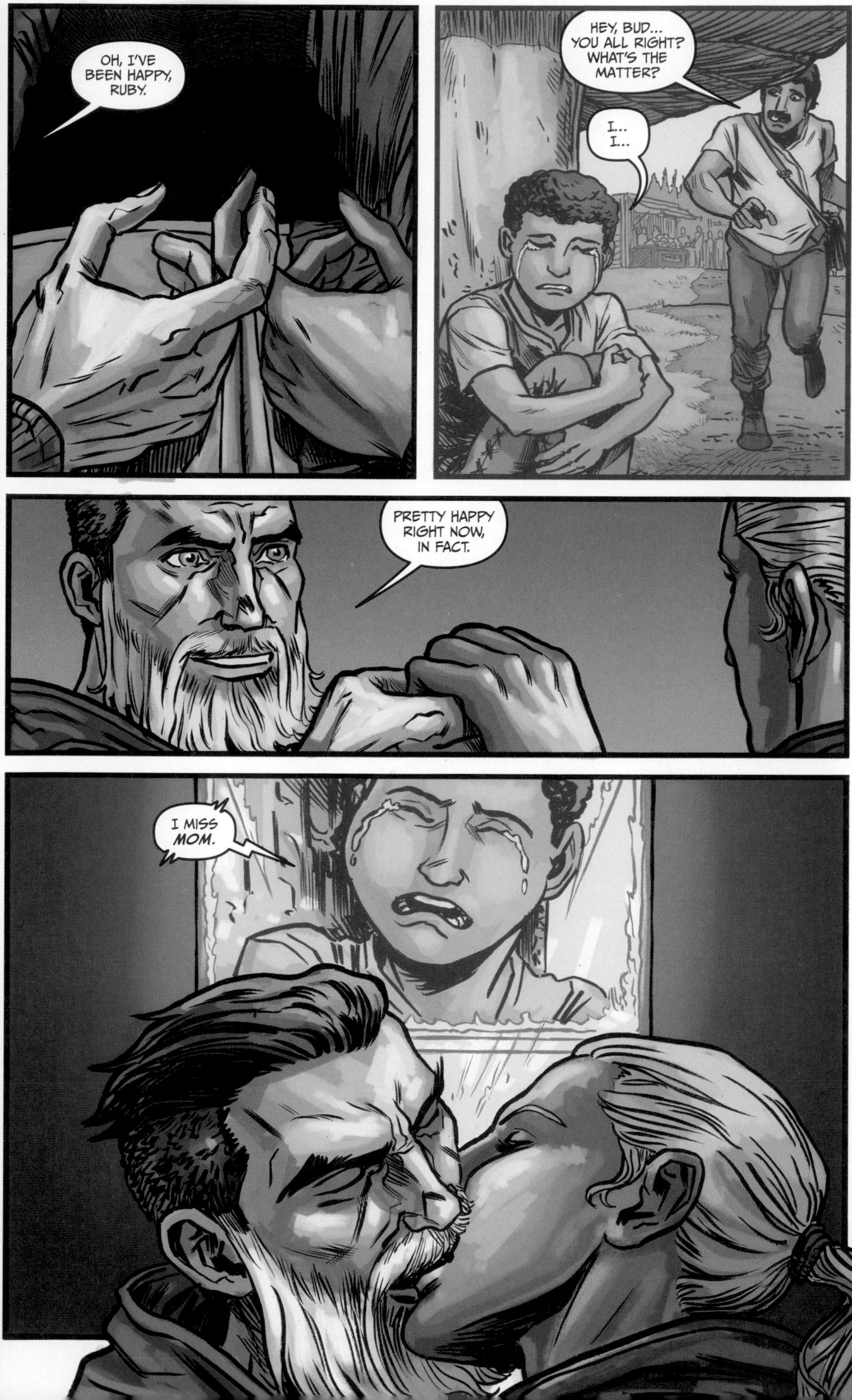
OH, I'VE BEEN HAPPY, RUBY.
HEY, BUD... YOU ALL RIGHT? WHAT'S THE MATTER?
I... I...
PRETTY HAPPY RIGHT NOW, IN FACT.
I MISS MOM.

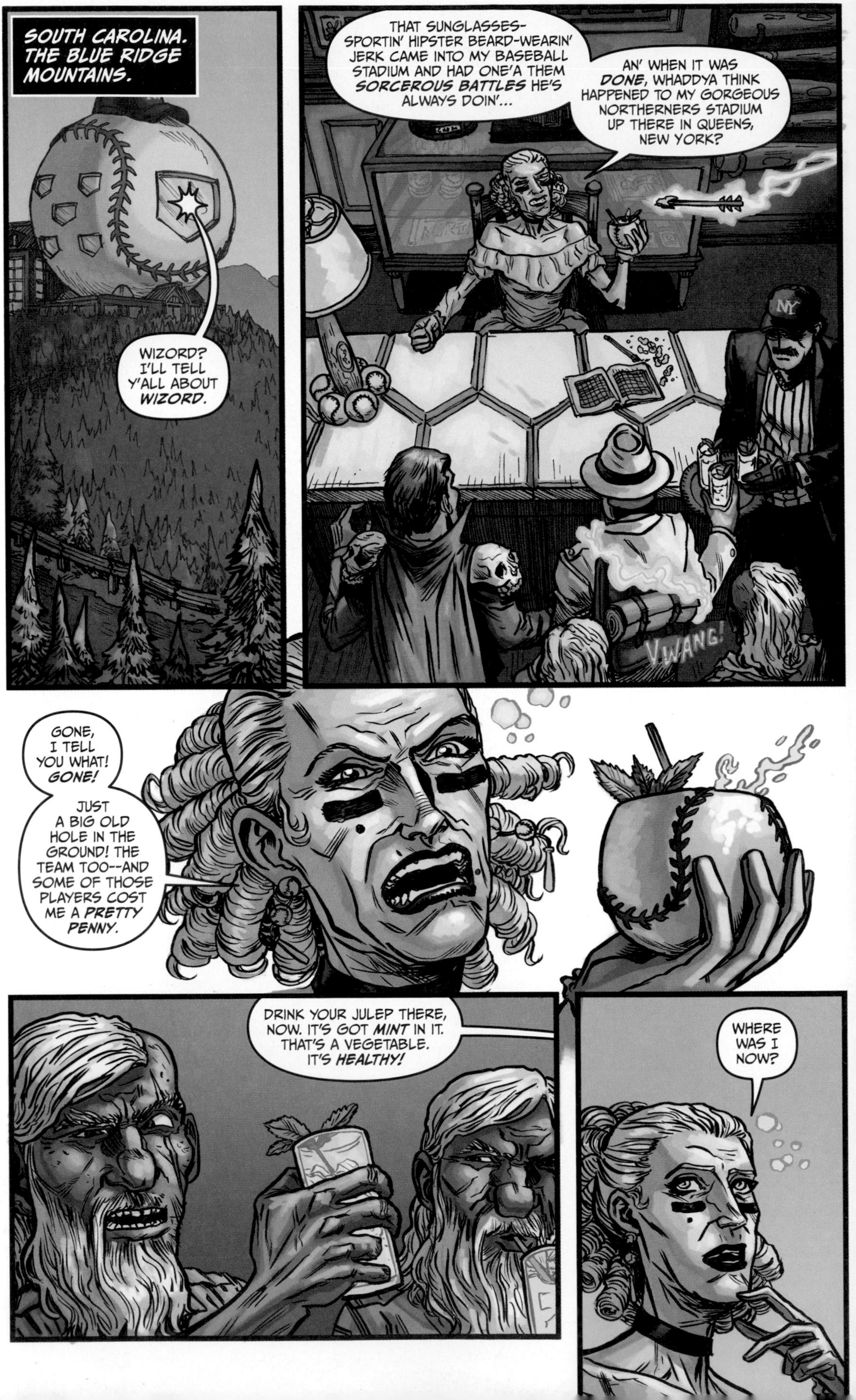
SOUTH CAROLINA. THE BLUE RIDGE MOUNTAINS.
WIZORD? I'LL TELL Y'ALL ABOUT WIZORD.
THAT SUNGLASSES-SPORTIN' HIPSTER BEARD-WEARIN' JERK CAME INTO MY BASEBALL STADIUM AND HAD ONE'A THEM SORCEROUS BATTLES HE'S ALWAYS DOIN'...
AN' WHEN IT WAS DONE, WHADDYA THINK HAPPENED TO MY GORGEOUS NORTHERNERS STADIUM UP THERE IN QUEENS, NEW YORK?
VWANG!
GONE, I TELL YOU WHAT! GONE!
JUST A BIG OLD HOLE IN THE GROUND! THE TEAM TOO--AND SOME OF THOSE PLAYERS COST ME A PRETTY PENNY.
DRINK YOUR JULEP THERE, NOW. IT'S GOT MINT IN IT. THAT'S A VEGETABLE. IT'S HEALTHY!
WHERE WAS I NOW?

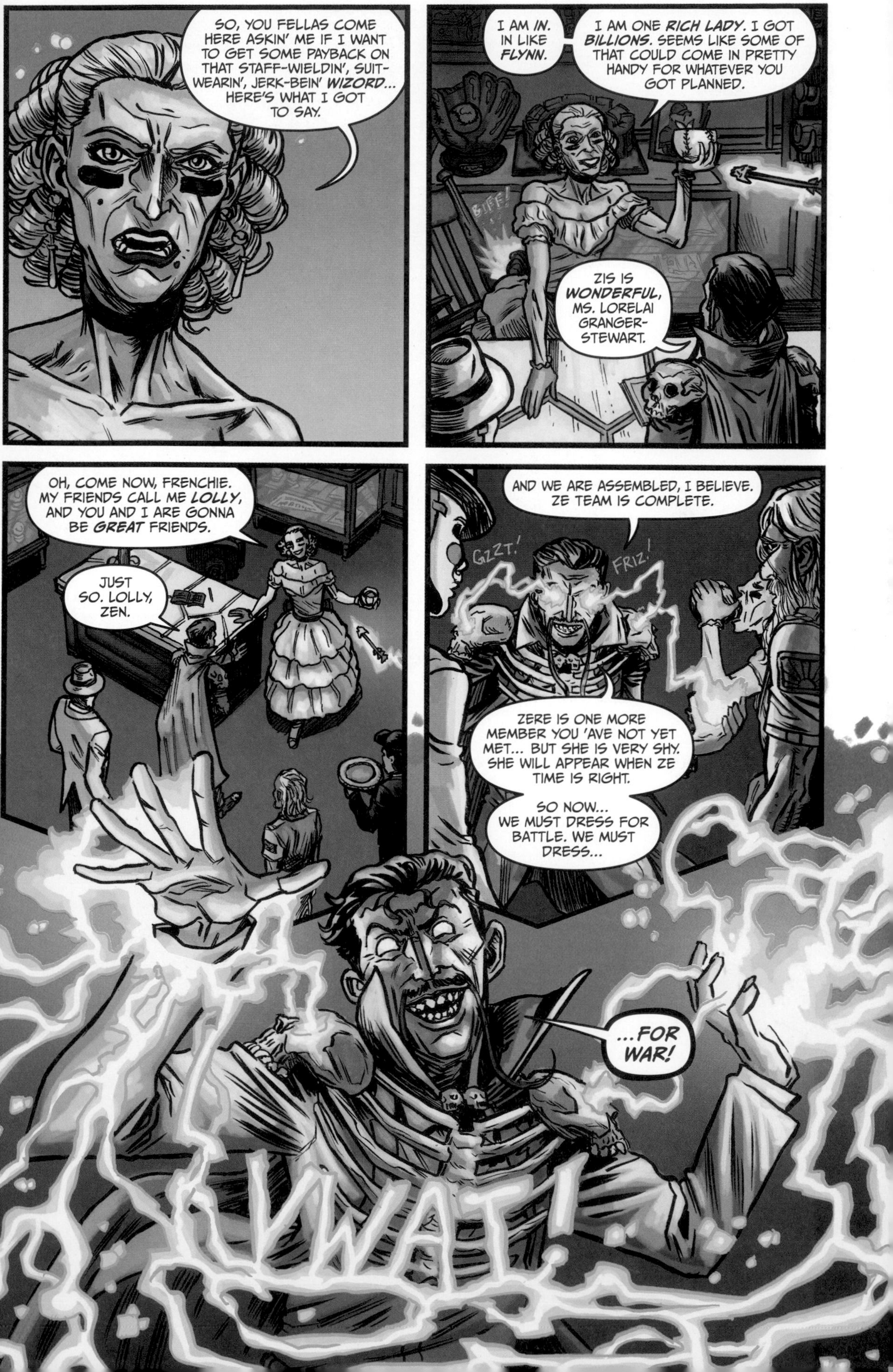
SO, YOU FELLAS COME HERE ASKIN' ME IF I WANT TO GET SOME PAYBACK ON THAT STAFF-WIELDIN', SUIT-WEARIN', JERK-BEIN' WIZORD... HERE'S WHAT I GOT TO SAY.
I AM IN. IN LIKE FLYNN.
I AM ONE RICH LADY. I GOT BILLIONS. SEEMS LIKE SOME OF THAT COULD COME IN PRETTY HANDY FOR WHATEVER YOU GOT PLANNED.
ZIS IS WONDERFUL, MS. LORELAI GRANGER-STEWART.
OH, COME NOW, FRENCHIE. MY FRIENDS CALL ME LOLLY, AND YOU AND I ARE GONNA BE GREAT FRIENDS.
JUST SO. LOLLY, ZEN.
AND WE ARE ASSEMBLED, I BELIEVE. ZE TEAM IS COMPLETE.
GZZT!
FRIZ!
ZERE IS ONE MORE MEMBER YOU 'AVE NOT YET MET... BUT SHE IS VERY SHY. SHE WILL APPEAR WHEN ZE TIME IS RIGHT.
SO NOW... WE MUST DRESS FOR BATTLE. WE MUST DRESS...
...FOR WAR!
VWAT!

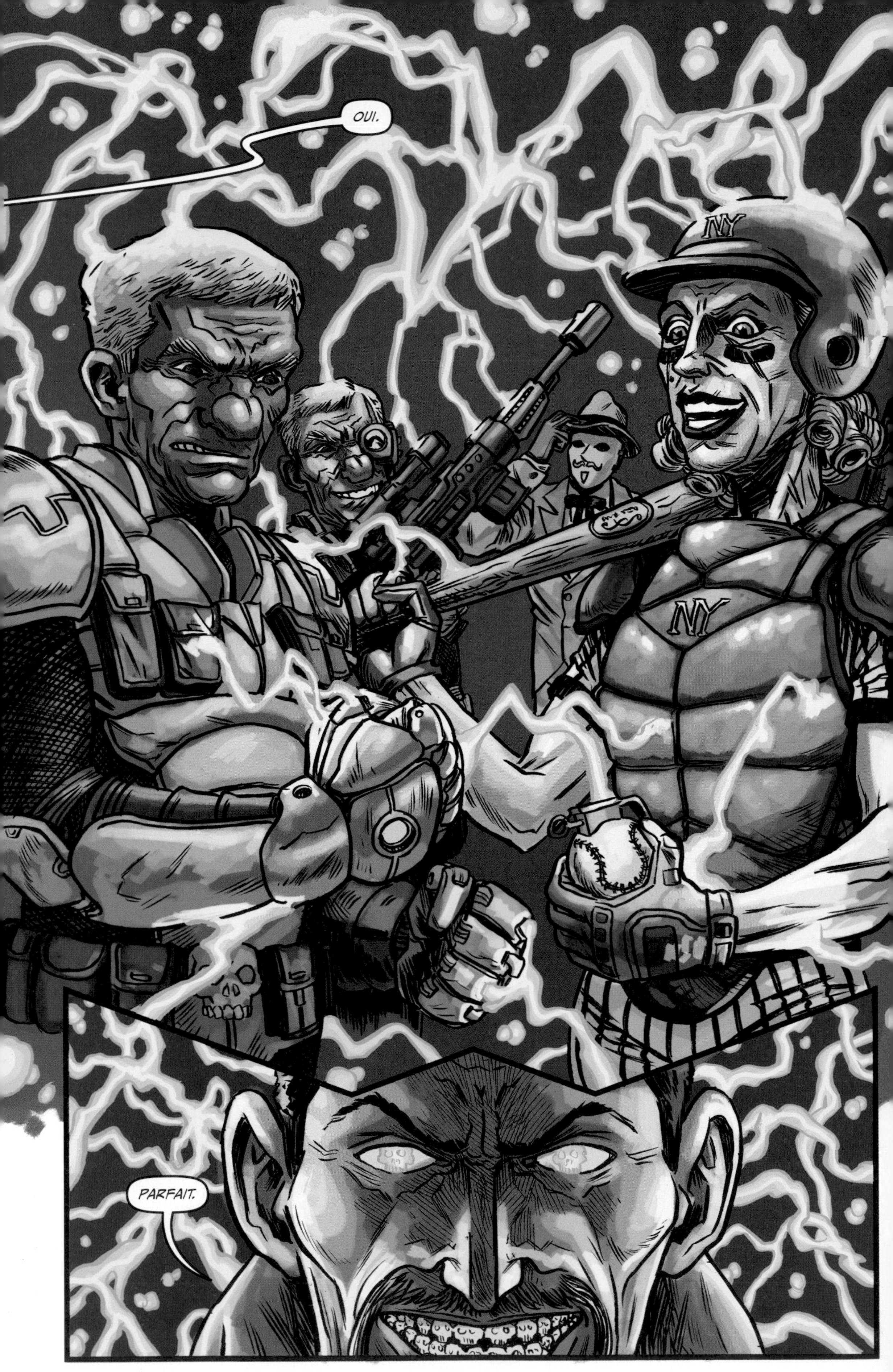
OUI.
PARFAIT.

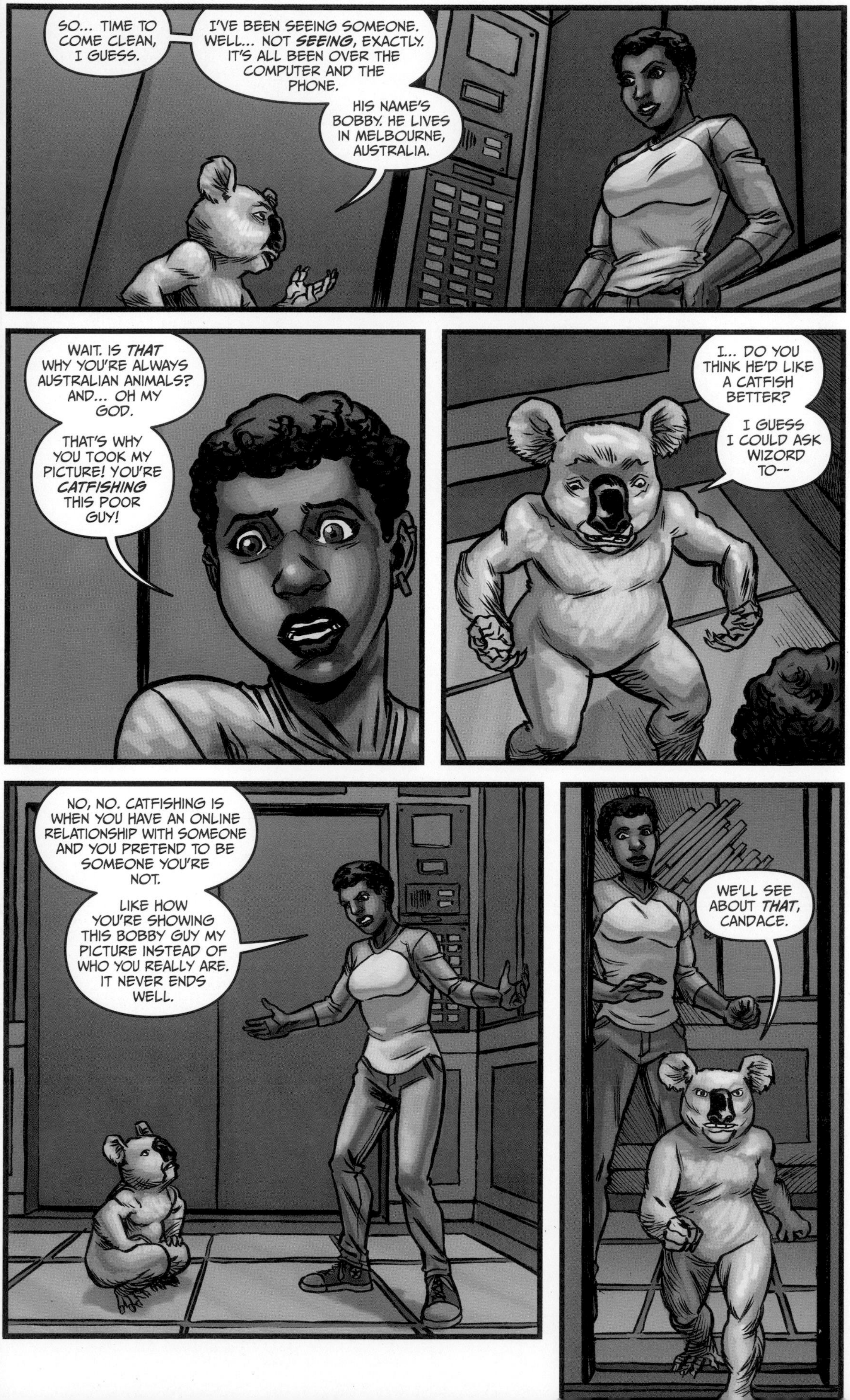

SO... TIME TO COME CLEAN, I GUESS.
I'VE BEEN SEEING SOMEONE. WELL... NOT *SEEING*, EXACTLY. IT'S ALL BEEN OVER THE COMPUTER AND THE PHONE.
HIS NAME'S BOBBY. HE LIVES IN MELBOURNE, AUSTRALIA.
WAIT. IS *THAT* WHY YOU'RE ALWAYS AUSTRALIAN ANIMALS? AND... OH MY GOD.
THAT'S WHY YOU TOOK MY PICTURE! YOU'RE *CATFISHING* THIS POOR GUY!
I... DO YOU THINK HE'D LIKE A CATFISH BETTER?
I GUESS I COULD ASK WIZORD TO--
NO, NO. CATFISHING IS WHEN YOU HAVE AN ONLINE RELATIONSHIP WITH SOMEONE AND YOU PRETEND TO BE SOMEONE YOU'RE NOT.
LIKE HOW YOU'RE SHOWING THIS BOBBY GUY MY PICTURE INSTEAD OF WHO YOU REALLY ARE. IT NEVER ENDS WELL.
WE'LL SEE ABOUT *THAT*, CANDACE.

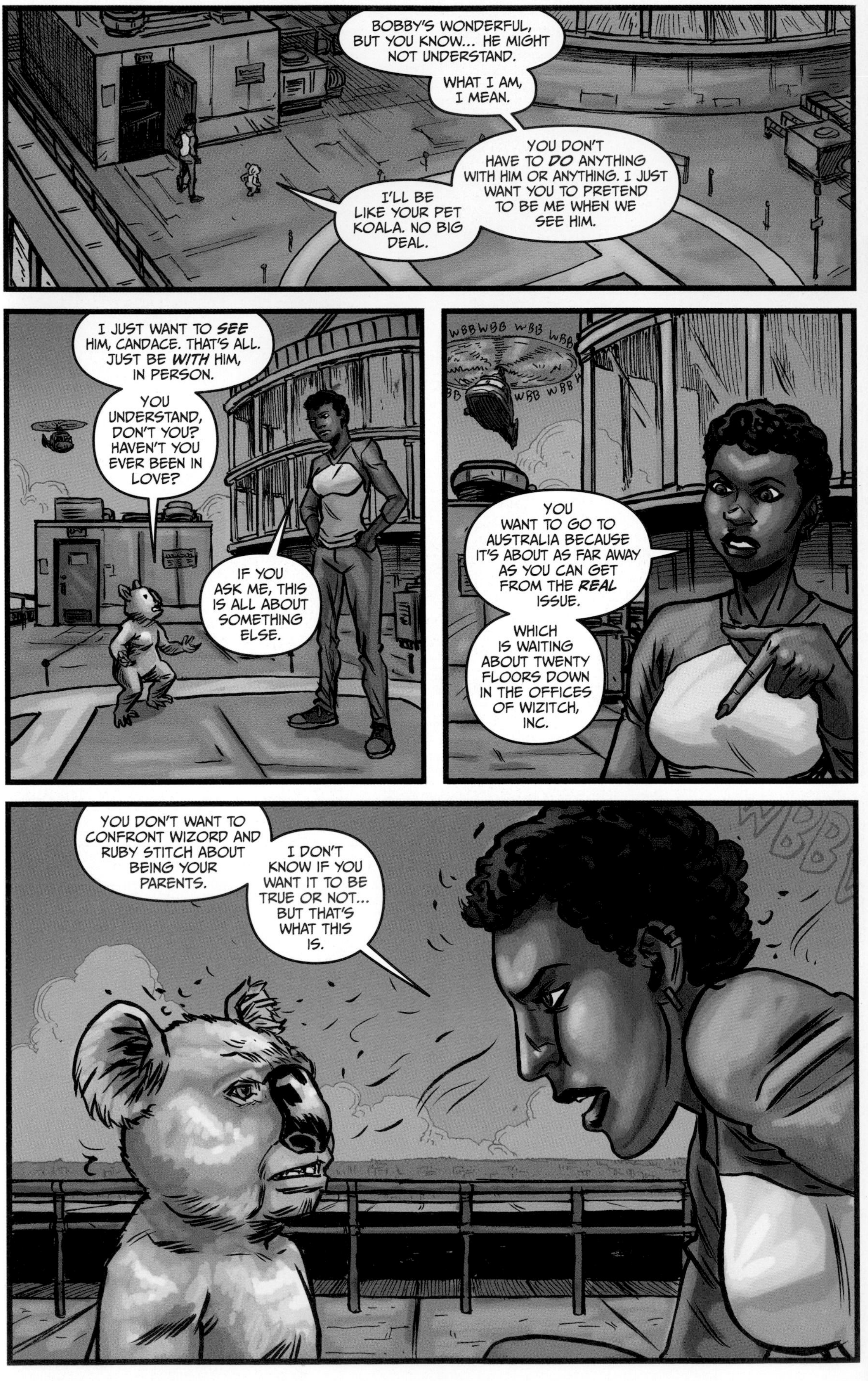
BOBBY'S WONDERFUL, BUT YOU KNOW... HE MIGHT NOT UNDERSTAND.
WHAT I AM, I MEAN.
YOU DON'T HAVE TO DO ANYTHING WITH HIM OR ANYTHING. I JUST WANT YOU TO PRETEND TO BE ME WHEN WE SEE HIM.
I'LL BE LIKE YOUR PET KOALA. NO BIG DEAL.
I JUST WANT TO SEE HIM, CANDACE. THAT'S ALL. JUST BE WITH HIM, IN PERSON.
YOU UNDERSTAND, DON'T YOU? HAVEN'T YOU EVER BEEN IN LOVE?
IF YOU ASK ME, THIS IS ALL ABOUT SOMETHING ELSE.
WBB WBB WBB WBB
YOU WANT TO GO TO AUSTRALIA BECAUSE IT'S ABOUT AS FAR AWAY AS YOU CAN GET FROM THE REAL ISSUE.
WHICH IS WAITING ABOUT TWENTY FLOORS DOWN IN THE OFFICES OF WIZITCH, INC.
YOU DON'T WANT TO CONFRONT WIZORD AND RUBY STITCH ABOUT BEING YOUR PARENTS.
I DON'T KNOW IF YOU WANT IT TO BE TRUE OR NOT... BUT THAT'S WHAT THIS IS.

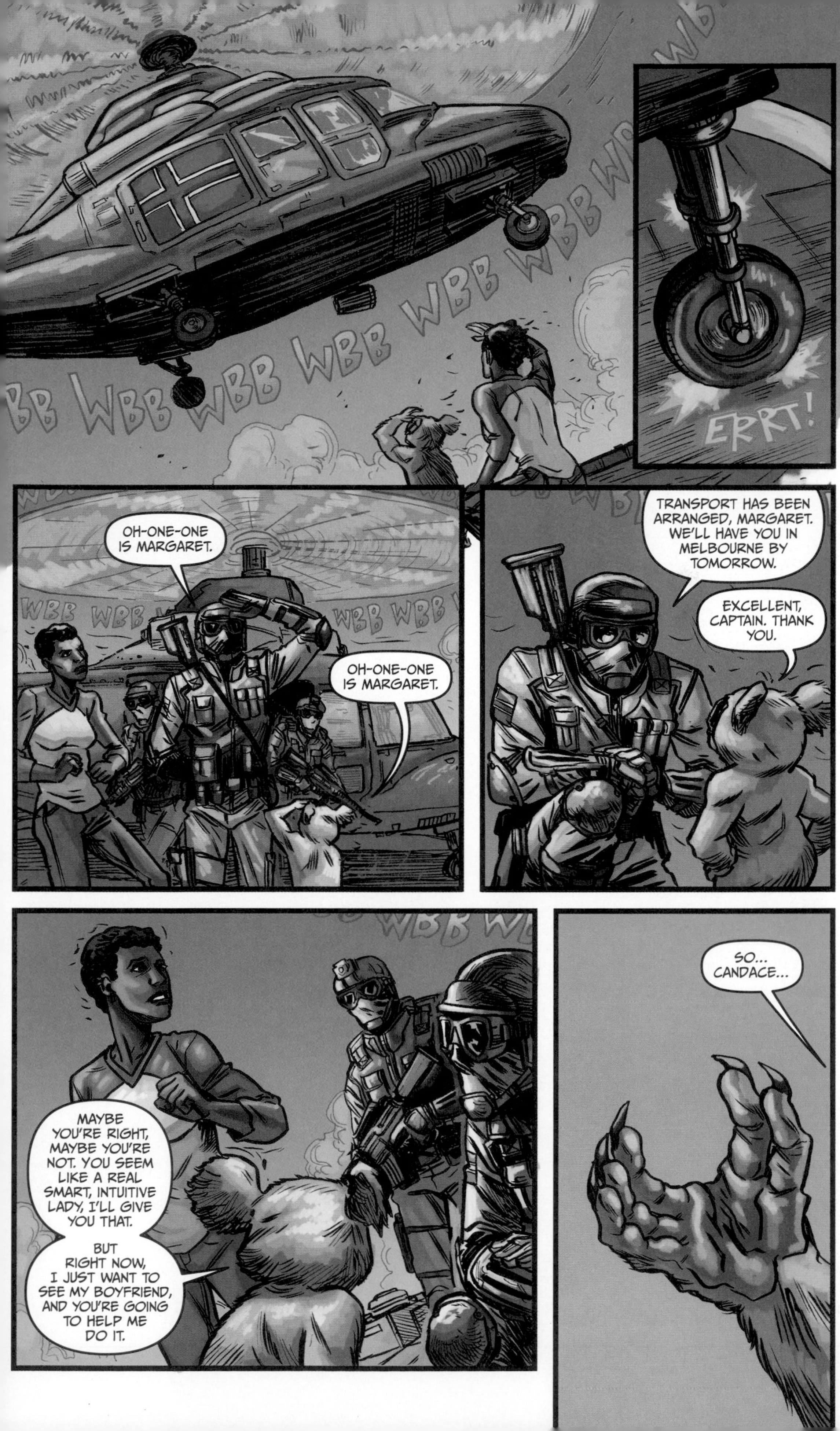
WBB WBB WBB WBB WBB WBB
ERRT!
OH-ONE-ONE IS MARGARET.
WBB WBB
WBB WBB
OH-ONE-ONE IS MARGARET.
TRANSPORT HAS BEEN ARRANGED, MARGARET. WE'LL HAVE YOU IN MELBOURNE BY TOMORROW.
EXCELLENT, CAPTAIN. THANK YOU.
WBB
MAYBE YOU'RE RIGHT, MAYBE YOU'RE NOT. YOU SEEM LIKE A REAL SMART, INTUITIVE LADY, I'LL GIVE YOU THAT.
BUT RIGHT NOW, I JUST WANT TO SEE MY BOYFRIEND, AND YOU'RE GOING TO HELP ME DO IT.
SO... CANDACE...

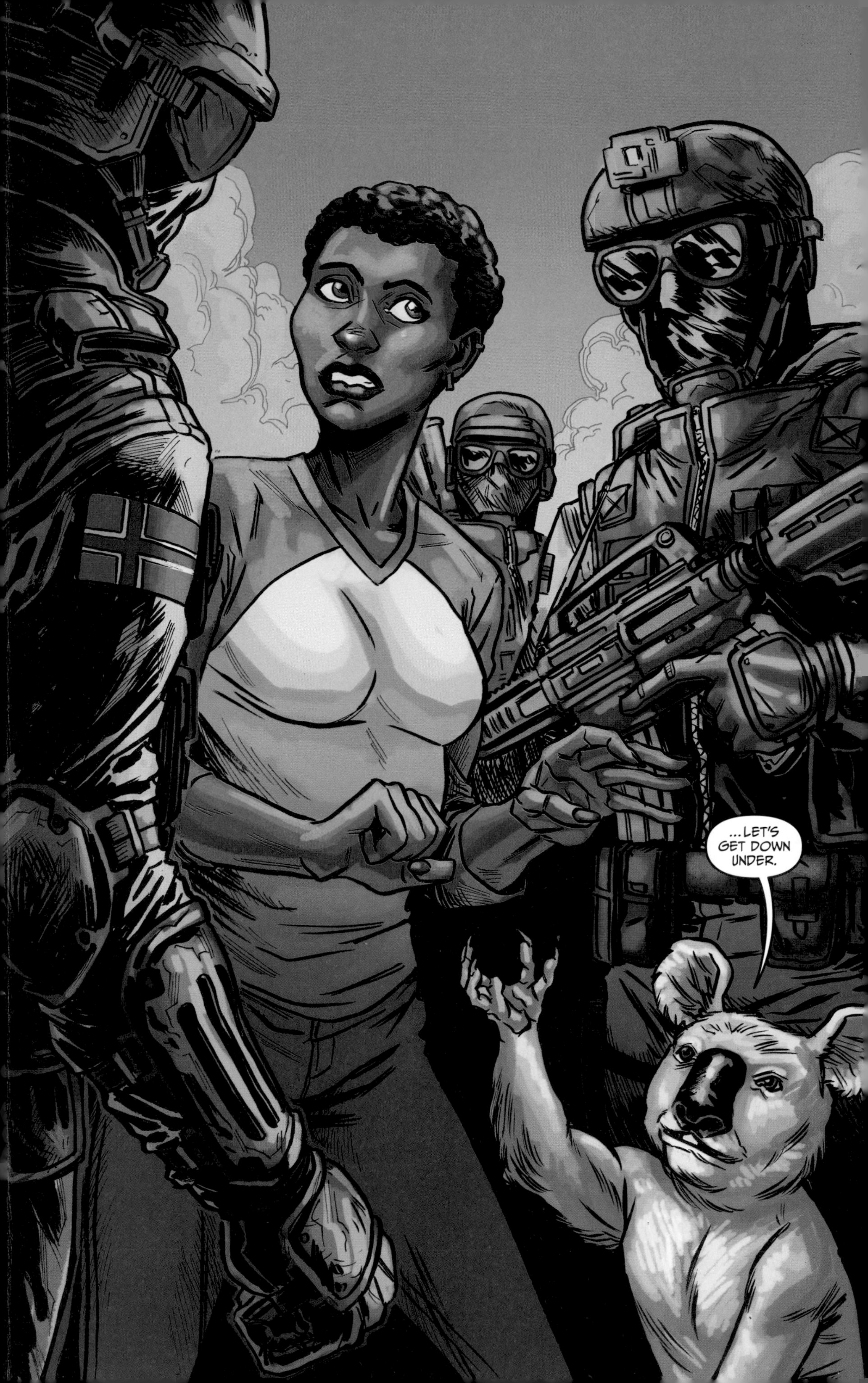
...LET'S GET DOWN UNDER.

NINETEEN

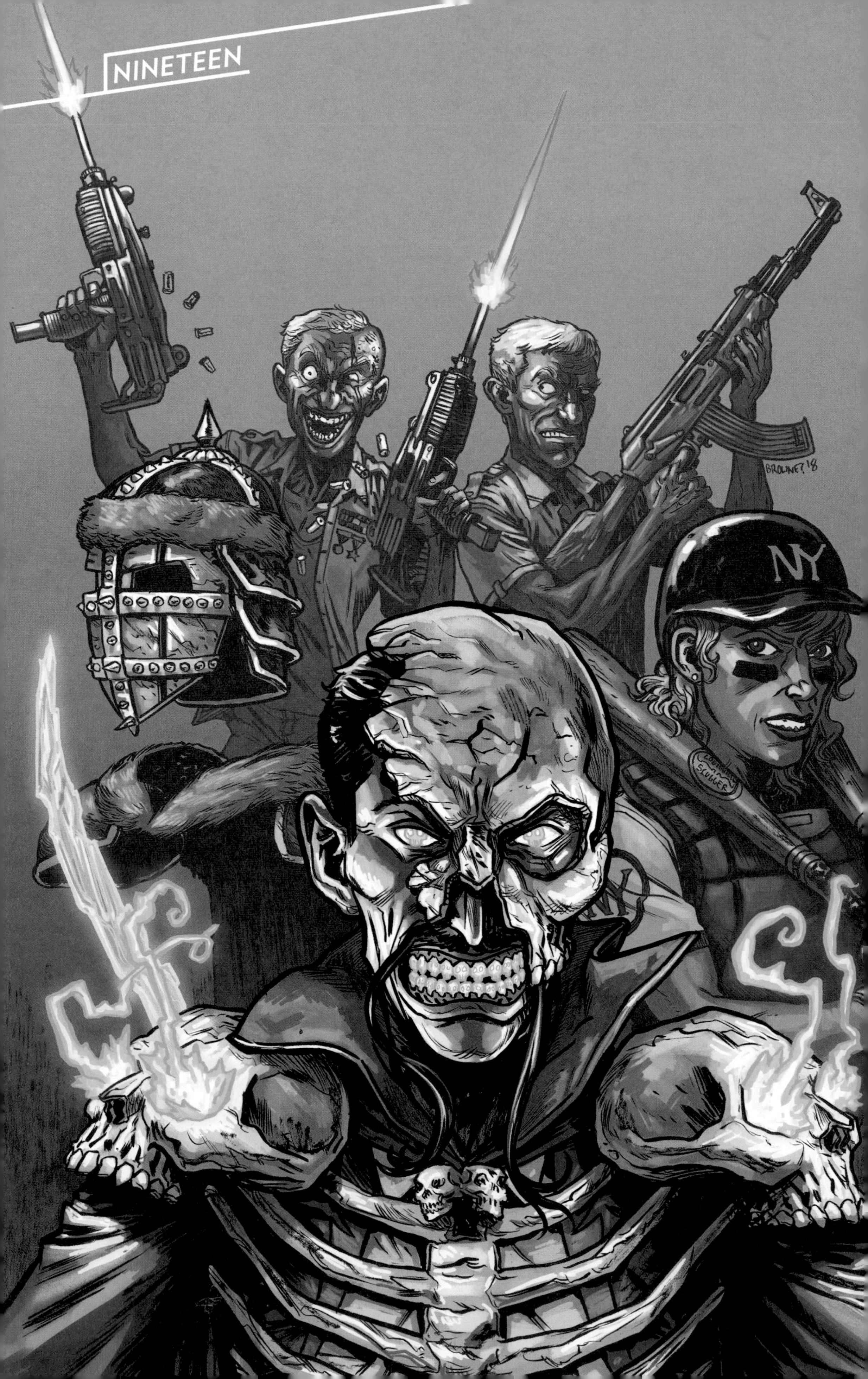
NY

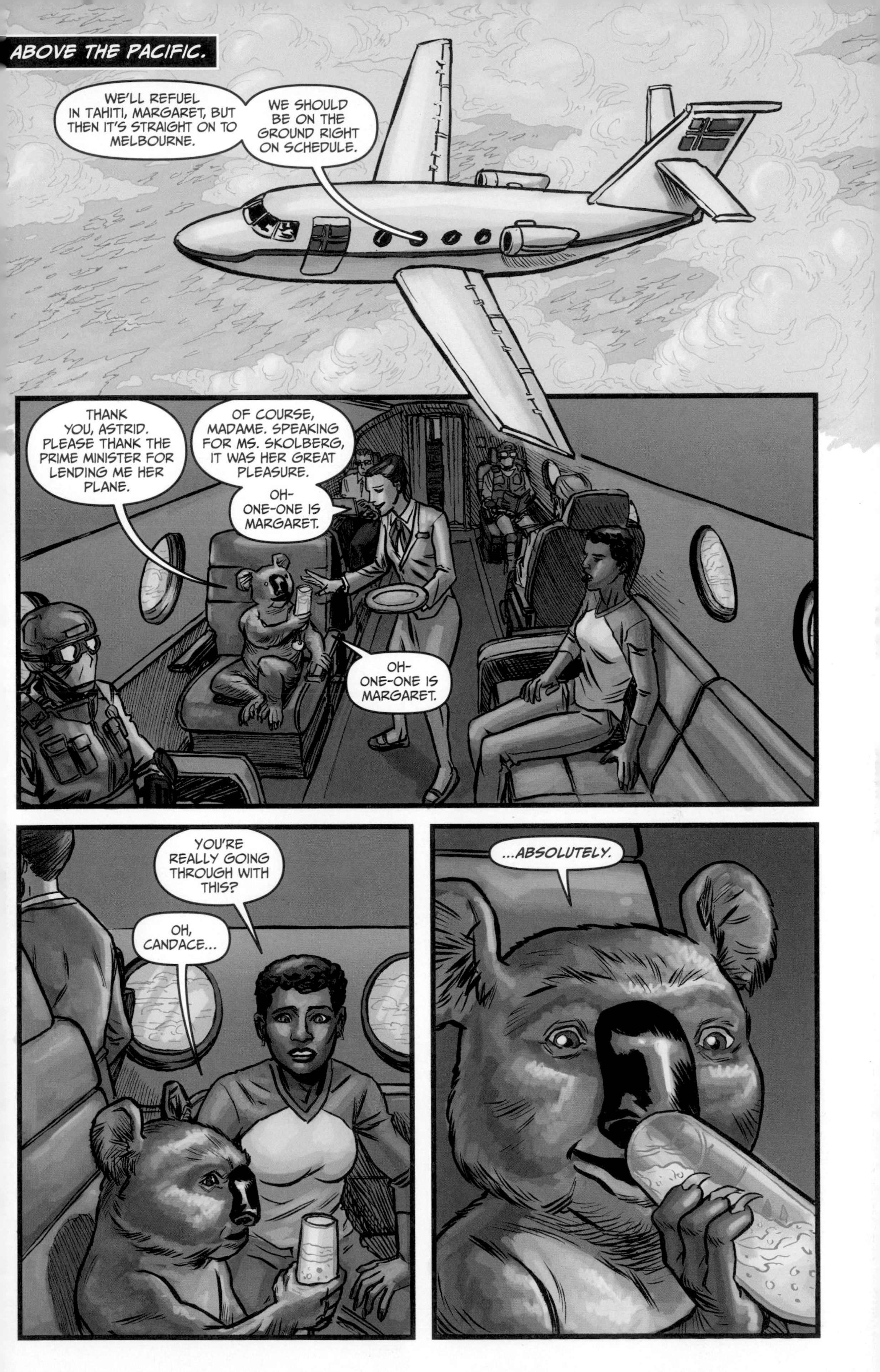
ABOVE THE PACIFIC.
WE'LL REFUEL IN TAHITI, MARGARET, BUT THEN IT'S STRAIGHT ON TO MELBOURNE.
WE SHOULD BE ON THE GROUND RIGHT ON SCHEDULE.
THANK YOU, ASTRID. PLEASE THANK THE PRIME MINISTER FOR LENDING ME HER PLANE.
OF COURSE, MADAME. SPEAKING FOR MS. SKOLBERG, IT WAS HER GREAT PLEASURE.
OH-ONE-ONE IS MARGARET.
OH-ONE-ONE IS MARGARET.
YOU'RE REALLY GOING THROUGH WITH THIS?
OH, CANDACE...
...ABSOLUTELY.

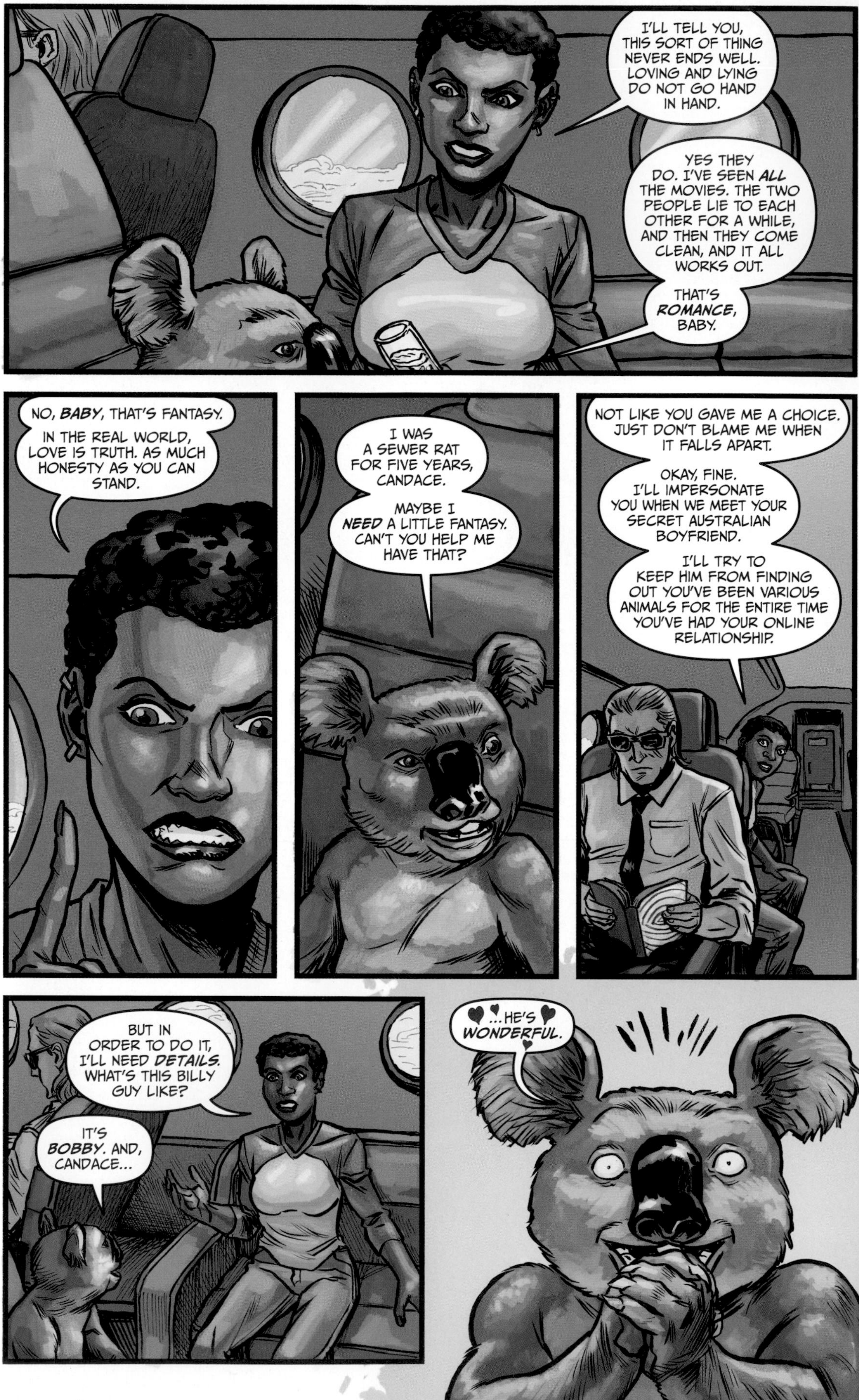
I'LL TELL YOU, THIS SORT OF THING NEVER ENDS WELL. LOVING AND LYING DO NOT GO HAND IN HAND.
YES THEY DO. I'VE SEEN ALL THE MOVIES. THE TWO PEOPLE LIE TO EACH OTHER FOR A WHILE, AND THEN THEY COME CLEAN, AND IT ALL WORKS OUT.
THAT'S ROMANCE, BABY.
NO, BABY, THAT'S FANTASY.
IN THE REAL WORLD, LOVE IS TRUTH. AS MUCH HONESTY AS YOU CAN STAND.
I WAS A SEWER RAT FOR FIVE YEARS, CANDACE.
MAYBE I NEED A LITTLE FANTASY. CAN'T YOU HELP ME HAVE THAT?
NOT LIKE YOU GAVE ME A CHOICE. JUST DON'T BLAME ME WHEN IT FALLS APART.
OKAY, FINE. I'LL IMPERSONATE YOU WHEN WE MEET YOUR SECRET AUSTRALIAN BOYFRIEND.
I'LL TRY TO KEEP HIM FROM FINDING OUT YOU'VE BEEN VARIOUS ANIMALS FOR THE ENTIRE TIME YOU'VE HAD YOUR ONLINE RELATIONSHIP.
BUT IN ORDER TO DO IT, I'LL NEED DETAILS. WHAT'S THIS BILLY GUY LIKE?
IT'S BOBBY. AND, CANDACE...
...HE'S WONDERFUL.

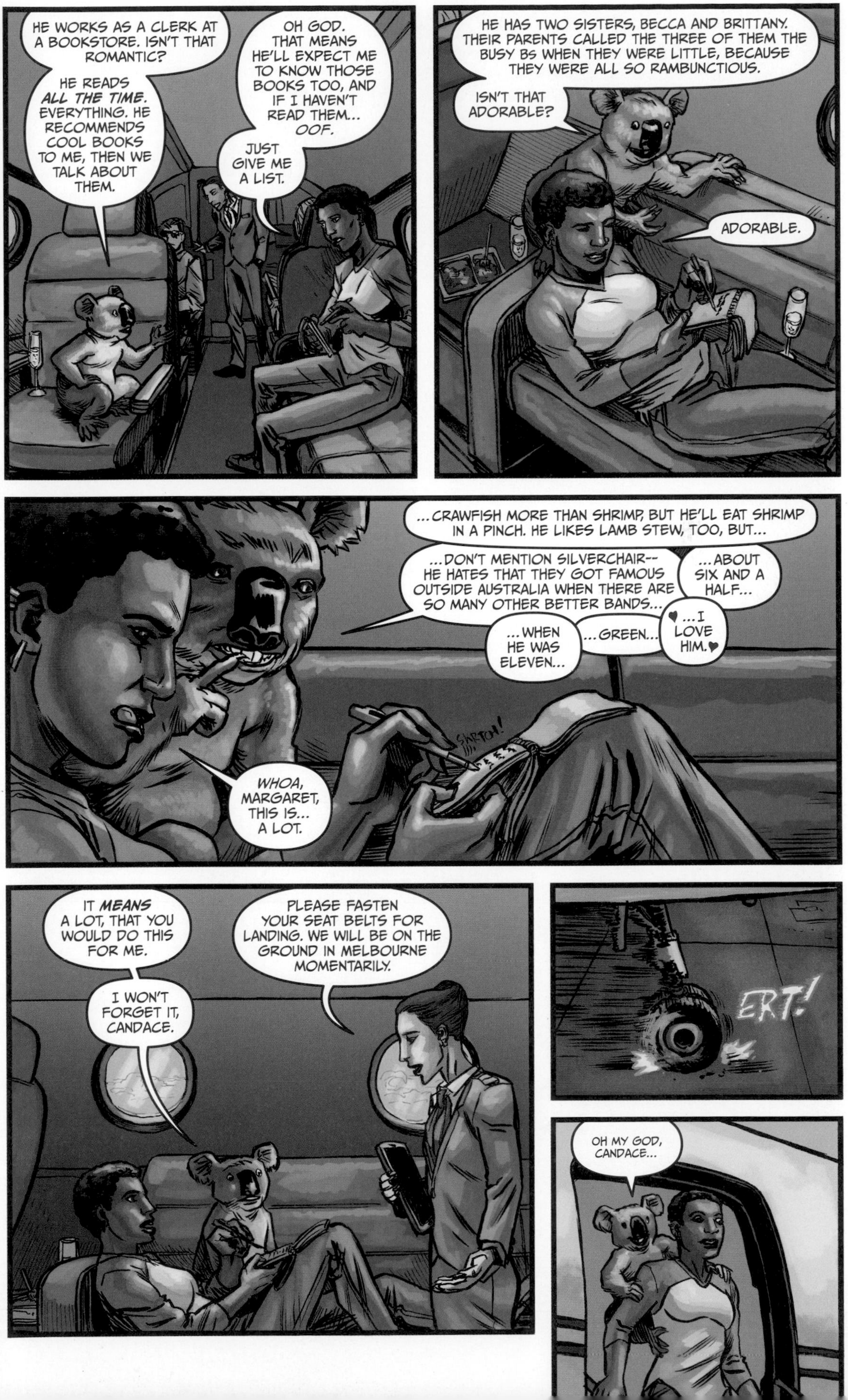
HE WORKS AS A CLERK AT A BOOKSTORE. ISN'T THAT ROMANTIC?
HE READS *ALL THE TIME*. EVERYTHING. HE RECOMMENDS COOL BOOKS TO ME, THEN WE TALK ABOUT THEM.
OH GOD. THAT MEANS HE'LL EXPECT ME TO KNOW THOSE BOOKS TOO, AND IF I HAVEN'T READ THEM... *OOF.*
JUST GIVE ME A LIST.
HE HAS TWO SISTERS, BECCA AND BRITTANY. THEIR PARENTS CALLED THE THREE OF THEM THE BUSY BS WHEN THEY WERE LITTLE, BECAUSE THEY WERE ALL SO RAMBUNCTIOUS.
ISN'T THAT ADORABLE?
ADORABLE.
...CRAWFISH MORE THAN SHRIMP, BUT HE'LL EAT SHRIMP IN A PINCH. HE LIKES LAMB STEW, TOO, BUT...
...DON'T MENTION SILVERCHAIR-- HE HATES THAT THEY GOT FAMOUS OUTSIDE AUSTRALIA WHEN THERE ARE SO MANY OTHER BETTER BANDS...
...ABOUT SIX AND A HALF...
...WHEN HE WAS ELEVEN...
...GREEN...
♥...I LOVE HIM.♥
SKRTCH!
WHOA, MARGARET, THIS IS... A LOT.
IT *MEANS* A LOT, THAT YOU WOULD DO THIS FOR ME.
I WON'T FORGET IT, CANDACE.
PLEASE FASTEN YOUR SEAT BELTS FOR LANDING. WE WILL BE ON THE GROUND IN MELBOURNE MOMENTARILY.
ERT!
OH MY GOD, CANDACE...

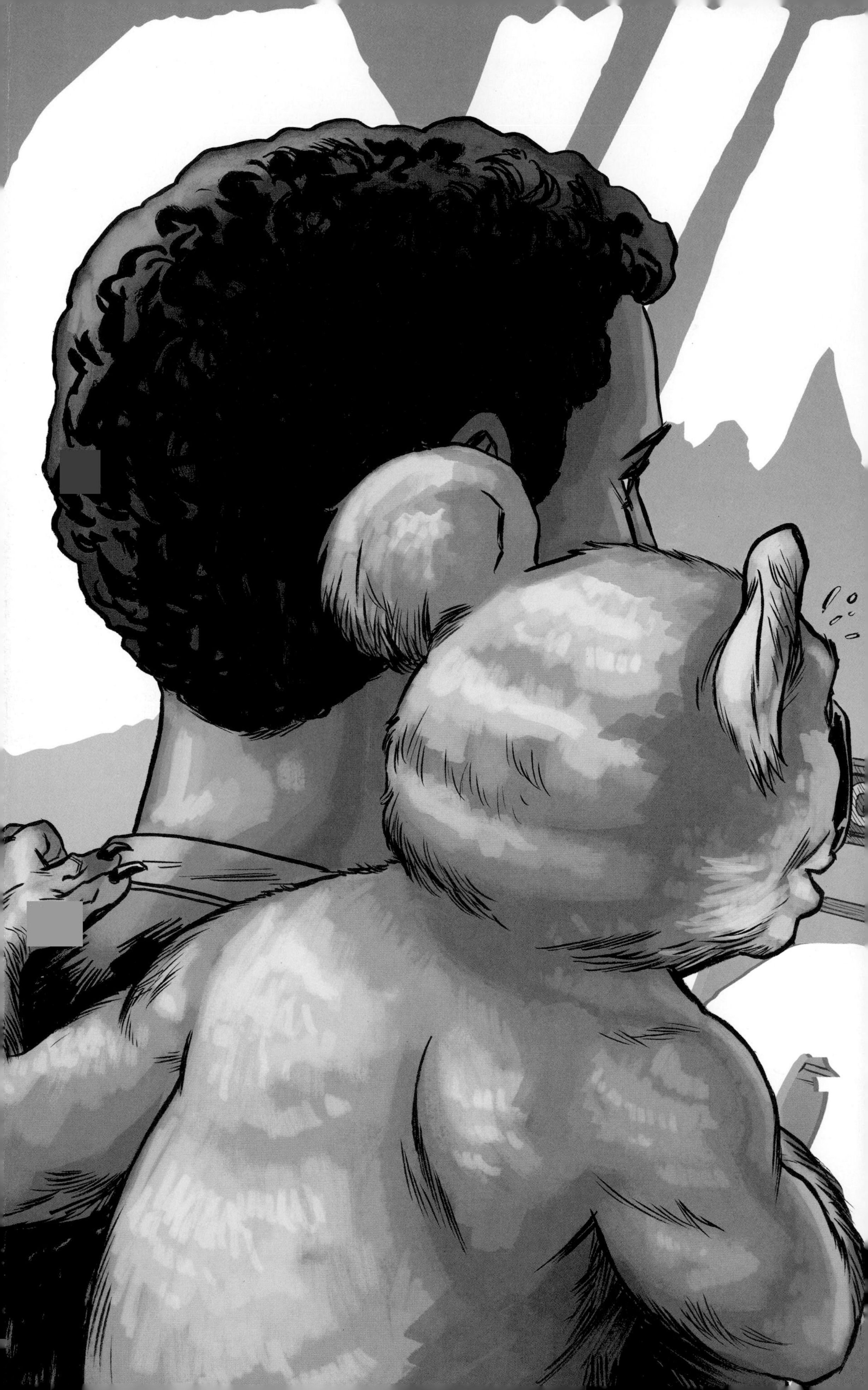

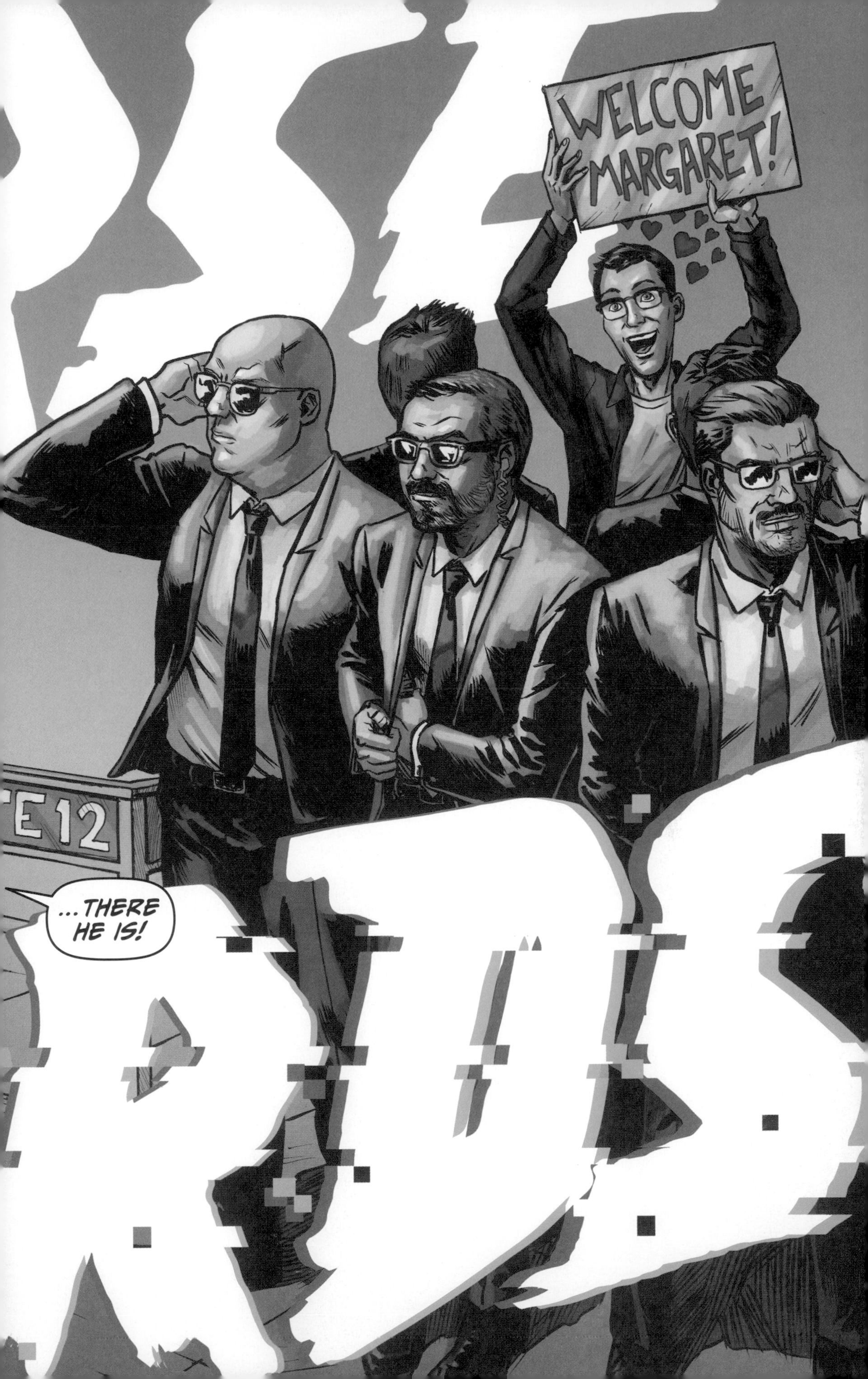
WELCOME MARGARET!
E 12
...THERE HE IS!

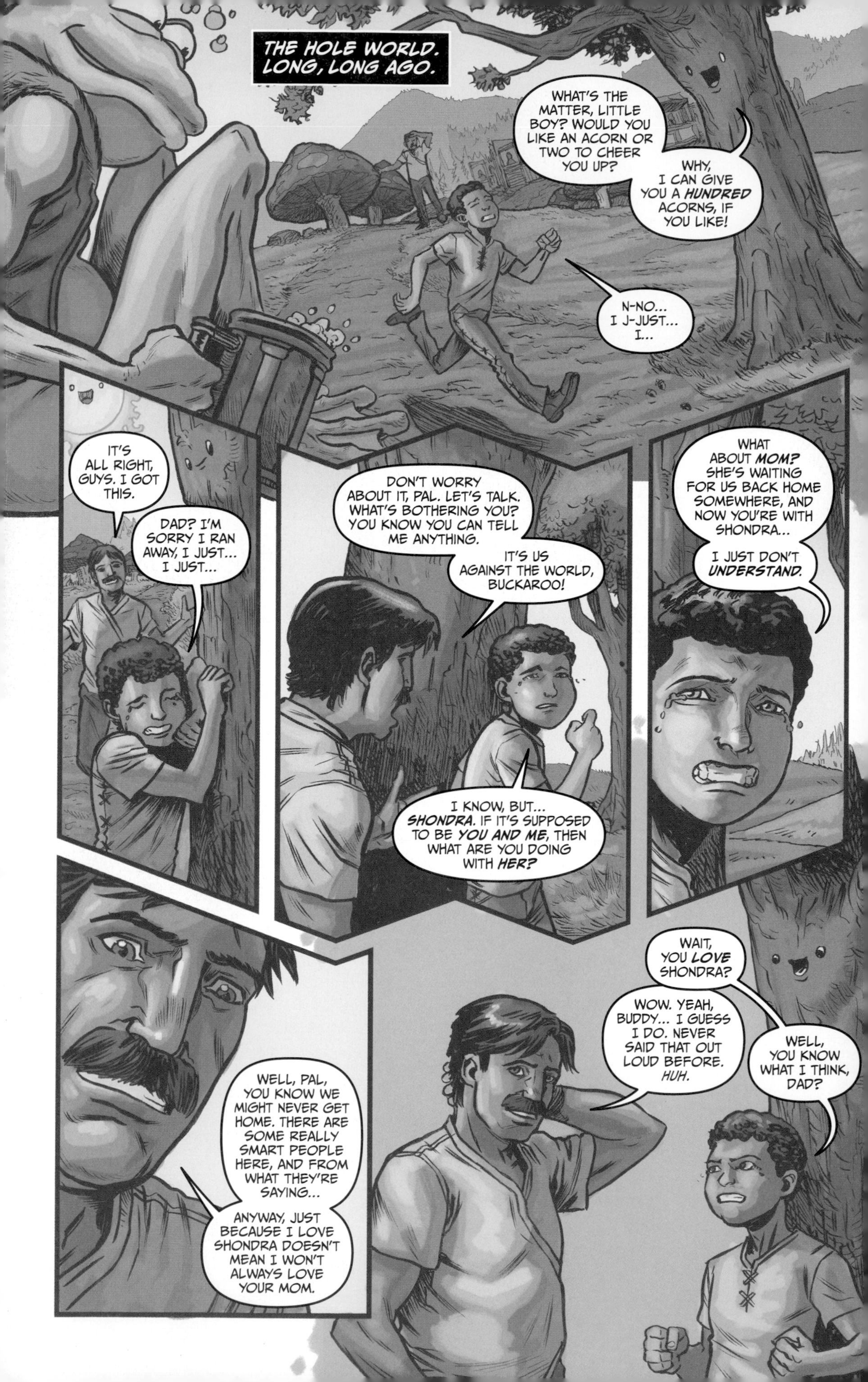
THE HOLE WORLD. LONG, LONG AGO.
WHAT'S THE MATTER, LITTLE BOY? WOULD YOU LIKE AN ACORN OR TWO TO CHEER YOU UP?
WHY, I CAN GIVE YOU A HUNDRED ACORNS, IF YOU LIKE!
N-NO... I J-JUST... I...
IT'S ALL RIGHT, GUYS. I GOT THIS.
DAD? I'M SORRY I RAN AWAY, I JUST... I JUST...
DON'T WORRY ABOUT IT, PAL. LET'S TALK. WHAT'S BOTHERING YOU? YOU KNOW YOU CAN TELL ME ANYTHING.
IT'S US AGAINST THE WORLD, BUCKAROO!
I KNOW, BUT... SHONDRA. IF IT'S SUPPOSED TO BE YOU AND ME, THEN WHAT ARE YOU DOING WITH HER?
WHAT ABOUT MOM? SHE'S WAITING FOR US BACK HOME SOMEWHERE, AND NOW YOU'RE WITH SHONDRA...
I JUST DON'T UNDERSTAND.
WELL, PAL, YOU KNOW WE MIGHT NEVER GET HOME. THERE ARE SOME REALLY SMART PEOPLE HERE, AND FROM WHAT THEY'RE SAYING...
ANYWAY, JUST BECAUSE I LOVE SHONDRA DOESN'T MEAN I WON'T ALWAYS LOVE YOUR MOM.
WAIT, YOU LOVE SHONDRA?
WOW. YEAH, BUDDY... I GUESS I DO. NEVER SAID THAT OUT LOUD BEFORE. HUH.
WELL, YOU KNOW WHAT I THINK, DAD?

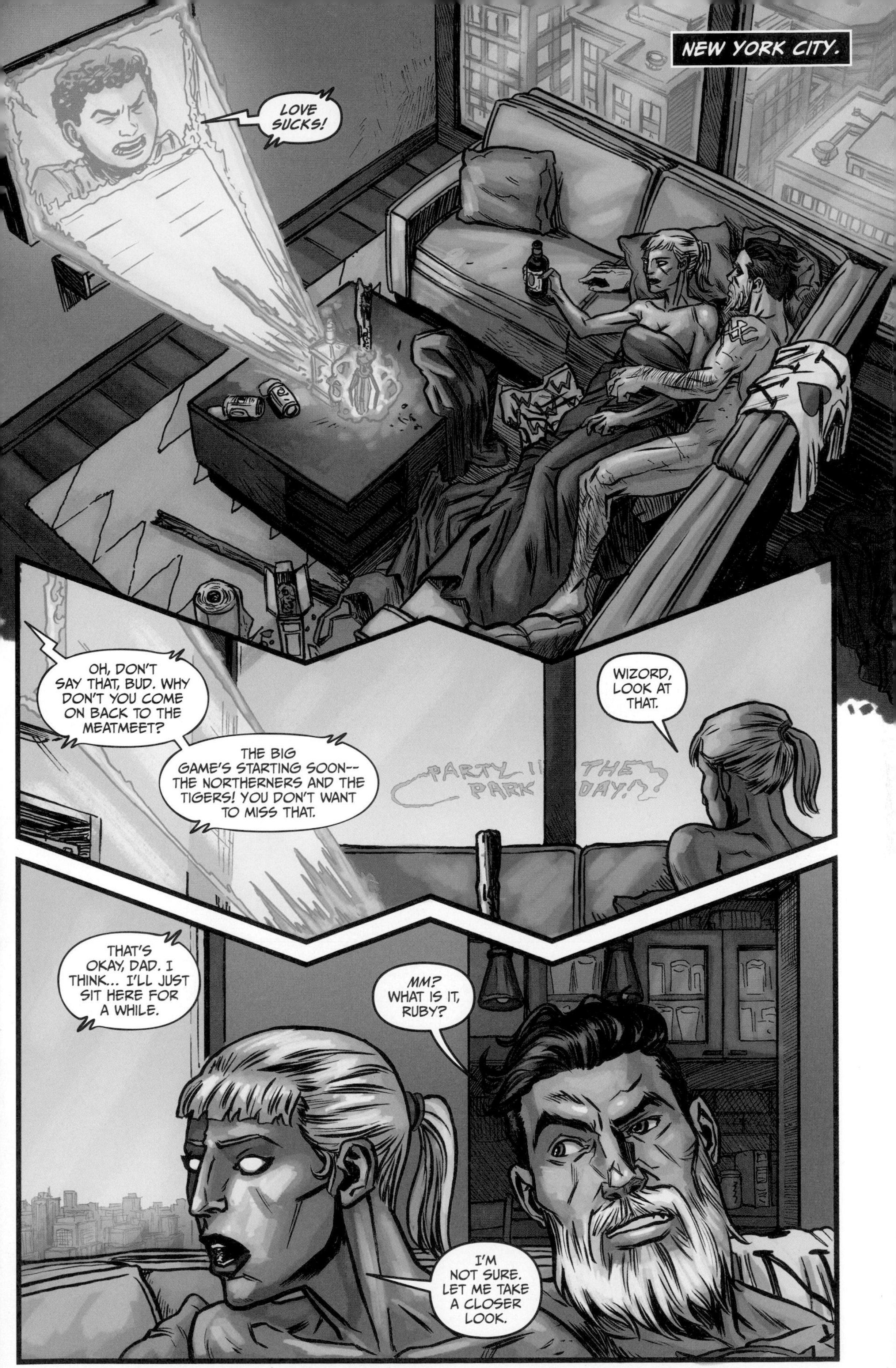
NEW YORK CITY.
LOVE SUCKS!
OH, DON'T SAY THAT, BUD. WHY DON'T YOU COME ON BACK TO THE MEATMEET?
THE BIG GAME'S STARTING SOON-- THE NORTHERNERS AND THE TIGERS! YOU DON'T WANT TO MISS THAT.
WIZORD, LOOK AT THAT.
THAT'S OKAY, DAD. I THINK... I'LL JUST SIT HERE FOR A WHILE.
MM? WHAT IS IT, RUBY?
I'M NOT SURE. LET ME TAKE A CLOSER LOOK.

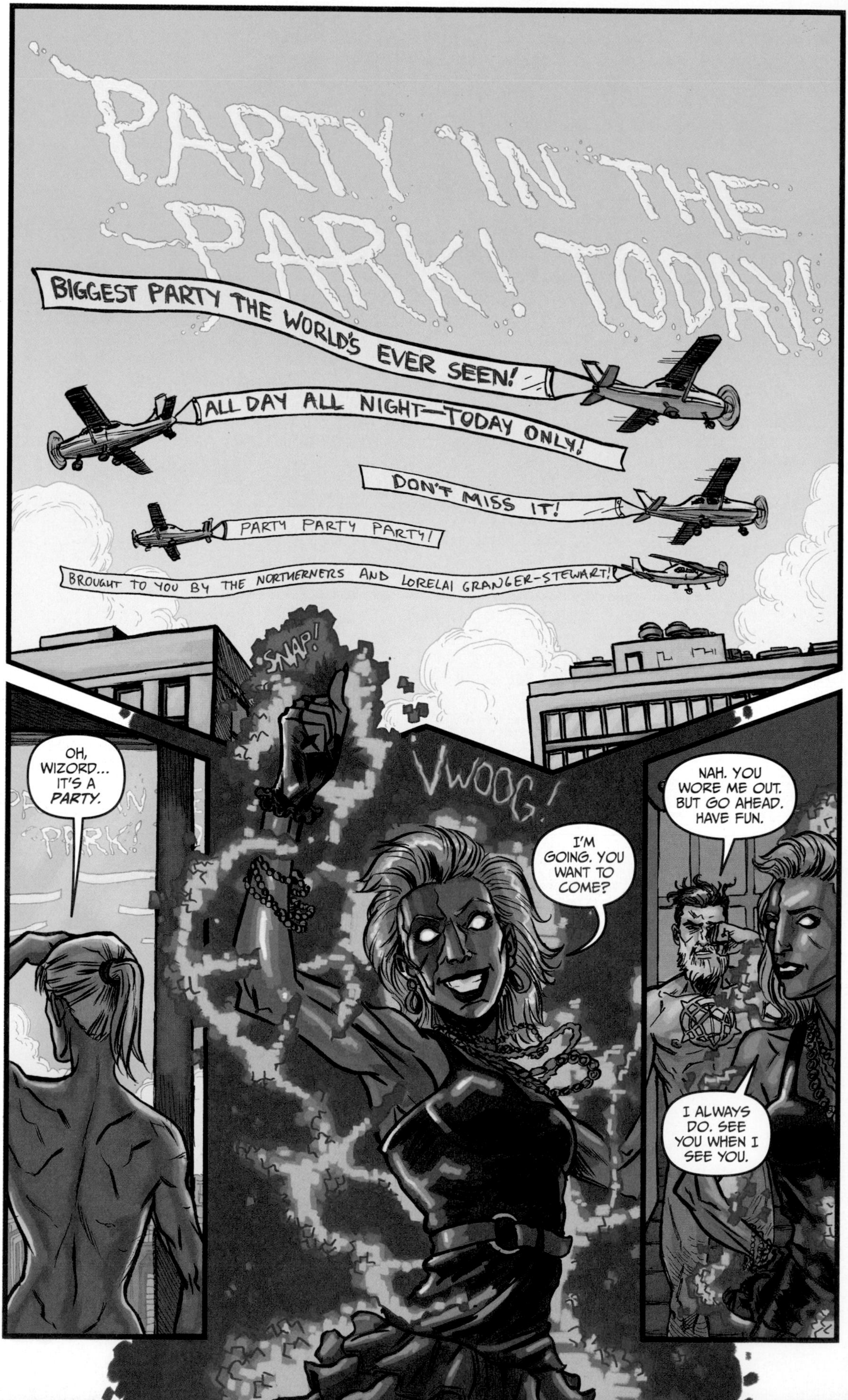
PARTY IN THE PARK! TODAY!
BIGGEST PARTY THE WORLD'S EVER SEEN!
ALL DAY ALL NIGHT—TODAY ONLY!
DON'T MISS IT!
PARTY PARTY PARTY!
BROUGHT TO YOU BY THE NORTHERNERS AND LORELAI GRANGER-STEWART!
SNAP!
OH, WIZORD... IT'S A PARTY.
VWOOG!
I'M GOING. YOU WANT TO COME?
NAH. YOU WORE ME OUT. BUT GO AHEAD. HAVE FUN.
I ALWAYS DO. SEE YOU WHEN I SEE YOU.

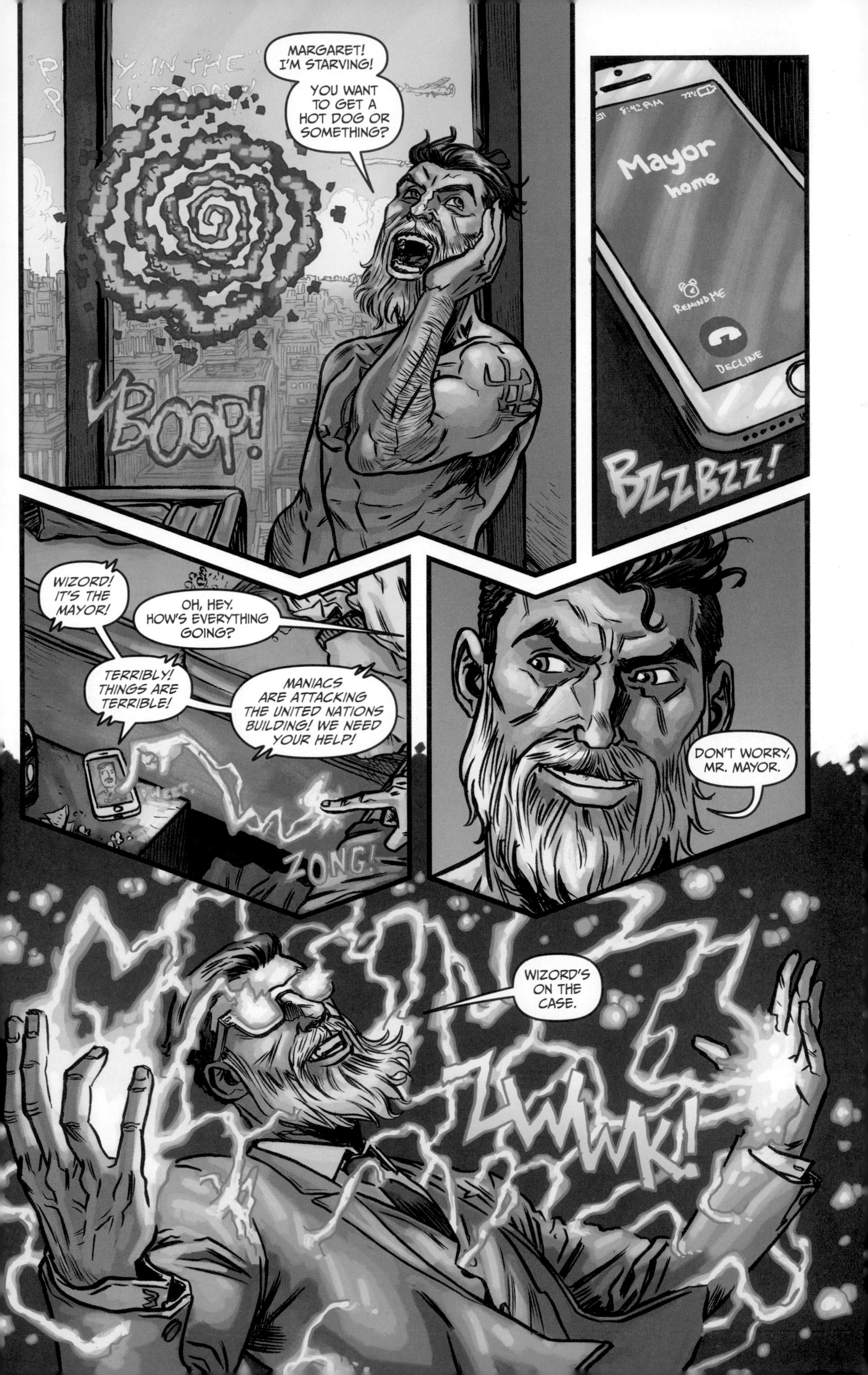
MARGARET! I'M STARVING!
YOU WANT TO GET A HOT DOG OR SOMETHING?
BOOP!
Mayor
home
REMIND ME
DECLINE
BZZBZZ!
WIZORD! IT'S THE MAYOR!
OH, HEY. HOW'S EVERYTHING GOING?
TERRIBLY! THINGS ARE TERRIBLE!
MANIACS ARE ATTACKING THE UNITED NATIONS BUILDING! WE NEED YOUR HELP!
ZONG!
DON'T WORRY, MR. MAYOR.
WIZORD'S ON THE CASE.
ZWAK!

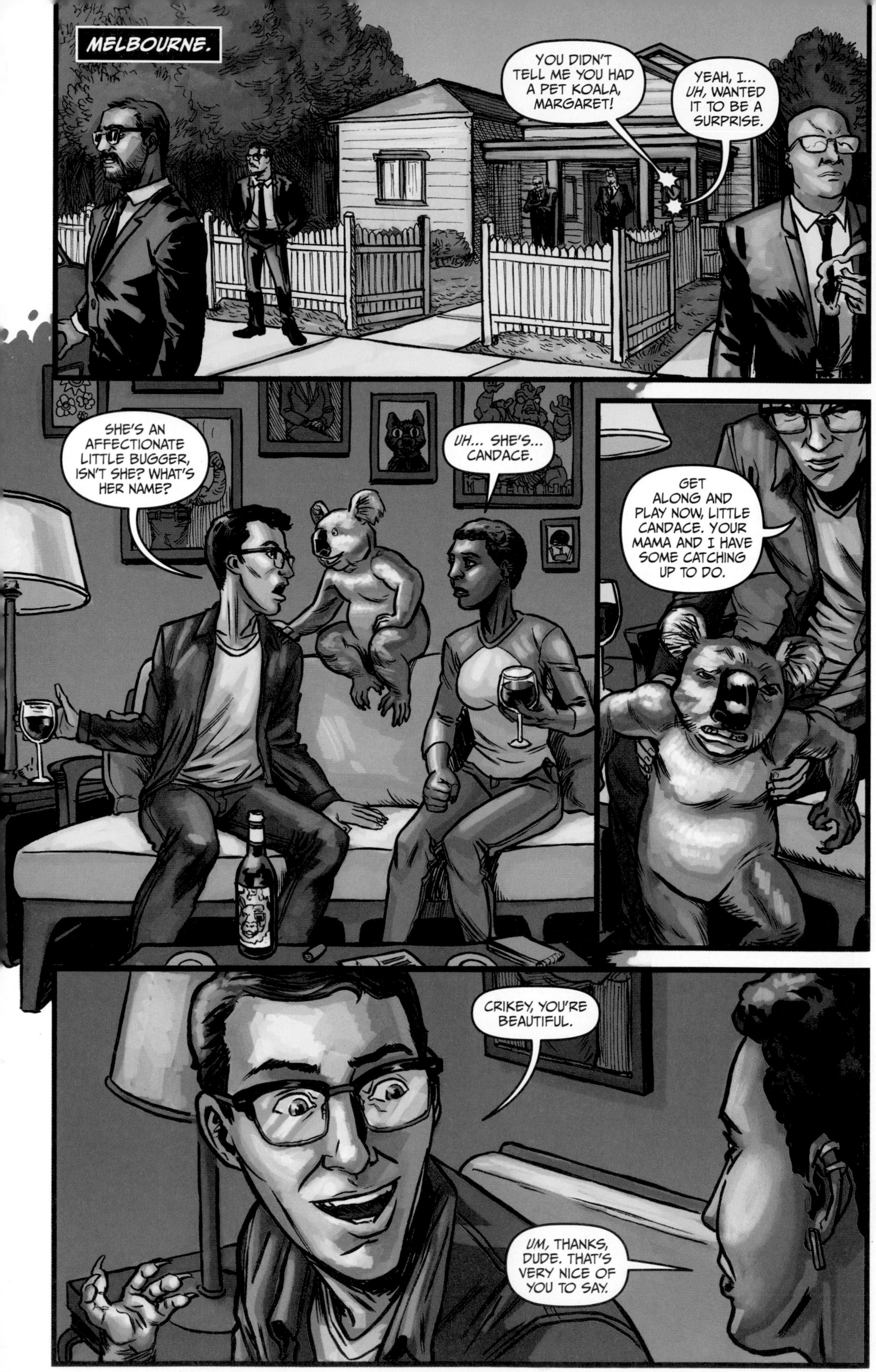
MELBOURNE.
YOU DIDN'T TELL ME YOU HAD A PET KOALA, MARGARET!
YEAH, I... UH, WANTED IT TO BE A SURPRISE.
SHE'S AN AFFECTIONATE LITTLE BUGGER, ISN'T SHE? WHAT'S HER NAME?
UH... SHE'S... CANDACE.
GET ALONG AND PLAY NOW, LITTLE CANDACE. YOUR MAMA AND I HAVE SOME CATCHING UP TO DO.
CRIKEY, YOU'RE BEAUTIFUL.
UM, THANKS, DUDE. THAT'S VERY NICE OF YOU TO SAY.

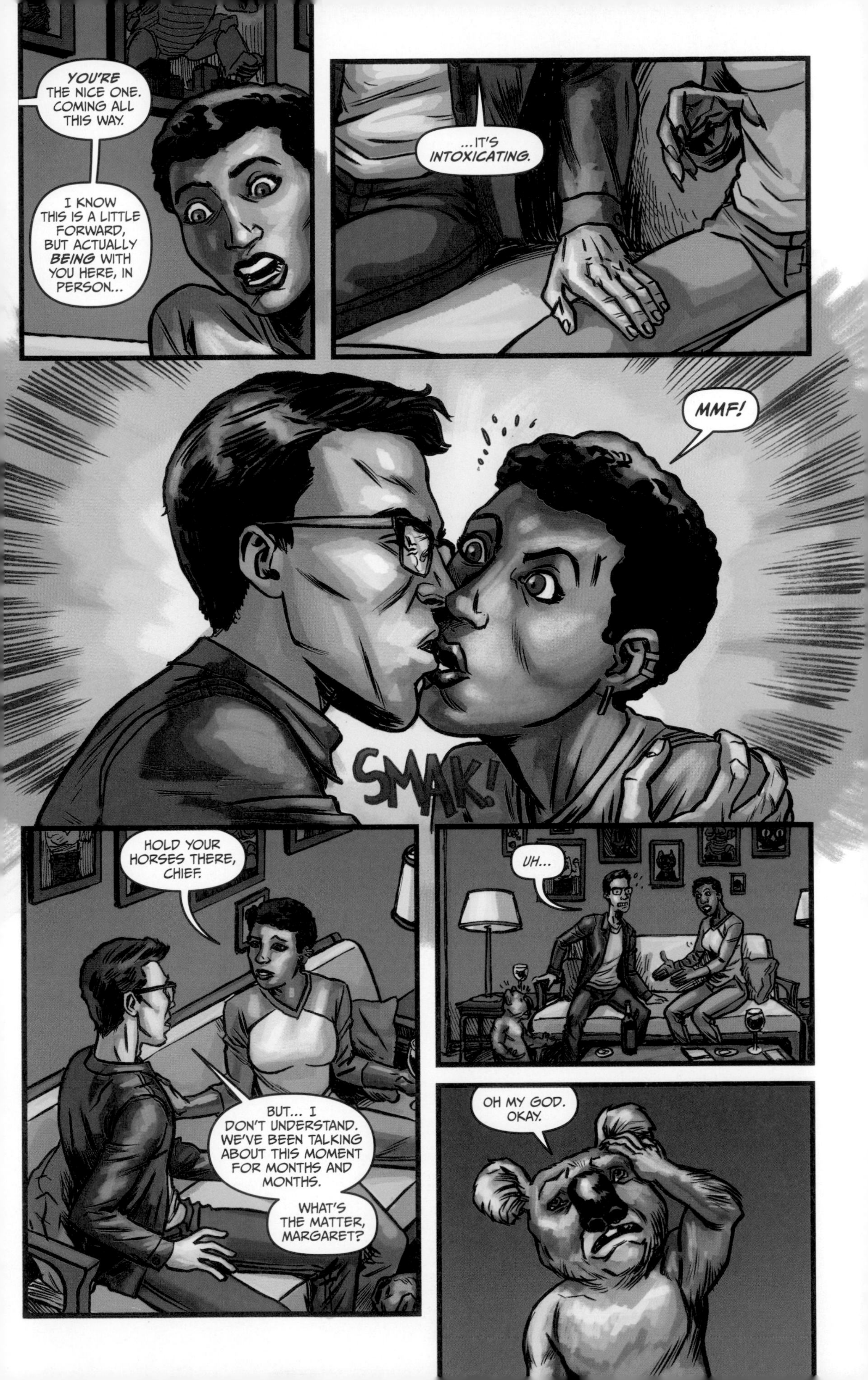
YOU'RE THE NICE ONE. COMING ALL THIS WAY.
I KNOW THIS IS A LITTLE FORWARD, BUT ACTUALLY BEING WITH YOU HERE, IN PERSON...
...IT'S INTOXICATING.
MMF!
SMAK!
HOLD YOUR HORSES THERE, CHIEF.
BUT... I DON'T UNDERSTAND. WE'VE BEEN TALKING ABOUT THIS MOMENT FOR MONTHS AND MONTHS.
WHAT'S THE MATTER, MARGARET?
UH...
OH MY GOD. OKAY.

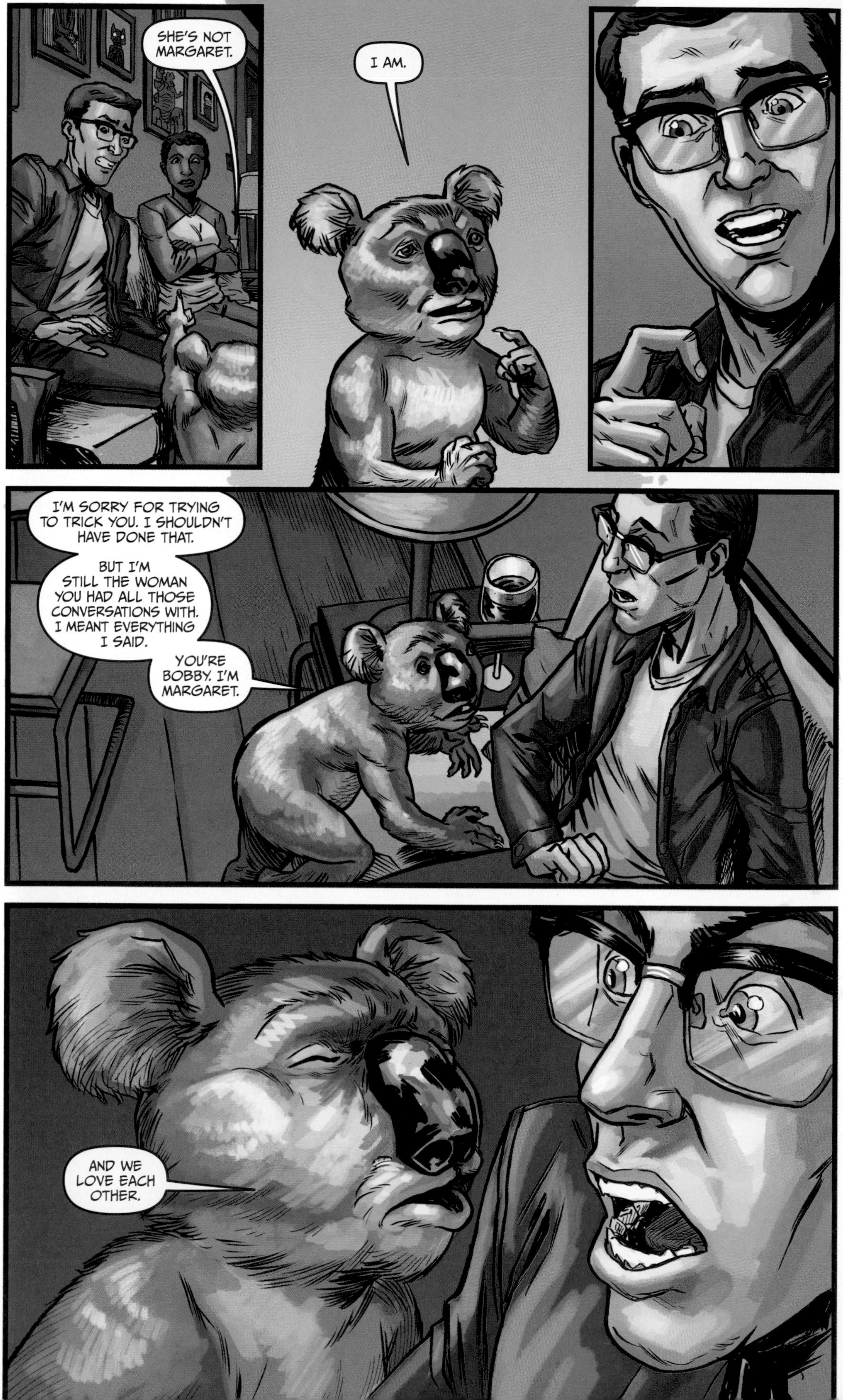
SHE'S NOT MARGARET.
I AM.
I'M SORRY FOR TRYING TO TRICK YOU. I SHOULDN'T HAVE DONE THAT.
BUT I'M STILL THE WOMAN YOU HAD ALL THOSE CONVERSATIONS WITH. I MEANT EVERYTHING I SAID.
YOU'RE BOBBY. I'M MARGARET.
AND WE LOVE EACH OTHER.

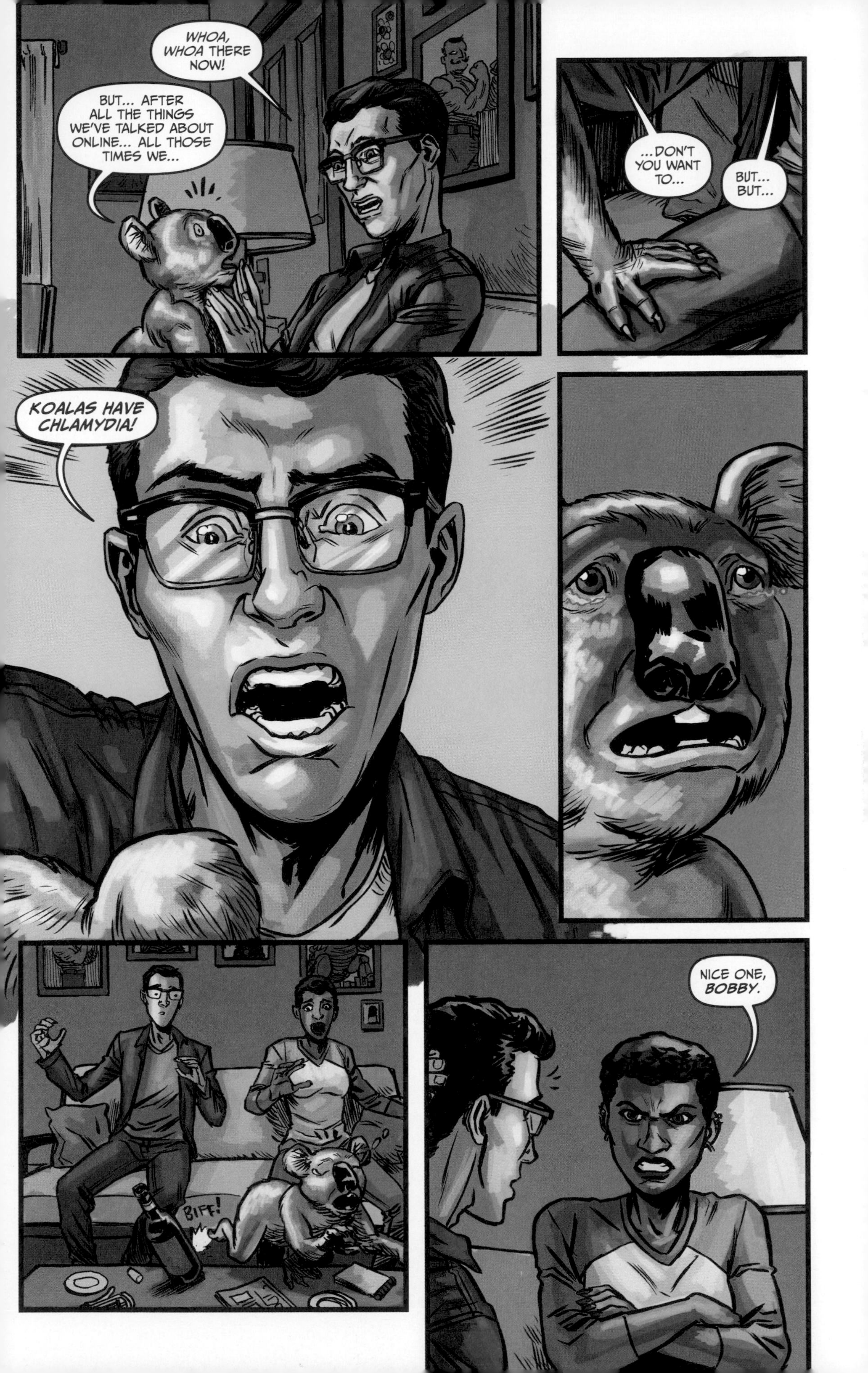
WHOA, WHOA THERE NOW!
BUT... AFTER ALL THE THINGS WE'VE TALKED ABOUT ONLINE... ALL THOSE TIMES WE...
...DON'T YOU WANT TO...
BUT... BUT...
KOALAS HAVE CHLAMYDIA!
BIFF!
NICE ONE, BOBBY.

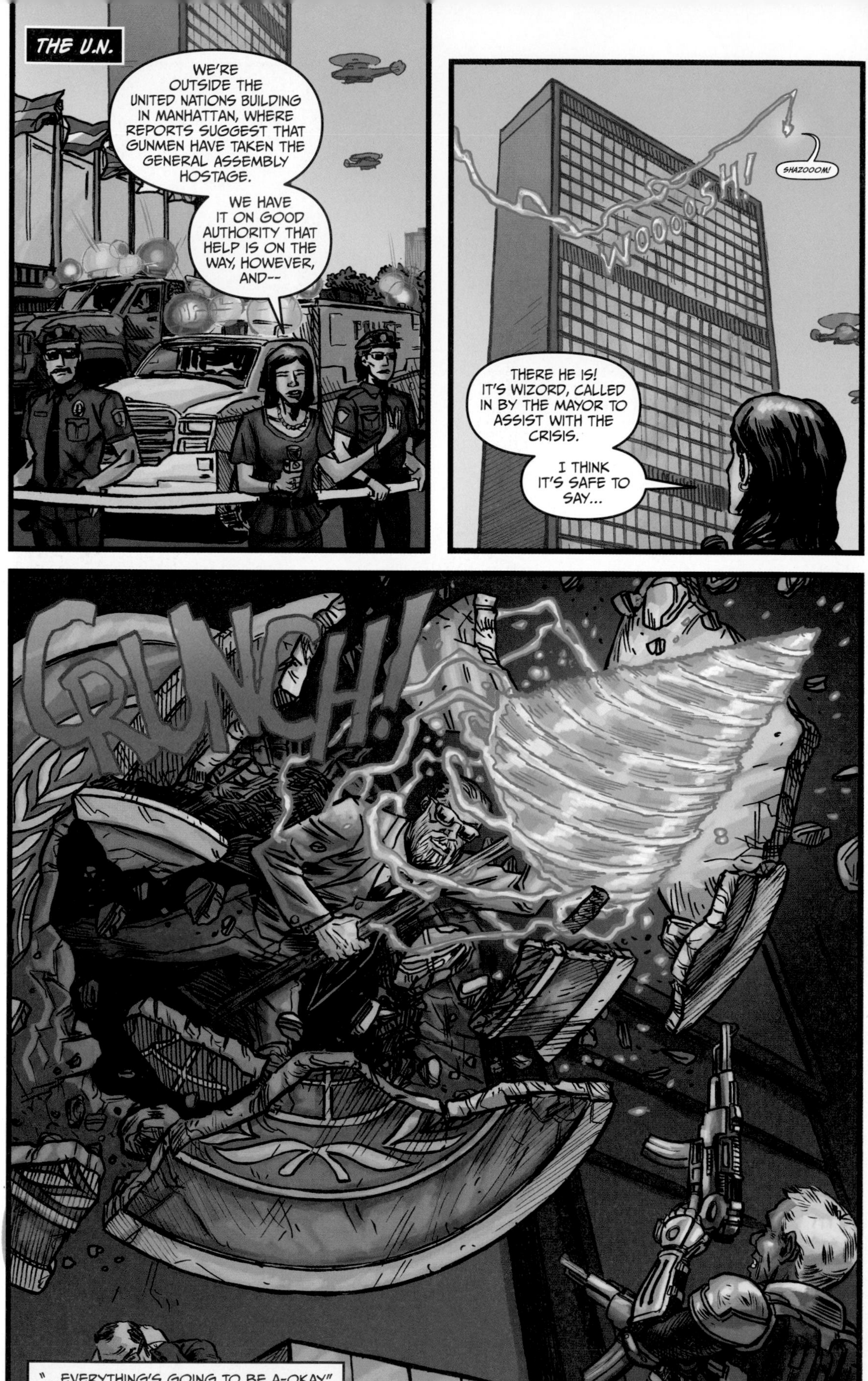
THE U.N.
WE'RE OUTSIDE THE UNITED NATIONS BUILDING IN MANHATTAN, WHERE REPORTS SUGGEST THAT GUNMEN HAVE TAKEN THE GENERAL ASSEMBLY HOSTAGE.
WE HAVE IT ON GOOD AUTHORITY THAT HELP IS ON THE WAY, HOWEVER, AND--
WOOOOSH!
SHAZOOOM!
THERE HE IS! IT'S WIZORD, CALLED IN BY THE MAYOR TO ASSIST WITH THE CRISIS.
I THINK IT'S SAFE TO SAY...
CRUNCH!
"...EVERYTHING'S GOING TO BE A-OKAY."

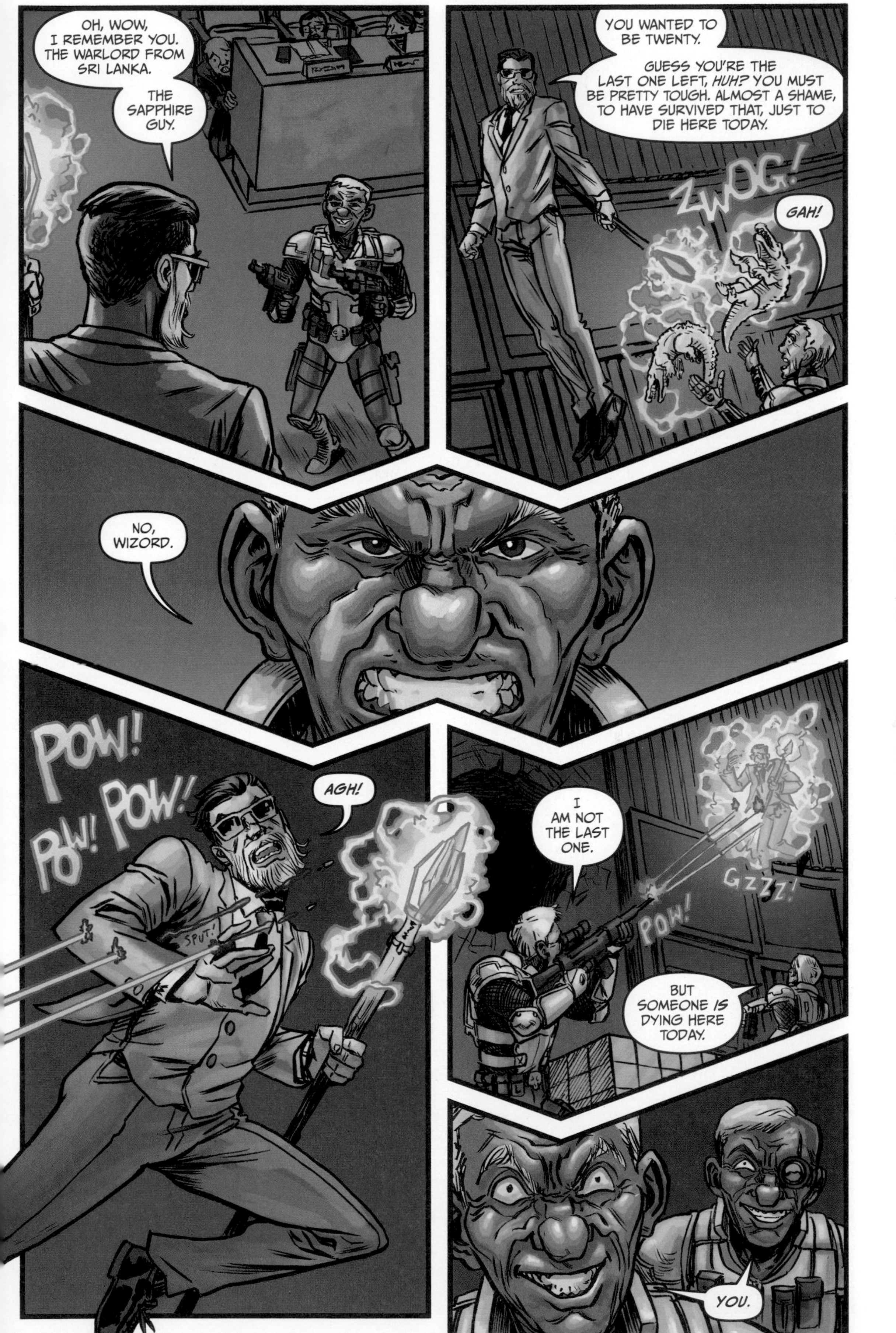

OH, WOW, I REMEMBER YOU. THE WARLORD FROM SRI LANKA.
THE SAPPHIRE GUY.
YOU WANTED TO BE TWENTY.
GUESS YOU'RE THE LAST ONE LEFT, *HUH?* YOU MUST BE PRETTY TOUGH. ALMOST A SHAME, TO HAVE SURVIVED THAT, JUST TO DIE HERE TODAY.
ZWOG!
GAH!
NO, WIZORD.
POW!
POW! POW!
AGH!
SPUT!
I AM NOT THE LAST ONE.
GZZZ!
POW!
BUT SOMEONE *IS* DYING HERE TODAY.
YOU.

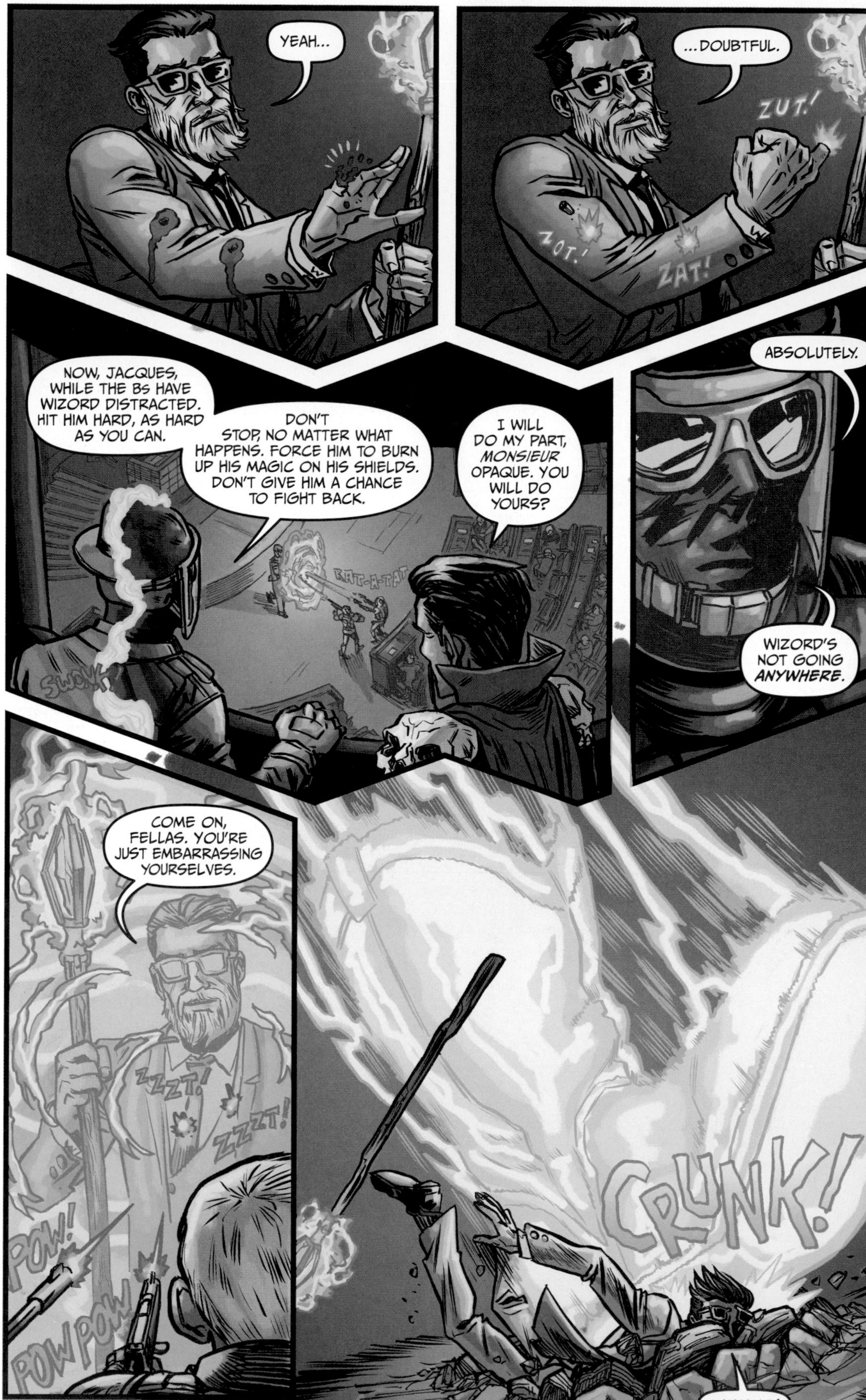
YEAH...
...DOUBTFUL.
ZUT!
ZOT!
ZAT!
NOW, JACQUES, WHILE THE Bs HAVE WIZORD DISTRACTED. HIT HIM HARD, AS HARD AS YOU CAN.
DON'T STOP, NO MATTER WHAT HAPPENS. FORCE HIM TO BURN UP HIS MAGIC ON HIS SHIELDS. DON'T GIVE HIM A CHANCE TO FIGHT BACK.
RAT-A-TAT
I WILL DO MY PART, *MONSIEUR* OPAQUE. YOU WILL DO YOURS?
ABSOLUTELY.
WIZORD'S NOT GOING *ANYWHERE*.
COME ON, FELLAS. YOU'RE JUST EMBARRASSING YOURSELVES.
ZZZT!
ZZZT!
POW!
POW POW
CRUNK!
WMMMF!

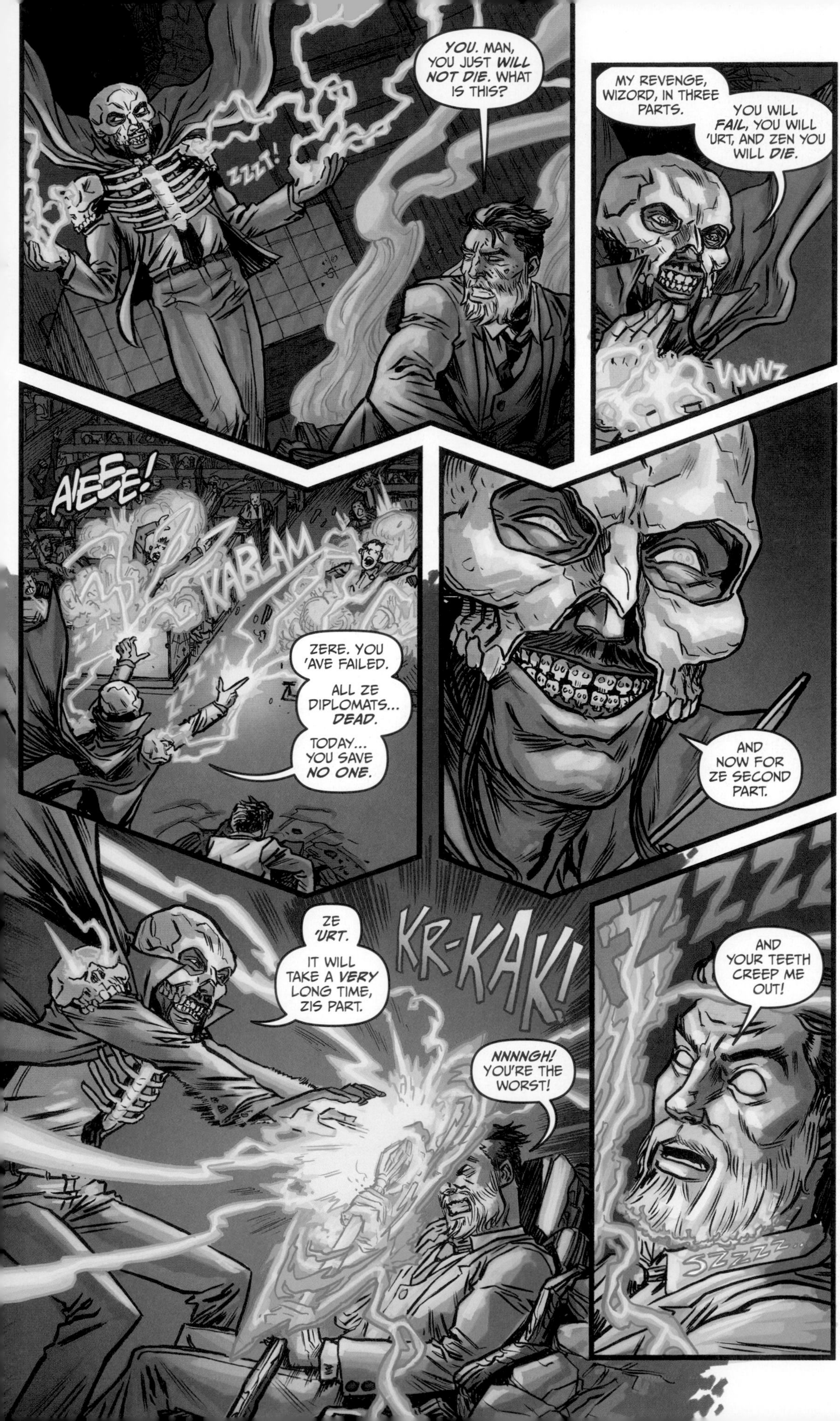

ZZZT!
YOU. MAN, YOU JUST WILL NOT DIE. WHAT IS THIS?
MY REVENGE, WIZORD, IN THREE PARTS.
YOU WILL FAIL, YOU WILL 'URT, AND ZEN YOU WILL DIE.
VUVVZ
AIEEEE!
KABLAM
ZERE. YOU 'AVE FAILED.
ALL ZE DIPLOMATS... DEAD.
TODAY... YOU SAVE NO ONE.
AND NOW FOR ZE SECOND PART.
ZE 'URT.
IT WILL TAKE A VERY LONG TIME, ZIS PART.
KR-KAK!
NNNNGH! YOU'RE THE WORST!
ZZZZ
AND YOUR TEETH CREEP ME OUT!
SZZZZ...

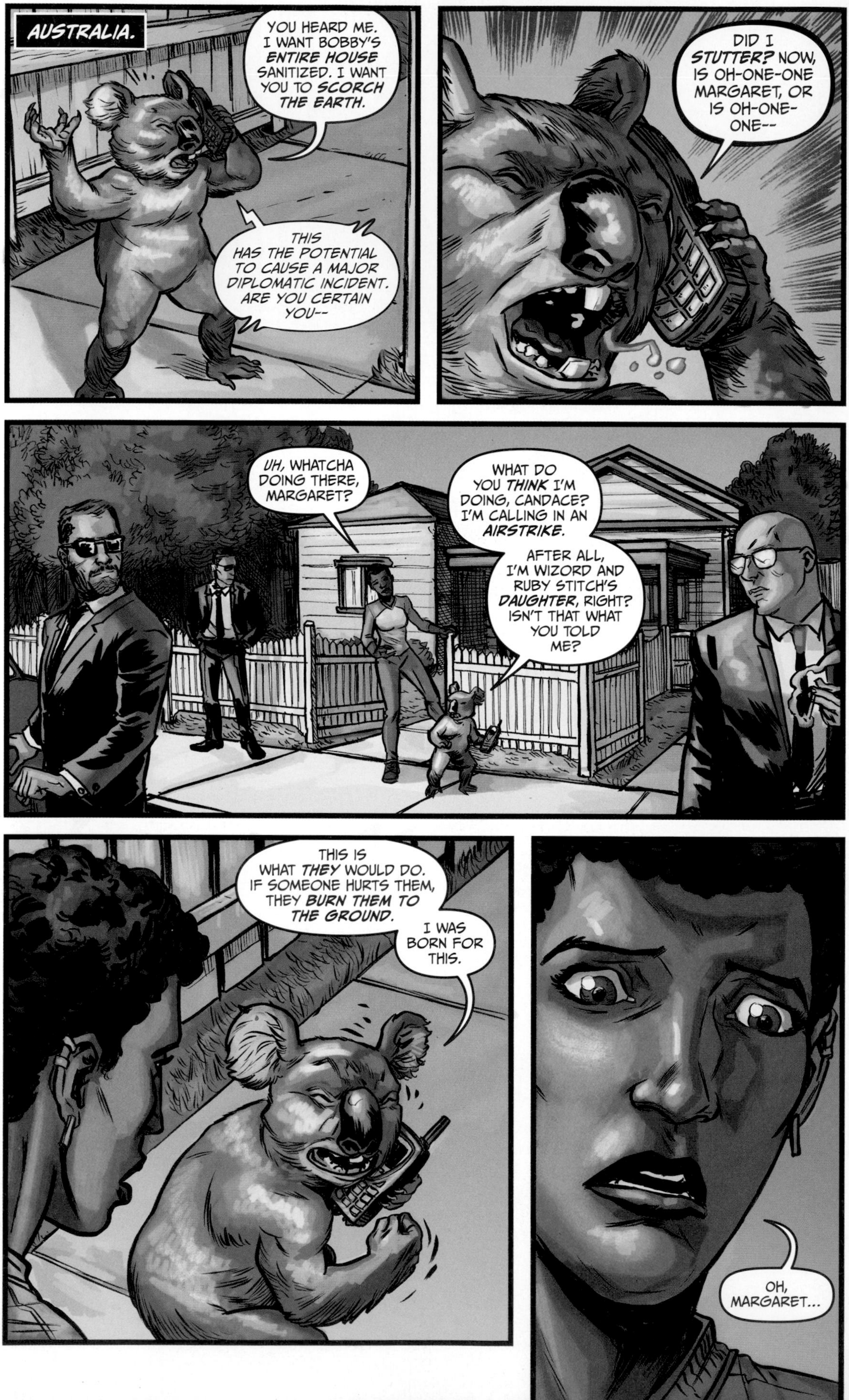
AUSTRALIA.
YOU HEARD ME. I WANT BOBBY'S ENTIRE HOUSE SANITIZED. I WANT YOU TO SCORCH THE EARTH.
THIS HAS THE POTENTIAL TO CAUSE A MAJOR DIPLOMATIC INCIDENT. ARE YOU CERTAIN YOU--
DID I STUTTER? NOW, IS OH-ONE-ONE MARGARET, OR IS OH-ONE-ONE--
UH, WHATCHA DOING THERE, MARGARET?
WHAT DO YOU THINK I'M DOING, CANDACE? I'M CALLING IN AN AIRSTRIKE.
AFTER ALL, I'M WIZORD AND RUBY STITCH'S DAUGHTER, RIGHT? ISN'T THAT WHAT YOU TOLD ME?
THIS IS WHAT THEY WOULD DO. IF SOMEONE HURTS THEM, THEY BURN THEM TO THE GROUND.
I WAS BORN FOR THIS.
OH, MARGARET...

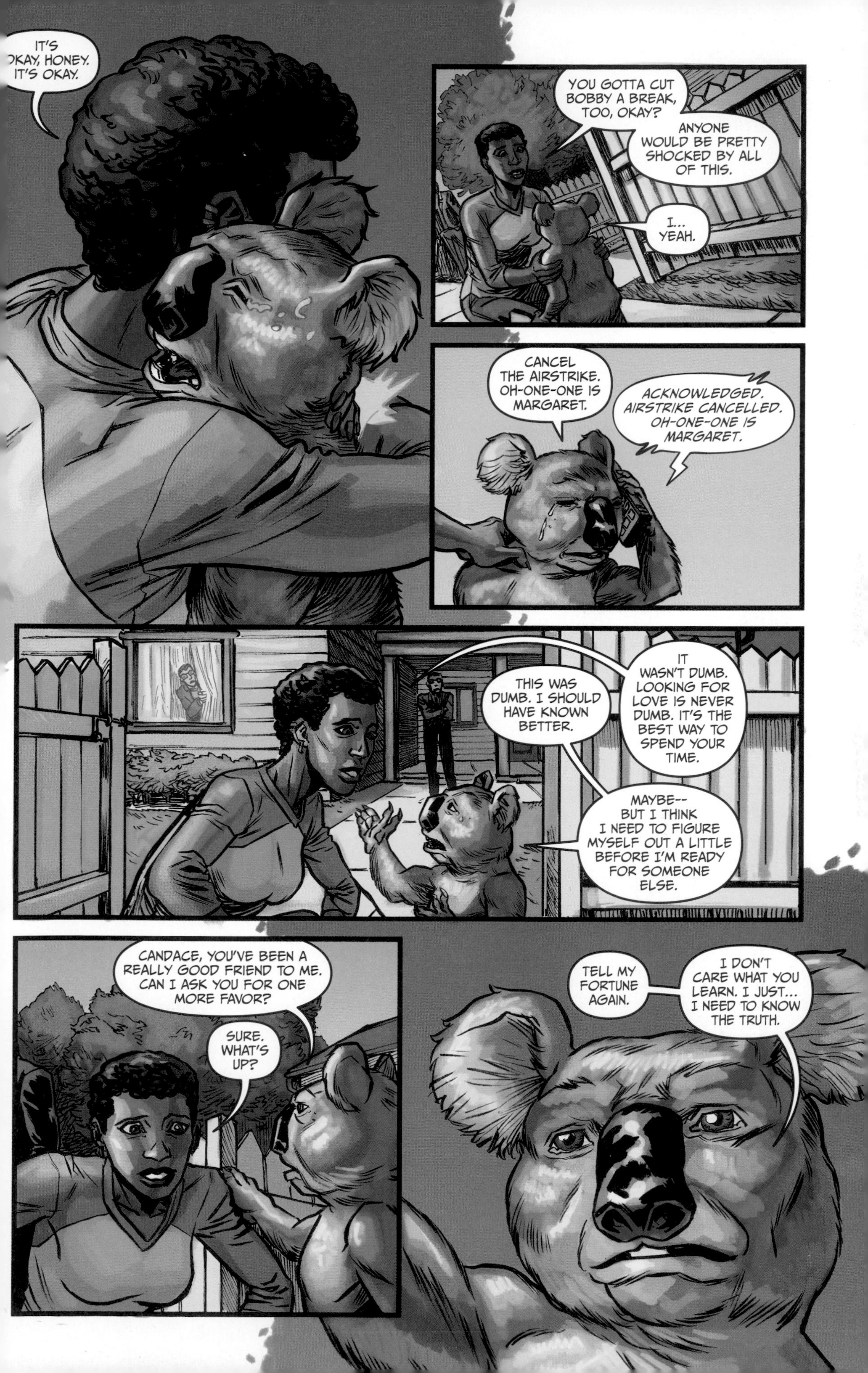
IT'S OKAY, HONEY. IT'S OKAY.
YOU GOTTA CUT BOBBY A BREAK, TOO, OKAY?
ANYONE WOULD BE PRETTY SHOCKED BY ALL OF THIS.
I... YEAH.
CANCEL THE AIRSTRIKE. OH-ONE-ONE IS MARGARET.
ACKNOWLEDGED. AIRSTRIKE CANCELLED. OH-ONE-ONE IS MARGARET.
THIS WAS DUMB. I SHOULD HAVE KNOWN BETTER.
IT WASN'T DUMB. LOOKING FOR LOVE IS NEVER DUMB. IT'S THE BEST WAY TO SPEND YOUR TIME.
MAYBE-- BUT I THINK I NEED TO FIGURE MYSELF OUT A LITTLE BEFORE I'M READY FOR SOMEONE ELSE.
CANDACE, YOU'VE BEEN A REALLY GOOD FRIEND TO ME. CAN I ASK YOU FOR ONE MORE FAVOR?
SURE. WHAT'S UP?
TELL MY FORTUNE AGAIN.
I DON'T CARE WHAT YOU LEARN. I JUST... I NEED TO KNOW THE TRUTH.

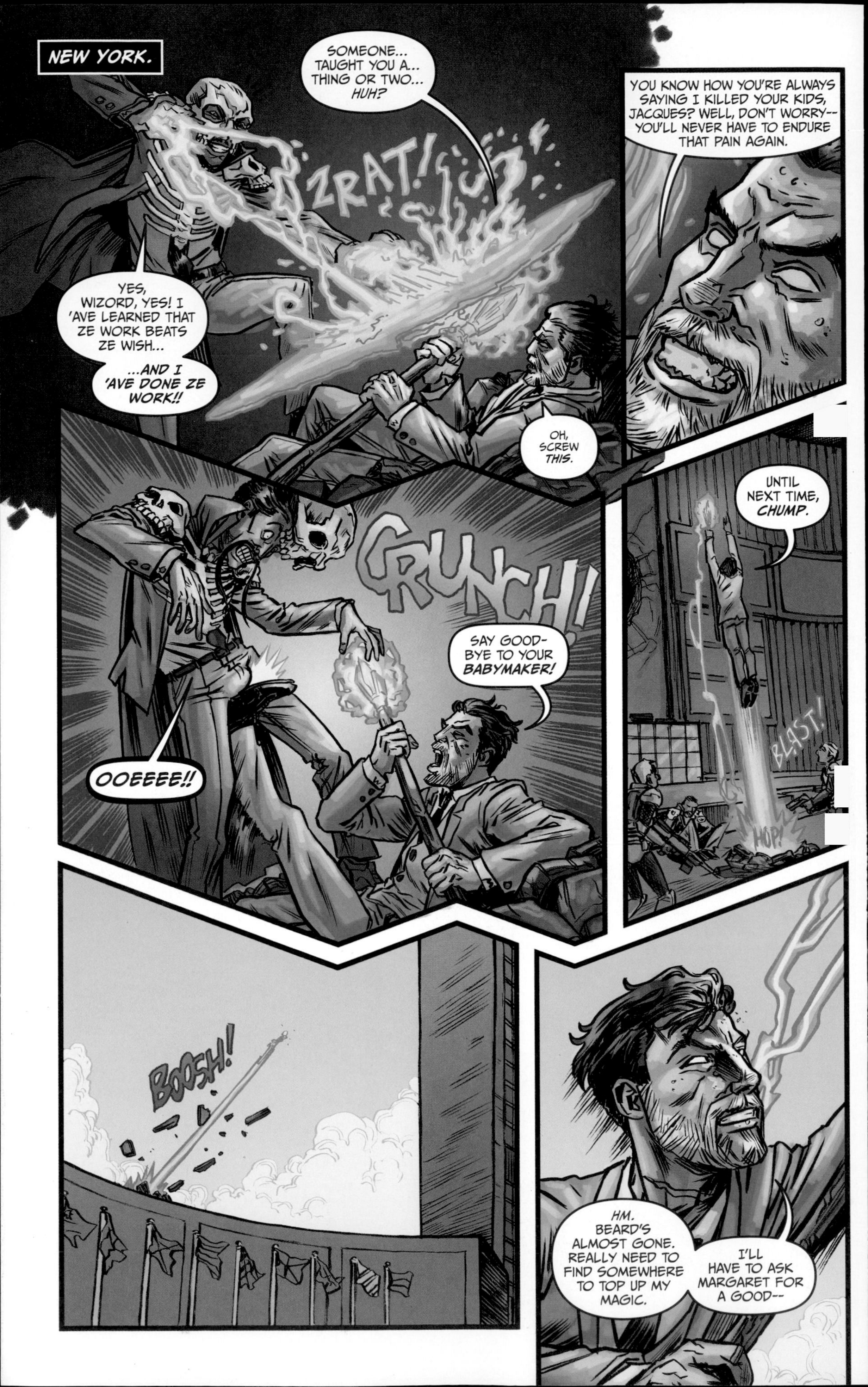
NEW YORK.
SOMEONE... TAUGHT YOU A... THING OR TWO... HUH?
ZRAT!
YES, WIZORD, YES! I 'AVE LEARNED THAT ZE WORK BEATS ZE WISH...
...AND I 'AVE DONE ZE WORK!!
OH, SCREW THIS.
YOU KNOW HOW YOU'RE ALWAYS SAYING I KILLED YOUR KIDS, JACQUES? WELL, DON'T WORRY-- YOU'LL NEVER HAVE TO ENDURE THAT PAIN AGAIN.
CRUNCH!
SAY GOOD-BYE TO YOUR BABYMAKER!
OOEEEEE!!
UNTIL NEXT TIME, CHUMP.
BLAST!
HOP!
BOOSH!
HM. BEARD'S ALMOST GONE. REALLY NEED TO FIND SOMEWHERE TO TOP UP MY MAGIC.
I'LL HAVE TO ASK MARGARET FOR A GOOD--

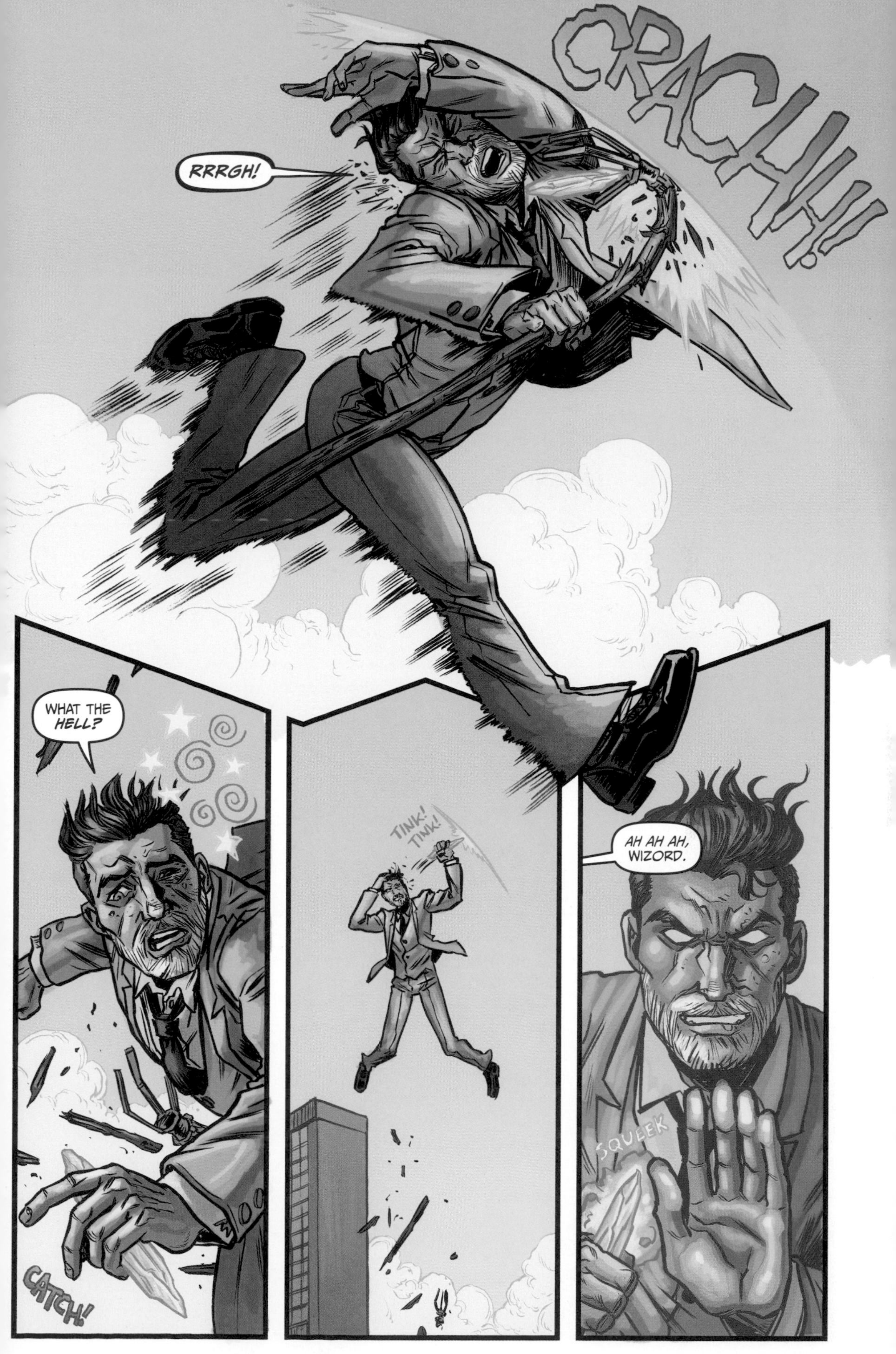
CRACHH!!
RRRGH!
WHAT THE HELL?
CATCH!
TINK! TINK!
AH AH AH, WIZORD.
SQUEEK

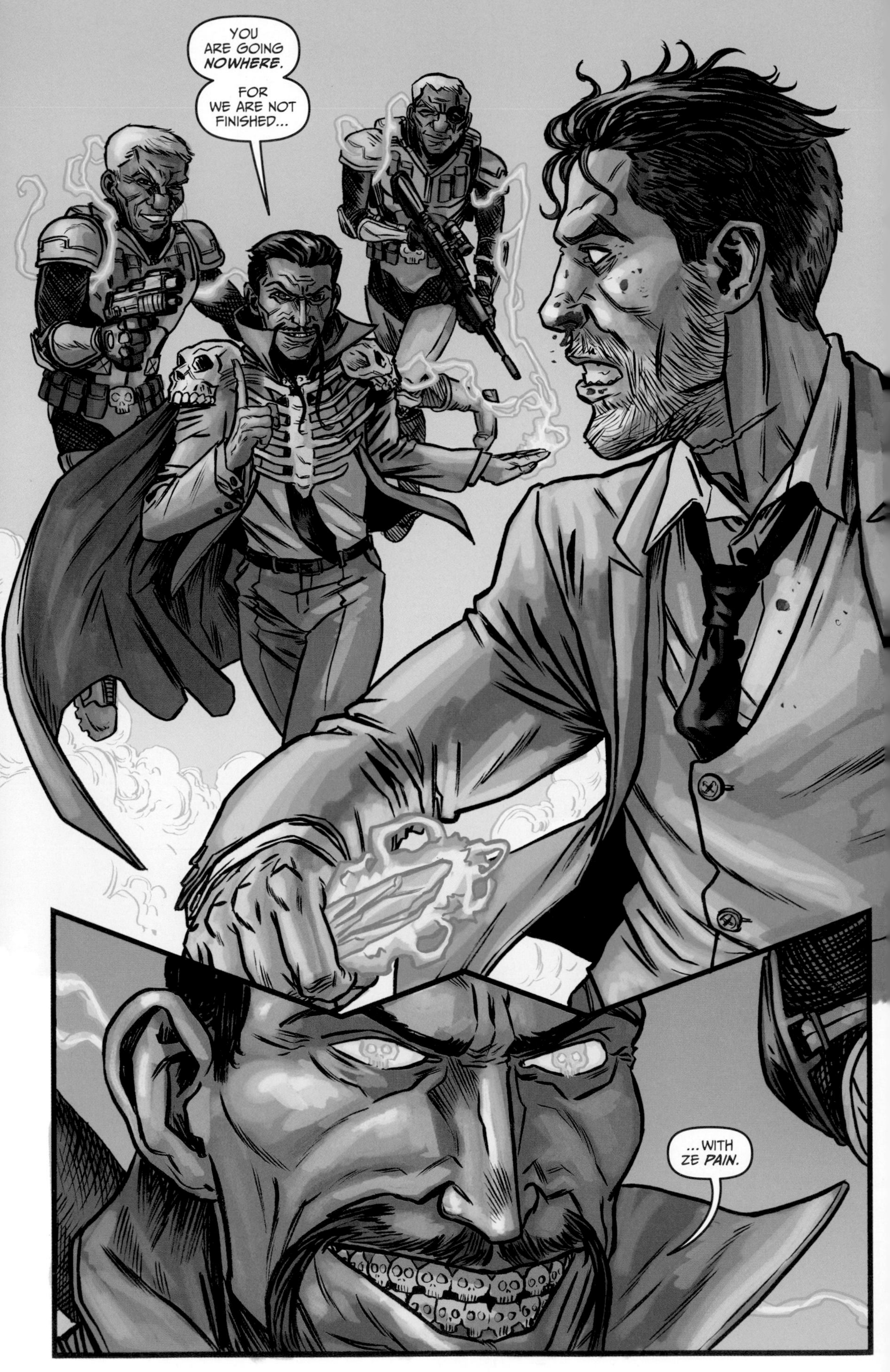
YOU ARE GOING NOWHERE.
FOR WE ARE NOT FINISHED...
...WITH ZE PAIN.

TWENTY

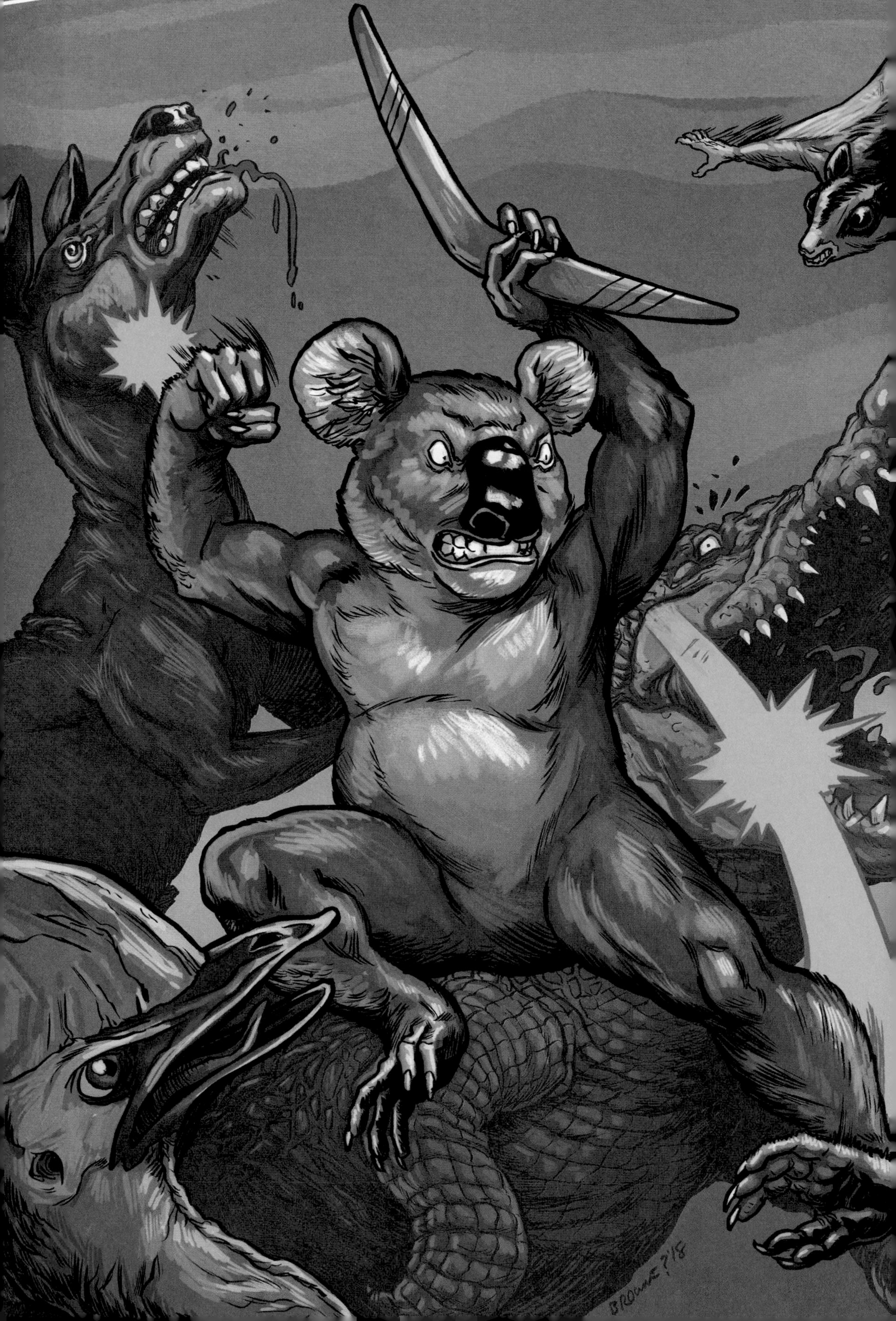

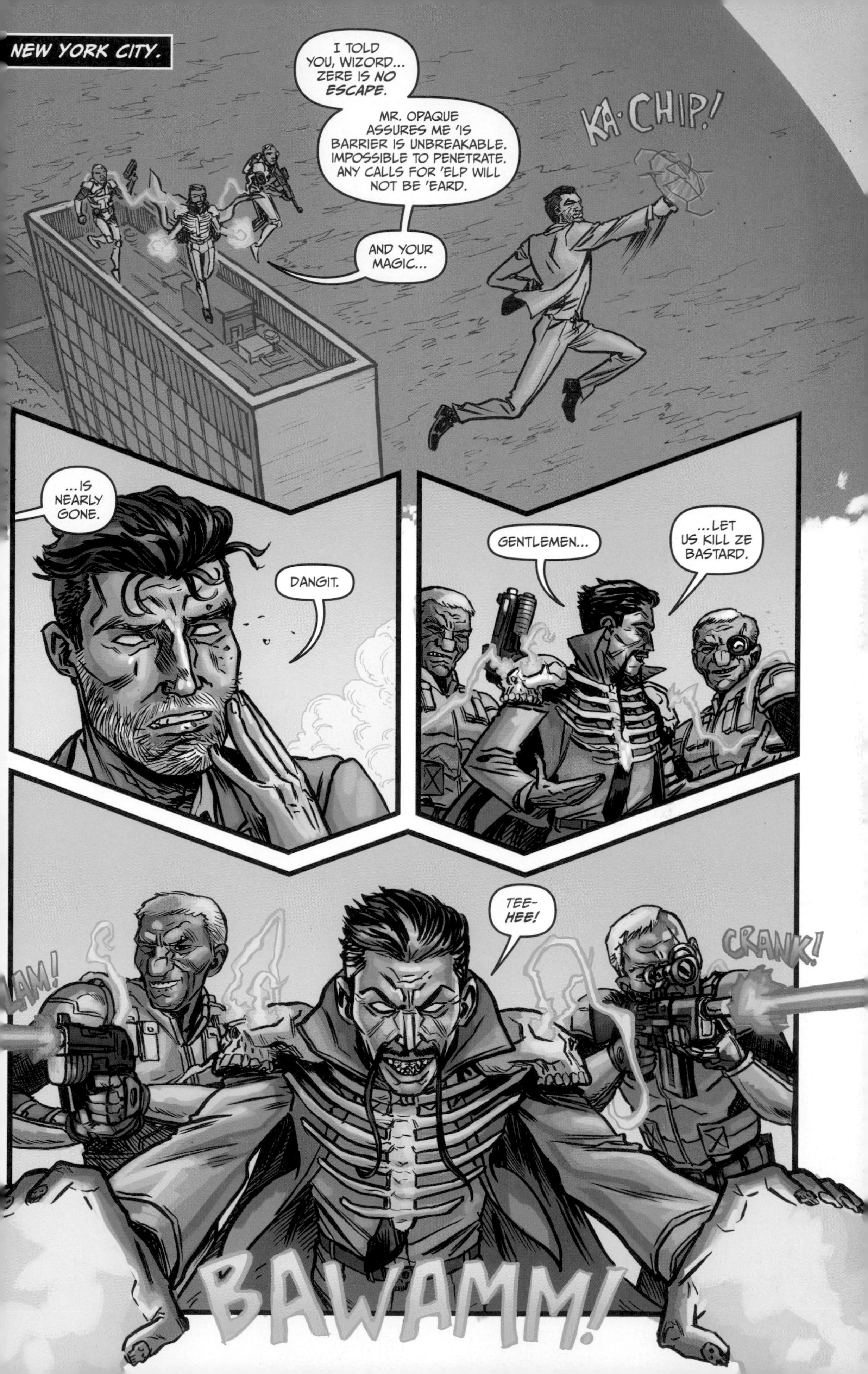
NEW YORK CITY.
I TOLD YOU, WIZORD... ZERE IS NO ESCAPE.
MR. OPAQUE ASSURES ME 'IS BARRIER IS UNBREAKABLE. IMPOSSIBLE TO PENETRATE. ANY CALLS FOR 'ELP WILL NOT BE 'EARD.
AND YOUR MAGIC...
KA-CHIP!
...IS NEARLY GONE.
DANGIT.
GENTLEMEN...
...LET US KILL ZE BASTARD.
TEE-HEE!
CRANK!
BAWAMM!

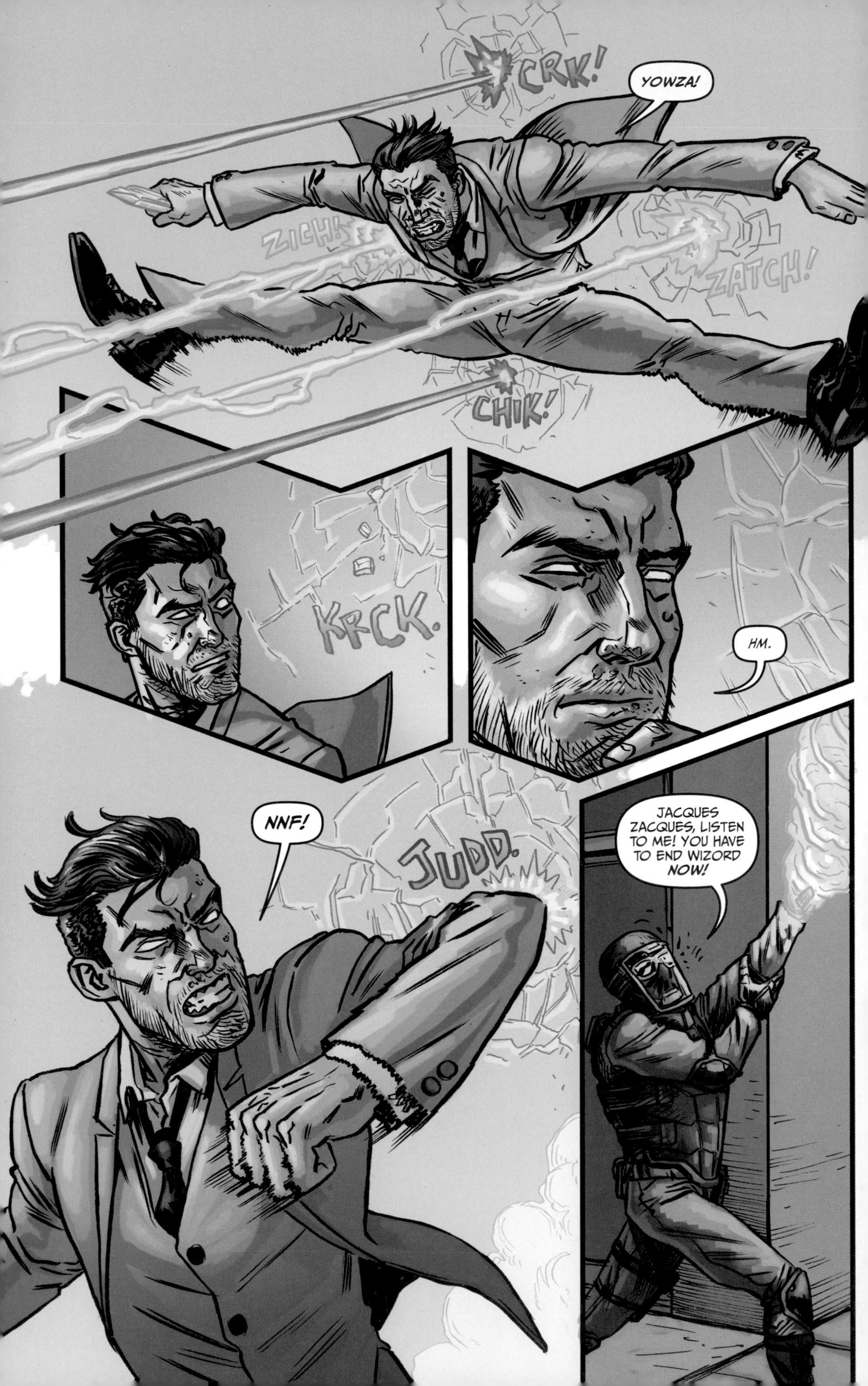
CRK!
YOWZA!
ZICH!
ZATCH!
CHIK!
KRCK.
HM.
NNF!
JUDD.
JACQUES ZACQUES, LISTEN TO ME! YOU HAVE TO END WIZORD NOW!

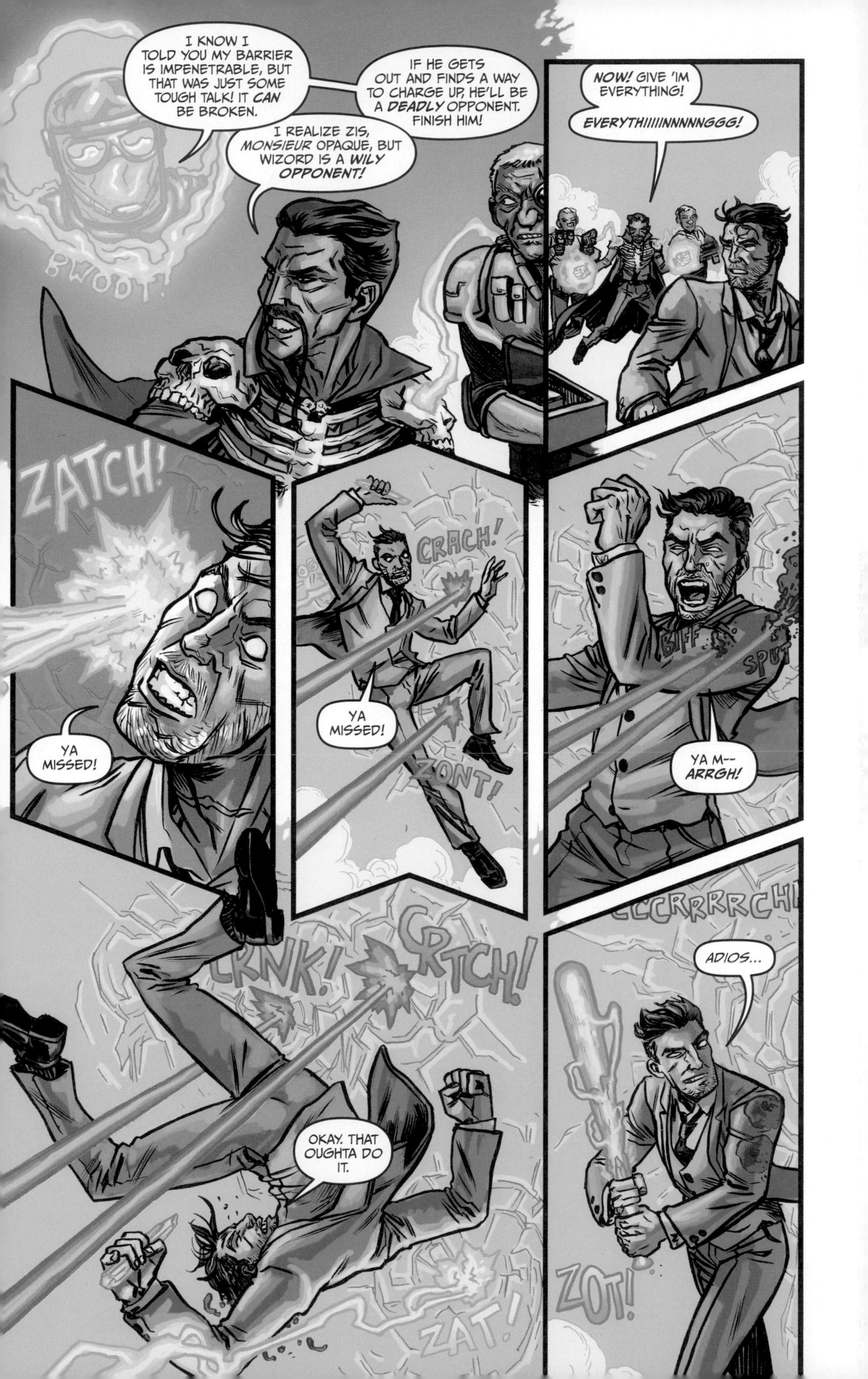
I KNOW I TOLD YOU MY BARRIER IS IMPENETRABLE, BUT THAT WAS JUST SOME TOUGH TALK! IT *CAN* BE BROKEN.
BWOOT!
I REALIZE ZIS, *MONSIEUR* OPAQUE, BUT WIZORD IS A *WILY OPPONENT!*
IF HE GETS OUT AND FINDS A WAY TO CHARGE UP, HE'LL BE A *DEADLY* OPPONENT. FINISH HIM!
NOW! GIVE 'IM EVERYTHING!
EVERYTHIIIIINNNNNGGG!
ZATCH!
YA MISSED!
CRACH!
YA MISSED!
ZONT!
BIFF
SPUT
YA M-- *ARRGH!*
CRNK!
CRTCH!
OKAY. THAT OUGHTA DO IT.
ZAT!
ADIOS...
ZOT!

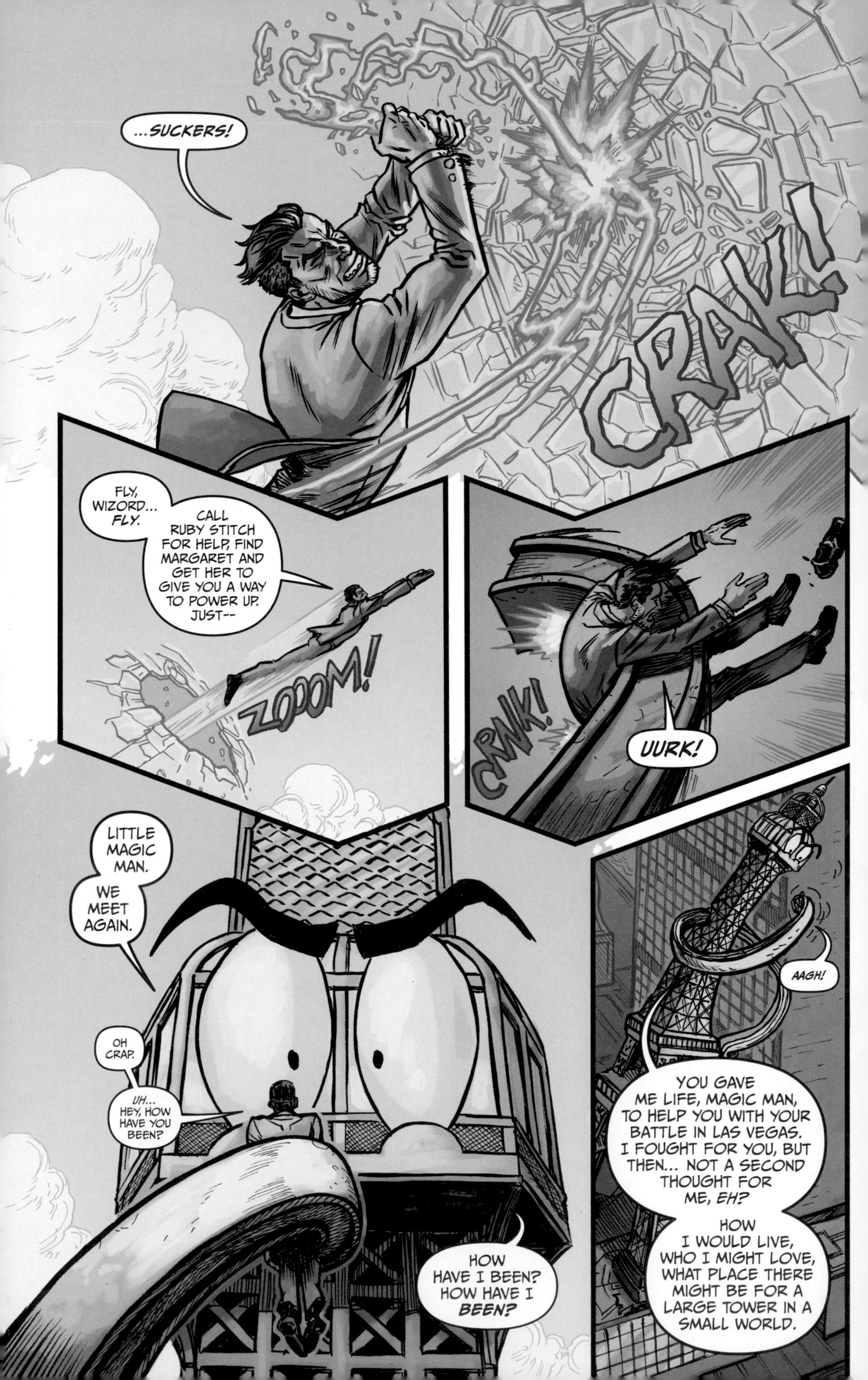
...SUCKERS!
CRAK!
FLY, WIZORD... FLY.
CALL RUBY STITCH FOR HELP, FIND MARGARET AND GET HER TO GIVE YOU A WAY TO POWER UP. JUST--
ZOOOM!
CRNK!
UURK!
LITTLE MAGIC MAN.
WE MEET AGAIN.
OH CRAP.
UH... HEY, HOW HAVE YOU BEEN?
HOW HAVE I BEEN? HOW HAVE I BEEN?
AAGH!
YOU GAVE ME LIFE, MAGIC MAN, TO HELP YOU WITH YOUR BATTLE IN LAS VEGAS. I FOUGHT FOR YOU, BUT THEN... NOT A SECOND THOUGHT FOR ME, EH?
HOW I WOULD LIVE, WHO I MIGHT LOVE, WHAT PLACE THERE MIGHT BE FOR A LARGE TOWER IN A SMALL WORLD.

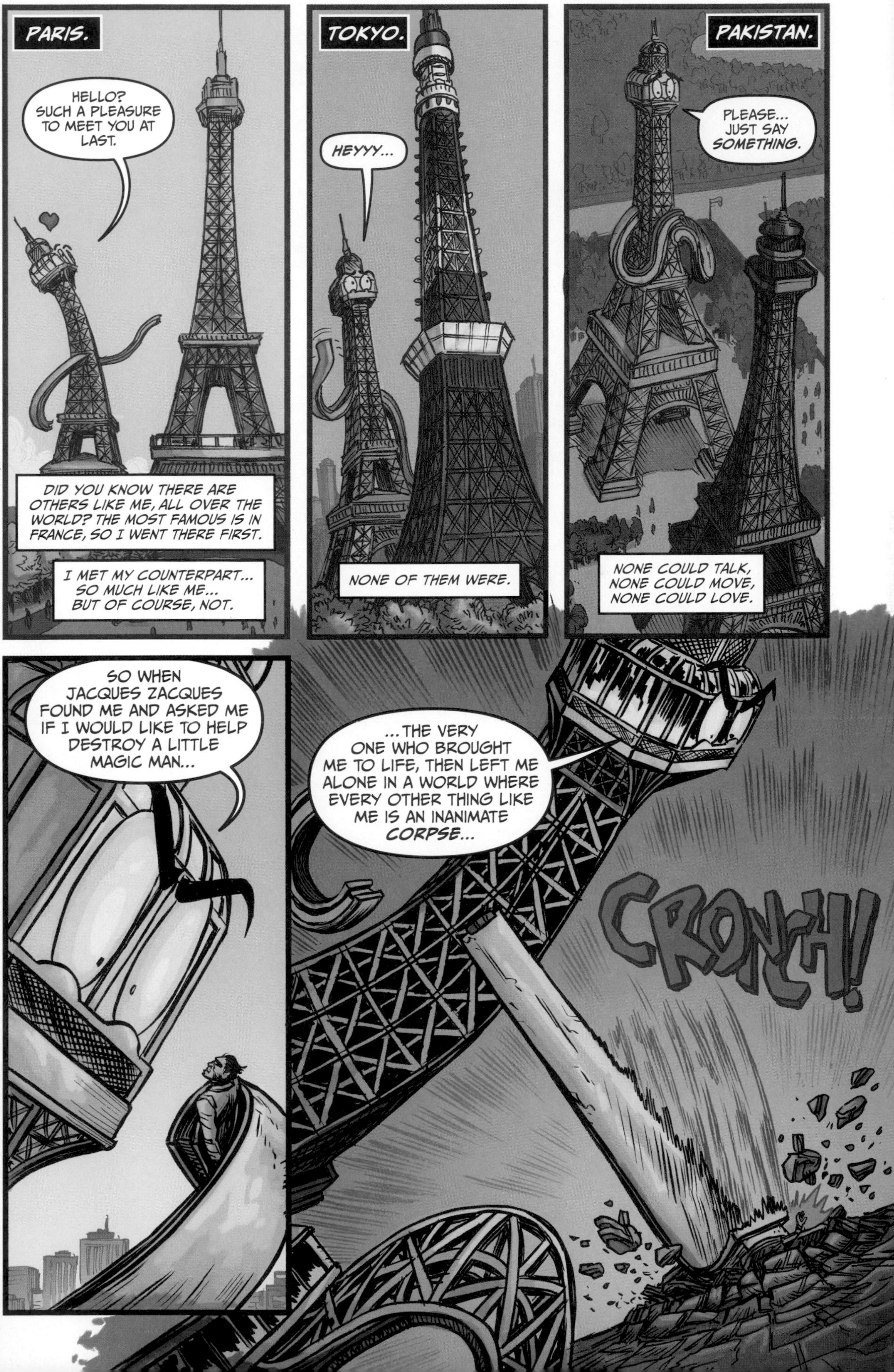
PARIS.
HELLO? SUCH A PLEASURE TO MEET YOU AT LAST.
DID YOU KNOW THERE ARE OTHERS LIKE ME, ALL OVER THE WORLD? THE MOST FAMOUS IS IN FRANCE, SO I WENT THERE FIRST.
I MET MY COUNTERPART... SO MUCH LIKE ME... BUT OF COURSE, NOT.
TOKYO.
HEYYY...
NONE OF THEM WERE.
PAKISTAN.
PLEASE... JUST SAY SOMETHING.
NONE COULD TALK, NONE COULD MOVE, NONE COULD LOVE.
SO WHEN JACQUES ZACQUES FOUND ME AND ASKED ME IF I WOULD LIKE TO HELP DESTROY A LITTLE MAGIC MAN...
...THE VERY ONE WHO BROUGHT ME TO LIFE, THEN LEFT ME ALONE IN A WORLD WHERE EVERY OTHER THING LIKE ME IS AN INANIMATE CORPSE...
CRONCH!

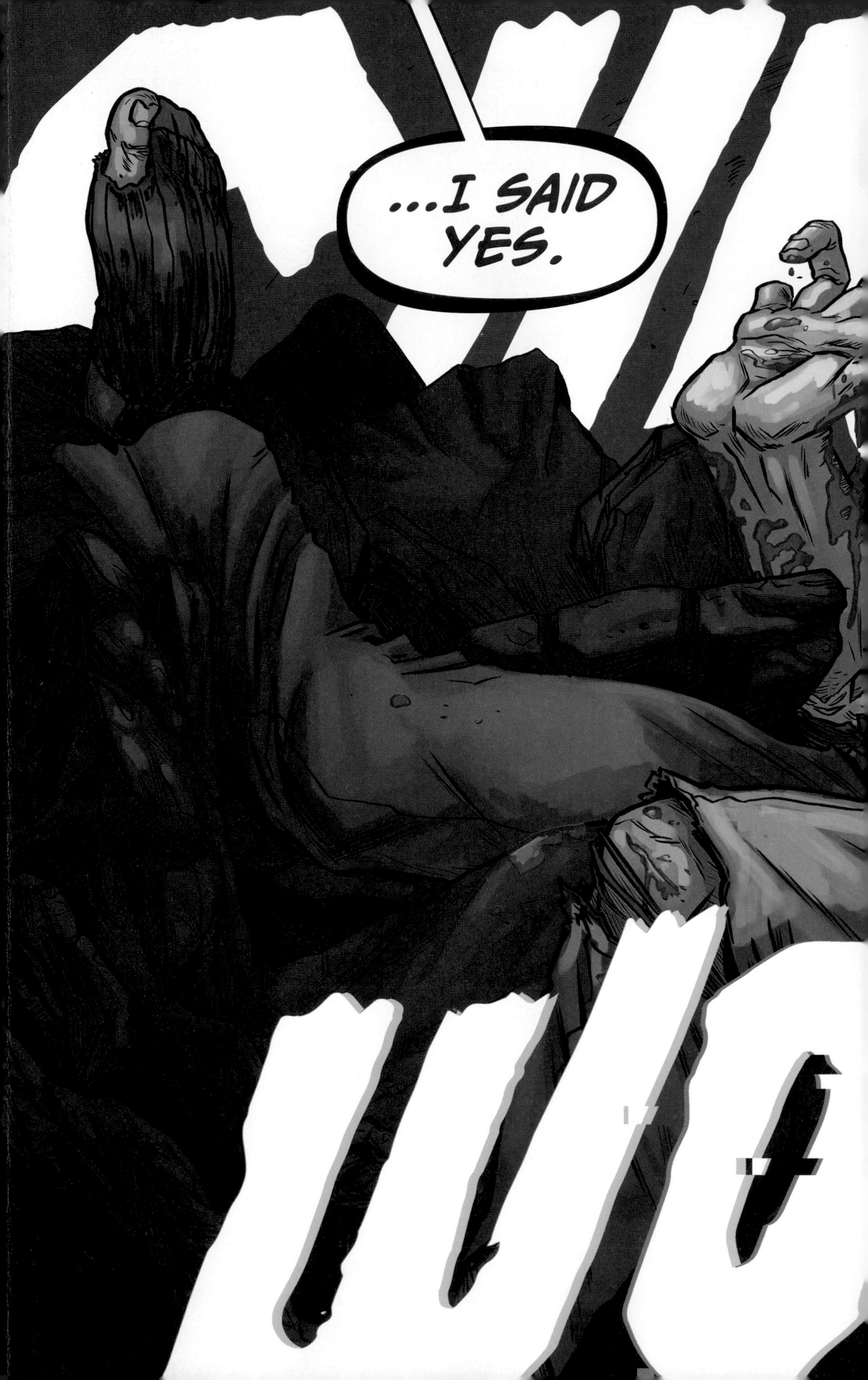
...I SAID YES.

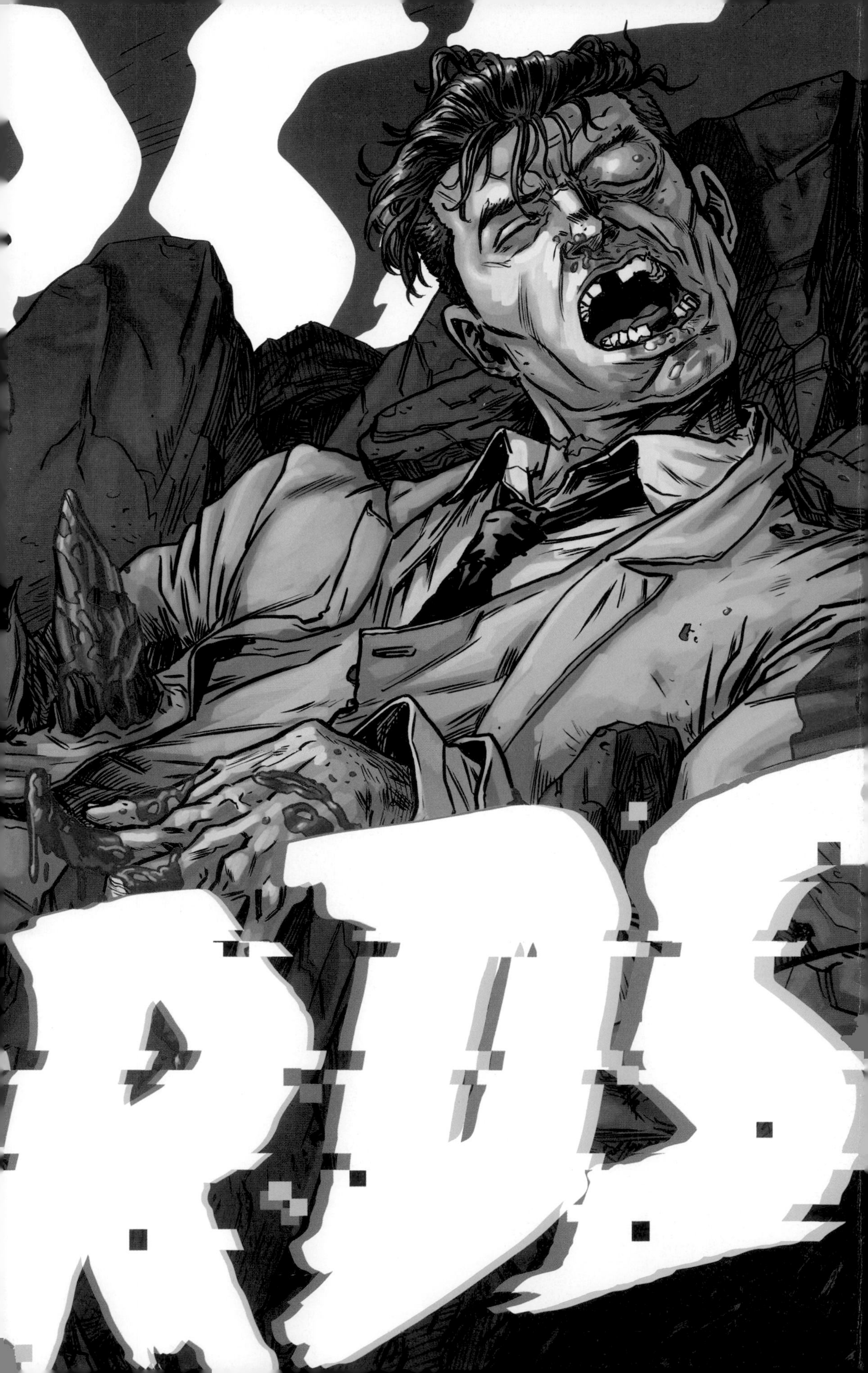

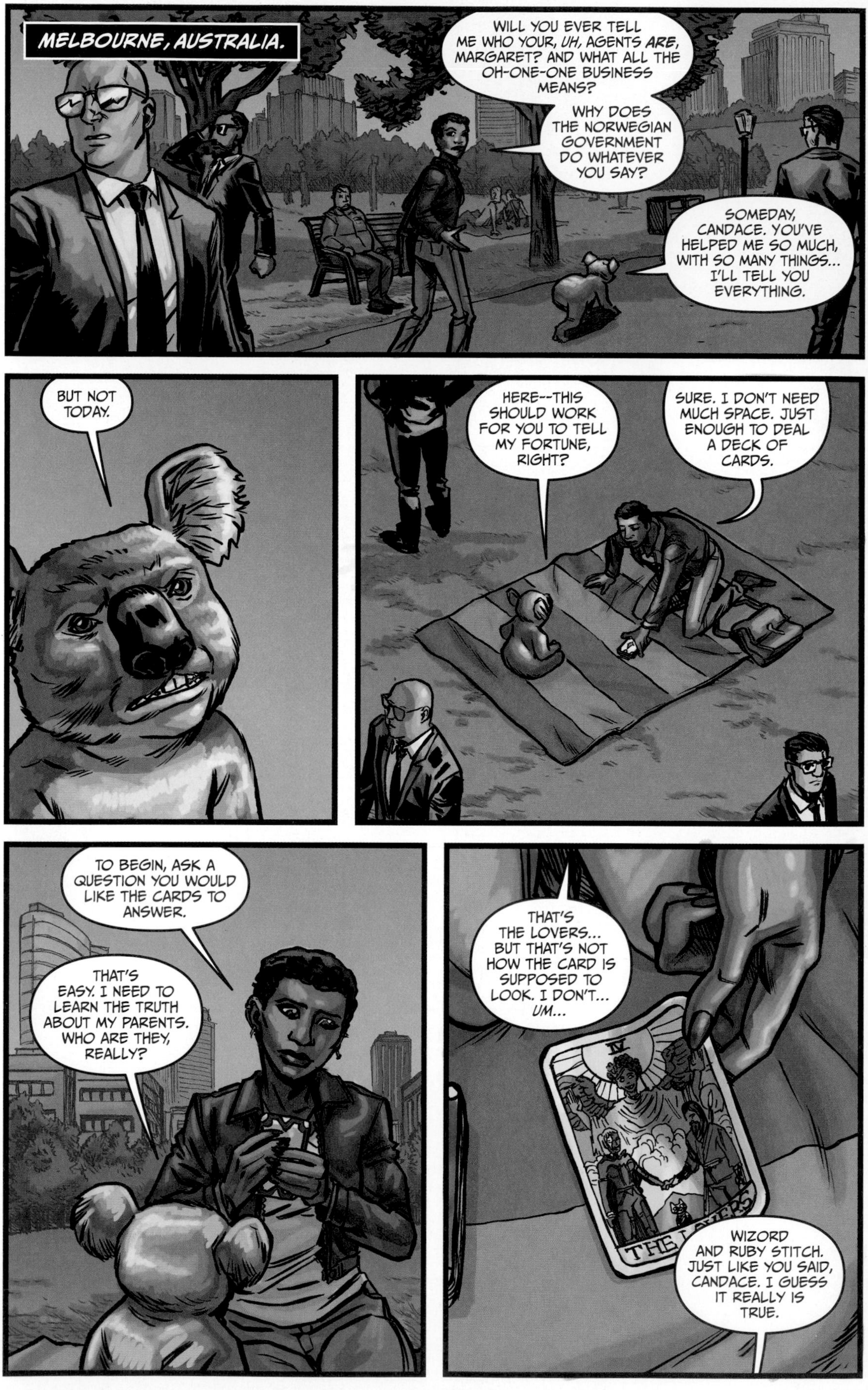

MELBOURNE, AUSTRALIA.
WILL YOU EVER TELL ME WHO YOUR, *UH*, AGENTS *ARE*, MARGARET? AND WHAT ALL THE OH-ONE-ONE BUSINESS MEANS?
WHY DOES THE NORWEGIAN GOVERNMENT DO WHATEVER YOU SAY?
SOMEDAY, CANDACE. YOU'VE HELPED ME SO MUCH, WITH SO MANY THINGS... I'LL TELL YOU EVERYTHING.
BUT NOT TODAY.
HERE--THIS SHOULD WORK FOR YOU TO TELL MY FORTUNE, RIGHT?
SURE. I DON'T NEED MUCH SPACE. JUST ENOUGH TO DEAL A DECK OF CARDS.
TO BEGIN, ASK A QUESTION YOU WOULD LIKE THE CARDS TO ANSWER.
THAT'S EASY. I NEED TO LEARN THE TRUTH ABOUT MY PARENTS. WHO ARE THEY, REALLY?
THAT'S THE LOVERS... BUT THAT'S NOT HOW THE CARD IS SUPPOSED TO LOOK. I DON'T... *UM*...
THE LOVERS
WIZORD AND RUBY STITCH. JUST LIKE YOU SAID, CANDACE. I GUESS IT REALLY IS TRUE.

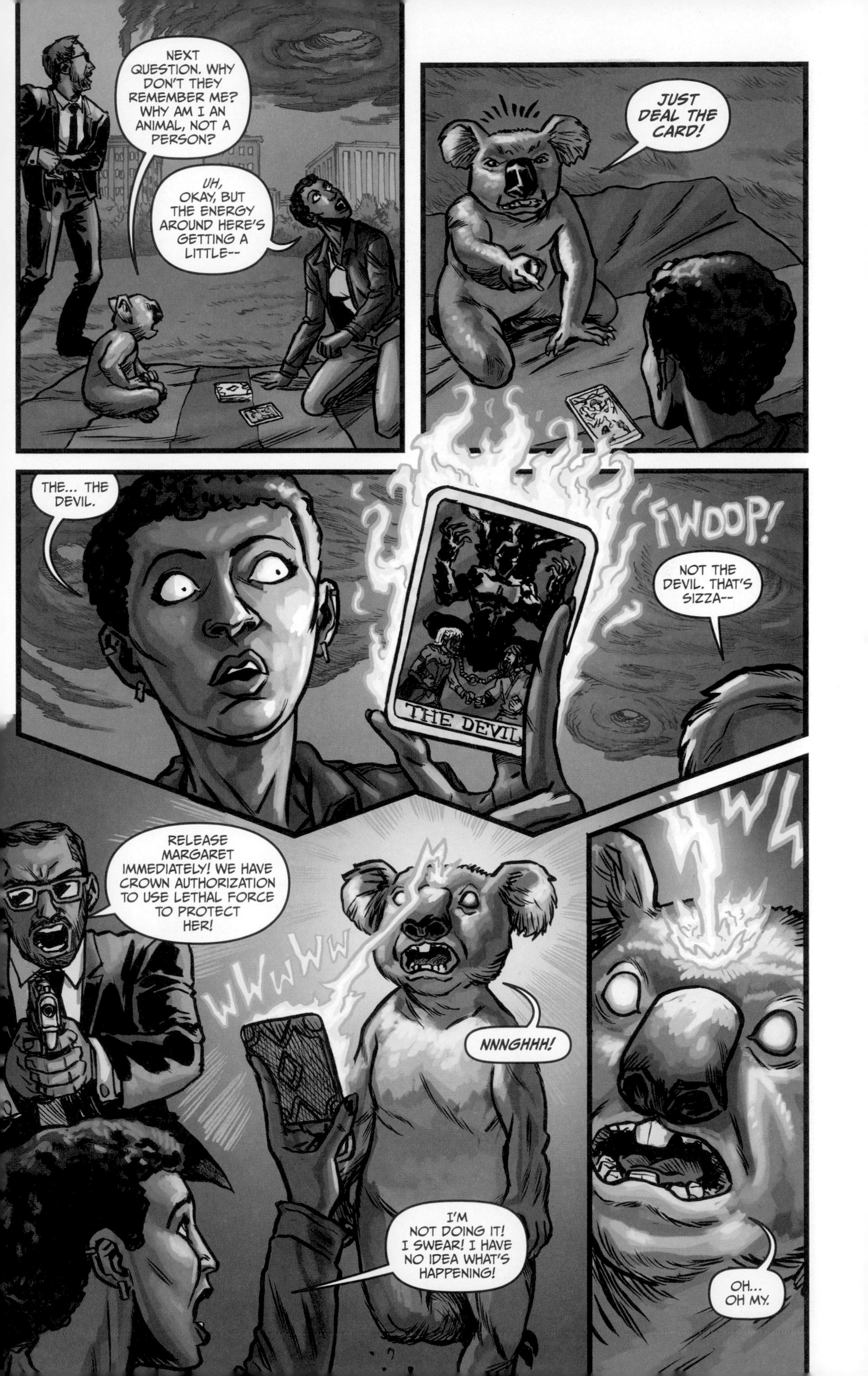

NEXT QUESTION. WHY DON'T THEY REMEMBER ME? WHY AM I AN ANIMAL, NOT A PERSON?
UH, OKAY, BUT THE ENERGY AROUND HERE'S GETTING A LITTLE--
JUST DEAL THE CARD!
THE... THE DEVIL.
THE DEVIL
FWOOP!
NOT THE DEVIL. THAT'S SIZZA--
RELEASE MARGARET IMMEDIATELY! WE HAVE CROWN AUTHORIZATION TO USE LETHAL FORCE TO PROTECT HER!
WWWWWW
NNNGHHH!
I'M NOT DOING IT! I SWEAR! I HAVE NO IDEA WHAT'S HAPPENING!
OH... OH MY.

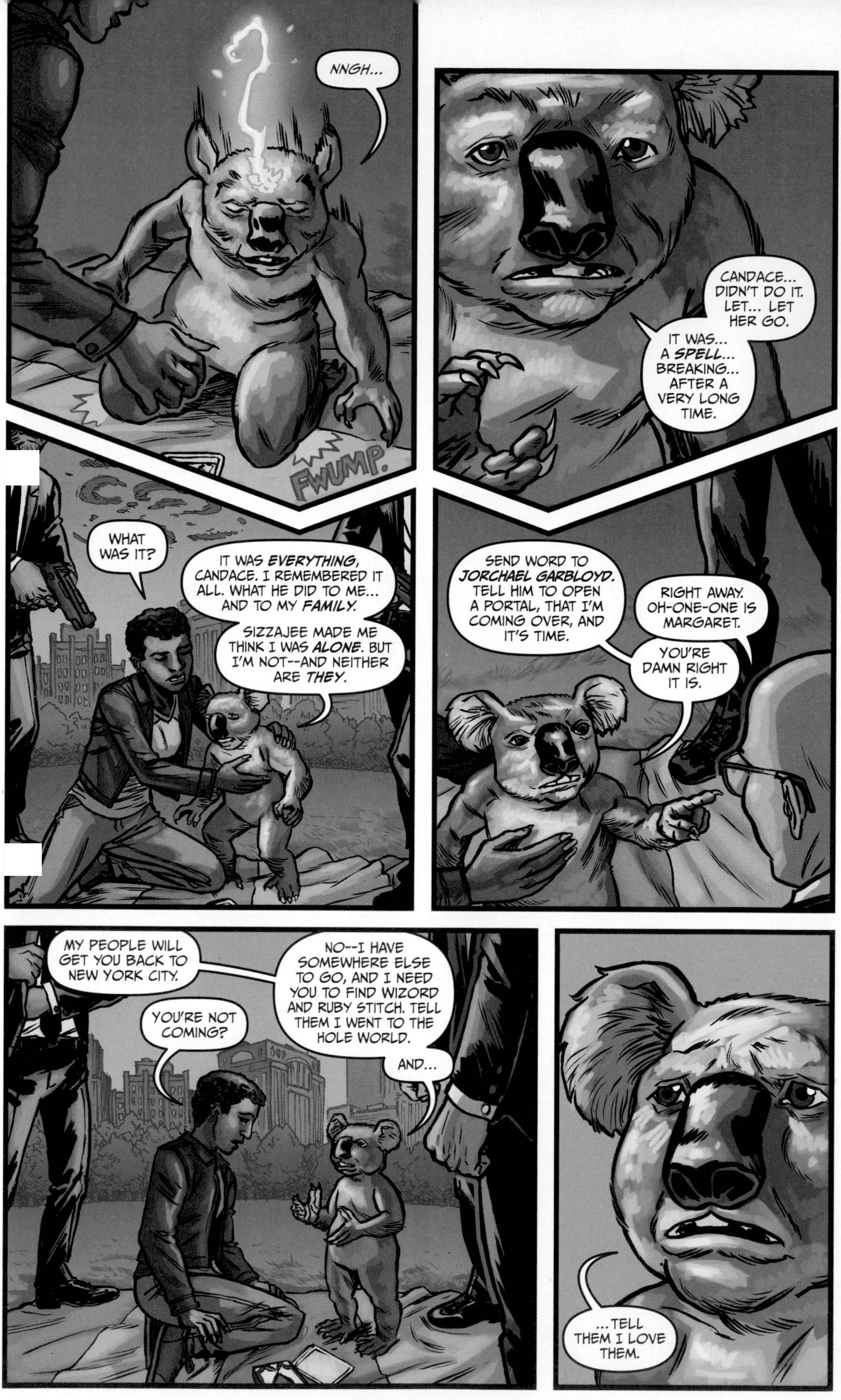
NNGH...
FWUMP.
CANDACE... DIDN'T DO IT. LET... LET HER GO.
IT WAS... A SPELL... BREAKING... AFTER A VERY LONG TIME.
WHAT WAS IT?
IT WAS EVERYTHING, CANDACE. I REMEMBERED IT ALL. WHAT HE DID TO ME... AND TO MY FAMILY.
SIZZAJEE MADE ME THINK I WAS ALONE. BUT I'M NOT--AND NEITHER ARE THEY.
SEND WORD TO JORCHAEL GARBLOYD. TELL HIM TO OPEN A PORTAL, THAT I'M COMING OVER, AND IT'S TIME.
RIGHT AWAY. OH-ONE-ONE IS MARGARET.
YOU'RE DAMN RIGHT IT IS.
MY PEOPLE WILL GET YOU BACK TO NEW YORK CITY.
YOU'RE NOT COMING?
NO--I HAVE SOMEWHERE ELSE TO GO, AND I NEED YOU TO FIND WIZORD AND RUBY STITCH. TELL THEM I WENT TO THE HOLE WORLD.
AND...
...TELL THEM I LOVE THEM.

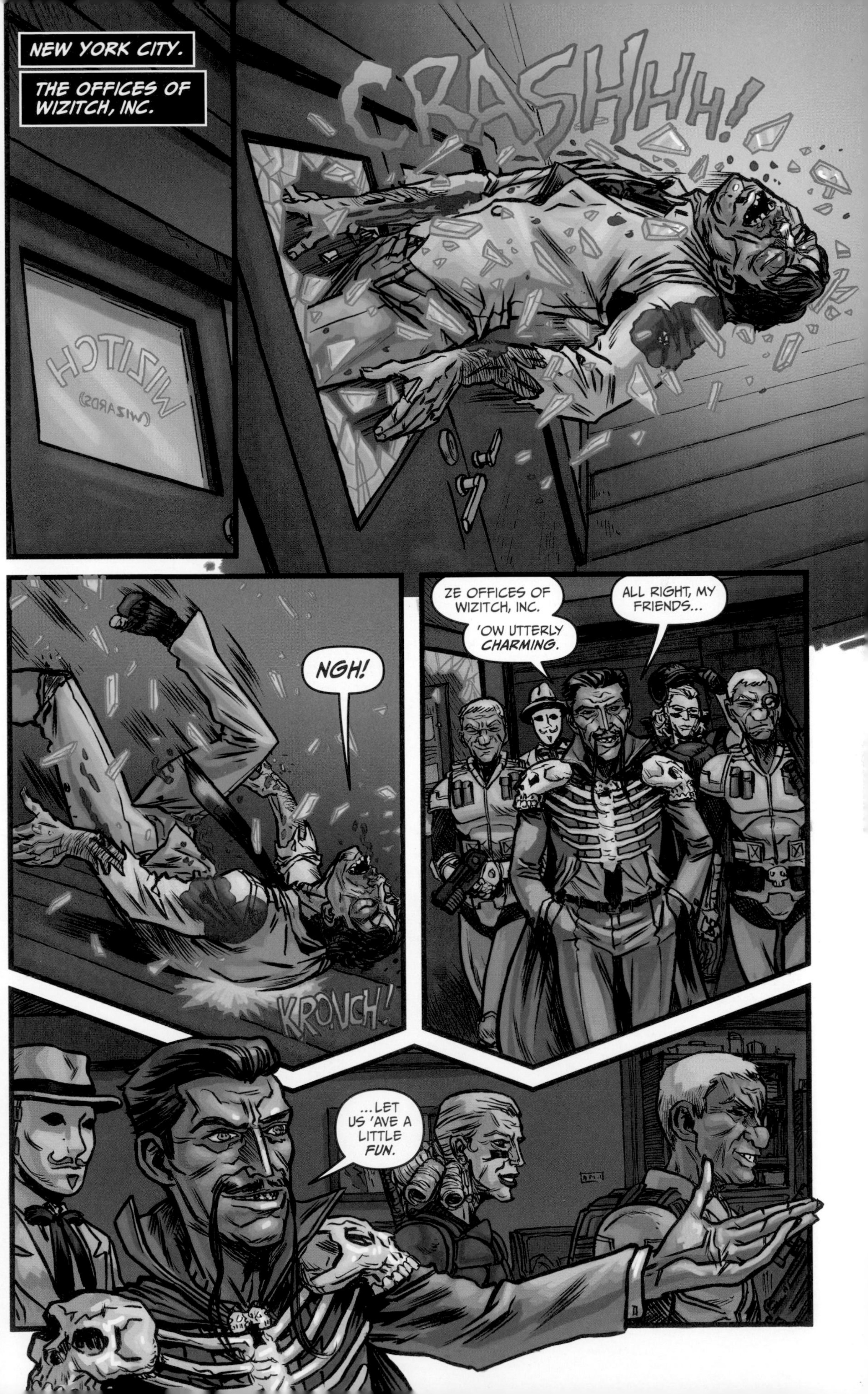
NEW YORK CITY.
THE OFFICES OF WIZITCH, INC.
CRASHHH!
WIZITCH (WIZARDS)
NGH!
KRONCH!
ZE OFFICES OF WIZITCH, INC.
'OW UTTERLY *CHARMING.*
ALL RIGHT, MY FRIENDS...
...LET US 'AVE A LITTLE *FUN.*

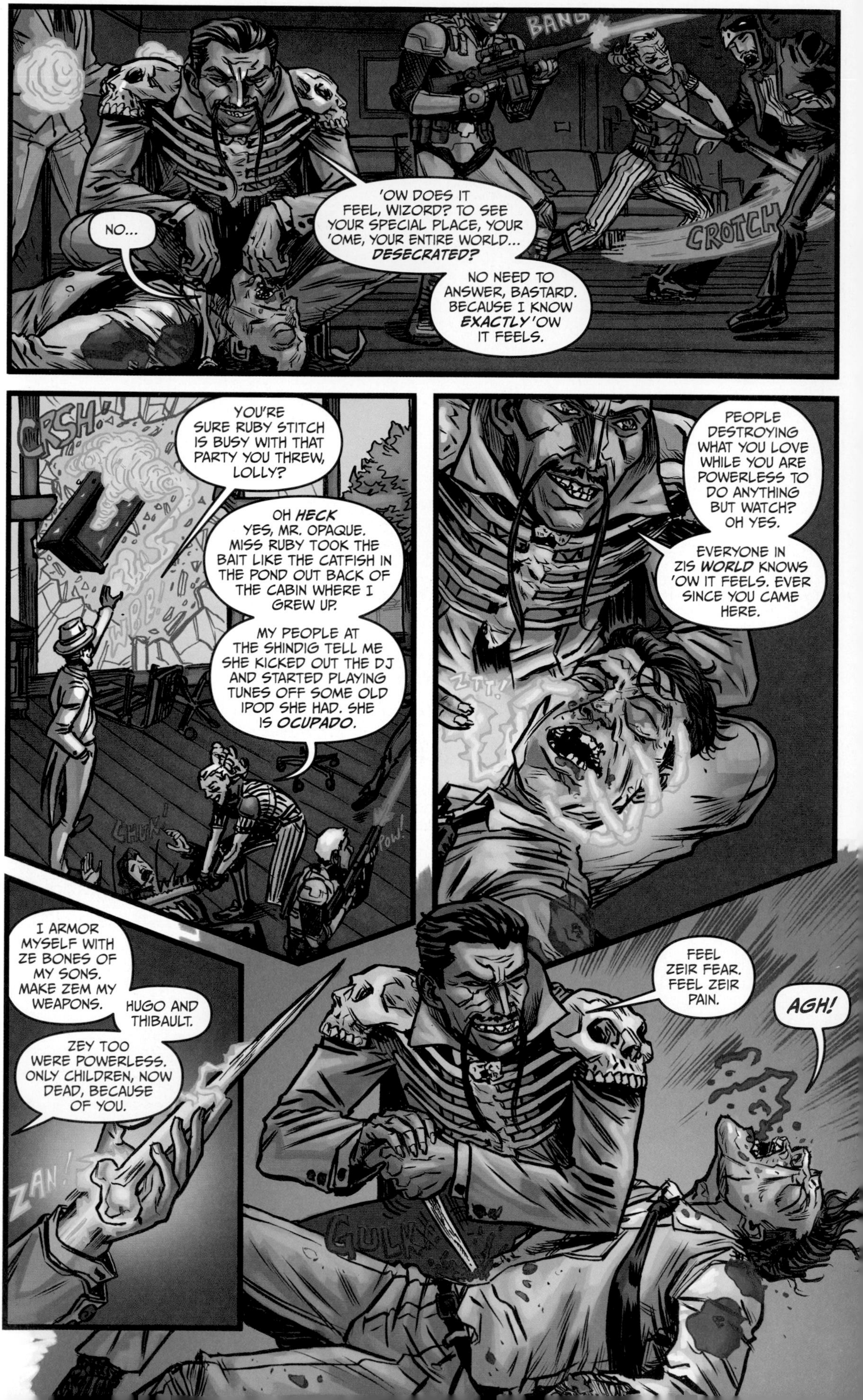
BANG
'OW DOES IT FEEL, WIZORD? TO SEE YOUR SPECIAL PLACE, YOUR 'OME, YOUR ENTIRE WORLD... DESECRATED?
NO...
NO NEED TO ANSWER, BASTARD. BECAUSE I KNOW EXACTLY 'OW IT FEELS.
CROTCH
CRSH
YOU'RE SURE RUBY STITCH IS BUSY WITH THAT PARTY YOU THREW, LOLLY?
OH HECK YES, MR. OPAQUE. MISS RUBY TOOK THE BAIT LIKE THE CATFISH IN THE POND OUT BACK OF THE CABIN WHERE I GREW UP.
MY PEOPLE AT THE SHINDIG TELL ME SHE KICKED OUT THE DJ AND STARTED PLAYING TUNES OFF SOME OLD IPOD SHE HAD. SHE IS OCUPADO.
POW!
PEOPLE DESTROYING WHAT YOU LOVE WHILE YOU ARE POWERLESS TO DO ANYTHING BUT WATCH? OH YES.
EVERYONE IN ZIS WORLD KNOWS 'OW IT FEELS. EVER SINCE YOU CAME HERE.
ZTT!
I ARMOR MYSELF WITH ZE BONES OF MY SONS. MAKE ZEM MY WEAPONS.
HUGO AND THIBAULT.
ZEY TOO WERE POWERLESS. ONLY CHILDREN, NOW DEAD, BECAUSE OF YOU.
FEEL ZEIR FEAR. FEEL ZEIR PAIN.
AGH!
ZAN!
GULK

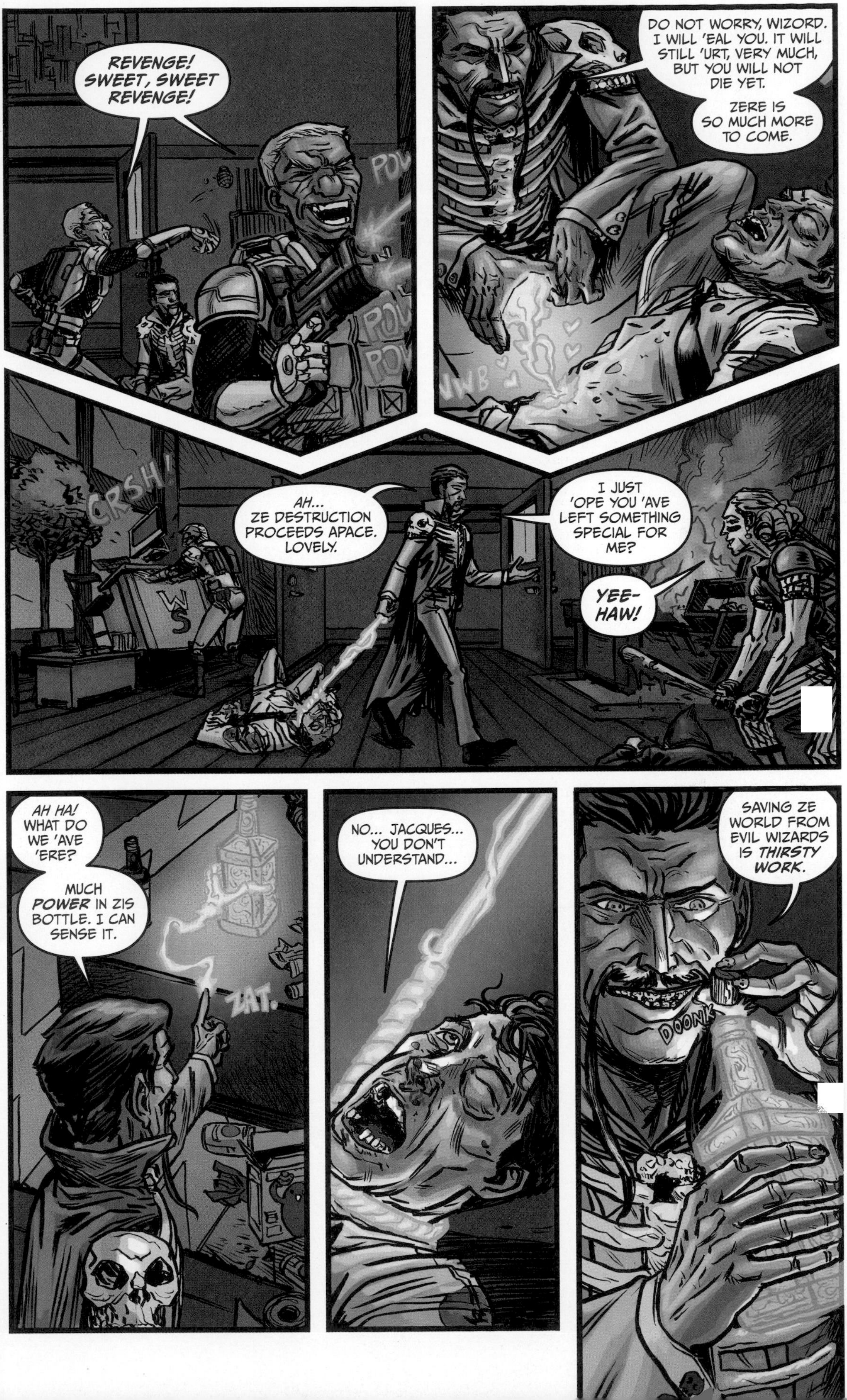
REVENGE! SWEET, SWEET REVENGE!
POW
POW
POW
DO NOT WORRY, WIZORD. I WILL 'EAL YOU. IT WILL STILL 'URT, VERY MUCH, BUT YOU WILL NOT DIE YET.
ZERE IS SO MUCH MORE TO COME.
CRSH!
AH... ZE DESTRUCTION PROCEEDS APACE. LOVELY.
I JUST 'OPE YOU 'AVE LEFT SOMETHING SPECIAL FOR ME?
YEE-HAW!
AH HA! WHAT DO WE 'AVE 'ERE?
MUCH POWER IN ZIS BOTTLE. I CAN SENSE IT.
ZAT.
NO... JACQUES... YOU DON'T UNDERSTAND...
SAVING ZE WORLD FROM EVIL WIZARDS IS THIRSTY WORK.
DOONK

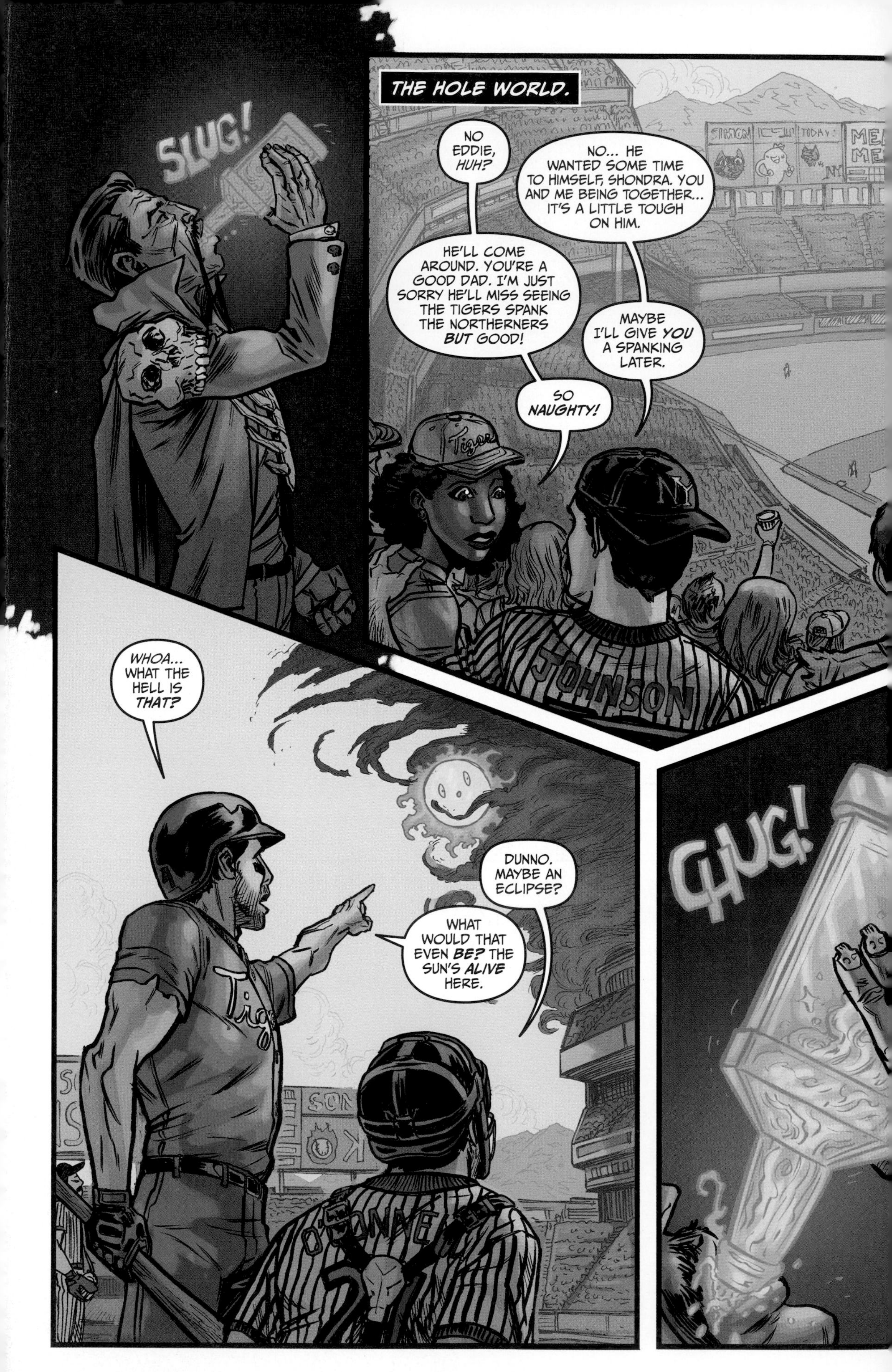
SLUG!
THE HOLE WORLD.
NO EDDIE, HUH?
NO... HE WANTED SOME TIME TO HIMSELF, SHONDRA. YOU AND ME BEING TOGETHER... IT'S A LITTLE TOUGH ON HIM.
HE'LL COME AROUND. YOU'RE A GOOD DAD. I'M JUST SORRY HE'LL MISS SEEING THE TIGERS SPANK THE NORTHERNERS BUT GOOD!
MAYBE I'LL GIVE YOU A SPANKING LATER.
SO NAUGHTY!
JOHNSON
WHOA... WHAT THE HELL IS THAT?
DUNNO. MAYBE AN ECLIPSE?
WHAT WOULD THAT EVEN BE? THE SUN'S ALIVE HERE.
GLUG!

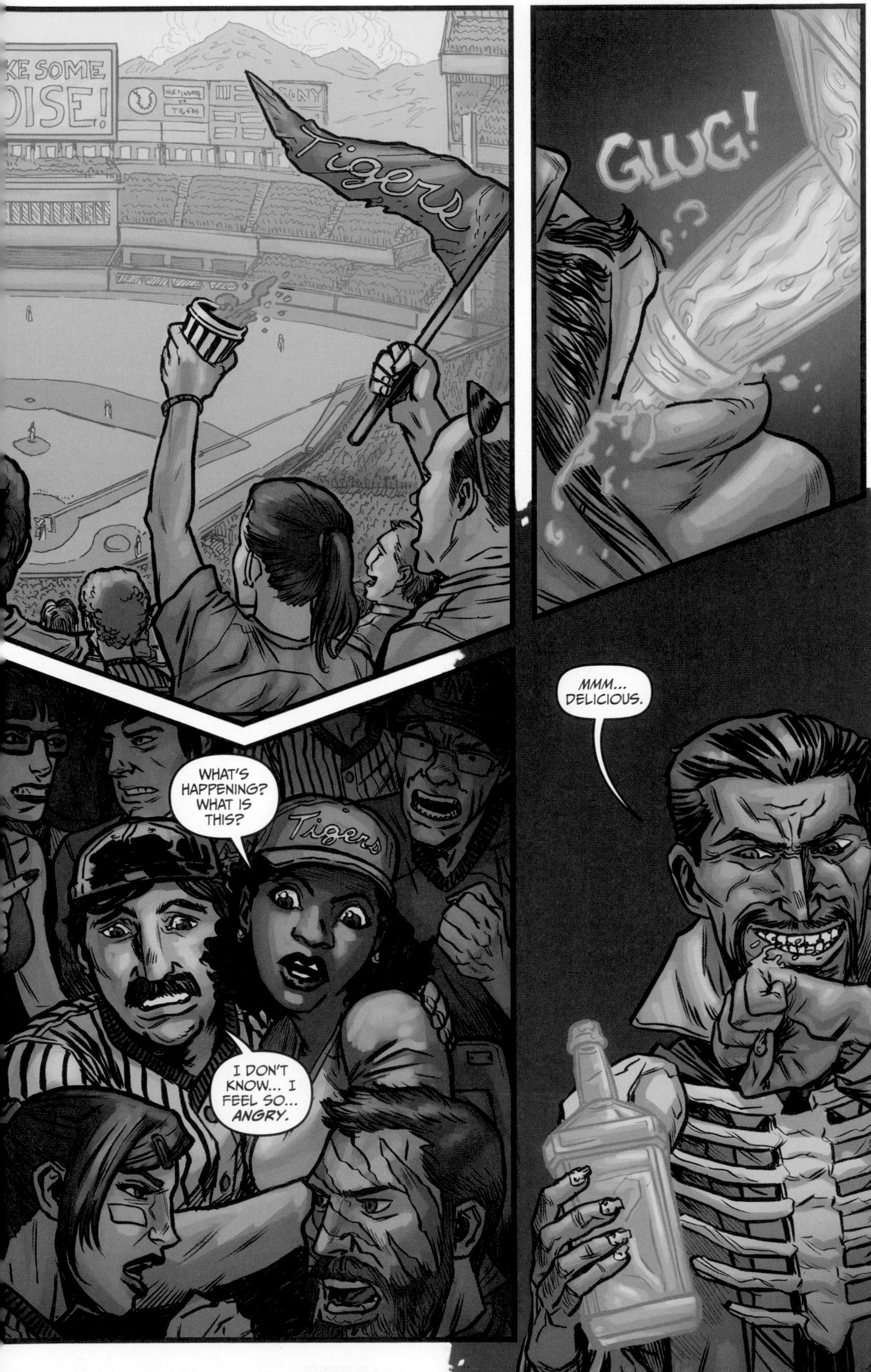
KE SOME
OISE!
Tigers
GLUG!
WHAT'S HAPPENING? WHAT IS THIS?
Tigers
I DON'T KNOW... I FEEL SO... ***ANGRY.***
MMM... DELICIOUS.

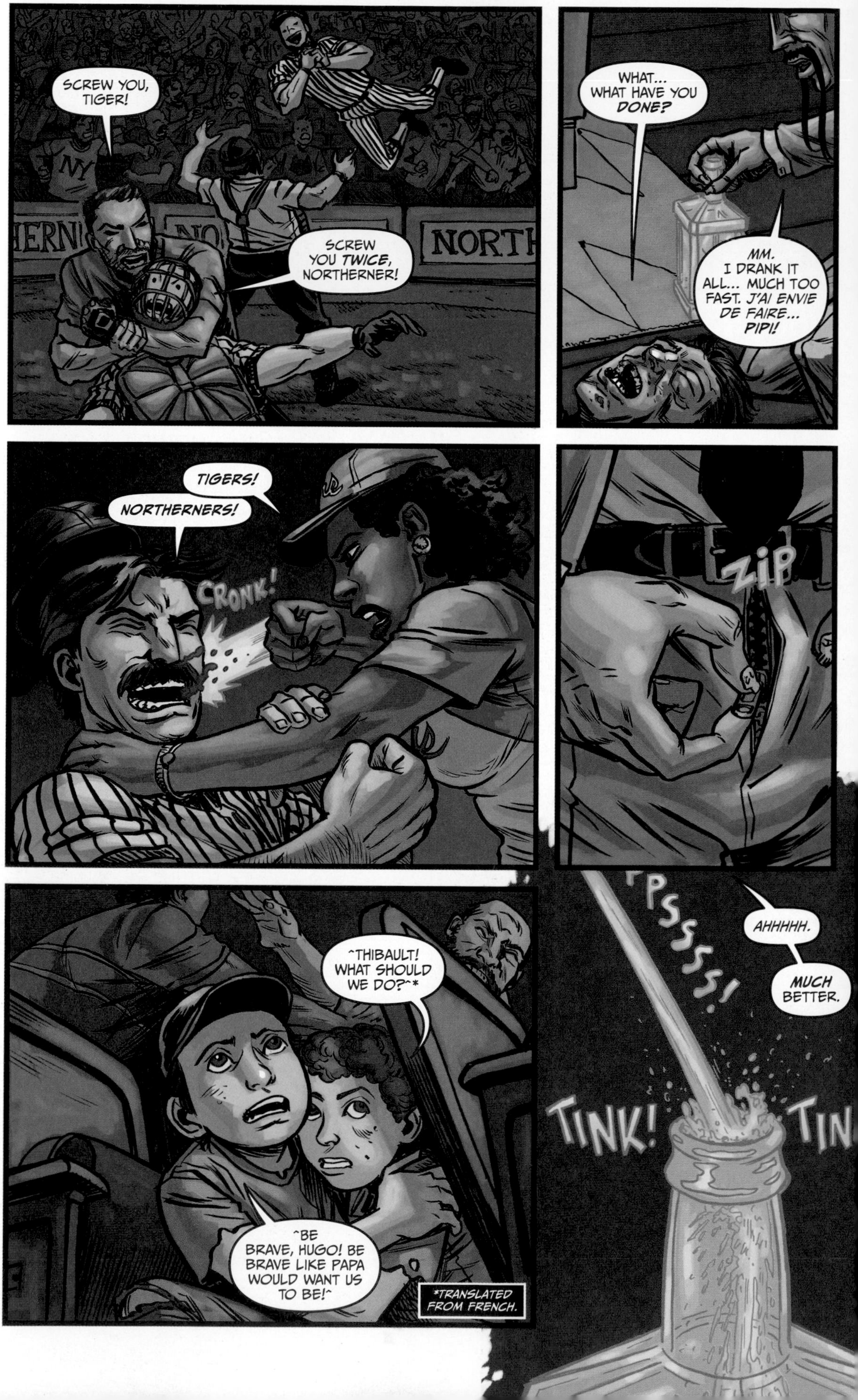
SCREW YOU, TIGER!
SCREW YOU TWICE, NORTHERNER!
WHAT... WHAT HAVE YOU DONE?
MM. I DRANK IT ALL... MUCH TOO FAST. J'AI ENVIE DE FAIRE... PIPI!
TIGERS!
NORTHERNERS!
CRONK!
ZIP
^THIBAULT! WHAT SHOULD WE DO?^*
^BE BRAVE, HUGO! BE BRAVE LIKE PAPA WOULD WANT US TO BE!^
*TRANSLATED FROM FRENCH.
PSSSSS!
AHHHHH.
MUCH BETTER.
TINK!
TIN

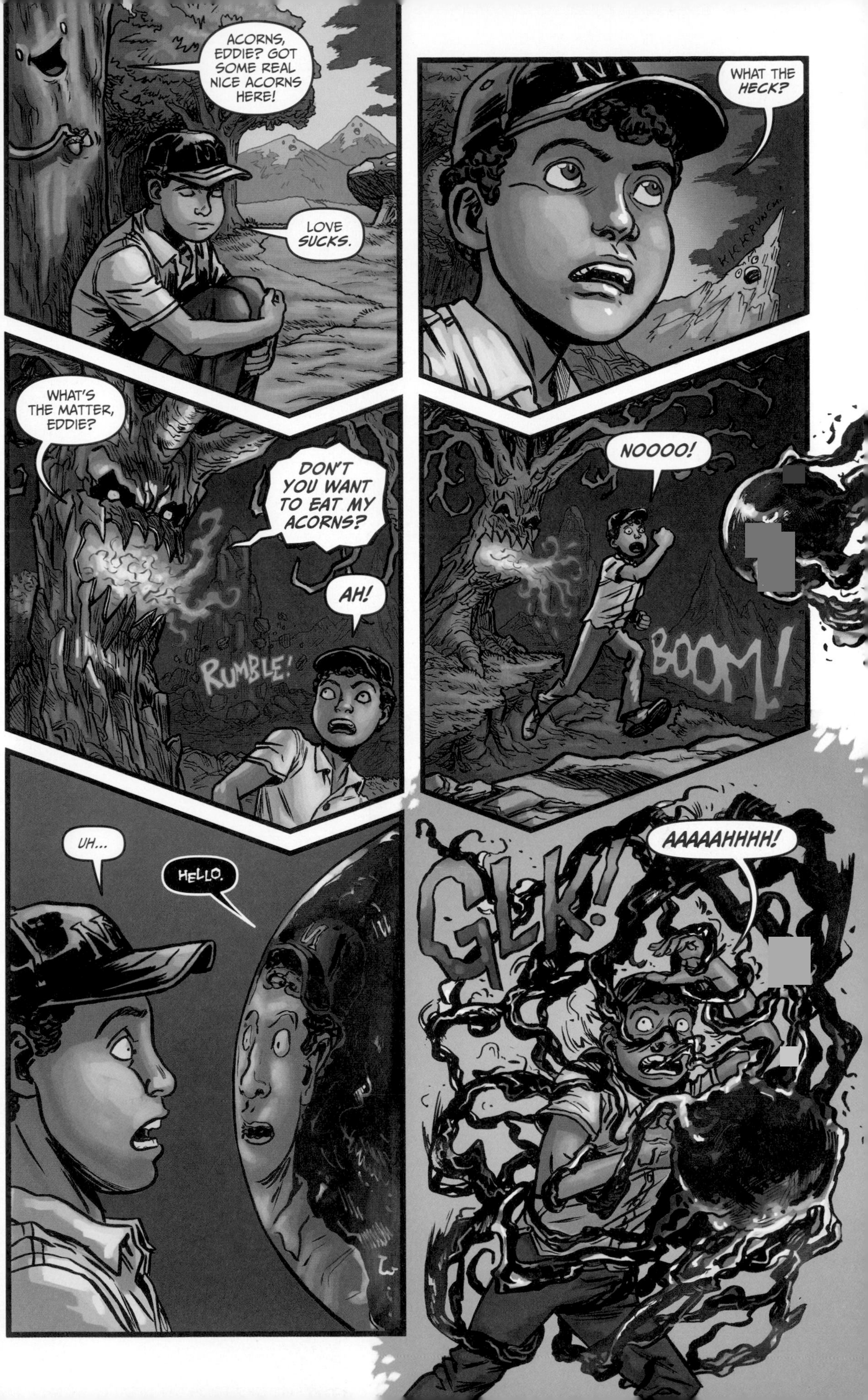
ACORNS, EDDIE? GOT SOME REAL NICE ACORNS HERE!
LOVE SUCKS.
WHAT THE HECK?
WHAT'S THE MATTER, EDDIE?
DON'T YOU WANT TO EAT MY ACORNS?
AH!
RUMBLE!
NOOOO!
BOOM!
UH...
HELLO.
GLK!
AAAAAHHHH!

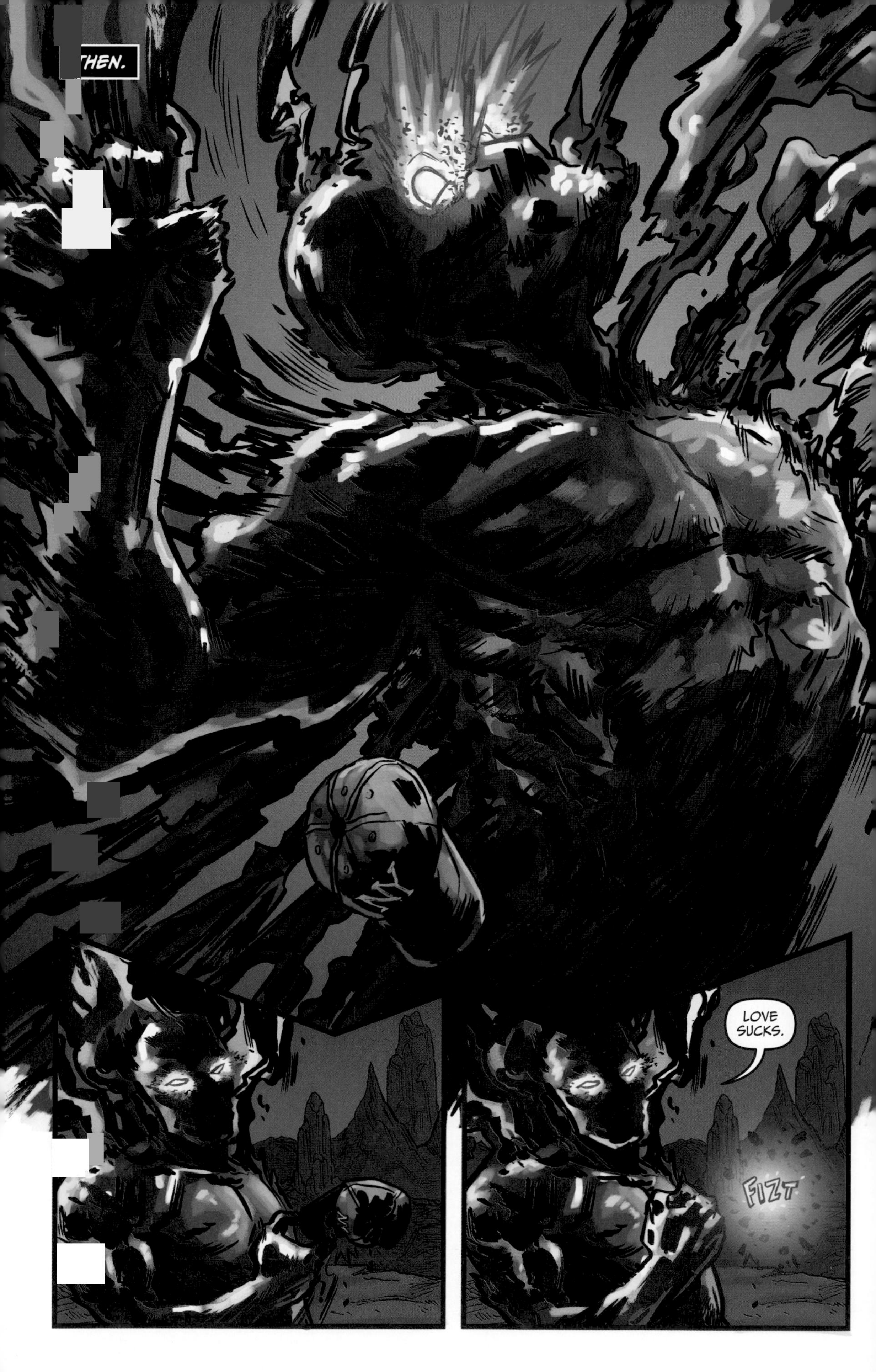
THEN.
LOVE SUCKS.
FIZT

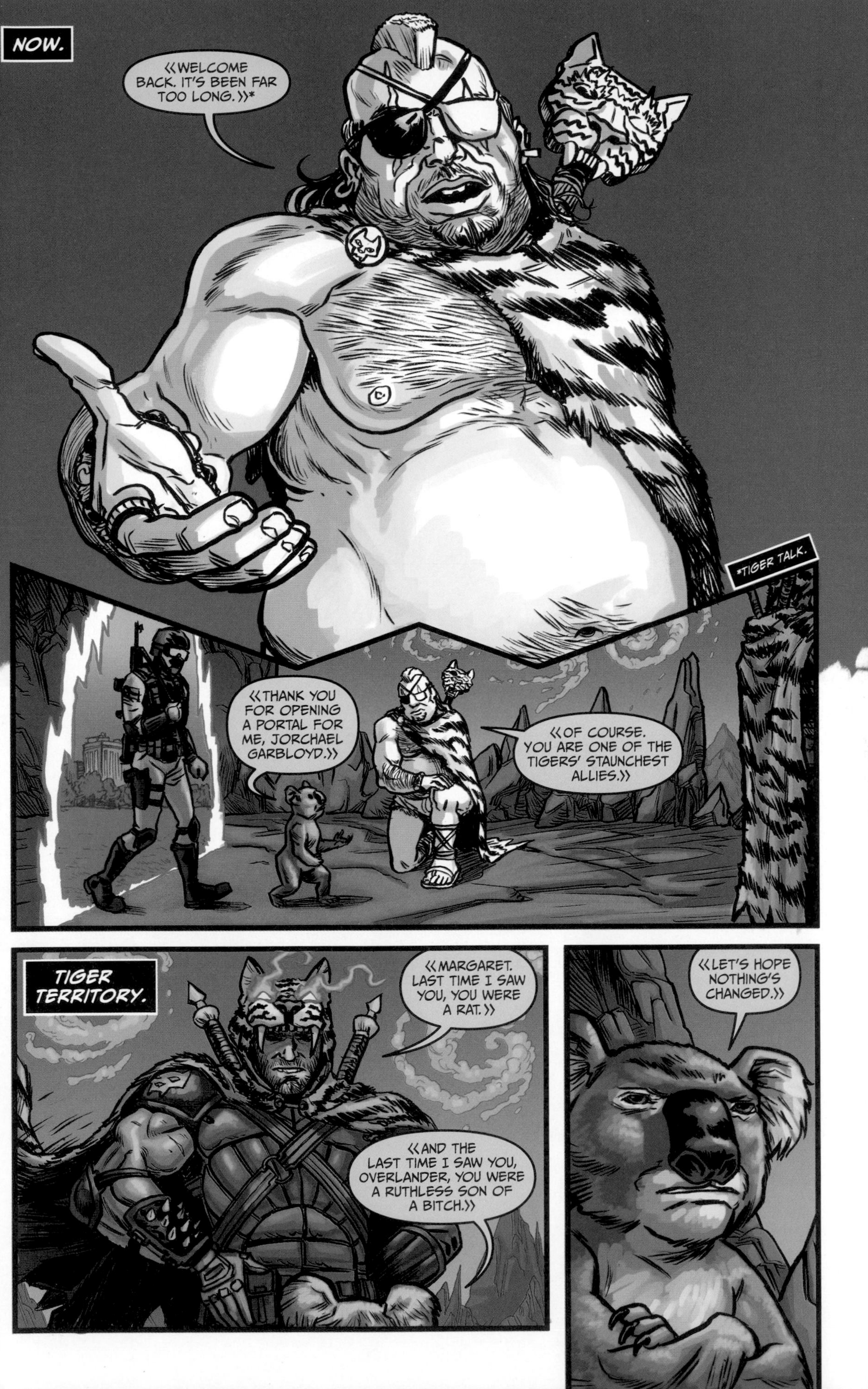
NOW.
<<WELCOME BACK. IT'S BEEN FAR TOO LONG.>>*
*TIGER TALK.
<<THANK YOU FOR OPENING A PORTAL FOR ME, JORCHAEL GARBLOYD.>>
<<OF COURSE. YOU ARE ONE OF THE TIGERS' STAUNCHEST ALLIES.>>
TIGER TERRITORY.
<<MARGARET. LAST TIME I SAW YOU, YOU WERE A RAT.>>
<<AND THE LAST TIME I SAW YOU, OVERLANDER, YOU WERE A RUTHLESS SON OF A BITCH.>>
<<LET'S HOPE NOTHING'S CHANGED.>>

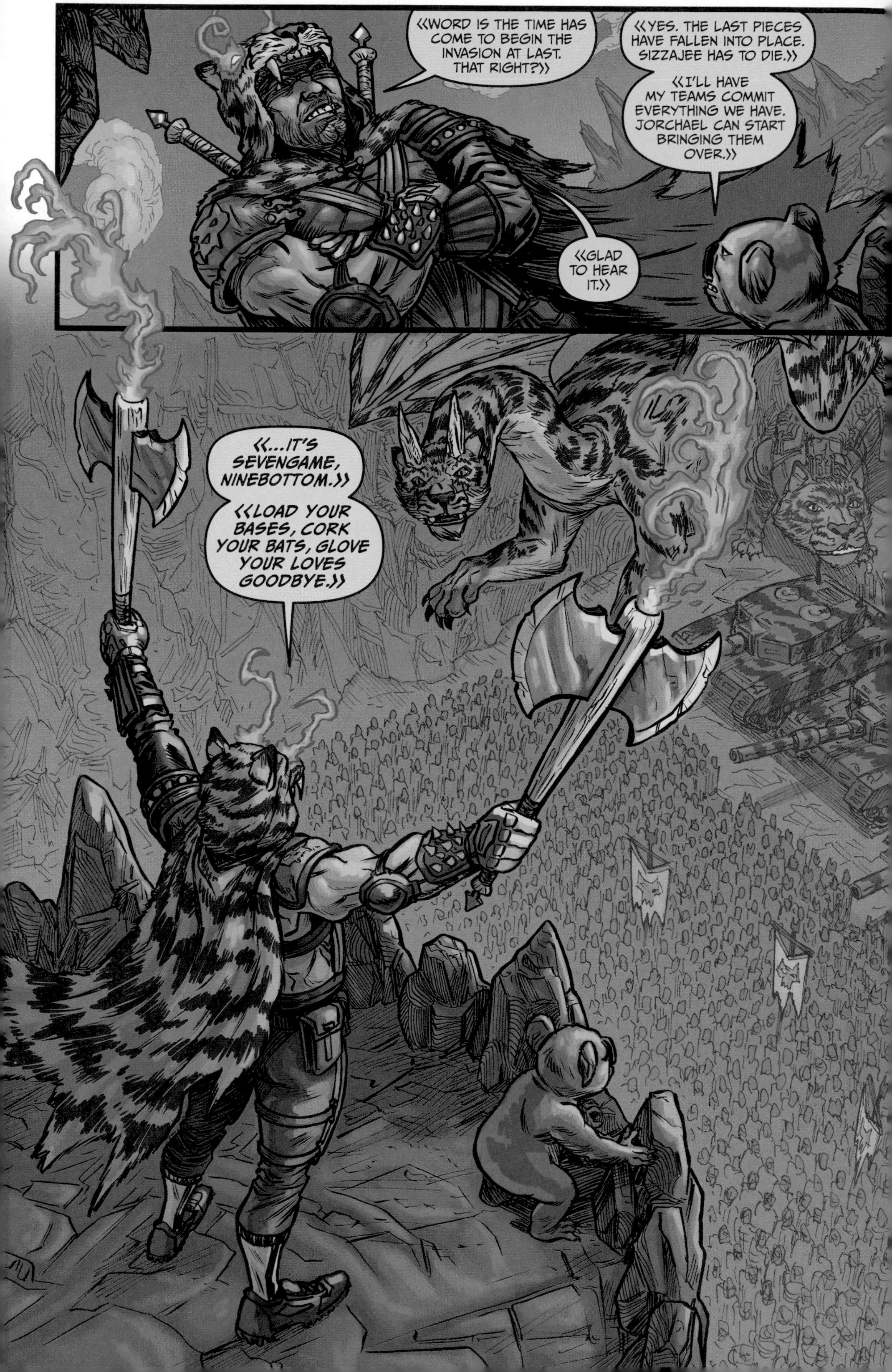

<<WORD IS THE TIME HAS COME TO BEGIN THE INVASION AT LAST. THAT RIGHT?>>
<<GLAD TO HEAR IT.>>
<<YES. THE LAST PIECES HAVE FALLEN INTO PLACE. SIZZAJEE HAS TO DIE.>>
<<I'LL HAVE MY TEAMS COMMIT EVERYTHING WE HAVE. JORCHAEL CAN START BRINGING THEM OVER.>>
<<...IT'S SEVENGAME, NINEBOTTOM.>>
<<LOAD YOUR BASES, CORK YOUR BATS, GLOVE YOUR LOVES GOODBYE.>>

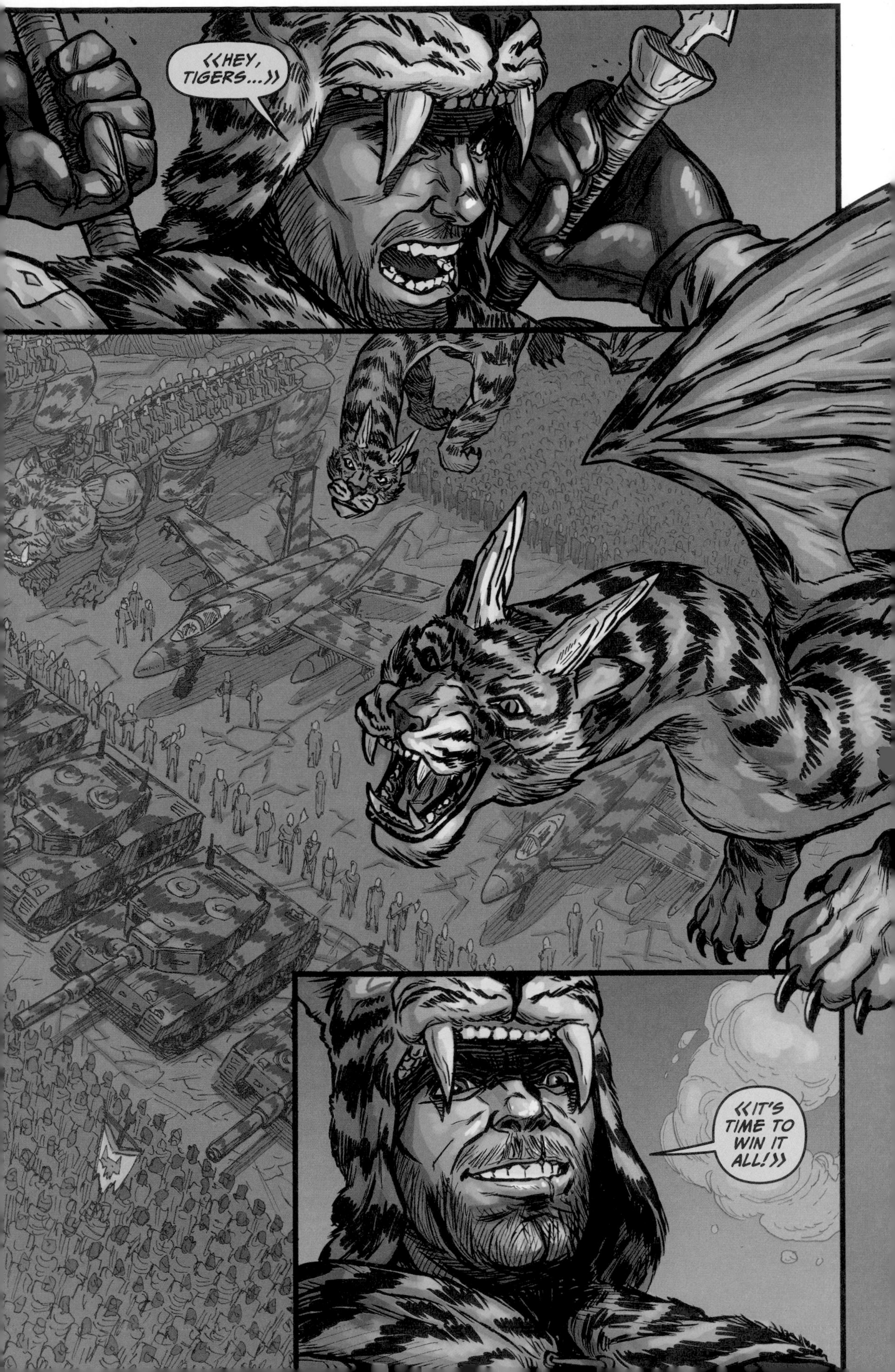
<<HEY, TIGERS...>>
<<IT'S TIME TO WIN IT ALL!>>

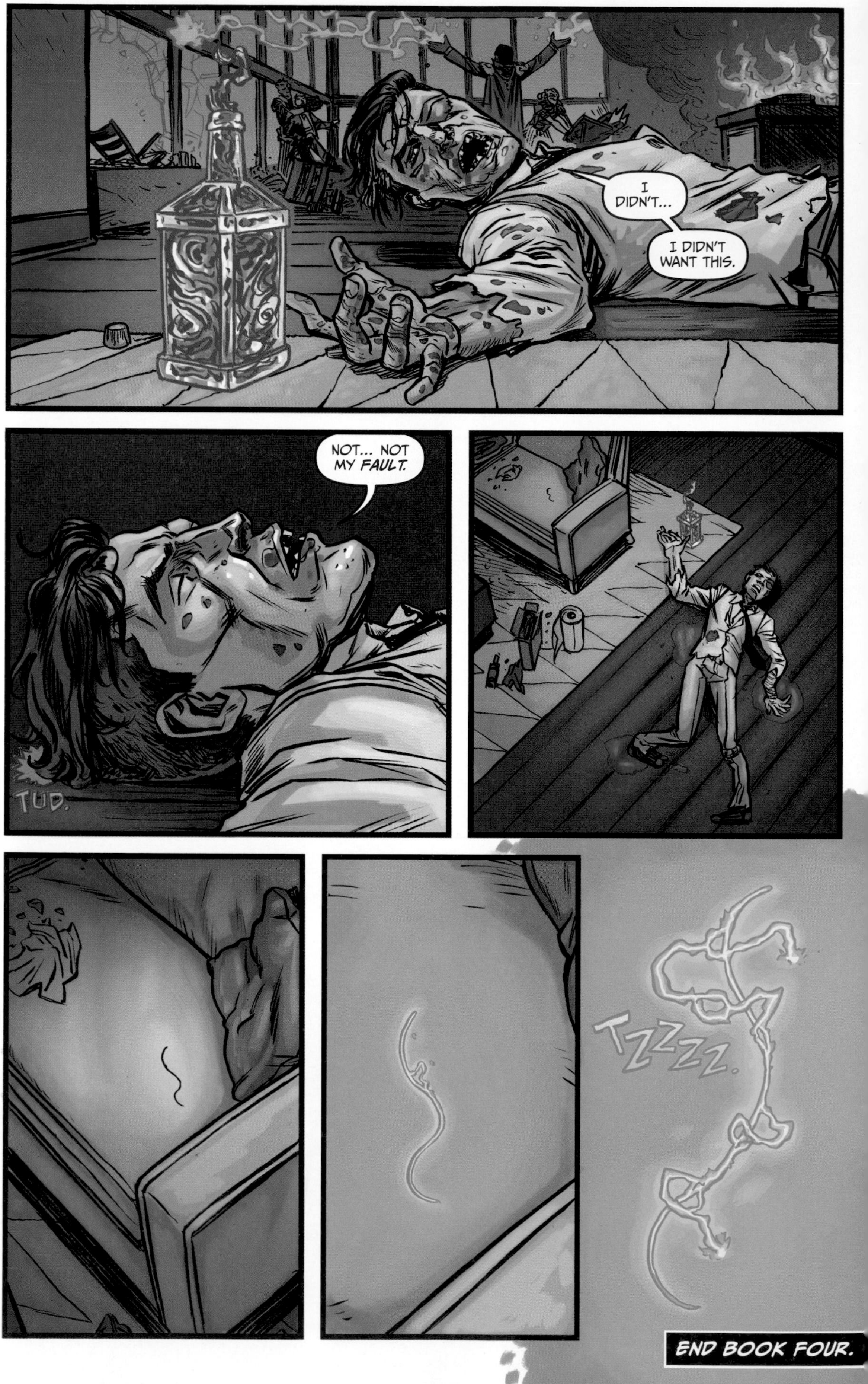
I DIDN'T...
I DIDN'T WANT THIS.
NOT... NOT MY *FAULT.*
TUD.
TZZZZ.
END BOOK FOUR.

SUMMER SWIMSUIT SPECIAL VARIANT
BY **JOE QUINONES, JOE RIVERA,**
AND **ADDISON DUKE**

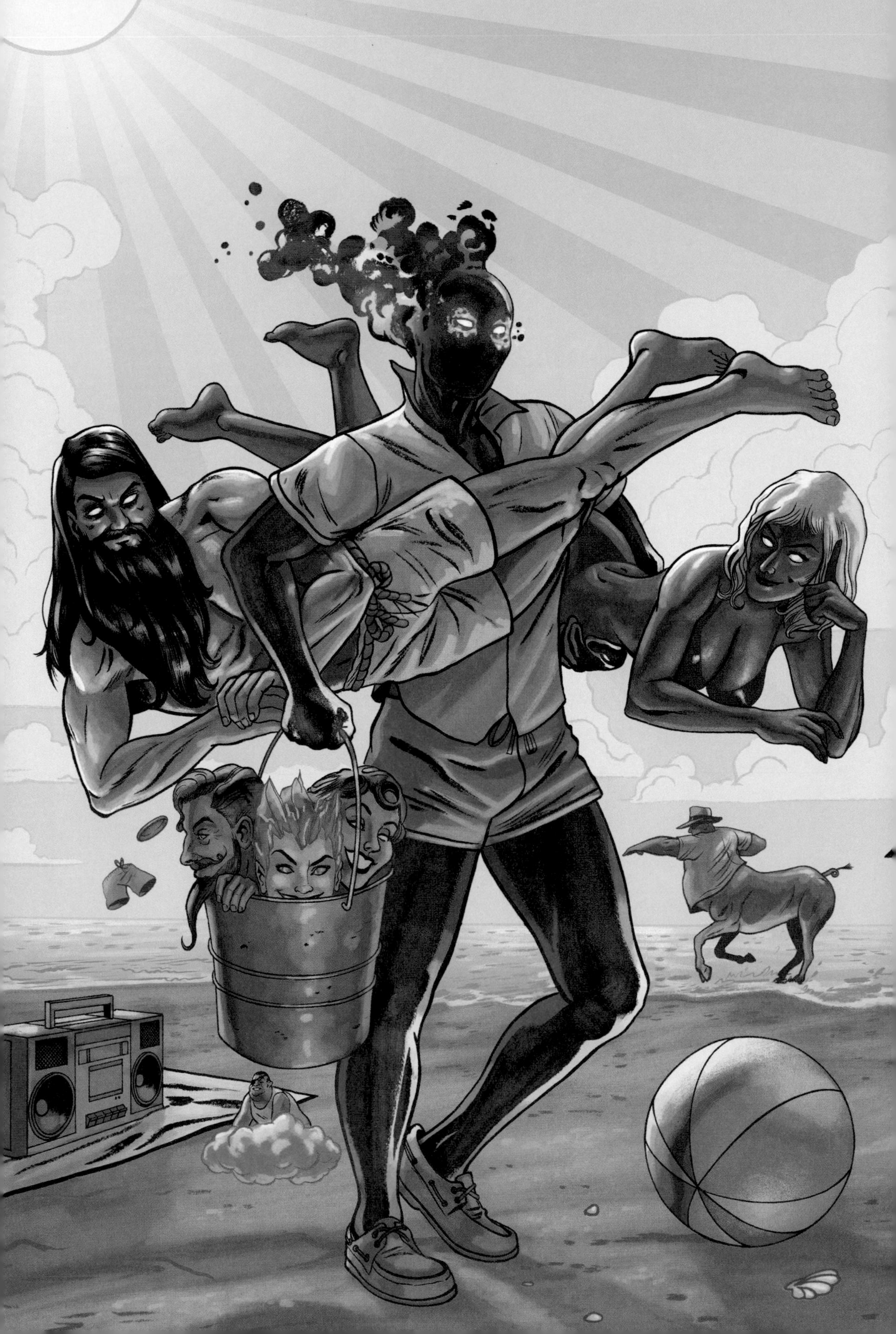

ISSUE 16 VARIANT COVER
BY **CHARLES SOULE**
AND **RYAN BROWNE**

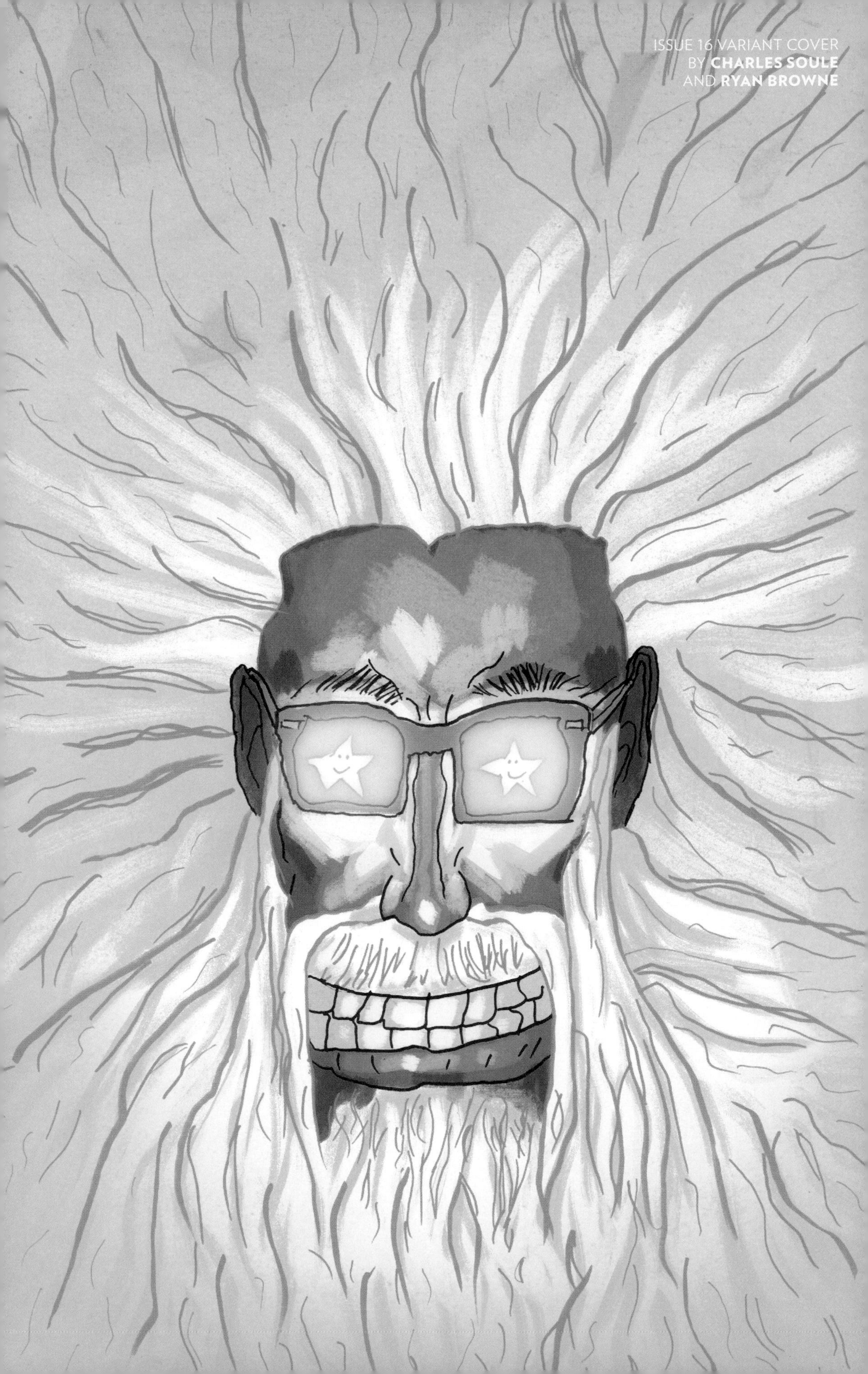

ISSUE 16 MAGICAL VARIANT
BY **RYAN BROWNE**

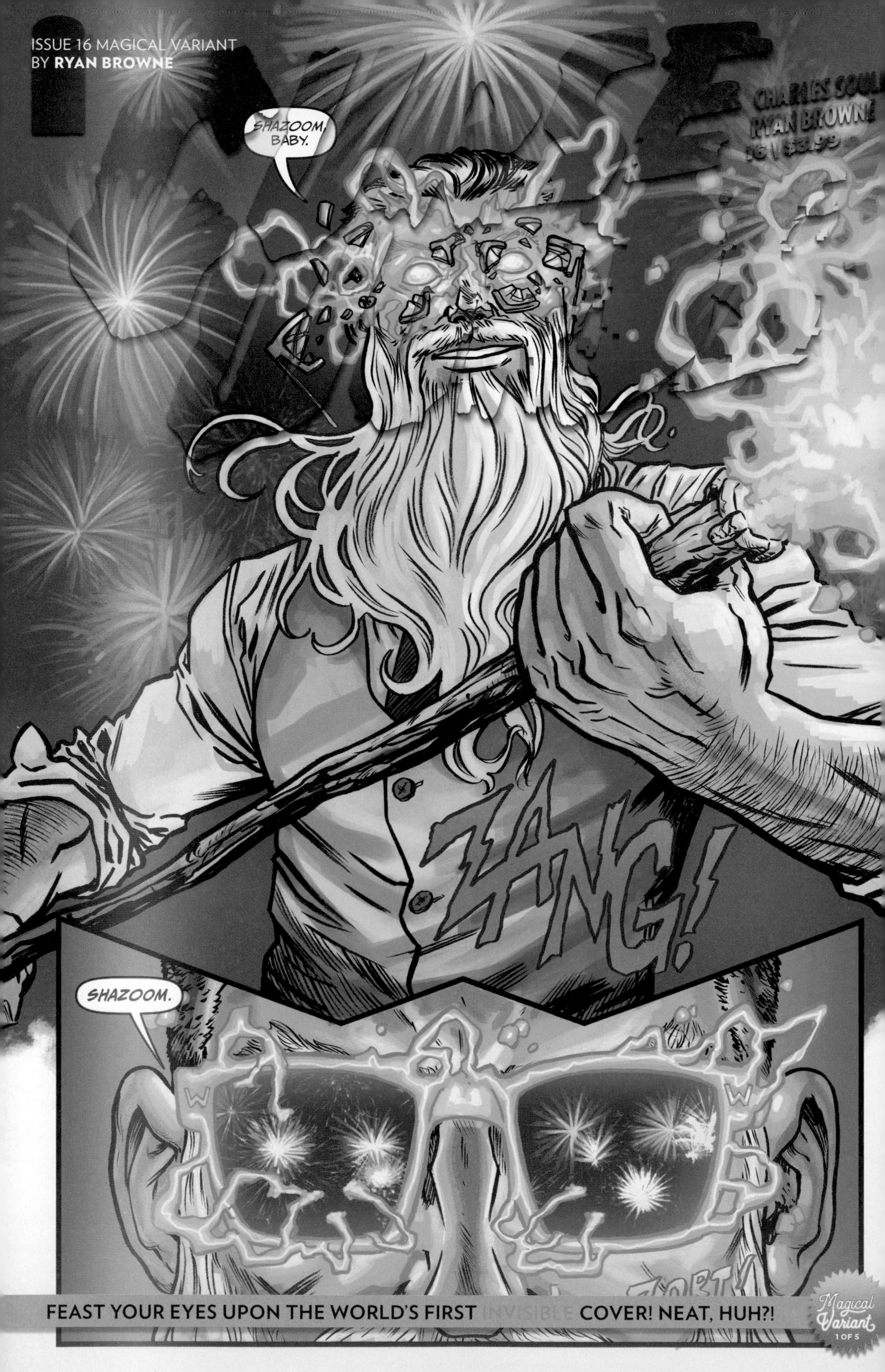
SHAZOOM, BABY.
ZANG!
SHAZOOM.
Magical Variant 1 OF 5

FEAST YOUR EYES UPON THE WORLD'S FIRST INVISIBLE COVER! NEAT, HUH?!

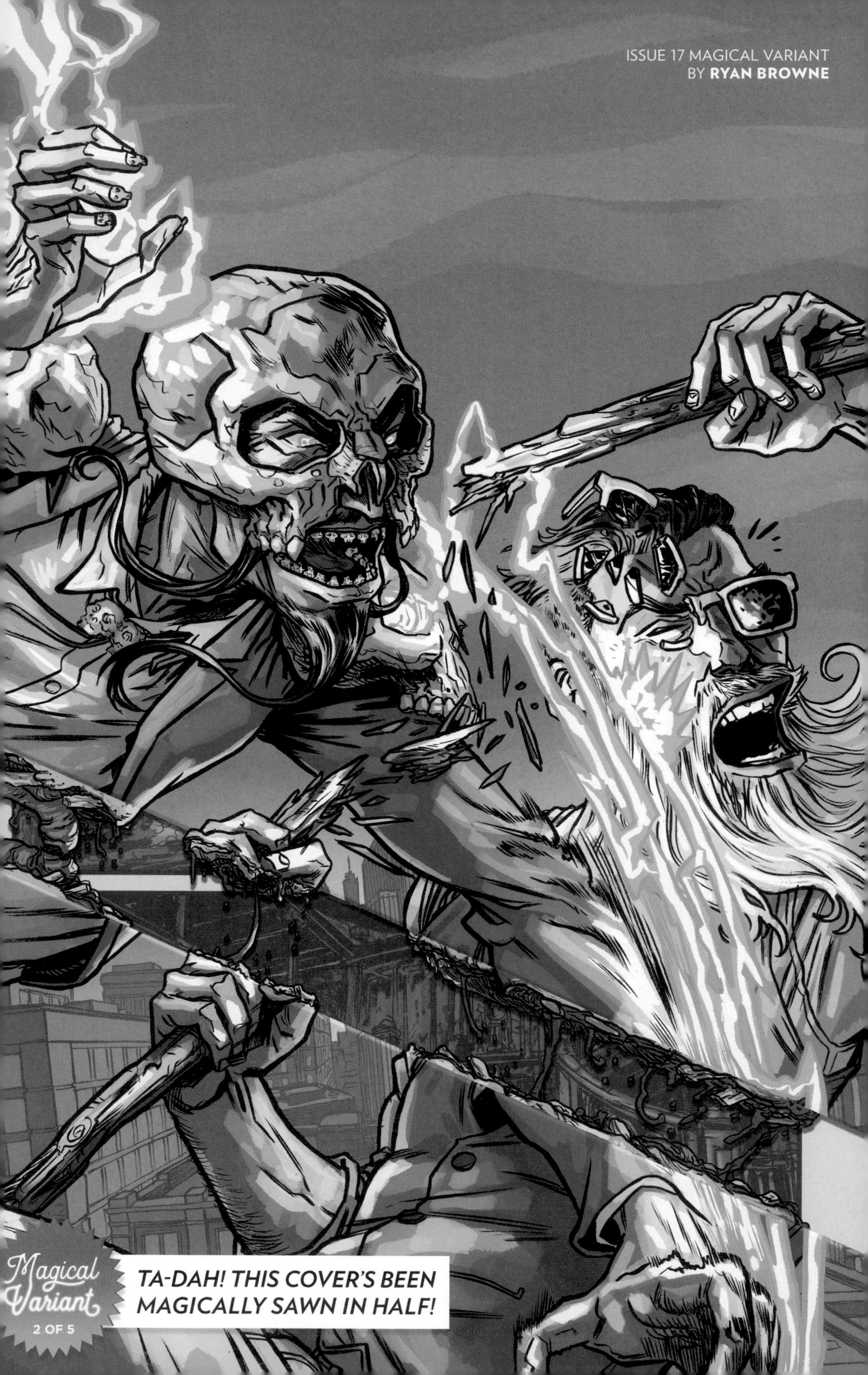
ISSUE 17 MAGICAL VARIANT
BY **RYAN BROWNE**
Magical Variant
2 OF 5
TA-DAH! THIS COVER'S BEEN MAGICALLY SAWN IN HALF!

ISSUE 18 MAGICAL VARIANT
BY **RYAN BROWNE**

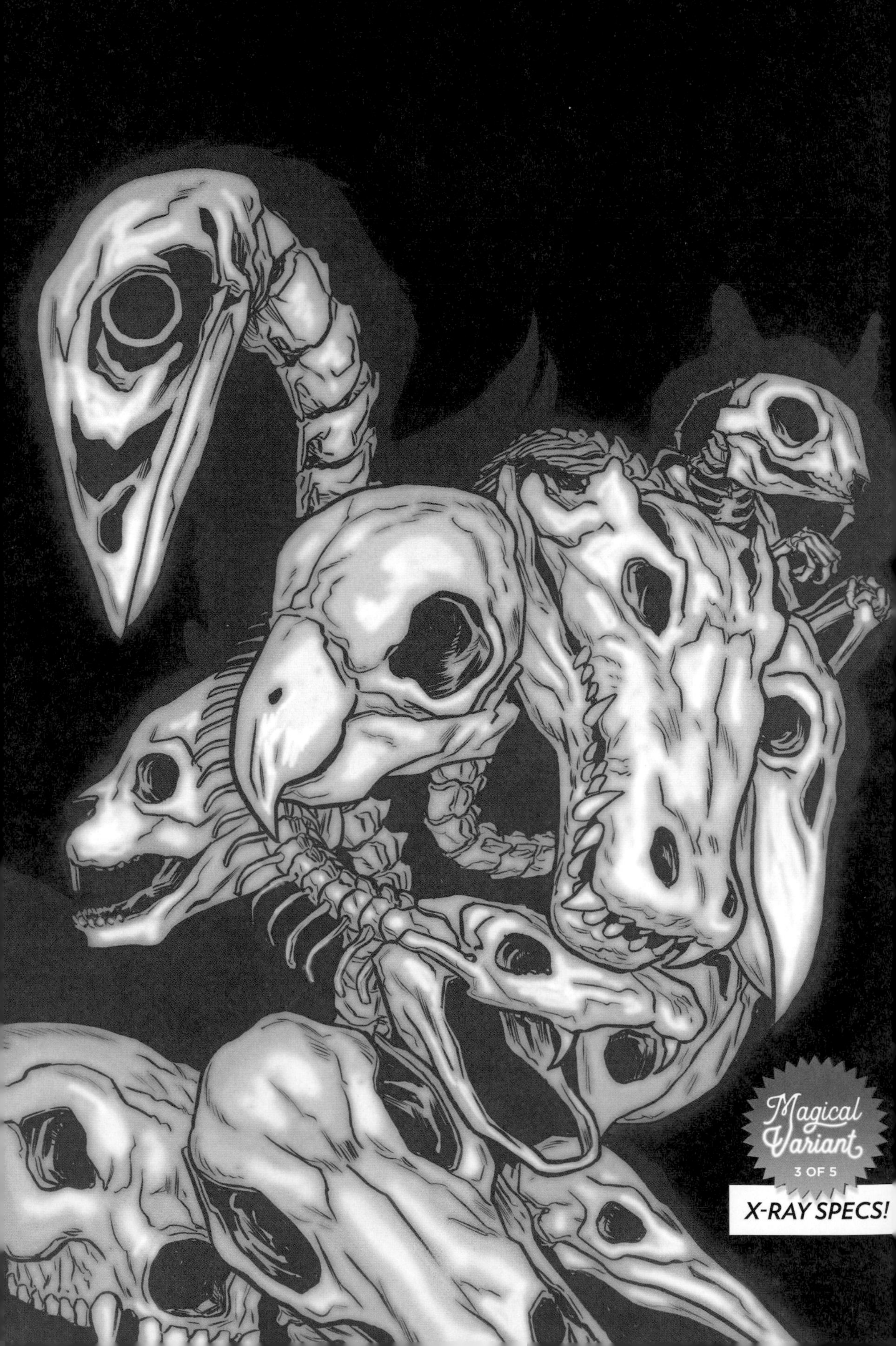

Magical Variant
3 OF 5
X-RAY SPECS!

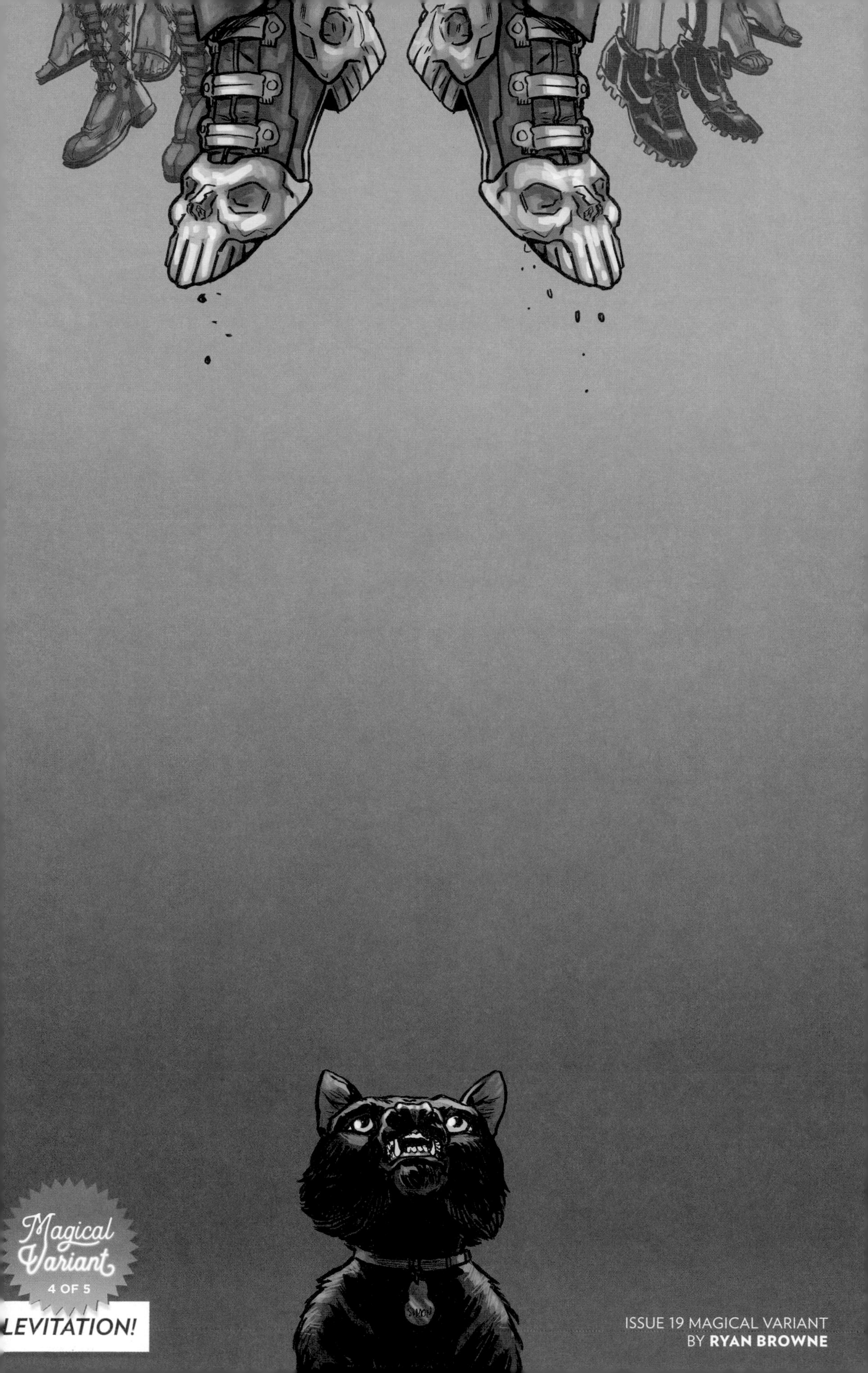
Magical Variant
4 OF 5
LEVITATION!

ISSUE 19 MAGICAL VARIANT
BY **RYAN BROWNE**

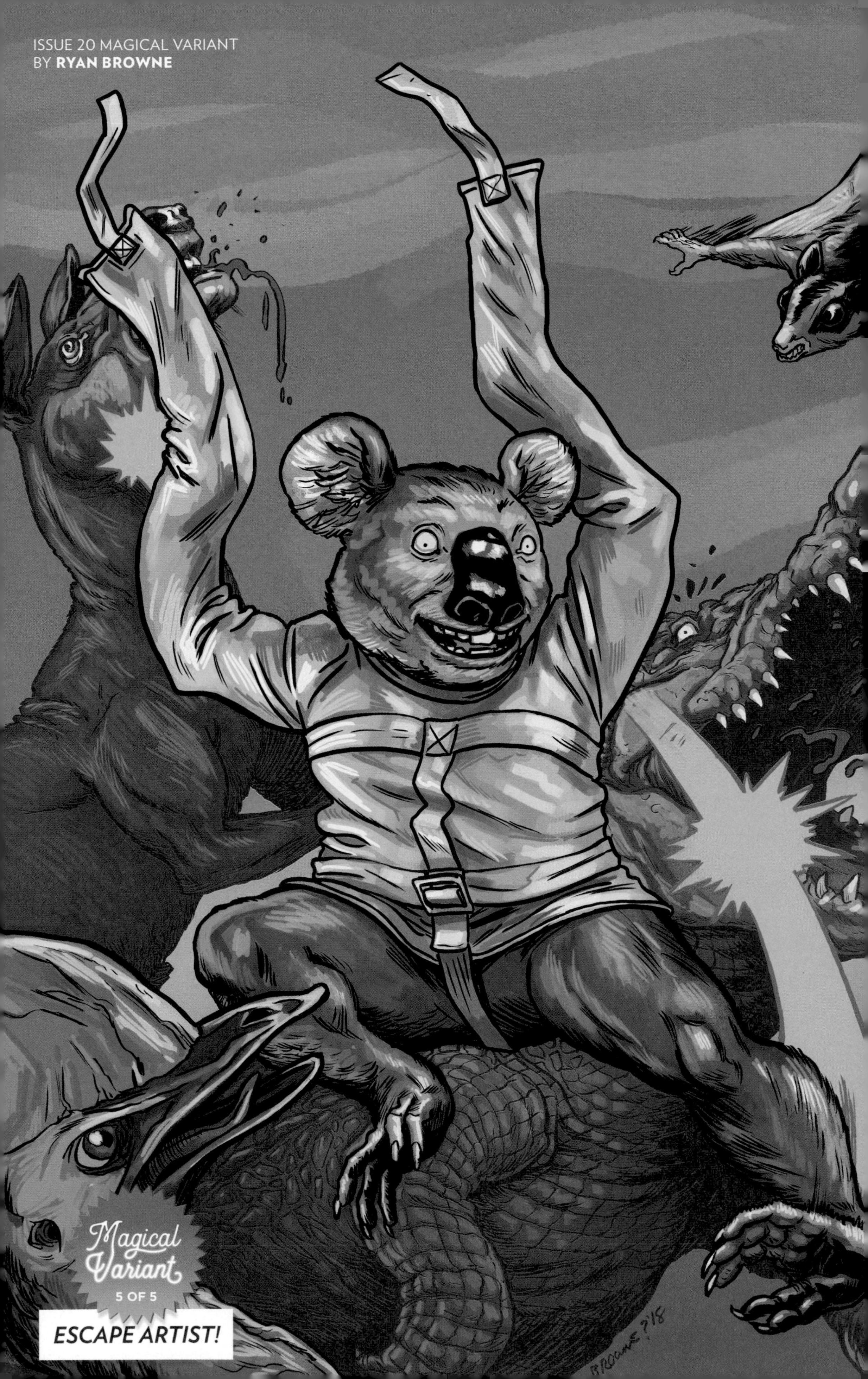
Magical
Variant
5 OF 5
ESCAPE ARTIST!
ISSUE 20 MAGICAL VARIANT
BY **RYAN BROWNE**

ISSUE 19 HERO INITIATIVE CHARITY VARIANT
BY **RYAN BROWNE**

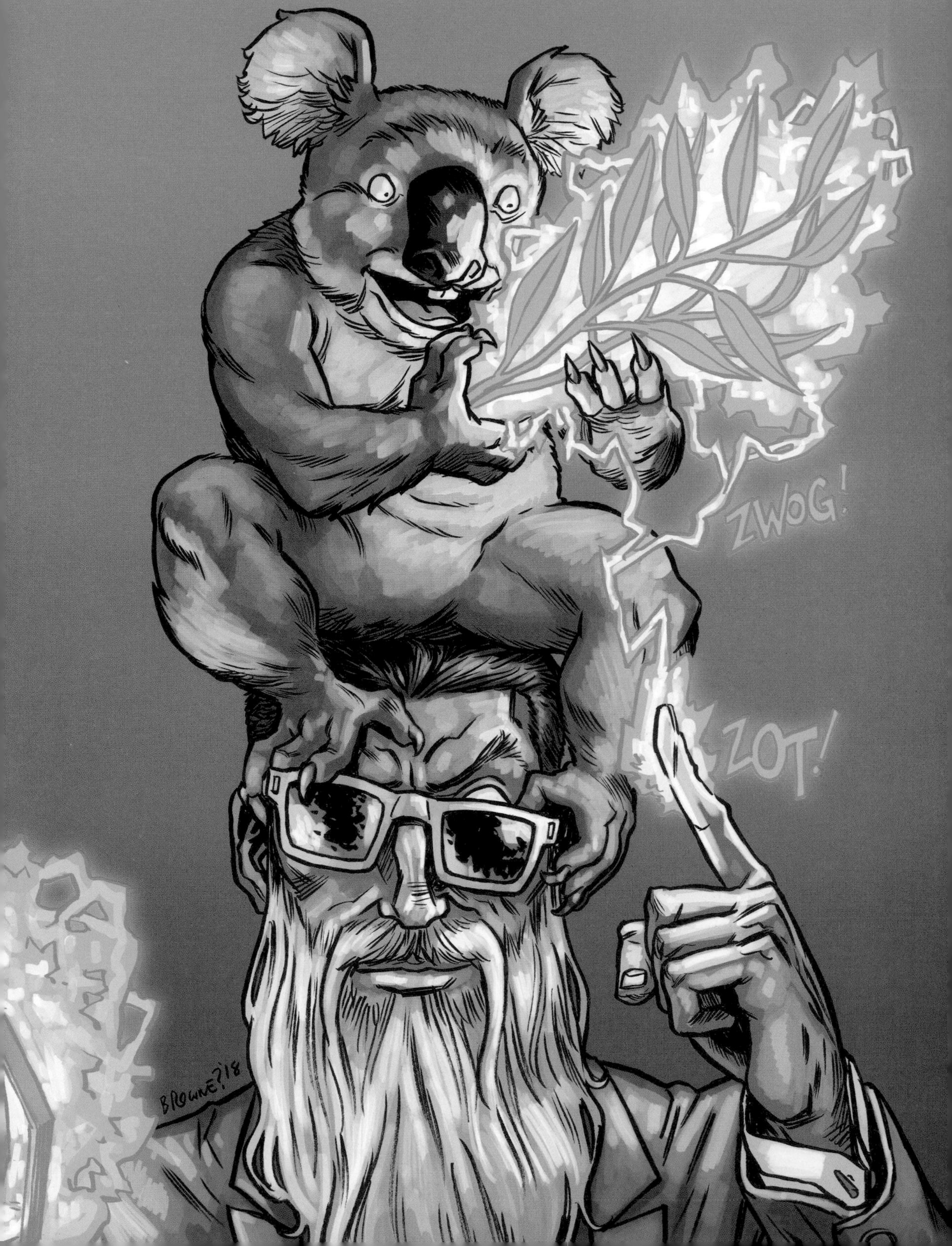
ZWOG!
ZOT!
BROWNE?18

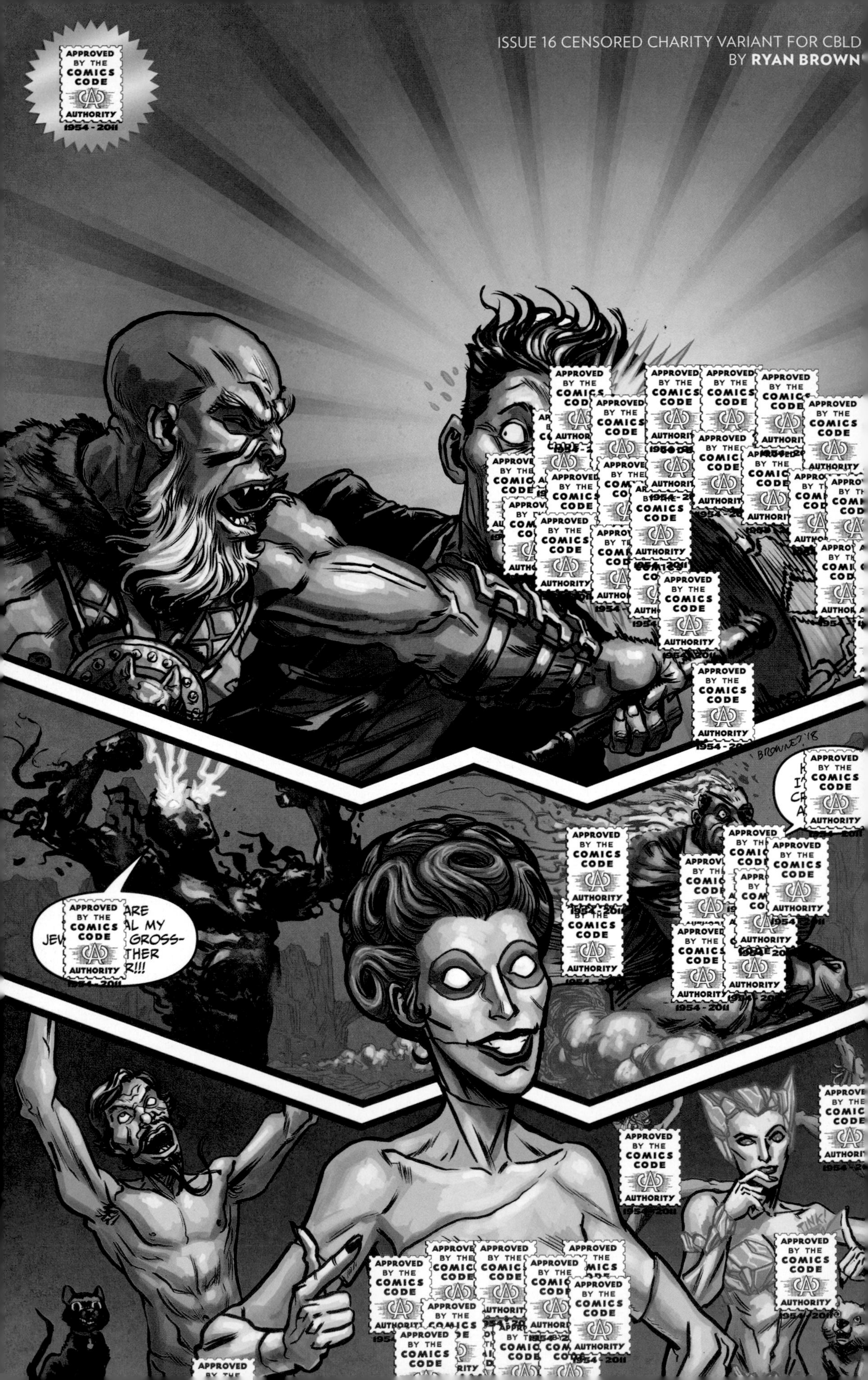
ISSUE 16 CENSORED CHARITY VARIANT FOR CBLD
BY RYAN BROWN
APPROVED BY THE COMICS CODE AUTHORITY 1954 - 2011

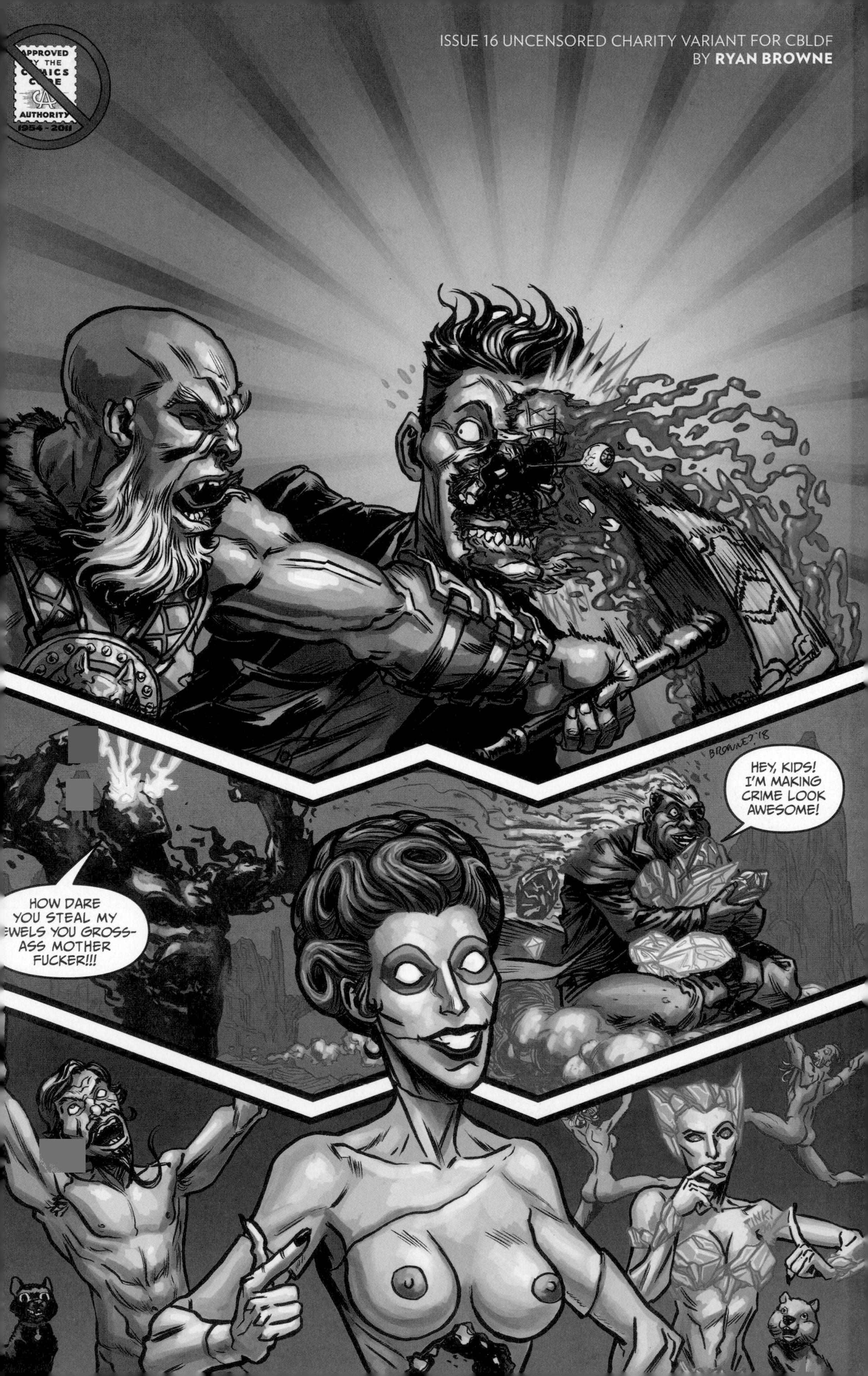
ISSUE 16 UNCENSORED CHARITY VARIANT FOR CBLDF
BY RYAN BROWNE
BROWNE?'18
HEY, KIDS! I'M MAKING CRIME LOOK AWESOME!
HOW DARE YOU STEAL MY EWELS YOU GROSS-ASS MOTHER FUCKER!!!

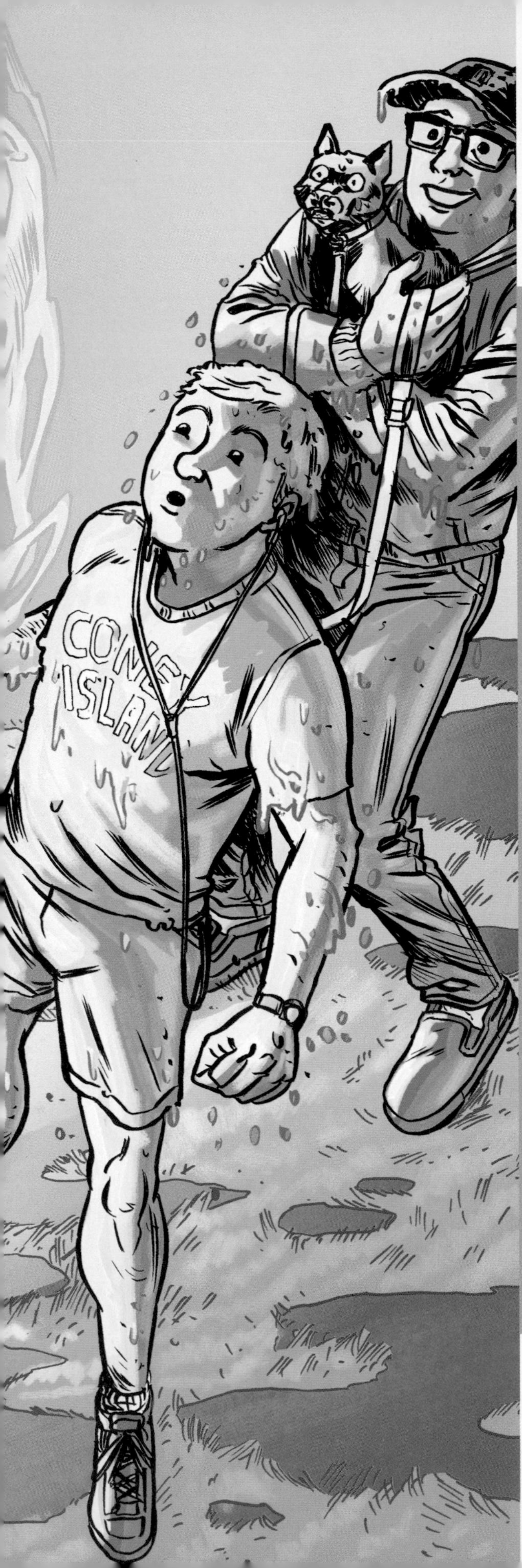
CONEY ISLAND

ABOUT THE AUTHORS

CHARLES SOULE has written many comics for Marvel, DC and others--*DAREDEVIL, STAR WARS, THE DEATH OF WOLVERINE, INHUMANS, SWAMP THING*... all kinds of stuff. He's also the creator of the award-winning epic sci-fi series *LETTER 44* for Oni Press, and his first (hopefully not last?) novel, *THE ORACLE YEAR*. (Don't tell any of those other projects, but *CURSE WORDS* is his favorite.)

He lives in Brooklyn, where he also plays music of various kinds and practices law from time to time.

Follow him on Twitter @CHARLESSOULE.

RYAN BROWNE is an American-born comicbookman who is co-responsible for *CURSE WORDS* (which you just read) and wholly responsible for *GOD HATES ASTRONAUTS* (which you should go read if you haven't). He currently lives in Chicago with his amazing wife and considerably less amazing cat. Also, he was once a guest on *The Montel Williams Show*--which is a great story and you should ask him about it.

Catch him on Twitter and Instagram @RYANBROWNEART.

GOTTA QUESTION FOR THE *CURSE WORDS* LETTERS PAGE? HIT US UP AT WIZORD@WIZORD.HORSE (YES, A .HORSE URL IS A REAL THING AND WE BOUGHT ONE).